Lord Bart and the Leagues of Sip and ALE

A BASEBALL STEAMPUNK ADVENTURE

Michael Barbato-Dunn

Setheridge
PRESS

For Aaron

I think you would have liked this.

You have only to play at Little Wars three or four times
to realize just what a blundering thing Great War must be.

H. G. Wells, *Little Wars*

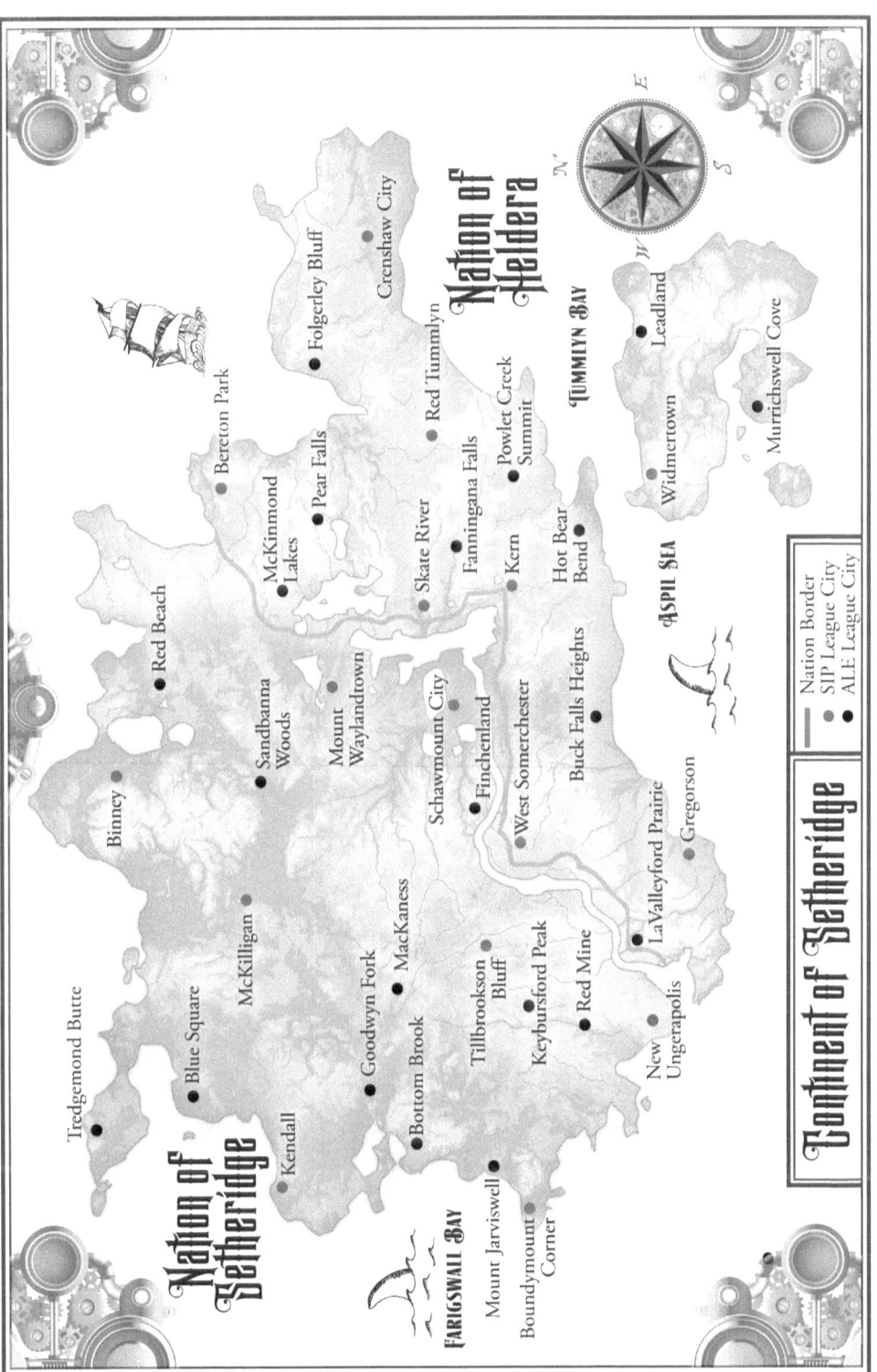

Continent of Setheridge

Nation of Setheridge

Tredgemond Butte

Blue Square
Kendall
McKilligan
Binney
Red Beach

Goodwyn Fork
MacKaness
Bottom Brook
Sandbanna Woods
Mount Waylandtown

Tillbrookson Bluff
Keybursford Peak
Red Mine
Schawmount City
Finchenland
West Somerchester
Buck Falls Heights

New Ungerapolis
LaValleyford Prairie
Gregorson

Mount Jarviswell
Boundymount Corner

Farigswall Bay

McKinmond Lakes
Pear Falls
Bereton Park
Folgerley Bluff
Crenshaw City

Skate River
Fanningana Falls
Red Tummlyn
Kern
Powlet Creek Summit
Hot Bear Bend

Nation of Heldera

Tummlyn Bay

Leadland
Widmertown
Murrichswell Cove

Aspil Sea

Compass Rose: N E S W

Legend
— Nation Border
● SIP League City
● ALE League City

Characters

The Office of the Commissioner of the Leagues of SIP and ALE

Lord Bartholomew J. H. Cunningham V, *His Excellency the Commissioner of the Leagues*

Andrew Gilpin Naughton, *Special Assistant to the Commissioner*

    Roderick Coyle, *Naughton's Chief of Staff*

    Inspector Enoch Gill, *Chief of Security*

Dr. Morgan Vinge, *the commissioner's personal physician*

Team Owners

Sir T. Broadlun Clay, *Executive of the Nation of Setheridge and owner of the Schawmount City Jackaloupes*

    Preston Dronwell, *Special Assistant to Executive Clay*

Clement Sands, *owner of the New Ungeropolis Fisher Cats*

Benedict Cheesley, *owner of the Tillbrookson Bluff Lizards*

Raymund Frun, *owner of the Kendall Griffins*

Sir R. Willison Caffrey, *Executive of the Nation of Heldera and owner of the Widmertown Flying Squirrels*

Morren Godwyn, *owner of the West Somerchester Rhinos*

Harry Gander, *owner of the Skate River Mad Dogs*

Alexander Fitton II, *owner of the Crenshaw City Warthogs*

    Tobias Droonan, *his personal assistant*

Dr. Granville Chanley, *owner of the Gregorson Monkeys*

Gerrold Patrick, Jr., *owner of the Fanningana Falls Park Toads*

Carroll Massey, *owner of the Bereton Park Hammerheads*

Others:

Amelia Naughton, *wife of Andrew Naughton*
    Their children, Isaac and Jack

Lady Vivian Packer Lynam, *friend and ex-oficio counselor to the commissioner*
Prof. Dr. Buford Wafer Northgood III, *leader of the Association of Scientificka*
Dr. Iphoneous Henry, *researcher, University of Kern*
Arbutus Chapp, *a steam master*

The Press

Ollo Ronnell, *national baseball columnist, The Chronicle*
Cromwell "Crom" Corcoran Jr., *managing editor of the Chronicle*
Bennet Rinkins, *publisher of the Chronicle*
Rowland Warde, *columnist for the Tillbrookson Bluff Register Times*
Gallahad Berry, *baseball writer for the Leadland Leader*
Obediah Noone, *baseball writer for the Widmertown Herald-Leader*
Maddy Looper, *baseball writer for the Skate River Post*
Blakeford Gash, *columnist for the Blue Square Noble Daily*
Samuel Cutty, *baseball writer for the Fanningana Falls Park News of the Day*

The Underworld

Phangorious Hood, *of the Magera*
C.T. Muldoon and Silas Pounds, *Hood's associates*
Hardwin Jellum, *bookmaker*

The 1923 Widmertown Flying Squirrels

Sir R. Willison Caffrey, *owner*
Eldon Langford, *General Manager*
Sander Halloway, *Manager*
Gabriel Keating, *Hurling Coach*
Archibald Ferns, *Striking Coach*

THE STRIKERS:
    Gillighan Alley 1B
    Silas Berbery RF

Lucius Cameron 3B

Regan Comber 1B-3B

Samuel Cook LF

Frederick Dunbar 2B

Morris Flaherty LF

Ike Gamp SS-2B

Ambrose Goldwell CF

Gerard Hermon RF

Haly Kelly Jr C

Pyce Marsh RF

Jeremy Minnocks C

Nicholas Wrye SS

THE HURLERS:

Ketter "The Count" Asgar, starter

Cokely Broughan, starter

Benjamin Harald, starter

George "Larry" Skelly, starter

Morris Treesparrow, middleman

Ryan Foreman, closer

October 15, 1923

Dearest Amelia:

If the arrival of this letter finds you in the company of others, please remove yourself from their presence and return to my words when you are alone. Suffice it to say that I have gone to great lengths to have this delivered to you to in such a manner that my whereabouts could never be traced. Please destroy this note once you have read it, lest it fall into the view of prying eyes. But I urge you to read it in its entirety.

My heart, of course, yearns to be telling you this in person, but that would risk the safety of you and the boys. And my heart, of course, yearns to be next to you, to be embracing you, to be telling you how so very sorry I am that circumstance — horrible, and horribly avoidable — led to this. So this paltry missive will have to serve.

Months ago you told me, "Don't get yourself into something that has no good outcome." I admit to you now that I have done precisely that. I put myself in a position where I had to choose between two courses of action, neither of which could have had a good outcome. The course I selected was intended to save our beloved continent. The price, as you no doubt have by now realized, is that I can never see you, or Jack or Isaac, again.

To write those words brings pain both unmitigated and unfathomable. I am not so bold as to ask for your absolution, nor your compassion. I do, though, tender this detailed explanation. I write this now to tell you the full story, the true story, so that even if you can never forgive me, at least you can understand…

March 7

O N THIS DAY, THE 30TH anniversary of the founding of the Setheridge Island Professional League of Baseball, thousands filled Schawmount Stadium, bedecked in their finest formalwear and chattering in anticipation of the celebration to come. Luminous sunshine graced the lush field, and Andrew Naughton knew no foul elements would dampen the spirits and goodwill of the day. Yet he found it difficult — nay, impossible — to appreciate the good fortune brought by the weather, for the register of his worries was voluminous.

Not the least of his concerns was the safety of the commissioner himself, the Lord Bartholomew J. H. Cunningham V — 'Lord Bart' they called him — who would shortly be making his way to the podium behind the home bag. Naughton glanced at members of the League security force posted around the perimeter of the VIP section: some in uniform, firmly at attention, gazing in all directions; others in plainclothes, blending in amongst the owners, politicians and other dignitaries. Their eyes prowled for suspicious movements. He motioned for Coyle, his chief of staff.

"Anything thus far?" He spoke in a whisper.

"Nothing, sir. We're still frisking at the gates, at least the men. Suffice it to say that none of the guests is pleased about it, but everyone to this point has been generally cooperative. One arrest, a drunk. We confiscated a few pocket knives."

"Has there been anything else? Anything remotely suspicious?"

"No. Not to this point."

"Fine. Proceed."

Coyle retreated, and Naughton paused in his ruminations to finally take in the entirety of the scene. The thousands of details to which his staff had attended over the past many months were complete, and he could not help but admit that the result was every bit as glorious as he'd envisioned. Bunting in red and blue — the colors of the hometown Jackaloupes — hung throughout the stands, from the reserved sections with their cushioned velvet seats to the rows of splintering wooden bleachers that crowded the stadium's upper levels. The brass railings and banisters that encircled the field's perimeter gleamed as if ablaze. Gold and white flags embroidered with the numbers '3' and '0' — denoting the anniversary year — snapped on high poles as a breeze nestled through the rafters.

The attendees in the park — more than 40,000 in all — were every bit as regal. Naughton saw ladies adjusting towering cherry plume hats and folding yellow-and-white parasols as they lowered themselves into their seats, while their mustachioed and bearded male companions straightened felt derbies and woolen top hats in preparation for the ceremony about to unfold. None of the attendees — particularly those who fancied themselves as members of the aristocracy — had arrived adorned in anything less than what their tailors would describe as resplendent perfection.

Above, in the nearly cloudless sky, four airships slipped across the breadth of the oblong park: luxury craft with tubular gondolas fastened below the oblong balloons and separate, smaller nacelles for the engines on the sides. An array of lamps festooned on each side of the balloons, near the nacelles, formed images of the insignias of the Twin Nations, Setheridge and Heldera. The ships glided at a leisurely pace, their paths criss-crossing, and Naughton found their presence calming.

It was truly a festive day.

Then came the first words of the public address announcer, a deep disembodied voice carried over the thousands of footlengths of pneumatic tubing that snaked throughout the stadium's steel structure and poured out from cone-shaped speakers posted high as the flags. "Kind people, please devote your attention to the stage behind the home bag…"

The throng of conversations throughout the ballpark transmuted into applause and cheers. Concessionaires hawking fried dough sticks and ice-cooled fruit ade, hoping to squeeze in extra sales before the ceremony began, silenced their efforts. Children in the furthest bleachers, scurrying about and mimicking the professional ball-players they idolized, were silenced by their parents. The droning of the airships merged imperceptibly with the omnipresent humming of the steam-station below the ballpark itself.

"…as we present on this august occasion the founder and Commissioner of the Leagues of SIP and ALE, his most excellent Master and Gentleman, Lord Batholomew Cunningham!"

From behind Naughton, two of Coyle's aides escorted Lord Bart from a curtained waiting area toward the podium. The old man, while increasingly frail, had insisted on speaking from that ornate pedestal alone. He would hear no arguments: he said it was vital to do so without help, to appear strong. The Twin Nations needed to see this. It was the only way.

So despite weeks of protestations, Naughton could only now observe from his seat a dozen rows away. He dug his fingers into his palm of his left hand, then reached down with his right to stroke Crandy, motionless at his feet. The petting was more than therapeutic: it prompted the servohound to emerge from his low-power state. His companion needed to be ready; a steady wag of his hinged tail and small wisps of steam from his exterior tubing provided Naughton that assurance.

After a few steps, Cunningham waved off the aides and emerged from the shadows of the stadium overhang into the basking sun.

And then tens of thousands saw their hero.

The applause was rapturous, cascading across the manicured field like a wave at high tide, and every man, woman, and child in attendance craned forward. Lord Bart moved only with the help of his walking stick, sliding his feet toward the front of the stage, then inching up the four small steps of the riser. He wore a tuxedo and tails, as was his preference, and his top hat seemed to engulf his balding head. Wire-framed glasses hung on the tip of his thin nose, and in the sunlight his pallid skin appeared almost translucent.

The commissioner removed the script of his speech from a jacket pocket and placed the papers on the sloped incline of the podium top. The old man's hands shook, but Naughton knew the tremors were slight and likely imperceptible to any but those seated closest to the stage.

He looks so small. So vulnerable.

Still, the adoration of the thousands was palpable. Tremendous cheers and jubilant whistles came from every section and row, and many held handwritten signs aloft. "Our Commissioner," read one. "Eternally Grateful," said another. And to the left of Naughton, up several dozen rows, five young men wore masks of the old man's characteristic visage: top hat, monocle, thin and large ears. It was a caricature, certainly, but one of reverence rather than ridicule.

He was not simply Lord Bart. He was *their* Lord Bart.

The commissioner steadied himself at the podium, looked upward in acknowledgment of the crowd's anticipation, and smiled. He adjusted his top hat and cleared his throat. Cunningham had written the speech out longhand. Despite his long tenure as the commissioner's Special Assistant, Naughton had not seen it. The old man flicked his index finger against the microphone, and the resulting click reverberated throughout the stadium. And then Bartholomew Cunningham began.

"Kind people, if you are old enough to have been there, you may not need to be reminded. But I direct this to those who are younger, who only learned this in school: three decades ago when I first proposed that the continent of Setheridge unite under a single baseball league, we had already endured 50 years of strife, and the Great Insurrection had no end in sight. Many feared we could be headed toward extinction. We had lost sense of what we'd been fighting over." Many in the crowd nodded and murmured assent. "My proposal, you should recall, was not singular but three-fold: not just the creation of a professional league of baseball but, nearly simultaneously, the declaration of a ceasefire and independence for the Helderan people."

More cheers came, but Naughton wondered if the history lesson was necessary. He turned his gaze and studied familiar faces scattered throughout the VIP section nearest the podium. These were the very people who most depended on the peace flourishing throughout the continent: the team owners, 36 of them, the de facto governing body of the Twin Nations. To his right, the eighteen owners from the nation of Setheridge, all men, all in sedate tweed suits and black top hats that seemed to rise above that of the commissioner. All beaming in pride. To their left, their Helderan counterparts. Some stared at the ground, others watched Lord Bart with dour grimaces and furrowed brows. Naughton noticed that Alexander Fitton II, the young owner of the Warthogs of Crenshaw City, kept his top hat resting on his lap. A coarse sign of disrespect.

Cunningham continued. "We resolved to channel our endless aggressions into a far less bloody pursuit: a smaller war if you will, or rather thousands of little wars, played out with bats on ballfields rather than muskets on battlefields. And the plan proved to be much more, for the formation of organized baseball reminded our disparate peoples of things that had been woefully forgotten: the thrill of athletics, the value of gentlemanly competition, and most of all — the sheer fun of the game."

Then, with voice raised, the old man exclaimed: "And so with baseball, joy returned to all our lives."

At that the crowd whooped and howled, and Naughton had no doubt that thousands more listening on the audiocasters in plazas and publick houses across the continent had broken into celebrations as well. Crandy stirred at the crowd's eruption and rotated his aluminum-clad ears front to back.

MICHAEL BARBATO-DUNN

"But—" Cunningham raised his hand. The cheers dissipated as that weighty single word reverberated throughout the ballpark.

Naughton cringed. *Must there be a 'but'? Can't he just end it there? Let this be a mirthful day.*

"But," Cunningham repeated, for emphasis, "we have far still to go. We all know there are forces throughout the continent that would have us return to our warring ways. Some sitting here amongst us." The entire audience seemed to shift at that thought, as though the spectators were suddenly uncomfortable being seated near strangers, even if dressed in fine linen and jewelry. Naughton shook his head. There was no need to sow distrust. Not now. Not today.

"We cannot allow this to be," Cunningham continued. "And I say this to each of you now: today, the 30th anniversary of the inception of the SIP and ALE leagues, must be not just an occasion for celebration. Rather, it must be a day in which we resolve again to let this sport heal our wounds."

Naughton could see the old man's withered hands clasping the podium's brass-rimmed edges. "Let our resolve quash the doubters. Let our resolve silence the skeptics. Let our resolve ring forth!" Shouts of agreement scattered through the park, and with the crowd at a fever pitch, old Lord Bart raised his voice to exclaim: "I urge you. I beg you. We need — once and for all — to dispel the hatred."

Out of the corner of his eye, Naughton spied a scuffle of guests back in the upper reaches of the stands. A shadow cast by one of the airships made details unclear. A fistfight between opposing fans perhaps, or some drunken Amandeans. He hoped it was nothing worse.

Naughton snapped his fingers. Crandy rose and wagged his metallic tail. "Section 351," Naughton whispered. "Get me a report." The servohound bowed his head and was gone in an instant.

"Do not let all our work so far crumble in weakness. Let the baseball endure. And…" Cunningham's timber rose, his hands steadied, his words projected forward like a line drive to deep center. "And as baseball endures, so will the continent!"

Cheers and near-hysterical shouts cascaded through the stands. Some began chanting "baseball" in unison, others did the same with "Lord Bart" and "Play ball!" A horn ensemble struck up the league anthem, "War No More," carried over the tinny amplification system.

The commissioner seemed oblivious to the rhapsodic jubilation that had enveloped every level of the ballpark. He gathered the papers of the speech and turned away from the stands, head bowed, then began shuffling toward his seat.

The speech was complete; an exhibition game would now be played. Naughton studied each step intently. If he noticed one hint of a stumble...

But there was none: Cunningham bridged the short divide between the podium and his chair without fault. Naughton unclenched his fists. The clapping, chanting and fanfare continued unabated. The adoration for the old man was effusive: women cried, men thrust young children in the air for a glimpse of the commissioner, older children blew into penny-whistles and danced in aisles. Even the Helderan owners in the leftmost portion of the VIP section, the very owners least supportive of Cunningham, were now applauding.

Except the upstart, Fitton. He sat motionless, hands still clasped around the top hat on his lap, his stare narrowed, his long sideburns meeting at the edges of his pursed lips. Naughton pondered the man's reticence, and then realized that Fitton had spied his gaze. The Helderan owner's eyes bore down on him. Naughton did not flinch. After a moment Fitton smirked, then looked away.

Only then did Naughton notice that the rumble of one of the airships had escalated in volume, and that its shadow had expanded to rapidly envelope them in near darkness. It was plummeting from the brilliant blue skies, seemingly out of control, bearing down directly at the crowded bleachers. Naughton could not tell if it was headed toward the commissioner's section, but he took no time to consider the question: he was immediately at Cunningham's side, as were four of the guards.

Just as quickly, the realization of the airship's descent spread through the mammoth ballpark. The band halted, as did the remnants of the cheering and laughter. Some guests stood, grabbed family members and began to flee; others simply sat transfixed. The young players who were about to take part in the exhibition game emerged from the dugout, perplexed at the sudden shift in the crowd's mood. The stadium was suddenly, remarkably, silent.

Then the lurking craft began to gather speed, its shadow passing across thousands of seats, its droning steam engines merging with a growing cacophony of cries and shouts. In that moment the organist struck up a rousing march, as if in hopes a performance could calm the rising fears.

Three thoughts struck Naughton in that instant: that many were about to die, that this was unlikely to be accidental, and that the Leagues — indeed, the Eternal Ceasefire — could be shattered, eradicated as instantaneously as the ship itself now blotted out the day's glorious sun. And then, a fourth thought: relief that Amelia and the boys had stayed home.

There was no time to reflect beyond that. Naughton and the four guards

surrounded the confused commissioner like a phalanx. With his right foot Naughton flicked a switch embedded in a wooden tile under the commissioner's chair. In seconds a panel in the aisle floor slid open and a carriage large enough to hold the six rose upward. Its mesh wire door sprang open, and the guards ushered the frail man inside. Naughton squeezed in with them and grasped the silver-plated lever on the door to close it.

The cage descended, burrowing into the bowels of the stadium. Naughton had ordered the lift's covert construction months ago for precisely this possibility — the need to quickly extricate the commissioner from the anniversary celebration. He'd hoped it would never be needed. Now it worked flawlessly.

No one spoke. The old man's labored breathing was the only sound, and two of the guards held his arms in support. Naughton felt his own heart racing, and he struggled to unclench his fists. He looked down at Cunningham but his benefactor's gaze was vacant, expressionless. After two minutes the cage slowed and came to a rest at the stadium's lowest basement, a level just above churning steam generators that made up the substation.

The door sprang open. A small corridor lit by gas lamps hanging at sporadic intervals lay before them. Two of the guards immediately stepped into the corridor, but just as the rest were about to follow when the walls shook. Then came the booms of crashing, of smashing, of metal twisting and tearing, rippling far above them like thunderclaps.

None of the six moved. They all knew what the noises meant.

Naughton exhaled. *At least the old man is safe.*

But what he heard next was far worse: the anguished screams, unbridled shouts of panic, and despairing cries of guests who had only short moments ago been cheering shouts of adulation. These sounds echoed through the dim hallway, obliterating the droning of the steam-station below them.

None of the men spoke, seemingly rendered immobile as the piercing shrieks continued unabated.

Naughton shuddered. Yes, the commissioner of the Leagues of SIP and ALE was safe, but he expected that in the coming days and weeks little else on the continent would be.

March 9

WIDMERTOWN

FOR MANY IT WAS THE light-and-dark criss cross cut into the outfield by the groundskeeper. For some it was the distinctive odor of tar on the bat, or the leather of the mitt. For Halloway, though, the most evocative moment of the start of spring training was this very instant: the sight of the clubhouse attendants slinging canvas bags of balls and bats, then unloading them onto the field in a heap. He watched now from a distance. Two young clubhouse attendants, barely twenty, carried out this task without hesitation, as though it were just another day, and the clatter of dozens of bats falling to ground echoed throughout the park.

To the workers, it was a necessary chore. To Halloway it meant, 'And now we begin.'

A new start: each spring brought that. Hope for all teams, no matter how lacking in talent. Hope especially for his team, the Flying Squirrels of Widmertown, predicted by many to win the division. Perhaps to win it all.

Halloway chewed on the end of a toothpick and adjusted his cap as he surveyed the field. *But predictions are so often wrong. Hope is so easily dashed.*

"Cheesely!" he yelled at one of the young attendants. "The mitts are labeled. Put them in their proper lockers." The boy nodded and grinned. It was the youngster's first day on the job, and he'd be thrilled to hand out equipment used by the hurlers and backstops, who were reporting tomorrow.

But neither Halloway nor anyone involved in the Setheridge Island Professional League of Baseball — the SIP — knew whether any games would be played this spring. Nor his counterparts in the ALE — the Amandean League of Everyman. Even as a team manager he had no special insight into what the commissioners' office would decide. Those who died in airship crash — 30 in all, by horrible coincidence the same number as the anniversary year — would be buried over the next few days. Rumors now flew as to whether it was an accident or, if intentional, who was to blame. Setherians hinted at Helderan forces, while his own countrymen, particularly descendants of hardline Helderan insurgents, spoke in whispers of a Setherian conspiracy. And some of the columnists wrote that whatever the cause, whoever was to blame, the season should be canceled out of respect for the dead.

That, thought Halloway, would be the worst outcome.

Off to his right Eldon Langford, the Squirrels' general manager, studied detailed notes. The team would be a strong one, they both knew. Langford and Halloway had spent countless hours in the off-season debating personnel, mulling trades. Langford, in fact, had been able to pull off two major swaps, acquiring Ketter 'Count' Asgar, the 28-year old starting hurler, to shore up the rotation, as well as first bagger Gillighan Alley, also 28. No power there, thought Halloway, but he's got great contact and can sit atop the line-up. Hell of a striker. It had cost them four decent prospects.

"Anxious?" he called out.

Langford, who had run the Squirrels since '16, managed a laugh. "Am I ever not?"

He settled down next to his boss. "Have you heard anything?"

"Nothing. Silence. I've 'tubed every team general manager in the Helderan Division, and all they've heard are the same blengin' rumors flying about. And I'll ignore those rumors for now, thank you."

The field manager nodded. They would proceed as though it were a routine spring training. They would assume a full season would be played. Yet Halloway knew it would be hard for his players not to be distracted by the uncertainty. If warring did return, some of them could be drafted. Others might willingly enlist.

He sighed. The practices and exhibitions of spring training probably wouldn't matter at that point, of course. If fighting did reignite, there'd be no league in which to play. Baseball would be over. And the predictions of a championship season for the Squirrels would be moot. It seemed unfathomable.

Sander Halloway cared little about political and military matters. Though his grandfather and great-grandfather had died in the Insurrection, and his father had survived years of service with life and limbs intact, Halloway himself cared of little else but the game. Not just the competition, the camaraderie, but the small things: the sight of balls scattered near the dugout during batting practice, the graceful slope of the hurler's mound, the swath of dirt across a batsman's uniform after he'd slid into third. The sights and sounds that brought him instant comfort.

"I will address the clubhouse after the strikers report," he told Langford. "Until then, we will proceed apace."

———————— ————————

CHEESELY BROUGHT IN COPIES OF that day's SIP and ALE *Chronicle*, the national baseball broadsheet. Included were the pre-season predictions of Ollo Ronnell, their veteran columnist and the commissioner's most vocal critic. Halloway settled in at his desk in the cramped office behind the clubhouse and grimaced at the article. The old scribe — once a top striker himself — had projected the Squirrels to finish second in the Helderan South Division, behind the West Somerchester Rhinos:

> *The Squirrels, I daresay, are trending in the wrong direction, winning the division three years ago, then slipping to second in '21 and third last season. From this vantage point, we believe they'll rebound, at least back to second, and possibly will give the Rhinos a run for the division crown.*

That made no sense — trending in the wrong direction, yet at the same time a possible contender? Ronnell must be slipping in his advanced years. Halloway read on:

> *Highlighting the Widmertown off-season have been huge trades by long-time team general manager Eldon Langford for two players in their prime: Gillighan Alley and Ketter 'The Count' Asgar. Alley, 28, has little power but will be tremendous at or near the top of the Squirrels' line-up. The Count arrives in Widmertown after six years as the ace in Red Tummlyn. Asgar suffered through an off year last season, but prior to that was a consistent 15-game winner for the Grizzlies. We think the Count and Alley are the two deals that the Squirrels very much needed to do, and so from this hot corner comes a tip of the cap to old Langford for pulling them off.*

Langford will like that, Halloway knew, for the assessment would have Langford's fellow general managers grimacing, and his boss reveled in the jealousy of his peers.

Halloway stood from his desk, put the papers aside, and lay down on the wooden cot on the far side of his office. He had put it there originally for those rare times when the team played an evening game followed the next day by an afternoon contest. There'd be little point, he felt, in returning to his apartment in downtown Widmertown for just a brief bit of sleep. But last year he had slept on the cot far more often, particularly as the season wore. The constant travel for road games, the anxiety of making decisions during the games, his self-evaluation of

MICHAEL BARBATO-DUNN

those decisions and the players' performances, and the annoying and irresponsible questioning of reporters: all of that exhausted him as the season wore on.

So he had little energy to make the 30-minute trip downtown, and with the apartment empty anyway — his second marriage had ended seven years ago — he also had little motivation to do so.

Now he lay on the cot and pondered those off-season trades. He was thrilled to see Alley come aboard. The bulky first bagger was precisely what his line-up needed — a steady striker who drew walks as well. Great eye. And a positive clubhouse presence.

But not so Ketter Asgar. Halloway knew that the hurler's nickname 'The Count' had not been bestowed by his Red Tummlyn teammates for his prowess on the field. "The man is a malcontent," one scout had warned him privately after the trade. "He'll sow discord." The Grizzlies, in the midst of rebuilding with a younger core of players, could not afford to have such negativity in the clubhouse and traded him.

But dealing with a malcontent was, unfortunately, part of Halloway's job. Anyone could fill out the line-up card, even the kid Cheesely. Managers faced a bigger hurdle off the field, keeping 20 egos intact, keeping discord to a minimum.

He closed the newspaper and went back out to the field. Turf workers were painting the team's colors — ocean blue and black — on the foul lines. Others tended to the grass, patching along the lines where the infield dirt ended.

Catalinaside Stadium looked fresh, expectant; he breathed it in. Yes, the hurlers and backstops arrived tomorrow. Strikers, next week. Spring training would be underway. A new season was to begin.

Halloway thought again of the airship attack. And of his grandfather: dead at the hands of Setherian forces in 1849 at age 29. His father had been ten at the time. By that point the Great Insurrection — as the uprising of the Helderan people was known — had been raging for a dozen years. No one at that point could have imagined it would last for nearly forty more.

A spring breeze rippled over the field.

Sander Halloway shuddered. If only a malcontent hurler would be his sole worry as the new season got underway. If only the sounds in the air would be not gunfire, but the crack of bats on balls and the fireworks of a championship victory.

SCHAWMOUNT CITY

A CARRIAGE DRAWN BY TWO oak-brown mares carried Naughton and Coyle from the League headquarters. The thick panes of the cab offered shelter from blustering breezes that poured in to the city from Lake Leoran, but Naughton nonetheless shuddered in the leather seat.

Coyle ruffled through a sheath of papers compiled by investigators, sorting them for the presentation. He was 34 but, with pock-marked cheeks and a wisp of a mustache, appeared far more youthful. A quiet man, Naughton knew, not prone to anger or histrionics. He valued those qualities in his assistant, particularly at a time like this.

They were to brief the commissioner, and out of deference to Dr. Morgan Vinge, Lord Bart's personal physician, the meeting was to be at his residence rather than headquarters. The old man had not been injured during the airship crash or its aftermath, yet the doctor was concerned that the stress of those difficult hours might have lingering effects. Cunningham had protested that he was fine, but he gave Vinge his due and remained at home. His health was paramount, they'd told him. On that point he did not argue.

Now in the carriage, Naughton allowed himself a minute to close his eyes. In the two days since the incident, Naughton and his deputy had been ensconced in matters both complex and unpleasant, assigning tasks, preparing statements, sending and receiving communiques delivered by courier or pneumatube. Assessing the damage both physical and political. Neither had been out of doors in that time, nor had either much chance to sleep.

It had taken most of those 48 hours to fully assess the toll of dead and injured. The final count: 30 fatalities, 148 others suffering a range of mostly minor problems, from scrapes and bruises to broken limbs. None of the injured faced life-threatening situations, so the death toll was unlikely to rise, at least from the airship crash; a far greater question was whether more incidents were to come.

They arrived after an hour's ride, the carriage shifting side to side as it passed up the steep entryway. Naughton had worked for the commissioner for 20 years but rarely had been to his estate, and now he studied the gleaming brick-and-stucco mansion that rose above them during the trip. Baseball has been quite good to Bartholomew Cunningham. Quite good indeed. But few argued that Cunningham didn't deserve the riches. After all, he had saved their world.

Inside, the two were ushered by the solemn housemaster through an immaculate foyer crested with a massive, glimmering chandelier, then into a brass-and-wood paneled club room. Coyle sat, still immersed in his notes, while Naughton paced and pondered the memorabilia on the walls. A lifetime of gifts and plaques. Honors bestowed from every corner of the continent. Cases with bats, balls, and gloves of seasons past. Paintings by the greatest artists of the Twin Nations — Julius Mandible, Keiron Killeby, even one by W. Coulter Marmol — depictions of Cunningham himself during key moments of the formation of the SIP and ALE leagues. The paintings had been donated by the artists themselves, for they deemed that the privilege — and publicity — of Cunningham owning their work outweighed the value those pieces could easily command. To the right was shelving that occupied the entire north wall of the club room, filled with books only about Cunningham. Biographies, hagiographies, picture books, and masters theses. Naughton smirked. Cunningham's vanity knew no bounds.

The housemaster returned. "They are ready."

"They?" he asked. He did not know others would be present.

The man cast a stern look and turned to the inner door. "Yes, I said: they are ready."

"My dear Naughton!" A woman's voice reached him: a brash, piercing bellow. A voice he had not heard in two years.

Lady Vivian Packer Lynam strode toward him, arms outstretched. Taller than him by several thumblengths and boosted further by high-heeled leather boots, she leaned over him and brushed her cheek against his. "It is horrible, Naughton, just horrible."

He murmured agreement. "But the commissioner is fine, Lady Lynam. At least we have that."

The woman dabbed a handkerchief to her eyes and nodded. "Yes, Naughton. I am here to help him through this. I will always be there for Bartholomew." She sniffled demonstrably, then slid onto a couch, smoothed her burgundy hoop skirt, removed her lace veil and placed her bonnet at her side. The ensemble was of silk and lace, with a paisley scarf that ended in tassels. A necklace of large pearls was matched with equally substantial pearl earrings. Her hair, graying and thin, was tied in an elaborate bun and held with a gold clasp.

Amid this tragedy, she was immaculate.

Naughton clenched his teeth. Lady Lynam had been absent from the commissioner's life since '21, a departure that had prompted much speculation in the gossip columns of the tabloids that their long relationship had disintegrated in acrimony. He wasn't certain if that was the case; as Lord Bart's top adviser he was never able to learn the true cause of her absence.

To Naughton, though, the reason was irrelevant. He'd simply been relieved that Lynam would no longer be a voice in the commissioner's ear, and a hindrance to proper decision making.

But now she'd returned.

This will not do, not at the very moment of crisis. "Lady Lynam, I was not expecting your appearance in Schawmount so soon after the incident. Don't you think it would be safer—"

"I asked her here, Naughton."

With that declaration Bartholomew Cunningham, the Commissioner of the Leagues of SIP and ALE, entered the parlor, a servant trailing. He wore a pin-striped, double-breasted black suit, a kerchief folded into the breast pocket. But the formal attire did little to counter the image of frailty, the hobbled gait, the twitching of his jaw, the pallor of his skin. It was little wonder the doctors were concerned.

"Lady Lynam returned to Schawmount City yesterday at my request, gentlemen." She began to rise, but the old man motioned for her to stay seated even as they briefly embraced. Naughton glanced toward Coyle, careful not to let his countenance betray his dismay.

Lynam clasped the old man's hands after receiving a kiss on her cheek. "Bartholomew, did you sleep enough last night? Are you napping as your physician ordered?"

Cunningham scoffed at the question. "I am fine. Please, this is not a medical call. The health of the Twin Nations is the only matter to which we must attend."

"Oh, you!" She turned toward Naughton and Coyle. "I have never been so distraught as when I heard this news. Not even in the worst days of the Insurrection—"

"Vivian, please. I need your guidance, not dramatics." This silenced the woman, and the commissioner joined her on the couch. Naughton and Coyle pulled up chairs nearby. Lord Bart then signaled the attendant, who flipped several switches embedded into a side table. A panel in a neighboring wall slid upward, and an automated wait-table covered in a red velvet cloth ambled out and over to the gathering, its four hinged legs moving in precision. On its top was a bottle of what appeared to be ale and four glasses. The attendant poured, bowed, and left the room, and the wait-table retreated as well.

"Commissioner," Naughton began, with some hesitancy. "I believe that some of what we must discuss should remain confidential, for League officials only." He glanced at Lady Lynam, then back to the old man.

"Andrew," Cunningham laughed. "You are ever the dutiful soldier. Please understand that I have asked Lady Lynam here not for personal, um, comfort, but rather to serve as a key adviser as we weather this storm. What I will hear, she will hear."

Lady Lynam arched her back upward, her jaw jutted out toward Naughton.

"I understand," he replied. "Coyle, let's begin."

His chief of staff retrieved a yellow folder and read from the papers within. "The *Lady Crym* was a tourist craft like the other three airships hired to appear at the anniversary event. It had been fully tested and inspected before the flight. Other than the crew, no others were aboard, at least none that appeared on the official manifest. The *Lady Crym* was staffed by Smit Braggs, the pneumaticist, Burnell Hersey, the wingman, and Branford Stenzel, the commander. All three were military veterans, having served as members of the Setherian peacetime defense force roughly during the years of '14 through '19. None had any previous records in our files. Helderan security officials claim to have no records on them either."

"Any evidence of Magera involvement?" Naughton asked.

Cunningham winced at the question; the Magera was the dominant force in the underworld of the continent, with utterance of that very name inciting fear among citizens. It was a reputation cultivated by the Magera over more than one hundred years, dating back to long before the Great Insurrection. Disparate Magera clans relied on an underground economy with a wide range of activities: from gambling and alcohol running to kidnapping and extortion, with a bit of murder thrown in. And when the Eternal Ceasefire was declared 30 years ago, when Bartholomew Cunningham first formed the Leagues of SIP and ALE, he very quickly settled on a policy of co-existence with the Magera leader, Phangorious Hood. So long as Magera operations did not impede the Ceasefire or the Leagues, the Commissioner's Office, from which all laws were administered, often looked the other way. A wink and a nod.

"None at this point," Coyle replied, "nor any routine criminal involvement. The three had served as a crew together for the last five years. The company that owned the airship, Skygear Dirigible Air Tours, had hired them within a few months of each other. They had a spotless record working together. I don't yet know if they were friends or even acquaintances. We will be talking soon with family members, but obviously that will wait until after the funerals."

"No." Lady Lynam shook her head, sending her earrings swaying.

"Excuse me?"

"No. The investigation will be handled by another," the woman replied.

Naughton stared at her, then cocked his head slightly as Lynam continued. "With the commissioner's approval, I have engaged the services of a Monystian security expert to take charge of the internal investigation. I believe it is best to have this probe conducted by an independent agency, to ensure its veracity."

"Veracity?" Naughton said, turning toward the old man. "Commissioner, are you doubting that my aides and I can be impartial?"

"Not at all, Andrew. I do, though, doubt that you can be thorough as you tend to the Leagues' many other issues, including the question of whether the season proceeds. Heading the investigation will be Enoch Gill. You may remember his father, Hargate."

Naughton did. Hargate Gill had been Cunningham's primary covert investigator during the first two decades of the Ceasefire. Never formally on the payroll, the elder Gill was effectively the commissioner's chief spy. Naughton had had no idea, though, that the son was following that career path. "I assume the retention of the Monystian is to remain confidential?"

"Of course." The Commissioner finished the last of his ale, then flipped several switches on the arm of the couch to summon the wait-table for more. The old man was gaunt in the wake of the incident, and Naughton wondered if Dr. Vinge approved of even moderate drinking. He let it go unquestioned.

Lynam, now assuming full stewardship of the meeting, continued. "And you, Coyle," she motioned toward his aide, "shall be responsible for preparing a separate report that will be made public."

Again Naughton cocked his head. He felt out of sorts. This woman had interjected herself at the very moment of the continent's greatest crisis, and seemed to have concocted her own plans ahead of time, with Cunningham's apparent assent. "Two reports? What? Why?"

"Naughton, you must understand," she replied with a slight grin. "There are two separate questions here. First, what truly caused this disaster? Determining that will be Gill's task. Second, what is needed to preserve the peace?"

Lady Lynam grabbed the arm of the satin-covered couch and rose slightly as if in emphasis. "We all know there is a great likelihood it was not an accident. And that the forces who precipitated this would like nothing more than to see a return to war. If we pronounce publicly the true culprits, then they succeed. So what is needed to preserve the peace right now is the declaration that airship *Lady Crym* fell from the skies by accident.

"And imagine how the conspirators will feel to see us proclaim this a fluke!" Now she was standing fully, waving her arms about. "They will be denied the very thing they seek!"

Naughton pursed his lips and turned to Cunningham. "Do you want me to create a sham investigation? Commissioner, you know my very being is dedicated to the preservation of the peace. But 30 people died! Their families deserve justice. The truth must be known."

The old man said nothing, again leaving Lady Lynam herself to counter. "We are saving lives by doing this. How many tens of thousands died in the Great Insurrection? How many tens of thousands more will die if the Twin Nations again return to warring? Yes, their families deserve and will get justice. That will be the third part of task, once the two reports are complete."

"Yes, once the culprits are identified," Lord Bart interjected, "they are to be removed. Quietly, without public acknowledgment. Permanently removed." His words seemed to reverberate through the suddenly quiet meeting room.

Naughton took a deep breath and held it. *They've already worked this out in its entirety. She's now a decision maker.* He rose from his seat and glowered at the two. "Commissioner. I beseech you." He spoke in a low monotone, a near whisper. "How can you be ordering this? How has it come to this? What has happened?"

Bartholomew Cunningham, 86 years old, sports promoter, peacemaker, hero to millions across the Twin Nations, nodded and matched Naughton's tone with his own whisper. "Protest all you wish. I'd expect nothing less from you, Andrew Naughton. But you know there is no other choice."

With that the old man grabbed his cane and shuffled slowly out of the parlor, head bowed. Lady Lynam rose, gathered her shawl and purse, then exited as well without the slightest nod in their direction.

Eventually, Naughton and his deputy made their way back to the carriage. "League Headquarters," he ordered the driver, "with haste, my man. With haste."

March 12

O LLO RONNELL PULLED ANOTHER CIGAR from the top drawer of his desk and studied the release from the commissioner's office. It had come through the Schawmount priority pneumatube minutes earlier, only the second dispatch from the Leagues since the airship disaster. The relative silence from Cunningham had been fodder for Ronnell's *Chronicle* columns already. This was better than more silence: some meat to chew on. In fact, as he read the statement, Ronnell was already formulating his next piece.

SIP AND ALE LEAGUES FORM MEMORIAL FUND FOR FAMILIES OF VICTIMS

(Schawmount City) — The Commissioner of the SIP and ALE Leagues, His Excellency Lord Bartholomew Cunningham, today announced the creation of a memorial fund to aid the families of victims of the recent airship crash and survivors.

The fund will be seeded with a one million yore endowment from the Leagues. Any families seeking assistance are urged to apply by August 31st.

"We are, of course, heartbroken by the tragedy," said the commissioner. "While the deceased are forever lost, we in the sport of baseball hope this fund can ease certain burdens the families will face."

The commissioner also announced that the formal League investigation into the disaster will be complete in one month, at which point the findings will be made public. Commissioner Cunningham urges residents of both nations to reserve judgment until that probe is complete.

"We should all go about our normal routines," he said. "Harbor no

suspicions, cast no aspersions. Take comfort that the Twin Nations of Setheridge and Heldera will endure."

Requests for assistance should be forwarded by post or pneumatube to the Office of the Commissioner in Schawmount City, Setheridge.

Clever, thought Ronnell. Everyone will focus on the fund. On the great magnanimity of Commissioner Bartholomew Cunningham, and his ever-so reassuring words. A diversion, to be sure.

But there was this: "our normal routines." That was as close to confirmation that the baseball season would take place as he'd heard since the abortive anniversary event. Ronnell had written three columns since the airship crash, all of which lambasted Cunningham for failing to pronounce firmly on the fate of the season. Spring training had begun, but the silence on the question of the season itself made no sense to him. "Isn't uncertainty throughout the continent increased by the lack of a definitive answer?" he'd written.

Ronnell's desk occupied a wide, raised corner of the *Chronicle's* newsroom. No one questioned that the columnist deserved the prominent location; he commanded attention. Now he stood and called out to Corcoran, the managing editor, to expect another column for the next day's broadsheet. "Front page, Crom. You won't want to bury this one." The others, pecking away at their mechascribes, laughed, for Ronnell never wanted anything less than front page.

He settled in to write, but a familiar hiss and rumble rose as Corcoran's wheeled steamchair glided toward him. The editor had lost both legs in '90 stepping on a mine while posted to an infantry. Only one year later came the Ceasefire.

"I've got three men still in Schawmount City," he told Ronnell, "trying to come up with something on the airship company — the men flying it, who owns the firm. I've got two more talking to League owners, pumping them for some sense of where the investigation will head. I've got four others talking to families of the victims and trying to get in to Schawmount Stadium where the repairs are proceeding. My whole blengin' staff is on this, Ollo. So I may not have room tomorrow for your column, certainly not on Page One."

"Your blengin' staff, Crom, has been coming up quite dry, wouldn't you say? How much are you paying them?"

"They're reporting, Ollo. Reporting doesn't always yield results after just a day

or two. Not everyone can just sit back on his duff with a cigar and write only what's on his mind."

"Yes, I hear very few have that talent. Anyway, you'd be best to set aside at least eighteen thumblengths for my column."

"I don't have the space."

"Fourteen."

"Ten. That's it."

"Twelve."

The editor sighed, shifted in his chair and squinted at Ronnell. "Fine, but go easy on him for once."

"Pardon me?"

"Ollo, you cannot argue that the continent sits in a precarious state. I am simply asking you to be fair to Lord Bart. Be responsible. We don't need to be inciting passions on either side of the border any further than they are now."

"Cromwell Corcoran. Are you getting soft in your old age? I thought our goal was to sell newspapers."

"Ollo, every blengin' morning when I wake up, I forget I have no legs and try to stand. I don't particularly care to be the editor of the broadsheet that prompted another 50-year conflict. Your words carry weight, and you know it. Don't abuse it."

Ronnell began to voice a quick retort, then thought better of it. He glanced down at the outline of Corcoran's stumps, then back toward the editor's bitter countenance. They'd worked together from the day Ronnell had been hired, fresh after retiring from baseball. He'd never known Crom to complain about his injury. Not once.

"Twelve?"

"Twelve. Not a thumblength more." With that Corcoran rotated two brass switches on the right handle of his chair. The wheels rotated in a semi-circle, small whisps of steam emerging from tubes in the back, and the chair glided back to the national desk midway across the dim and cluttered newsroom. Other reporters who'd stopped to eavesdrop on the exchange quickly returned to their mechascribes and avoided Ronnell's gaze.

His cigar hung from the edge of lips, the burning tollar weed offering a cascade of white-gray smoke that circled his balding head. Ronnell would write out this column, as he did all his pieces, longhand. He abhorred the mechascribes that cluttered the newsroom and left their operation to the copy boys. He dipped the quill in the well, but then sat back and wondered how to begin.

After a few minutes, words came to him. He had no doubt that what he was about to write would infuriate the commissioner of the sport he loved. He sighed and re-lit the soggy cigar, then picked up the quill once more. "Oh, my old friend Bart," he mumbled to himself. "We'll sell some papers with this one." The words flowed with ease.

Dozens of batsmen take swings in the hitting box. Dozens of hurlers loosen up in the bullpen. And tens of thousands of ticket buyers hover in their homes and publick houses. Two nations worth, in fact.

And deep inside the League offices, the great and beloved Lord Bartholomew J. H. Cunningham V keeps all of us waiting.

Needlessly waiting.

The commissioner's continued silence is perhaps the greatest single testament to his inability to lead, greater even than the 30 funerals which are to come. At a time when the Twin Nations desperately need bold leadership, our old hero has retreated behind his brassy doors.

It is time for Lord Bart to come out and face the anxious people who revere him so.

March 13

SCHAWMOUNT CITY

THE NEWLY HIRED SECURITY CHIEF, Inspector Enoch Gill, arrived in Schawmount City on March 13th, six days after the airship crash. He was led through League Headquarters to Naughton's office, his traditional Monystian dreadlocks swaying across his shoulders, a revolver on his hip. He wore a military-style blazer, its olive coloring overshadowed by the deep bronze of his skin, and the effect only accentuated his profound height. Three aides — also brought in from Gill's private firm, just as towering — followed at his side.

After introductions, Naughton asked the aides to wait in the outer room. He was pleased that Gill dispensed with introductory pleasantries. "Special Assistant

Naughton. I will need ready access to all facets of the investigation conducted so far. Nothing is to be held back. I'm sure you understand."

"Well, to be perfectly honest, Inspector Gill, I do not understand." He'd had no say in the hiring of this man, this outsider. That was all the commissioner, and perhaps also his companion, departed but now suddenly returned, the Lady Vivian Packer Lynam.

The Monsytian smiled, the grin stretching across the tremendous jawline common to his race. "Sir, I hear your reticence. I would feel the same. But there is no middle ground here. We have to work together; we have to cooperate. And that entails the sharing of all intelligence. It starts now. If you can't, I'll immediately return to the Schawmount port and leave your employ. It's as simple as that."

Naughton shook his head. "Obviously, you know I can't turn you away. The commissioner has asked you here, against my best judgment."

"With all due respect, sir, if he had asked me here sooner, before the Anniversary Celebration, 30 people would still be alive."

Naughton looked out, beyond the other man, to the wide range of plaques and awards that filled one office wall. *Thirty people would still be alive.* Had he failed at the security for the event? Could the incident have been prevented?

He sighed. He was not prone to self-doubt. Perhaps this tragedy had changed that. "Very well. You will have full access to all private files and dossiers concerning this incident. You will lead the probe. But you will have no access to other League documents and records without my express approval."

Gill nodded and rubbed the exposed magazine end of his pistol. "Very well. Please inform all necessary staff members of this arrangement as soon as is feasible. And one other thing, sir."

"Yes?"

"It won't work."

Naughton cocked his head. "What won't work?"

"The commissioner's tactic of procrastination. Delaying any public pronouncements about the future of the league to make the conspirators — whoever they may be — anxious, and therefore more likely to make themselves known to us. A clever plan; I admire it. But this attack has likely been long in the making and quite detailed. Every eventuality may have been predicted, including the possibility that the commissioner simply declares it an accident. You may be naïve in expecting that tactic to provoke a mistake on their part."

Naughton evaluated the thought. Naïve? Of that he doubted. During the

30 years of the Eternal Ceasefire, including the 20 of his own tenure, no single insurgent, no group or person seeking to provoke a return to warring, had successfully outmaneuvered the Office of the Commissioner of the SIP and ALE Leagues. There had been many who tried. Many more than anyone outside the commissioner's Office ever knew.

He scowled and bid the Monystian farewell.

———————————————

CRANDY HAD RETURNED.

A technician with the manufacturer, Metallidogs of Mount Waylandtown, arrived at Naughton's office mid-day and unpacked the servohound. It lay motionless on the floor as the man slipped three pneumatic condensers into slots on his underbelly. Five minutes needed to elapse before the charge was complete.

Naughton cringed. He abhorred seeing Crandy in an unpowered state. At least he had been spared the sight of the damage inflicted on the hound in the airship crash. Pieces had been found scattered among the remnants of Section 351 and neighboring seating. Scattered among the bodies.

"He's good as new," the technician chortled. "In fact, we replaced so many parts, you might as well call him new." The man's smile disappeared as he saw Naughton glowering.

Coyle, watching from across the room, sensed the awkwardness of the exchange. "That'll be all," he waved at the man. "We'll send a courier if we require any further assistance."

They sat after the technician's hasty exit and watched Crandy rejuvenate: first an ear twitched, then one eye opened, then the other, and then the head raised. Naughton exhaled.

The hound rose to his feet, front paws first, and surveyed his surroundings. The torso, the portion of the device most damaged in the crash, had been fully replaced and encased in a sheath of new fur. Amid the artificial hide was an array of precision gear assemblies, four where each of the limbs attached to the torso, another above the hound's rear, where his tail pointed at attention, and another in an open slot on the hound's back, from which small steam exhaust pipes rose. His ears — thin layers of metal encased in leather — pointed upright and rotated forward and back on unseen ball bearings. The nose — a small knob of black leather — sniffed in expectation. His eyes — glass with microscopic light receptors — shifted to and fro, taking in the whole of the room.

The hound's gaze stopped at Naughton and his segmented tail wagged excitedly in recognition. The creature galloped toward him and Naughton found himself burying his face into Crandy's slightly pliant face.

"That is a relief, I'm sure, sir," Coyle observed.

Naughton sat upright, trying to regain a professional demeanor. "Yes. Indeed so."

His aide glanced at his notes and spoke in the awkward, halting manner that he used when most unsure of himself. "Sir, so I'm clear: your hound had been by your side throughout the anniversary ceremony, but then you spotted a fistfight in section 351 just as the commissioner completed his speech."

"Yes."

"And you dispatched the servohound."

"Yes. I sent him to report back."

Coyle was the only person to whom he'd revealed this. A fistfight — certainly not unprecedented at the games of the SIP and ALE leagues — had directly preceded the airship crash.

"Did you tell the commissioner?"

"No."

"Will you?"

"Yes. But first I must deal with this Monystian, Gill, and see how his internal probe proceeds."

"So," Coyle replied, as if just thinking out loud. "The fisticuffs are what make you certain that the crash was intentional?"

Naughton pursed his lips and nodded. "There are other indicators, of course. But the convergence of the two events is, in my view, too much to be a coincidence."

Coyle looked down at Crandy, now laying down and cleaning his paws, then again at his notes. "It is a shame. The technicians sent the hound's internal recorder annotations, which survived. But Crandy had arrived at the section just as the airship fell. Nothing was really usable. I had them wipe those annotations clean before re-assembly."

Naughton nodded, and, still kneeling, scratched the hound's soft underbelly.

Wiped clean. The phrase made Naughton swallow. But still Crandy's basic coding remained, literally hard-wired into the core assemblage of tubing and gears. The coding that was the hound's training. The coding that was the hound's memory, the understanding of who he was. Who his master was.

He stroked Crandy's ears, and the hound looked up as his tail swished side-to-

side. And Naughton realized with a pang how much he'd missed, even for six days, his hound's adoring gaze.

AMELIA'S CURT MESSAGE HAD ARRIVED by 'tube in the morning. "If you can't come home, you will take an hour away from the office, and I will come to you. Be at the *Backstop at noon." He knew by her tone there was no room for negotiation; they hadn't seen each other in a week.*

When Naughton entered, she was already seated at a table near the rear of the restaurant. He prolonged their hug, but after a few seconds felt her pull away.

"Thank you," he told her as they sat. "Thank you for coming in. I couldn't leave—"

She quieted him with a touch to his lips. "I know. I know what you must do."

Amelia wore a gray dress with small brass clasps running to the neckline. Her bonnet was equally modest and the only jewelry she wore was an unassuming brass brooch. "Are things settling down?" she asked, picking at some toast rounds the waiter had left.

"No. Not one bit. It's all far too precarious."

Naughton studied her face and saw that anxiety had engulfed her: the color in her cheeks was absent, darkened rings fell under her eyes. Even the smattering of freckles across the bridge of her nose was obscured. He knew she was worried not just for him, and not just for the future of the league. It was the boys. Jack was 12; he'd be of conscription age in just five years. Isaac, just six. Further off, but still—

She was worried, he knew, as all mothers now were. War was again a possibility.

They each ordered crawfish soup and within minutes their servings arrived, along with chunks of warm brown bread. He attacked the bowl; he'd barely eaten a full meal since the incident.

"You're eating too fast," she admonished.

"I'm starved."

"You're anxious."

"As are you."

Amelia frowned. "Perhaps. But I'm not in the middle of it all."

Naughton put down the spoon. Next to the plate, invitingly, she'd poured him some pulpar wine left by the waiter. He hadn't had a drink since the disaster; he'd been too fearful that he'd be called back at a moment's notice. He needed his wits fully about him. Now, though, just a sip.

Then, another. And a third. It flowed down his throat. She moved to the chair immediately next to him and rested her head on his shoulder. "Jack asked if there would be baseball this year."

"And what did you tell him?"

"I told him of course there will."

He wove his fingers through her fine hair as the wine's comfort took hold. He said nothing.

The silence caused her to pull away and look toward him. "Andrew, was I right to tell him that?"

"We will start the season, yes."

"But will it finish?"

Naughton leaned over and kissed his wife's forehead, but offered no reply. He swallowed the final drops of wine. A better man would have eased her angst, he thought. A better man would have simply lied.

April 2

WIDMERTOWN

SUNLIGHT SHOT THROUGH CORNERS OF the curtains, waking Halloway. He had slept fitfully and it was ten minutes before he rose and went to the sink to shave. Smells of mildew and sewage permeated the bathroom from vents of the old building, so he hurried through his rituals, as he did each morning. He would shower later, at the clubhouse.

The apartment had one bedroom and was drafty and poorly lit. That didn't bother Halloway; most of his time was spent at the ballpark. The furniture was rented as well, and the pieces showed the wear of countless past tenants. He kept his clothes and notes here, but little else. His possessions, mainly the keepsakes and memorabilia of his playing days, were back in his hometown, at the home of his late parents, now passed on to him and his brother.

None of that mattered, he reminded himself. The season was getting underway; the stadium would become his home. He'd be with his true family: his coaches, his players. The game, the team, the competition, the camaraderie: all would shortly consume every moment of his time.

MICHAEL BARBATO-DUNN

Yet his stomach wrenched. He gripped the sides of the porcelain sink and fought the urge to vomit.

He wiped steam from the mirror. The gas lamp to the right of the mirror cast shadows across his face, accentuating the creases of his forehead, the rings below his eyes. The ravages of years of managing.

And yet they still hailed him a hero.

———————

A CLUBHOUSE BOY, DISPATCHED WITH a small carriage, picked up him an hour later and took him to the ballpark. "Great morning to you, coach." Halloway tipped his cap and grumbled a reply.

The afternoon would bring another spring training exhibition, the Squirrels hosting the Mad Dogs of Skate River, a 1:05 start. The veteran hurler Benjamin Harald would start for Halloway's club. He tried sketching out a line-up on his notepad, but his attention wandered to the series of farm houses on the outskirts of the city that lined the road to the stadium. Each had workers in the field: planting season. Tollar weed, perhaps, as well as wheat and corn. He wondered if the field hands were focused at all on the baseball season, or even on the larger political turmoil that had engulfed the continent.

The Commissioner's Office was expected to issue Lord Bart's decision on whether the regular season would be played within the next few days. The answer would make it clear to all how precarious the political situation had become in the wake of the airship crash, the 30 dead.

Was that what had kept him from sleep? He couldn't recall.

He squinted in the sunshine, trying to concentrate, to isolate what gnawed at him. He knew it was more than the usual anxiety about the team, about the long line of games to come. About winning. That tension was ever present, even in the off season; it pervaded him. This was different.

Perhaps it was simply about the importance of the coming season. He'd been hired by the Flying Squirrels as striking coach back in 1914. The organization — then in the midst of yet another losing season — had needed a promotional boost. "Without the ability to contend," one scribe had written, "the Squirrels are relegated to selling tickets by hiring a Helderan hero. Let's see if Mr. Halloway, though revered throughout our country, has anything to offer as coach."

The words — mirrored by a host of other writers — stung, but he decided to take them as a challenge — to end the long string of losing in Widmertown.

It was the largest city on the Island of Heldera, thought to be the very birthplace of the Helderan people, and baseball was beloved here. Yet in the 30 years since the inception of the Leagues, the Flying Squirrels had claimed not one single championship. Buried in the team's media guide, Halloway had found this miserable fact: in the team's three decades, its combined record was 1528-2073. A paltry .425 winning percentage. There were teams in both SIP and ALE that had delivered worse results over that time, but Halloway was well aware that for a city as hallowed as Widmertown, the lack of success was a particularly bitter one.

Three years later, in 1917, he was promoted to manager, and three years after that the team did what had been unthinkable — it won the Helderan Division crown, and advanced to the Continental Series, the 9-game battle for the championship of the SIP League. There, the squad had fallen easily to the Terriers of McKilligan, a perennial powerhouse, but Halloway at least had proved he could navigate a team to the final round. The mood of the columnists, and by extension, the fans, changed remarkably. He was no longer an imposter, elevated to manager by virtue of heroic acts decades ago. He was now a capable manager, one who might actually prove capable of bringing the hallowed league championship to Widmertown.

That aura — that optimism — dissipated just as quickly. Two years ago, they'd slipped from first to second place. Then last year, from second to third. The local scribes began writing about the waning patience of the team's owner, Willison Caffrey. Halloway was signed to a contract through '25, but that meant nothing. Managers were hired to be fired, he knew, and contracts were readily ignored.

He heaved a deep sigh as the carriage pulled up to the stadium's clubhouse entrance. National hero be damned: without a championship, Sander Halloway knew this year would be his last in Widmertown.

THE MANAGER STOOD NEXT TO his hurling coach, Gabriel Keating, as Harald took final warm-ups off the mound.

"Do you want to leave him in as long as he can go?" Keating asked. SIP and ALE teams used four-man rotations, with just two or three in the bullpen, and starting hurlers were expected to remain in for the full nine innings. Now, during spring training, starters were working their way up to full stamina.

"If you think he's up to it," Halloway said. "I need him sharp next month. Assuming we even have Opening Day."

Keating picked at his teeth with a sliver of wood and nodded. "We will. And he'll be ready."

Halloway could only hope. Every team needed middle-of-the-rotation types like Harald, whose stuff was mediocre but who could be relied upon to throw every fourth game. Four pitches — fastball, curveball, slider, and forkball — and not one was particularly effective. His fastball chugged in toward the bag slower than a steam engine. The forkball fooled few and gave the backstop fits. Still, Benny was a veteran who could hold up under the pressures of throwing for a contender, perhaps even into the play-offs.

The two watched as Harald unleashed a wild one, sailing high above the backstop and into the fence that protected fans sitting behind the home bag.

"He'll be ready," repeated Keating with a wry smirk.

Back in the dugout, Halloway hung a card with the afternoon's line-up on the far wall.

F. Dunbar 2B
N. Wrye SS
J. Minnocks C
G. Alley 1B
P. Marsh RF
A. Goldwell CF
R. Comber 3B
M. Flaherty LF
B. Harald P

Lucius Cameron, the Squirrel's long-time third bagger, sauntered over and shook his head after not seeing his name. No longer was Cameron the starter; he really hadn't been for two seasons now, but Halloway knew it was still hard for the veteran to accept. Even in a spring training game.

"Coach," Cameron called out. "I need some at-bats."

"I'll get you in there soon enough," he called over. Cameron sneered. Halloway paid the infielder no mind. Managing well meant irritating players. During the course of the season it was inevitable, even in spring training. They all wanted to be on the card.

The starters rustled up their mitts and caps and rushed to the field for some soft tossing. Cameron stared at the nearly vacant wooden bench, as if trying to convince himself to sit down. "I'll get you in," Halloway repeated. The striker studied his bat and ignored the promise.

Halloway ground his teeth, then walked out to the railing beyond the dugout and offered signatures to a small group of waiting fans, mostly children. Two small boys asked him to sign their caps, jumping up and down as he complied, and their father stood behind them, beaming. "Coach, is this finally our season?"

"I just want to get through the year."

"I'm sure you will."

"No, I mean everyone. All of us. My hope is that we all can get through this year."

The father gleaned Halloway's true meaning and scowled, then ushered the boys away.

Why did I say that? Children don't need to hear such talk. He signed programs and caps for the few more minutes, then begged off. He stomped his way through the clubhouse and into his office, slamming the door.

Schawmount City

THE EXECUTIVE OF THE SOVEREIGN Nation of Heldera, the mercurial Willison Caffrey, arrived at League Headquarters amid a wind-whipped spring rainstorm. He was small for a Helderan, and coarse in complexion, but projected an air of refinement, with a dark silk jacket adorned with brass buttons. His sideburns were elaborately crafted, sloping inward to join with a bushy pepper-gray mustache. A gold-framed monocle remained affixed to his right eye, and he carried a hand-crafted cane of fine oak capped with a silver handpiece. His top hat towered a good three handlengths. Naughton wondered if a hat that size was the latest fashion, or Caffrey's own attempt to boost his stature.

He greeted the Helderan leader and his entourage in the ante room outside the commissioner's office, offering a small bow. "Sir, we appreciate your gracing us with your presence today."

Caffrey waved off the attempt at pleasantries. He had owned the Widmertown Flying Squirrels on the Island of Heldera since the inception of the Leagues, and had been appointed as Helderan Executive by his fellow owners 15 years ago. Over the course of those years Naughton had seen the man's patience for pomp and circumstance only diminish. "Spare me, Naughton. You know Lord Bart didn't call me here; I requested the meeting."

MICHAEL BARBATO-DUNN

"Of course." Naughton offered a nod of appeasement. "I will check on the commissioner."

He nodded as well to the Helderan owners who accompanied Caffrey. There was Morren Godwyn, the mercantile magnate who owned the West Somerchester Rhinos, and who in recent months had been lobbying for wholesale changes in league financial rules. Next to him stood Gerrold Patrick, Jr., owner of the Toads of Fanningana Falls in the ALE league. His was one of the smallest franchises, yet he remained one of the most influential owners on either side of the border. And further back with furrowed brow, the Warthogs owner, Sir Alexander Fitton. Naughton had not seen Fitton since their awkward glances just before the airship attack.

Naughton proceeded through one set of doors, where two uniformed guards stood at attention. The commissioner's secretary nodded toward him as she activated the switches to open the next set of doors. Tones sounded. Naughton entered the inner chamber.

"Sir, Executive Caffrey has arrived, with Godwyn, Patrick, and Fitton. The Executive's mood is most foul."

Cunningham paused from writing longhand at his desk and grimaced. "Well, I'll just have to see if I can outdo him." The response pleased Naughton; clearly, the old man was feeling better and was up to the task of holding potentially difficult meetings.

"You said Fitton was among them? Of Crenshaw City?"

"Yes, sir."

"That is rather odd, wouldn't you say? Usually Harry Gander rounds out Caffrey's entourage."

Naughton agreed. "Perhaps Gander is not well."

"And your guess as to Caffrey's agenda, Naughton?"

"Most likely he is simply trying to gauge our disposition."

"Testing *me*, no doubt." Cunningham flipped down a handle at the side of his writing desk, exposing the tubular end of an intercom. "Send them in, Janell."

The four appeared, lockstep as if choreographed. These men — and the other 14 Helderan team owners — ruled their nation, just as the Setherian owners controlled their country. Neither nation had a central government; such were the terms of the Proclamation of an Eternal Ceasefire. Legal and administrative power instead rested in the individual cities governed by the SIP and ALE League team owners, 36 in all, spread across the continent. Each nation's owners chose from their ranks a single leader to speak for them, an executive, a first among equals. For the Helderans, it was Willison Caffrey.

"Bartholomew! You have our warmest regards for your continued good health and leadership. We were vastly relieved you were spared from the hideous attack."

"Willison, my old friend, I trust the day finds you in good health. Morren and Gerrold, you as well." Cunningham offered the greetings in a deliberately neutral tone.

Alexander Fitton, towering above the rest, leaned forward and thrust his open hand to Cunningham. "Certainly better health than the 30 who died, Commissioner," he interjected.

The old man scowled. "Now, Sir Fitton. You don't need to be reminding me of that. It weighs on me every minute."

"What weighs on the Nation of Heldera, Commissioner, is that we are about to be blamed for it."

The others stood awkwardly in silence. Cunningham, undaunted by the barb, turned to face Caffrey. "Well, Willison, it seems tact is in short supply these days. Perhaps an ale would be in order for all of us."

This is off to a wondrous start. Naughton wondered if he'd have to summon guards. For now, he activated several switches on the half-butler, which retreated to the anteroom to prepare the drinks.

Cunningham motioned for the four to repair to the couch as he and Naughton pulled up chairs.

Caffrey began to speak but then glanced over at Naughton, who was sitting unobtrusively off to the side. "Does he need to be here?" he asked Cunningham.

"Yes, as a matter of fact, he does."

"We did not bring our aides, Bartholomew."

"This is my house, my chamber, Willison. Please proceed. I have a terrible amount of work ahead."

Caffrey sighed. "Fine. Commissioner, we are perplexed by the silence that has emanated from your office since the disaster."

"Silence? We issued a press release one month ago, five days after the, um, incident. I'm sure you saw it."

"Yes, but when are you going to pronounce yourself on the future of the season?"

"Spring training is already underway. Surely you and your Helderan brethren can extrapolate that the season will begin as scheduled."

The Helderan leader glanced at his fellow owners. Caffrey, nearly 70, wore a grimace masked only by his sculpted mustache and sideburns. "Let me tell you this, Commissioner: the situation cries out first and foremost not for a public relations announcement but for some comforting words from you, and only you. The Commissioner, the Founder, the Great Peacemaker. A swift declaration that the crash will be investigated, and that the season will proceed. Why in the continent's sake have you not done so?"

Naughton knew this was coming. Even with the *Chronicle* and other broadsheets screaming that the Twin Nations needed reassuring words directly from the commissioner, Cunningham had deliberately refused to make any pronouncements. The apparent agitation of Caffrey and the others was no surprise. Naughton waited to see how the old man finessed this.

"Oh, Willison. I would have thought you, of all people, would have realized why I'm silent."

Godwyn, seated next to Caffrey, shook his head. "No. I'm sorry. It makes no sense. The peoples of the continent are confused, angry, anxious. Yet you remain mute. So forgive me for being dense, and pray tell your reasoning for this."

"Its quite simple, really." Bartholomew Cunningham leaned forward. Naughton, at the commissioner's side for two decades now, stifled a grin. He knew the old man was vamping, making it up as he went along.

"Yes?"

"Out of respect for the dead. For their families."

The four Helderans jerked back simultaneously. "I don't—" said Godwyn.

"How would you feel if your loved ones had died and within days I was proclaiming that the season will go on? Oh, and it will go on, in case you were wondering. The peoples of the Twin Nations know it will go on. But stating the obvious, my dear friend, would accomplish little, other than to offend those who are grieving."

"So…" Caffrey stammered. It was clear this idea had not occurred to him, nor to any of his fellow Helderan owners. That the commissioner should place the sentiments of the families of the victims above the matters of baseball and war was… was simply inarguable. "So, I see." The glower was gone. The executive looked — ever-so-slightly — defeated. The other Helderans seemed to shrivel at the realization, except for Fitton, who merely pursed his lips as if in disgust.

At this point, Bartholomew Cunningham knew he had met the Helderans' challenge and, ever the showman, chose to end with a flourish. Naughton found himself enjoying the spectacle. "But Willison, you raise a valid point. I will have Mr. Naughton issue a statement this very afternoon, to be transmitted by courier and pneumatube to all corners of the continent, proclaiming that the 30th anniversary season will, in fact, proceed. Would that suffice?"

Clever, Naughton realized. *Lord Bart would have issued such a proclamation within a day or so anyway. Now he lets the Helderans leave believing they accomplished something.*

Caffrey fiddled with the end of his mustache and mulled the offer. "Yes, Commissioner, I would imagine that will be sufficient, at least for now."

The four owners glanced amongst themselves, then rose to leave, but Cunningham had his final punch. "But allow me to ask you a question."

"Of course, your Excellency."

Bartholomew Cunningham rose and leaned forward, appearing to tower over the seated Caffrey. "I need to know, Executive Caffrey: can you keep your people in line?"

The two men stared at one another. *'Your people.'* That phrase, Naughton knew, could be interpreted in any number of ways. The other owners. The Helderan governing council, known as the Second Tribunal. Or the entire populous of the Nation of Heldera. The question hung in the silence.

"In line?" Caffrey laughed. "Commissioner. You know full well that Heldera is more a coalition of city states than any unified country. And we... we are just owners of baseball teams."

"Your nation heeds the words of the owners," the commissioner countered. "You are the de facto governors. And you yourself, Willison, are the executive appointed by all of the owners."

"Please. Get to your point."

"My point is that this fragile peace hinges all too much on people like your colleague Mr. Fitton here — the younger owners who never experienced the Great Insurrection. Who have little recollection of the founding of the Eternal Ceasefire. Fitton and the other newcomers: industrialists, politicians, sportsmen. Willison, we have known each other for more than three decades. We have trusted each other for three decades. The fate of the continent is in your grasp. You could easily choose to seize this crisis as a means to foment unrest."

"Are you accusing us of complicity—"

"No, of course not. Nor am I accusing you of being the ones who are quietly

spreading talk that I should step down, that I am too old and feeble to remain as Commissioner—"

"Lord Cunningham, we would do no such thing!"

"Spare me your protestations, Willison. I am simply reminding you that all of us best tread carefully, for the continent is in a precarious state." Naughton cringed. He was not sure the old man's blunt tone was warranted at this point. Caffrey and the others appeared aghast.

Except Fitton, who stood and retrieved his top hat from the neighboring chair. Methodically, he drew his white gloves onto the length of each bony hand, and spoke directly to Cunningham. "You flatter us, Commissioner, but you vastly overstate our influence."

"I do no such thing." The commissioner's voice rose in volume and his face reddened. "Modesty has no place in this discussion."

"No doubt. Rest assured, kind sir, that the people of the Nation of Heldera remain committed to the ceasefire." Fitton turned and made his way to the office door, then swung back and added, "But do not for a moment assume that we will always be lulled into complacency by a good baseball game and a stout. There are limits to our support for the current arrangements, and they are very close to being reached." Then he bowed to each of them and departed, and his fellow owners, with bemused expressions, followed suit.

WIDMERTOWN

THE STANDS WERE STILL NEARLY empty when Benjamin Harald offered the first throw — a ball, low and outside — to the Mad Dogs' second bagger Bergan Wickes. Then another ball. Then a third. The strike zone was proving elusive, and suddenly Harald needed a strike to avoid walking the lead-off batsman on four throws.

Neither Halloway nor Keating flinched. Benny would settle down. Veterans often needed an inning to find their location. And it was just spring training.

The fourth of the hurler's offerings arrived solidly in for a strike, with Wickes looking all the way, and then Harald did in fact settle, coaxing Wickes into a pop-up and inducing two quick ground-outs from the second and third batsmen. Harald glided off the mound.

In the bottom of the inning, the Mad Dogs went with their own crafty veteran, the journeyman Lawrence Nayland. Skate River was his fifth team in five years after being cut by his original organization, West Somerchester. Like Harald,

Nayland had four decent pitches but little zip on his fastball, and he survived in the SIP League simply by trying to induce ground-outs. He too was wild a bit in the first, walking two, though those strikers were left stranded with a fly-out by the Squirrels right fielder Gerard Hermon.

That, in fact, is how the game proceeded: two aging, mediocre hurlers, ostensibly dueling each other but actually fighting to hold on to their rotation spots. The first two innings passed at a languid pace, and both hurlers kept their opponents scoreless. Next to Halloway was his striking coach, Archibald Ferns, who tried cajoling a bit of life into his batsmen. "We could use a little contact, gentlemen."

But Skate River got on the board in the third, as third bagger Jake Stratton walked on four straight pitches. Halloway could see Harald grimacing at the fourth throw, which looked to be just inside. The arbiter's strike zone was tight indeed. Stratton advanced to second on a bunt by Wickes. Next, left fielder Jed Chanley, the Mad Dog's two-hole striker, lashed a double to right and drove in Stratton. Halloway muttered a profanity under his breath.

Geoffrey Beech, the Mad Dogs' manager, lifted Nayland after four innings. An early hook, Halloway mused, since the hurler hadn't yielded but three hits and no runs. Relieving was Griffin Harrison, who'd come to Skate River through an off-season trade as well. Perhaps that explained the early hook for Naylad: Beech needed a longer look at Harrison. The newcomer proved to be just as solid as both Nayland and Harald, and over the next four innings batsmen on both squads were handcuffed. By the end of the eighth, the score remained 1-0 for Skate River.

"One more?" asked Keating. The pitching coach wanted to know whether Harald would go out for the ninth. Halloway's preference in spring training games was to go easy on the starters, usually no more than seven innings. But Harald so far had yielded just two hits and two walks over eight. "Yes, sure. But get Ryan up." Ryan Foreman, the Squirrels' closer, was dispatched to the bullpen to ready himself should Harald falter.

Foreman was not needed; Harald dispatched the Mad Dogs with ease in the ninth, yielding a solitary two-bagger to a pinch hitter who ended up stranded by the final striker. Harald's outing was complete: nine solid innings, just three hits and one run overall. Halloway was pleased, for he expected to rely heavily on the hurler during the upcoming season.

The score remained tied heading into the bottom of the ninth. Beech removed

Harrison in favor of the Mad Dogs' closer, Britton Ray, who induced lazy fly-outs from the Squirrels' first two batsmen.

Two outs. Extra innings seemed inevitable.

Halloway glanced over at Cameron, seated quietly on the bench, focused only on the round of his bat, still sulking after not getting the start. "Get in there," he yelled.

Cameron grinned, snapped up his tarred stick, and leaned over. "I'll take care of this," he predicted with a wink. He scampered up the dugout steps, dug in at home base and glared down at the hurler. What remained of the already sparse crowd cheered on.

———————— ————————

ONE SIMPLE SPEECH, SO MANY years ago.

It had come amid the Inaugural Draft, held in late 1892, a year before the first season. Sixteen teams took turns claiming the rights to hundreds of semi-professional ball players who had competed in regional leagues and brew-house tournaments during the the war. The best of the semis were about to become purely professional, the first crop of players for the Setheridge Island Professional League of Baseball, known simply as 'the SIP.' The draft played out over several weeks, with team general managers tendering meager offers to the semis who were still available, then relaying their choices by courier to the commissioner's office in Schawmount City.

And throughout the first weeks of the draft, one trend appeared: the Setherian owners were drafting Setherian players, the Helderan teams claimed only Helderans. It was not by mandate; Lord Bartholomew Cunningham had never proclaimed that team rosters should reflect the new political boundaries. But no one involved expected it to be otherwise.

Then came the announcement that reverberated for days, as if rattling the very pneumatic tubes that carried the message. Raymond Frun, the Setherian owner of the Kendall Griffins, chose in the 20th round a slugging first-bagger named Sander Halloway.

A Helderan.

At first many thought it was a clerical error. The Eternal Ceasefire was less than a year old, and some mocked the name, certain that the end of warring would in fact be quite short-lived. The very thought of a Helderan — a descendant of insurgents, whose great-grandfather and grandfather had died in the Insurrection — playing for a Setherian team was inconceivable. The war was still too fresh, too raw.

But Bartholomew Cunningham himself — as Halloway later came to learn — knew immediately this was no recording mistake: Frun was certain that the success of the Leagues, and of the Ceasefire, depended on putting a Helderan ballplayer onto his Setherian club.

So Halloway found himself a major figure: the first, the only, Helderan national to be drafted by a Setherian club. Dozens of reporters and political activists, and dozens more who were simply curious, flocked to his parents' home in Hot Bear Bend the day it was announced. The reporters demanded an answer: would he, in fact, play for a Setherian team? The crowd chanted his name, urging him to come out and speak.

For two hours he hid behind drawn curtains. Then Frun himself arrived and sat with Halloway for an hour as the chanting continued. "Come play for me," the owner asked. "We'll win some ball games." Halloway looked to his father, who simply nodded and smiled.

Frun then escorted his new player out to the press, and Sander Halloway, 31 years old, stepped onto the lawn and spoke words that ensured his place in the history of the continent.

"I will join the team of my ancestors' once-mortal enemies. I will play on their fields, and I will score them some runs. For nothing less will ensure that this newborn peace becomes eternal. For the Twin Nations, for the entire continent and for all the five races: I will play baseball for the Griffins of Kendall."

AFTER CAMERON'S SHOT SAILED OFF into the night sky, after the striker had circled the bases, jumping into the crowd of teammates around the home bag, Halloway felt himself finally, mercifully, relax. Ever so slightly.

An hour later, after meeting with reporters and issuing the usual platitudes about the importance of pinch batters, of players always being ready to contribute, Halloway returned to his small clubhouse office. On his desk was a 'tube communique, likely left there by a courier in the past few minutes. The terse note was from Langford, the Squirrels' general manager.

> *"The Commissioner's Office has confirmed that the season will begin as scheduled on May 2. New security measures at all ballparks will be in place. Otherwise, games will follow all normal procedures."*

Still chomping furiously on the wad of tollar tucked into his cheek, Halloway closed his eyes. This was good. This was what he'd wanted to hear. He took several deep breaths and his thoughts returned to the just-completed game.

"The dark secret of baseball managing," he'd once told his first wife, Kiara, "is that the better ones are just plain lucky. They come around at a time when a core of good players are coalescing and peaking. They know enough to just let those guys play and stay the hell out of their way." Kiara was long gone, as was his second wife, Ruth. The road trips, the job changes, the long hours. It never suited either of them. So be it.

So the season would go on. But did he have the right men to win it all? Halloway refused to allow himself an answer. But in his 20 years of coaching he had never quite felt this... what was the word?

It came to him. It was a word he hated. It was a word he refused to consider, much less speak. Why did it appear to him now? After all, it was only spring training. It was a word that hardened ball players would never be caught uttering.

The word was 'destiny.'

April 13

Leoran Lake

Naughton's next meeting with Security Chief Gill was on a lake.

It had been 11 days since the encounter with the Helderans and the commissioner's declaration that the season would proceed: a period of much-needed calm. During that time the funerals for the 30 victims had been held; Lord Bart and his entourage attended each one; some days included as many as three such services. Naughton insisted that Cunningham's personal physician accompany them; he feared the travel, the crowds, and the relentless grief would take its toll. But the old man seemed to hold up well.

Reporters massed around the commissioner at the first several funerals, but Naughton told told them his excellency would not comment out of deference to the mourning families. By the time the last dozen were held the press lost interest; the burials had become routine for all but the loved ones. In the meantime, spring training for all the teams of the SIP and ALE Leagues had continued, quietly, respectfully.

Uneventfully.

Gill had sent a message by pneumatube that he needed a private meeting at the soonest possible opportunity, and that they should meet on Lake Leoran, due east of Shawmount City. Just the two of them, in a small rowboat. He would have preferred his own office, within the depths of the cavernous League Headquarters. But the more he examined the demand, the more sense it made. If Gill's message had been intercepted, a meeting at a more convenient location could be observed, surveyed. Eavesdropped. Only on the wide lake could they truly be assured of absolute privacy if the time and location became known to others.

Coyle and Gill's aides waited on the shoreline as the security chief rowed for a full half-hour, his braided dreadlocks swaying front to back as he paddled. It was not until they reached what was certainly the center of the shimmering lake that Gill felt comfortable enough to talk. "Here," he said grimly, placing the oars within the hull.

Naughton watched small katydids dancing on bits of algae on the water's surface. The air was tepid. The bow rocked quietly in the slight westward breeze.

Gill glowered. "Sir, I have taken it upon myself to prepare a file for you, one I'm sure you will find worthwhile."

From a small hide case the Inspector retrieved a leather bound folder with a locked clasp, unlocked it, then handed it to Naughton.

Naughton took a deep breath, then began paging through the folder. It had been precisely a month since Gill first arrived, and since their initial, tense conversation over the extent of Gill's access, Naughton had seen little of him or his aides. Their prolonged absence had only exacerbated Naughton's unease over the commissioner's decision to hire the man. But now — here was the result of their work.

"We have interviewed the relatives of the crew members," Gill said. "We have interviewed all seven people who worked at the airship company. We have conducted background checks on everyone, and thus far we have found no links whatsoever to any insurgent or politically active groups. Nothing that would give cause for concern. We are in the midst of interviewing leaders of the three surviving Helderan insurgent groups. This incident, though, bears none of the hallmarks of their work."

Naughton smiled. "Yes. It was executed with far more competence than they could muster."

"Indeed. In the meantime, we are continuing our analysis of the remnants of the airship. Unfortunately, much of the wreckage was charred in the ensuing blaze. Stadium security successfully kept the fire from spreading beyond the neighboring sections of the ballpark, which of course is quite fortunate. But the cabin was fairly well consumed. This will thwart our ability to truly determine if there was sabotage. Still, the analysis continues."

"What is the state of the actual control panel within the cabin?"

"It was crushed in the impact, split into numerous sections."

"Can it be reconstructed?"

"We are trying. But it is unlikely."

"And I'm sure you have looked into whether the incident has any links to the Magera?"

"Yes. At this point, we can find none. But the tentacles of Phangorious Hood are long indeed."

"True." Naughton could sense Gill's disdain for Hood and his underworld organization. Some of that was racial: there was long distrust between the Monystians and the Rebular. The Monystian people prided themselves on being law-abiding, and thus despised the Magera, whose membership was primarily Rebularan. The antipathy was mutual.

"Now, Mr. Naughton, I have a question for you. When are you releasing the bogus report, the one that will claim the crash was an accident?"

"How do you know of that?"

"Part of the reason I've been retained, sir, is that I have at the ready a fairly extensive intelligence network that snakes throughout the continent. It is a network established decades ago by my father, and which I retain at great expense."

"And that network extends even into the Commissioner's Office."

"Correct."

A more difficult breeze curled past them and the tiny boat rocked side to side. He despised having to prepare a sham report. And to think word of its existence, and its lack of veracity, was already known to the Monystian made the plan more distasteful.

"So beyond Cunningham wanting your intelligence, he hired you to ensure that your intelligence is not available to others."

"That might also be correct."

"The false report is complete," Naughton admitted. "It was drafted by one of my most trustworthy men, Roderick Coyle. No one else has seen it."

"Will it withstand scrutiny?"

"Perhaps. But the critics will try their best to poke holes nonetheless."

"Ronnell first among them, no doubt," Gill said.

"No doubt." He was again impressed: the Monsytian was cognizant of the potential harm that the *Chronicle* columnist could bring. Ronnell — revered in both nations, first as a ballplayer and now as an acerbic scribe — frequently insisted on using his printed pulpit to sow unrest. There was nothing Naughton could do to stop him.

"Do you have someone watching him?" Gill asked.

"We do, and apparently that surveillance dates back the moment he went to work for that damned newspaper, though I doubt he has any ill-advised connections. He seems to simply enjoy riling people up."

"So when is this manufactured document being sent out?"

"In 10 or so days," Naughton explained. "The commissioner will present the document to the press and answer questions. We are preparing him for that now."

The boat had begun drifting slightly toward the other shore, the Helderan side, so Gill rowed for a minute, the movement sending ripples on the otherwise still water in all directions. "And, sir, I draw your attention to the final section in the folder."

Naughton examined it and was surprised. The man was good: he'd anticipated what Naughton was likely to request in a matter of days: a full surveillance report on the rude Helderan owner Alexander Fitton. Naughton rifled through the pages, which numbered fewer than two dozen. "Worth a read?"

"From an investigatory standpoint, sir, no. This is all grade three surveillance, from the greatest possible distance, with minimizing risk of discovery as the absolute priority. Therefore, the results are minimal."

"Minimal?"

"Well, there is the prurient. He seems to have several mistresses."

"Several?"

"Three that we know of."

"Fine. What else?"

"Really, the only thing I'll draw to your attention is something of which you are probably already aware. The political rumblings."

"Go on."

"Sir, political matters are normally outside my realm, but the crossover between forensic and political sometimes makes things murky…"

"Get to the point."

"I believe there is some covert fund-raising taking place to form a new political party in Heldera, with Fitton at its helm."

"That's not illegal."

"No, sir, of course not."

Still, Naughton understood Gill's point. The political leadership within Heldera has been quite fractured in recent years, with several of the SIP and ALE owners in that nation vying for control of the governing council, the Second Tribunal. Caffrey of Widmertown had managed to retain the executorship for 15 years, but only because he was palatable to factions that could not otherwise agree. "He is everyone's second choice," he'd once been told by a Helderan staffer.

Jockeying to succeed Caffrey had continued between Patrick and Godwyn, two of Caffrey's entourage when the Helderans met with Cunningham two weeks ago. Each — Caffrey, Patrick and Godwyn — had long controlled their own political parties, and those groups regularly engaged in political nastiness across the Helderan countryside. Now, with the possibility of Fitton forming and leading a fourth party, the current situation could become complicated in ways that Naughton couldn't imagine.

The wind picked up and the boat felt as though it was rocking violently. He lifted up the folder. "I will read it. Is there more?"

"Yes — my operatives in Kern have passed this on to me." Gill took out a handbill and handed it to Naughton.

It had been printed by the Opera House in Kern, one of the largest cities in Heldera and the one closest to the League Offices across the border in Setheridge. In fact, Naughton could glimpse the Kern skyline just beyond the eastern shore of the mammoth lake.

The handbill announced a coming lecture at the theater by a certain Dr. Iphonious Henry. Naughton vaguely knew the name. "*The Value of the Scientificka in Politically Unstable Times,*" the presentation was titled.

"Who's Henry?"

"He's an increasingly popular figure among certain factions of the Scientificka. Only 26 years old, already with several degrees, a prestigious position at the University of Kern, multiple publications to his credit, and now growing acclaim among some of the more politically minded scientists."

The Scientificka was the professional organization of researchers, physicians and theoreticians that arose after the declaration of the Eternal Ceasefire. The group claimed no national allegiance, no boundaries, no political agenda. Setherians and Helderan academicians alike dominated its leadership. The minority races — the Rebular, the Monystians, even the Amandeans — had only token representation.

The group had never been a threat, for over the past 30 years, Lord Bart had successfully found ways to ensure that the majority of the Scientificka's governing board included scientists who were deferential to the needs of the Leagues. And to him.

"Does this lecture concern you?" he asked Gill.

"Mr. Naughton, to the extent that the continent hangs precariously on the brink of warfare, everything concerns me."

"Fine," Naughton nodded. "I will send Coyle to this Dr. Henry's lecture next month. If you have further cause for concern, bring it to my attention promptly."

"Thank you, sir."

Naughton looked away from the Monystian, out toward the Helderan side of the shoreline. Carriages could been seen meandering down the river road. He swallowed and asked the difficult question.

"I need to know something, Gill."

"Of course, sir."

"It is well known that Monystians excel at intelligence operations."

"Indeed."

"And part of that reputation is that your people are not loathe to use, shall I say, extremely aggressive means of eliciting information."

"And you need my assurance that my men and I will avoid such tactics as we work in your employ."

"No. Not at all."

Gill cocked his head, confused.

Naughton shifted on the rowboat seat and looked at the clear water, lapping rhythmically against the side of the boat. "Do what you must do. Just don't get caught."

The Monsytian's mouth turned upward in the slightest of smiles. "Indeed. But tell me, sir: are you able to trust me?"

Naughton weighed his words. "I believe so. For better or worse, you are on the inside now, and thus I must place in you my complete trust. It may take time, but yes."

"Because, Mr. Naughton, as you know, half-trust could prove deadly."

"I know that."

"Then tell me — why haven't you mentioned that your servohound was found amid the wreckage of the airship? Why did you keep that from me?"

Above them, in the distance, Naughton spied an airship hovering above the city of Kern. He wondered momentarily if it was meant to be there. "I do not know. I honestly do not know. I suppose—"

Enoch Gill brushed back the braided locks of his thick hair, leaned forward and made his final point.

"I know why. Things are in chaos. The Continent's future is suddenly on the precipice. You don't know who to trust. So you withhold a vital piece of information from your new inspector. I don't blame you. I would have withheld the fact also. It was too important."

"Yes. That it is."

"But yet, while you are withholding this, you are wholly laying your trust about this with a group of people you don't even know."

Naughton cocked his head in confusion. "What do you mean? Who?"

"Do you know who repaired your hound?" Gill asked.

"Why, the manufacturer, Metallidogs. They've been fully vetted by my office."

"Yes, but were the technicians who carried out the repairs specifically cleared?"

"I— I assume so." Naughton stopped. Gill's point was clear. He had bungled this entirely: withholding from his new security expert the matter of the fistfight in Section 351, yet at the same time assuming that the repairs to Crandy were not compromised. He found himself reviewing how many meetings he'd attended, with Cunningham and others, since the hound was returned. How many meetings Crandy had laid next to him as the most confidential matters were discussed. Crandy, now waiting for him along with Coyle on the lake shoreline. And if a surveillance device had been implanted—

Gill, as if anticipating that very fear, quashed the concern immediately. "Don't worry, sir. I had the hound checked over two weeks ago, while you were in constant private meetings. He's fine. There's been no compromise."

Naughton exhaled. Now he understood why they were on the lake, away from any possible surveillance or listening device. "You need me to be on guard, yet to trust you, fully, and without reservation. That's why we're here, isn't it?"

"Yes. Because there's one thing of which I'm certain: whoever perpetuated this heinous act knows plenty. And knows enough to play off our own inherent failure to trust."

Naughton sighed, more despondent than at any point since being told the final death toll. "You are right. Thank you."

"Thank you, sir." Gill picked up the oars, paddling at first with only his right hand so the boat shifted back toward the Setherian shoreline.

After a few minutes, with their speed picking up, Naughton leaned back and relaxed slightly. "Is this solvable?" he asked.

"Only if they slip."

"Will they slip?"

But Gill spoke no more. He only rowed, back to the shoreline. Naughton watched as Schawmount City grew on the horizon, and wondered how well he could heed the Monystian's advice.

April 24

SCHAWMOUNT CITY

THE COMMISSIONER INSISTED HE WAS ready.

Naughton was unsure. He stood next to Coyle, off to the far right of the stage, and watched as reporters ambled into the auditorium. Crandy lay crouched at his feet, as if ready to spring. Crowds upset the servohound. Particularly scribes. The dailies of all the cities which hosted SIP and ALE teams had sent their beat reporters, and many had also sent columnists. The continent-wide paper, the *Chronicle*, had sent a team of four reporters and, of course, their belligerent columnist, Ollo Ronnell.

"Sharks, all of them," observed Coyle, in a whisper.

"Indeed. Today they smell blood."

It had been more than six weeks since the airship disaster, and though the document had long since been written, he and Cunningham had opted to wait until now to release it. Six weeks, he felt, was a credible amount of time to complete a probe. Ironically, the actual probe — the results of which would be kept private — had necessitated numerous interviews by Gill. Those, in turn, led to rumors on the street and gossip in the press about a wide-ranging investigation, talk that only gave credence to the manufactured document.

He made his way backstage to a small dressing room where Lord Bart sat, studying yet again his notes about the report. Next to him was a smirking Vivian Lynam. Naughton nodded toward her with a formal smile. He wanted the old man to remain focused on the task ahead. Her appearance would distract if not confuse the commissioner.

"Ah, Andrew," she said. "I'm so glad that you've backed away from your belief that the release of this document is quite ill-advised."

"What makes you believe I've changed my stance, Lady Lynam?"

"Why, I surmise that because you executed this flawlessly, the report is a gem. And because you're here, overseeing its release."

"Madam, I am the special assistant to the commissioner. It is my obligation and duty to carry out his commands." Naughton put emphasis on the word 'his.' "But I will restate what I only wish would be obvious to you — screens of smoke never work. They always fail in the end. Just look at the supposed Treaty of Calchas. What a mess that caused."

At this point the commissioner looked up from his notes and interjected a rebuttal. "We need to buy time, Andrew. You know that. We need tempers to calm, suspicions to ease. This is the only way. By the time the truth is revealed, both Setherians and Helderans will be again focused on baseball."

"Sir, with all due respect, this is most certainly not the only way. There is, of course, honesty." Crandy, sensing the rise in tension, stood on all fours and cocked his head sideways.

Lady Lynam stood and glared at him, her thin lips quivering as she spoke. "Such temerity surely cannot be countenanced, young sir. Lord Batholemew has guided two nations — the entire continent — through 30 years of peace. Not all have been easy years either, in ways that you'll never know. Yet we — he has been successful. And now all of that is threatened. That, I suggest, calls for extraordinary actions."

Crandy uttered a low growl. Lady Lynam wrapped her lace shawl over her shoulder and scowled at the servohound. "Must we have these vile devices around?"

"Vivian, please," said the commissioner. "Andrew is entitled to his opinion. I have no qualms with that. Let us all now focus on the immediate task: selling this document to the masses."

Ollo Ronnell sat in the back of the auditorium, as was his custom. The beat writers wanted to be up front, to be seen by Lord Bart and called upon with their carefully crafted questions. He did not blame them: they had swift deadlines to meet. He, on the other hand, had merely to devise a column, an opinion piece, and it was far easier to form an opinion while observing the entirety of an event, particularly when it was the commissioner who was speaking.

He had arrived early and nodded to his colleagues as they entered. They'd been in their respective positions nearly as long as he, and they felt like family: Samuel Cutty, beat reporter covering the ALE League Toads in Fanningana Falls; Blakeford Gash, veteran columnist for the *Blue Square Noble Daily;* Gallahad Berry, baseball writer for the *Leadland Leader.*

And of course, Maddy. The irascible Maddy Looper, who for 25 years had covered the Skate River Mad Dogs in the Helderan North Division of the SIP. She claimed the seat next to him. "Ollo, you look irritated as ever. It seems your latest hatchet jobs on the old man haven't changed his course." Her hair was gray now, and unkempt, but she'd never cared a wit about fashion. *If only,* Ronnell thought, *if only she lived a bit closer...*

"Oh, Maddy. I don't judge the value of my columns on how they affect their subjects. I simply want to help sell newspapers."

"Yes. As we all do."

"And how is... Harold?"

She smiled. "Martin. Harold was my fourth husband."

"You're on number five?"

"I do believe I managed to get it right this time." This brought them both to laughter.

"And what, my dear Maddy, do you hear about today's grand announcement from his excellency?" He pronounced Cunningham's honorific with sarcasm.

"Most likely the same things that you are hearing. We're about to receive the results of the investigation of the *Lady Crym* disaster. That should provide enough fodder for your pieces for several weeks, I daresay."

"Maddy Looper, you've always been jealous that I get to opine while you merely report the supposed facts."

She snorted a laugh. "Ollo Ronnell. You've never stopped quite being so impressed with yourself, have you?"

"And you never let the facts get in the way of a good story, do you?"

She smiled and studied his face. "No, Ollo. Not one bit."

They both leaned back in the wooden auditorium seats and surveyed the front of the room. The podium from which the commissioner would speak was on a small riser at the front, and doors to the right and left of the stage were open. On the left, they spied the commissioner's top assistant, Andrew Naughton, as well as a well-coiffed older woman.

Simultaneously, Ronnell and Maddy voiced the same question, "Is that Vivian Lynam?" And again they laughed.

"So she's back," said Maddy.

"Yes, so it would seem." He pursed his lips, then realized his grip on the chair's armrest had tightened.

"She left Lord Bart, what, two years ago?"

"Yes," he replied. "1921, in the middle of the season. I never could determine why."

"Nor could I. Not for want of trying. And my editor ultimately felt it was a personal falling out that was best left unreported."

"But now she is back at his side, suddenly, as the continent veers toward chaos."

"How convenient," she said.

"Indeed." Ronnell found himself wishing he could light a cigar, but to do so would be frowned upon in the now-crowded room.

"You knew her, didn't you?"

"Yes."

Maddy turned toward him and furrowed her brow, clearly curious at the curtness of his response. "You knew her 30 years ago, back when the leagues were first formed?"

"Yes."

"Were you… were you two together?"

He looked away, then down at his feet, then away again. "You could say that. For a time."

"Oh. I see. Before she was with him?"

Ollo Ronnell shook his head and frowned. "Maddy, stop asking questions. It was all a very long time ago. Let's focus only on today."

Maddy stood and retrieved her bag from the floor, then tapped him lightly on the shoulder. "I know as well as you, Ollo Ronnell, that 30 years is not so very long ago." She left and took an open seat toward the front of the hall, the better to get Lord Bart's attention.

He closed his eyes. She was right, of course. It still seemed so very recent.

From the earliest moments, Ronnell had wanted to be a striker. A batsman. His family's farm on the outskirts of Kendall had vast open fields, and the neighborhood children played daily after schooling was complete, improvising their own rules, making do with wooden sticks for bats and scraps of rawhide for gloves. The fieldwork was all well and good — he reveled in diving catches that other children couldn't manage — but it was as a striker that Ronnell had found most joy. The satisfaction of the solid thunk of making contact, the arc of the ball ascending beyond the outfield, the relaxing trot around the bases: nothing else mattered as much.

Of course, there were always adults nearby, stationed on patrol. Parents, delegated by committee, to be on guard. Free play would be allowed, but restricted. Attacks on civilians, though never officially described as intentional, were an ever-present risk.

And over time many of the men on guard would whisper to themselves about Ronnell's prowess, his strength and agility, motioning in his direction as they spoke.

He became known.

By the time he was 23, Ronnell was one of the top Setherian ball players, a sterling batsman and even, when needed, a formidable hurler on several squads. Independent baseball leagues had dotted the countryside of the continent for eons, but no one would have described the sport as organized. They were all technically amateurs, playing for a pittance here and there, or at least for a free dinner after the game. It was not a living, and he supplemented his earnings with shifts as a machinist.

In '84 came the draft notice; he was surprised it had taken so long. Most of his teammates — whichever team he happened to be on that month — had long since shuffled off at various times for tours of duty. His lasted four years, mostly spent on the Front, the strip of land along the Valencroft River that witnessed the heaviest fighting on the entire Continent. Four years: from which he emerged, unlike many of his teammates, without serious injury, and with the rank of Lieutenant for the United Setheridge Forces, Retired.

He returned to civilian life as the war still raged, quickly picking up work again in the machine shops and on the ballfields for several of the independent teams.

It was during that time that Ollo Ronnell met Vivian Packer Lynam.

And not long after that, he shared with her a rather astounding idea.

Michael Barbato-Dunn

NAUGHTON RETURNED TO THE WINGS of the main auditorium. Nearly all the 200 seats were filled, mostly with columnists, beat writers and hangers-on, but also with team employees, dispatched by curious owners to take notes and report back directly. Most appeared to have been sent by Helderan owners. The murmuring escalated into a sizable din. It was time.

He took a deep breath and nodded to Cunningham's attendants. Within seconds the old man, cane in one hand and notes in the other, made his way to the front, his countenance grim. The room quieted as the commissioner began.

"Gentlemen, in a moment you will hear the results of the league's formal inquiry into the tragic airship disaster of last month. I will make a statement before copies are handed out. At that point, I will avail myself of your questions. But heed this caution: I will deal only with the facts at hand. I will answer nothing that is speculative or hypothetical."

Off to the far left Naughton spied Ollo Ronnell, bedecked in a top hat and gray suit every bit as formal as the commissioner's, chewing on his ever-present cigar, jotting already in his notepad. Convincing the annoying columnist of the veracity of the bogus report was key. His influence was considerable. Naughton had resisted the temptation to call Ronnell in for a private discussion; that could have easily backfired.

"The Leagues of SIP and ALE, through their highly trained security detail, have conducted an exhaustive investigation of the crash of the Airship *Lady Crym*, with scores of people interviewed. In addition, League technicians reassembled much of the ship's fuselage and were able to postulate the final moments of the zeppelin."

Cunningham looked up from his notes. "The report concludes, without a shadow of a doubt, that the crash was caused by a mechanical defect in the craft, and was not — as too many have openly speculated — the result of tampering."

The scribes broke into shouts, even as they wrote down quotes, and several began lobbing questions. Naughton interceded. "Gentlemen, as he stated, the commissioner will take questions at the end of his statement. Please show some respect." The din lessened to a rumbling murmur.

The Commissioner resumed. "We have identified a crack in one of the airship's three main pneumatic drivers — the devices that keep the craft responsive to the cockpit controls. Suffice it to say, cracks have occurred in past incidents, though usually the remaining two drivers provide sufficient pressure to retain operation of the controls. Why did the pilot then lose control? For that, we have the most unfortunate answer. The coroner's autopsy found that the pilot, 42-year old Branford Stenzel, had suffered a heart attack. A heart attack brought on, no doubt, by the loss of controls."

This information prompted astounded silence from the crowd. "A confluence of two very different matters," Cunningham continued. "A mechanical defect — not common, though not rare — combined with a very medical defect: a shaky heart, pushed beyond its limit by a sudden crisis. We view this is a great tragedy. But an unavoidable one."

The old man looked up. Jaws were agape; quills frozen in clenched hands. "This report will remove, once and for all, any suspicions or taint of political malfeasance. Quite simply, gentlemen and ladies, accidents happen. And the greater tragedy would be if you continue to make the populace fear that this disaster was anything more than an accident."

Cunningham's voice rose and he made his final point. "We've enjoyed 30 years of peace. Thirty more could come if we muddle through this very moment. You can help us do that. Or, you can sell newspapers by sensationalizing and rumor mongering." Several of the reporters shifted uncomfortably; they were here to do a job, not to carry a national duty. "It is, gentlemen and ladies, your choice. Now I will be happy to entertain your questions."

A cacophony of shouts rose from the mass of scribes. Some raised their hands, others stood, all seemed to be shouting. Bartholomew pointed to the youngest of the group, Samuel Cutty, beat reporter covering the ALE League Toads in the Helderan city of Fanningana Falls.

If he had hoped the youthful reporter might offer a relatively easy question, he was wrong. "Mr. Commissioner, throughout Fanningana, indeed throughout most of Heldera, it is believed that Setherians will use this incident as an excuse to rekindle the warring. Even with your findings here, how can you convince Helderans that they are not at risk, that they should not raise up arms?"

"A fair question, Mr. Cutty. If I were Helderan, I would be alarmed. But you were not yet born, so you would not recall, that the very same question arose — repeatedly — 30 years ago when we first established the SIP and ALE Leagues. Many Helderans were fearful that I — a native of Setheridge — had devised the leagues merely as a ruse to disarm your new nation. They had right to be fearful, just as you do now. All I can say to you is what I said to them three decades ago: you must take this leap of faith, and place your trust in me. I proved then that I am a man of my word, and I will prove it again to the people of the Heldera. To the people of Setheridge."

"So we all should simply trust you?" More shouting from behind Cutty ensued.

"Yes. You cannot dispute that I have earned it."

"Commissioner! Commissioner!" Now it was Blakeford Gash, veteran columnist for the *Blue Square Noble Daily*, a Setherian newspaper covering the ALE League Gophers. "Mr. Commissioner, you know that many are going to doubt this report. The skeptics number in the millions already! Do you expect us to convince them of the crazy scenario — a broken pipe and then a heart attack? We will be laughingstocks!"

"Mr. Gash, all I can say is: yes. I do expect you to convince them of this scenario. But it is anything but crazy. My staff has assembled a list of quite similar events throughout the past century — a confluence of small mishaps that suddenly leads to a far greater disaster. It is, I'm afraid to say, the very nature of history. You can quote me on that. This is the very nature of history."

"But—"

"Wait." Cunningham raised his palm to the reporter. "You can also quote me on this: the easy thing for all of us to do here is to return to the warring ways of our less sophisticated forefathers. The easy thing. Conversely, the far more challenging course here is to stop doubting, and to place your faith in the Leagues, in the sanctity of this office. That's the more difficult thing. Ask your readers if they are ready to rise to that challenge."

"Mr. Commissioner—" Now it was one of the few female reporters in the lot, Maddy Looper of the *Skate River Post*. "Suppose the pilot was poisoned? Suppose he was knocked out with a pipe? What if the pneumatic driver had been sabotaged—"

Cunningham cut her off. "My assistant Mr. Naughton made clear at the onset that I will not deal with hypothetical scenarios, Miss Looper. What will guide our office are the facts. And the facts are in this report. I urge you to disseminate the report to all your readers — charge for it if you so desire — but you and they will quickly see that these facts bear the weight of scrutiny."

The cavalcade of shouting resumed for several minutes until one voice rose above the rest: Ollo Ronnell. The commissioner smiled in anticipation. "Ah, Ollo, you've been awfully quiet today. I wouldn't think that your colleagues had shouted you down until now. What is your question?"

Naughton bit down on his lip and leaned forward.

"Mr. Commissioner," Ronnell asked, "My question is quite simple: what if you are wrong?"

A sudden silence enveloped the auditorium. It was a question that even the most combative Helderan reporter dare not ask. It would have been taken as too overtly critical of the one man who was rarely, if ever, criticized in public.

But the old man seemed to be smiling. "A fair point. Fair indeed. If I am wrong — and I assure you that I am not — but if I am wrong, then all we will have suffered is more weeks or months or even years of peace. So ask your readers this, my old friend: is that such a bad thing?"

Ronnell rolled the butt of an unlit cigar from one side of his mouth to the other. "Mr. Commissioner, dare I say that you exhaust me? Would that all the peoples of the Twin Nations had your energy at half your age." The crowd laughed. The tensions of the announcement dissipated.

The conference went on for another half hour. Naughton at times stepped toward the commissioner, ready to cut off the questioning, but Cunningham would wave him off. The old man indeed seemed indefatigable, rejuvenated for the first time since the airship disaster. And as the tone of the questioning became less belligerent, Cunningham brightened. The dour expression was gone. He reveled in the moment.

Later, backstage, Cunningham's assistants helped lower the commissioner into his chair, while his physician examined his breathing, heart rate and pupils. Naughton stepped forward, Coyle at his side, Crandy trailing them both. "Commissioner, are you feeling faint? Do you need water?"

"No, no, I am fine."

But Naughton could see the old man was short of breath and pale. This would not be the time for a discussion of how the proceedings had gone. "Take him home," Naughton directed Vinge. "There will be no more League business today." That the normally strong-willed Cunningham did not argue his underling's command was proof enough that the old man's fortitude had indeed been exhausted.

Naughton tapped his thigh, signaling Crandy to attention, and the two made their way down a narrow flight of stairs that led back to his office.

Selling this to the masses. That is how the commissioner had described the task. It was an apt term, particularly for Cunningham. And Naughton knew that the morning's newspapers would foretell if the continent's greatest salesman — who three decades ago sold millions on the very idea of peace — still had his touch.

April 29

KERN

GAS LAMPS LINED THE BANISTER of the curving ivory staircase that led to the Kern Opera House. Dozens of gilded carriages snailed forward on the cramped roadways that surrounded the towering building. Brilliantly dressed couples moved across the rough-hewn sidewalks toward the steps, the men puffing their tuxedoed chests outward, the women wrapping their gloved arms around the elbows of their mates.

Naughton situated Crandy near an outside railing. Other servohounds had been left there in low-power, but Naughton commanded his to remain at alert. Then he navigated the steps with care, fearful of slipping in the uncomfortable evening jacket and stiff leather boots. His career had often brought him to this world of wealth, culture and society, but he'd always been more at home in the staid offices of the commissioner and the far less formal retinue of ballparks and locker rooms. Fortunately, his task tonight was not to socialize; in fact, if all went well, he'd not have to speak to a soul. He was here simply to gather information.

At the top of the stairway, outside the triple sets of glass doors, half-sized autonomic ushers in mock tuxedos greeted guests, their tubular steel appendages both receiving tickets and dispensing programs. Naughton's seat was on the third level of the mezzanine, far to the back. He wanted to be unobtrusive. Amid such a crowd, that would not be difficult.

As he arrived near his section, he looked down beyond the railings and surveyed the entire auditorium. The Opera House held nearly 2,000 and Naughton had little doubt that it would easily be filled. But more noteworthy than the size of the crowd was its constitution: Naughton recognized the faces of the writers, thinkers, social critics, and the very wealthy. Academics and millionaires. The intelligentsia of both the Setheridge and Helderan nations. In fact, there — in the front row — he spied Professor Doctor Buford Wafer Northgood III, the current leader of the Association of Scientificka, with other members of its governing board seated on either side of the revered researcher. For what had they come? To hear a young scientist who, until recently, was not even known outside Kern?

But from his high perch in the Opera House, he surmised the reason: there was tension in the air. *People are worried. And they're looking for answers.*

He had originally planned to send Coyle to the lecture, or one of Gill's men, so he'd later receive a full report. But Coyle suggested that he himself go, for two reasons: first, to gauge the intangibles: the make-up of the audience and their reception to the lecturer. And secondly, Coyle suggested, he needed a night away.

He could not argue. Naughton had worked virtually non-stop since the airship disaster, and though he'd been able to keep up on his sleep — he traditionally took no more than five hours a night — he agreed that a respite from the pressure of the past six weeks would be welcome. Amelia had laughed. "So going to a scientific lecture in another city is your idea of a respite?"

She had had a point. This really was no respite; he had felt a tightness of chest from the moment he arrived.

A detailed pencil sketch of Iphonious Henry adorned the front cover of the printed program. A shock of curls bulged out from under his top hat. Dark brows masked narrow eyes, just as a thick looping mustache hid a tight frown. At his side the scientist clasped a thick sheath of ruffled papers, and his bow tie was askew, giving the impression he was unaware he was being sketched. *Very deliberate,* Naughton thought. *He wants to appear serious, brilliant, and very much in a hurry.*

The elderly woman next to him pointed to the picture in his program, eager to converse. "A dashing young man, won't you say? And I hear he's so full of ideas; a bright light for Heldera."

"Hush, Nandy," interjected her husband, seated to her left. "Leave the man be."

Naughton merely smiled and nodded, attempting to be polite, but making it clear he desired solitude. The graying woman had one last word before turning back. "Let's hope the Setherians get no word of this. We need every advantage."

Every advantage. Were the Twin Nations already so braced for confrontation that even a well-to-do Helderan, who likely had everything to lose by a return to warring, was looking for opportunities for advantage? He sighed, wishing he were instead at a ballpark, a meade in hand, surrounded by rowdy Amandeans, cheering as a contest lasted into extra innings.

———————————————

THE APPLAUSE BEGAN AS A small ripple, then grew as Dr. Iphonious Henry strode onto the stage. Conversations ceased mid-sentence. Naughton retrieved his monocular from his jacket pocket. A double-breasted evening coat, most likely linen, encompassed the doctor's lanky frame, and he appeared thinner than depicted in the program's sketch.

"Kind people, thank you for taking time out of your hectic schedules to hear my words tonight," he began. "I had planned this lecture long before the terrible events of the last month. But I will tell you: that tragedy only makes my message all the more timely, all the more vital.

"I am, perhaps to my detriment, a man of few words. And so I find it necessary now to get directly to the reason I sought to speak today."

He paused, clearly for appropriate dramatic effect. The audience, already grasping onto every word, seemed motionless as he held the momentary silence.

"Simply put, kind people, the political precipice on which we all sit today makes this abundantly clear: the Twin Nations need once again to embrace the value of science. We have turned our backs on it for too long. And while that segregation of science from mainstream life has — in the view of some — helped ensure three decades of relative peace, it has come at a cost. A tremendous one.

"What is that cost, you wonder?" Henry waved his right arm in a sweeping motion.

"Ask yourself this: would you not have expected that after three decades, the wonderfully titled Eternal Ceasefire would have easily withstood the ramifications of the airship crash? Why is the ceasefire so tenuous after all these many years?

"The answer, in my humble opinion, is that the premise of the peace — that both nations would sublimate their animosity into baseball, through the Leagues of SIP and ALE — is very much a faulty one. Baseball? As a means of channeling aggression? My reaction is not so much to scoff at the notion as to voice amazement that this outlandish concept has, in fact, managed to hold the peace for so long. And the fact that we stand again on the brink of war after just a single untoward incident is proof enough that the premise is flawed. Fatally flawed, if it is not inappropriate to use that adjective in light of that tragedy."

The young doctor paused for dramatic effect. Naughton shifted in his seat. The neckline of his shirt collar felt increasingly constricted. Others in the crowd leaned toward companions, whispering and nodding.

"Think about it: the nations of Setheridge and Heldera came to love the peacetime advances of science while turning their backs on the very scientists who created them. Yet please don't be so naïve to think that members of the Scientificka have huddled quietly in basements for 30 years. I am here to tell you that in locations far from the public eye, in parts of the continent unseen by most of us, the march of science has moved on unrelentingly. And that progress, as I'm sure you can imagine, has not necessarily been for the public good.

"That's right. Just because the forces on the continent devoted to peace chose to sublimate science, just because the formal Association of Scientificka has willingly served as lackeys to the Leagues, don't believe for an instant that science stalled. No. It merely went underground."

By this point murmuring rose to a palpable clamor. It seemed as if these well-adorned patrons — the wealthy, the artistic, those who fancied themselves proponents of progress — felt threatened by Dr. Henry's warning.

"Rest assured when I tell you, it is this fact — more so than the inherent distrust between the Setherian and Helderan peoples — that will be our undoing. Science has progressed, and those who would seek to topple both our nations will use it to their devices."

At this the crowd became unruly. Several couples got up to leave, hissing echoed from the upper seats, and shouts of disdain rose as if in a chorus. "Prove it!" came one voluminous challenge. Others picked up the dare. "Yes — prove it!" "Prove it, or you're a phony!"

None of this seemed to perturb the doctor, who stood unwavering, hands planted in his jacket pockets. "I will give you your proof."

The blue velvet curtain behind Henry pulled back, and the audience gasped. An enormous, gleaming device rose behind him, a steel cylinder in three sections, each smaller in circumference than the one below it, with brass casing lining the edges of each portion. Atop the third cylinder, a cone-like object that began, at its lower rim, as wide as the cylinder, but then tapered upward to a point. And atop its end, a shining brass ball-bearing the size of a large man's fist.

The crowd was increasingly raucous. Some who had begun to leave moved back to their seats, curiosity overwhelming their disgust at Dr. Henry's message.

Naughton craned forward and attempted to study details of the device through his monocular. Small capstans lined the perimeter of each large section, and he surmised the contraption was driven both by pneumatics and clockwork.

The doctor let the cacophony continue unabated for several minutes. He walked around the side of the device, his gaze alternating between the strange machine and the audience. He waited for the shock to subside, then resumed. "Does anyone in the audience have an object about which they care little? Something they don't mind losing."

"Here," said an elderly man in the front row. "I brought this pulpar along in

case I tired." The small, oblong fruit was known to provide short bursts of energy. *How very convenient,* Naughton thought.

"Excellent," said Henry, accepting the fruit as he leaned over. "Perfect."

Finally the audience hushed. Two assistants appeared off from the wings of the stage. One took the pulpar from Henry and placed it on a cloth-covered box about half the stage away. The other helped Henry adjust the rotation of the mechanical creation so that it faced the box directly. Then both assistants wheeled out a wooden cart, polished in a gleaming lacquer. The doctor made his way to the rear of the cart and pulled back its cover, revealing a series of dials and knobs. He retrieved from his jacket pocket protective goggles, like those worn by an airship commander, and donned them.

"I don't have a name for this device. I don't have a purpose for it. Other than, of course, to prove my point."

He adjusted four knobs and the uppermost cone of the structure rotated to the right. He flipped six switches on the panel in succession, a cascade of interwoven gears began moving, and the cone pointed itself directly downward at the fruit. Four more switches were turned upward, and then Henry took hold of a large gray knob in the center of the panel.

"Kind people, prepare yourselves to witness: the progress of the Scientificka."

He turned the knob clockwise and a shrill whistle began emanating from the massive object. Within seconds, a red light, a beam straight as an ruler, precise as an arrow, shot from the brass ball at the tip of the cone. At the terminus of the beam was the pulpar fruit, unmoving.

Women screamed; men cried out in confusion, a few raised their walking sticks. "Oh my. Oh my," cried the elderly woman sitting next to him. She delivered an anguished look to her husband and the two fled for the exit. Others followed.

The beam pulsed without let-up. Those who remained in the Opera House settled down as if mesmerized.

Then, from the pulpar's core, from the very point at which the red light reached it, came smoke. First, a wisp. Then, a steady plume.

And then the fruit exploded.

———————————

IT TOOK A FULL HALF hour for the panic to subside. Police had been summoned, as had the fire marshall, and officials huddled in intense discussion, perhaps, Naughton guessed, as to whether Henry should be placed under arrest.

Only after the manager of the Opera House convinced the detectives that only a small piece of fruit had been harmed, and that he had everything fully under control, did the authorities disperse. Less than one third of the original crowd remained, and most of those who had been seated in the upper and rear levels had moved down.

As the special assistant to the commissioner, Naughton himself could have risen from his seat, identified himself and taken charge. But he chose not to. Neither did he flee, nor move his seat closer. Most of the mezzanine, which had nary a vacant seat at the onset of the lecture, was now abandoned. He sat in solitude, in the highest reaches of the grand chamber, studying the smirking Henry.

Clever man. A very clever man.

Eventually, the scientist returned to the front of the stage and resumed his presentation. "To those of you who I have scared or offended, I apologize. But I daresay anyone in either category has probably already left. To those of you who remain, I thank you for your patience, and your open-mindedness.

"And of course the truth is that no apology should be necessary, for better that all of you be exposed to some easy amplification of modern science in this setting than a far more brutal one."

He swept his hand back toward the hulking object, its breath-taking emission long since complete. "I created this not to advance technology but simply to prove a point." The young doctor shuffled his feet stage right and peered out at the crowd. "It is far too easy for new weapons that employ even modest advances in science to be manufactured. The truth is that I created this device in my spare time, using readily available materials, and readily available theories of present-day science.

"What is this science? Not the science taught in our advanced grade schools, our colleges, or our universities. No, that science, sublimated for three decades by the public prejudice against the Scientificka, is woefully out of date. The science of which I speak is underground, growing and progressing out of the public view.

"Gentlemen and ladies, the nations of Setheridge and Heldera, in the name of preserving the peace, have for three decades sought to hinder the advancement of science. But all they managed to do was to push it into the dank alleys and dangerous crevices of our society. That, of course, is the worst possible outcome.

"So now you see. If I, working alone, could devise a new and potentially devastating weapon in a mere six months, what have the worst elements of our society done in the past 30 years?"

Exclamations arose. What remained of the audience seemed more unnerved by

Henry's conclusion than the device itself. Henry himself remained as animated as he was at the start of his lecture. "Think about it. Is it not possible that a weapon far more powerful than this already exists? One that could emit a beam that could strike a man dead? Or one that could fell an airship from the sky in an instant?"

"No!" several shouted at once. "It can't be!" said others.

"Perhaps, gentlemen, you're right." Henry turned, retrieved his top hat from a nearby stool, adjusted the vest below his jacket, and checked to make sure his cuff links were still in place. "It probably can't be," he said with another smirk. "I bid you good night."

And with that, the man was gone.

<hr />

Naughton remained in his seat for nearly half an hour. Others in the audience scurried out, checking their timepieces, shaking their heads, and arguing with acquaintances over what they'd seen.

Then he rose and retrieved Crandy from the railing in front of the lobby. They made their way down the steps to the sidewalk, at which point he stopped, looking for a carriage that could take them to the Schawmount ferry. The Opera House was deserted by this point and Naughton had little doubt that many of those who'd seen the doctor's conclusion had repaired quickly to a nearby publick house for hours of heated debate.

"Mr. Naughton." He turned back. It was Iphonious Henry, greeting him by name though they'd never been introduced. Crandy growled, but the doctor offered his hand to be sniffed, and the hound relaxed. Clearly he was familiar with servohounds.

"Dr. Henry, a pleasure to meet you." They shook. "Quite an interesting evening, to say the least. You'll be the talk of the Twin Nations in short order."

"Sir, I wished you had introduced yourself beforehand. I'd have loved to have told the crowd that a high League official was in attendance. Perhaps fewer women would have fainted."

"I daresay you had a few men fainting as well. Was that your goal?"

"My goal, I trust you realize, is to make a point, to deliver a warning. Not to gain fame and certainly not to upset the fair of heart."

"Ah, yes. I'm sure, Dr. Henry. Though a bit of fame can go a long way for a young scientist. Perhaps one with political ambitions."

The doctor shifted closer to him. "Mr. Naughton, you assume too much. My ambitions are the very same as Commissioner Cunningham's — the preservation of the peace."

"Of that, I'm sure," Naughton acknowledged with a grin. "And the good Dr. Northgood, and the others on the governing board of the Association of Scientificka — were they aware of all this beforehand?"

"Not in the slightest." The young scientist smirked. "Else I daresay they would have prevented my appearance in the first place."

"And did Northgood speak to you afterward?"

"Indeed. He said I am to report in three days' time for a private hearing."

Now it was Naughton who was grinning. "That should prove interesting."

"It would if I were to actually appear. I have no plans to do so. The board is irrelevant."

"Are you not a member in good standing of the organization? You must abide by its jurisdiction."

"Mr. Naughton, I have come to the conclusion that the Scientificka does little for me and other free-thinking theoreticians. For 30 years they have deliberately sought to quash true progress."

Crandy, sensing the heightened animosity, edged toward Naughton and uttered a low-level growl. "Quiet, Crandy. We're fine." He patted the hound's head. "Dr. Henry, surely you are aware that your position here at the University of Kern is entirely dependent on funding from the Scientificka, and I sincerely doubt the the University's own trustees are going to continue to provide space and time, not to mention professorial tenure, to one who flouts the Scientificka's precepts."

A light rain began to fall and both men adjusted their top hats. Henry looked at his timepiece. Finally he replied, "Mr. Naughton, you needn't threaten me. I mean no harm."

"I wasn't threatening at all. I was simply stating the political reality. You know full well the true reason that the Association of Scientificka maintains jurisdiction over research on the continent."

"Yes, an anachronistic remnant of the long-held notion that scientists fueled the war."

"That's correct. The scientists — your predecessors — worked for both Setherians and Helderans. They knew no allegiance. They cared not who won the war. They simply used it to grow rich as both sides tried to find technological advantage. To find better weaponry. Better communication. Better intelligence."

Henry shook his head. "But let us not ignore the fact that wartime research

led directly to the great advances that now make modern life so glorious. The great harnessing of steam, and the resulting technologies of pneumatics, automation, and propulsion. Why, that very servohound at your side would not have been possible without the work of my predecessors. Surely you would not want to be without your loyal companion, now, would you?"

"Yes, but there is a reason the Twin Nations limit automatons to hounds and butlers."

"And that is?"

"You know reason, Dr. Henry. Servohound technology is precisely the sort of science that could, in the wrong hands, get out of control."

"Ah, yes. And the members of the governing board very much enjoy control."

"Dr. Henry, the Proclamation of an Eternal Ceasefire explicitly states that scientific research must be only for non-violent purposes. I am not certain how that beam device meets that restriction. That is what the governing board must determine. That is the case you must prove."

Henry scoffed. "Ah, yes, I see. Five decades of war our continent endured, and now you're concerned about a contraption that took two full minutes to fry a piece of fruit."

Now it was Naughton checking his timepiece. "Good doctor, we can debate the value of the Scientificka until the sun rises. But I have a ferry to catch, so I must make haste. Just remember that those who choose to ignore the association's jurisdiction may quickly find themselves without position, without salary, and indeed without even a laboratory. I beseech you, then: attend the hearing of the governing board. And keep your public demonstrations to a minimum."

Henry shifted his gaze down to Crandy, staring for long seconds. "Mr. Naughton, I appreciate your suggestions, even if I choose to ignore them. And remember, the clockworks always move forward. Even if some would do their best to stop them, they always move forward."

The pace of the rain had picked up, and the two men turned and rushed off in opposite directions.

April 30

AUGHTON WOKE EXHAUSTED. HIS SLEEP had been fitful.

Amelia had been asleep when he'd returned from Dr. Henry's lecture in Kern, and he chose not to wake her despite his desire to discuss the difficult evening. He'd been left instead with his own thoughts, so sleep proved long in coming and was never deep.

In the carriage now on the way to the League offices, he yearned for his morning black tea and churned over the question of the scientist. The lecture, the political rhetoric, the demonstration of this disturbing beam device: all seemed at the surface purely coincidental with the events of the disastrous Anniversary Celebration. He could not decide whether viewing the two matters as linked was paranoid or practical.

But he had no doubt that the matter was serious and warranted personal attention, so he was relieved he'd personally attended. And then another realization: it had been Enoch Gill who'd brought the lecture to his attention in the first place. Perhaps the Monystian's appointment as Security Chief would prove valuable.

Or perhaps, he wondered, *Gill is the link between the two events.*

It had been six days since the release of the fabricated report and, much to his relief, public acceptance of its findings seemed only to have grown. Reports received from all SIP and ALE team general managers pointed to a heartening increase in ticket sales and of sponsor advertising. Neither would have been feasible in the days immediately after the airship incident. His misgivings about the commissioner's decision to deceive the public had eased, if only slightly.

Several things could account for the response. First and foremost was their decision to distribute copies of the report at center squares in all SIP and ALE cities. Letting members of the public read their account directly was a clever way to bypass the press.

He still had copies of the hysterical tabloids and broadsheets from the morning after the report's release. *"ACCIDENT?"* screamed the *Skate River Journal* in Heldera. *"Unavoidable?"* cried the *Pear Falls Herald*, also in Heldera, mocking the commissioner's claim. Even the Setherian papers seemed intent on ramping up fears. The *Sandbanna Woods Register* blared, *"Commish Claims Accident,"* and offered a far-from-supportive recounting of the news conference. That was paired with a separate front page editorial titled, "*A Probe with Many Questions.*"

"This is being driven by the editors," Coyle had cautioned that morning. "This is all about competition, about selling papers. They're playing on the innate fears of residents of both nations."

But then came a surprisingly calming, rational piece by the *Chronicle's* usually difficult Ollo Ronnell. It had been rushed to Naughton's office moments after publication, and the anxiety in his stomach dissipated as he read the column:

"*The Hot Corner,*"
by Ollo Ronnell, National Baseball Correspondent

'WHAT IF YOU ARE WRONG?'

(Schawmount City, April 24) — "What if you are wrong?"

I posed that question to our esteemed commissioner, His Excellency Lord Bart, the wily old gent, feisty as ever. It came at the very end of his news conference on this fine spring afternoon. He'd convened scribes from throughout the land to convince us of the veracity of his report that deemed the horrible airship crash an accident.

I have no doubt that many of my colleagues in the Setherian and Helderan press have, by the time you read my words, already blasted the report as a fraud. I don't blame them. The work looks hurried and full of holes. The claims that the crash was a result of a coincidental failure of pneumatics and physiology are, to say the least, a stretch to accept. After all, none of us forgets that Lord Bart began his career as a showman, leader of a circus troupe, promoter of all manner of contrivances and fabrications.

But I also give our hallowed commissioner credit. He did not feign offense at my abrupt question, nor did he scoff at it. He answered it directly, without equivocation. And he brushed off attempts by his overly protective staff to end our interrogatory.

His answer to my query was succinct: "If I am wrong, then all we will have suffered is more weeks or months or even years of peace. Ask your readers: is that such a bad thing?"

So I sit back in the Hot Corner of my newsroom, ready to blast this slipshod report with the four letters it deserves — sham — and yet I find myself taken by the logic of his point. Is it such a bad thing that we give the commissioner the benefit of the doubt? Are the remnants of our years of warring, of centuries of mutual distrust before that, so strong that we simply can't wait this out?

No — to both. For the moment anyway, Bartholomew Cunningham, despite his foibles, his vanity, and his failings, does deserve the benefit of the doubt. And I will argue that we — the Twin Nations — deserve it as well.

So I am filing the League's report on my bookshelf, where it will gather dust along with the media guides issued by all the SIP and ALE League teams for the past 30 years. They are filled with statistics and stories of ball games gone by. They remind me that there are plenty more games to be played. Opening Day, thankfully, is around the corner.

If there was one thing that Naughton understood about the press, it was that most so-called columnists were all too happy to follow the tide of public opinion. They feared angry editors and publishers, after all. They feared for their cushy, three-columns-a-week jobs. So Ronnell's piece, though it slashed away at the veracity of the report, prompted other scribes to back off. And that, in turn, quickly snowballed into outright acceptance of the commissioner's position.

"He's giving us some breathing room," Naughton had said at the time.

"Yes," agreed Coyle. "I can't imagine why. Does he even speak to the commissioner?"

"Not that I'm aware. Their animosity is quite deep."

It had been a close call, no doubt. Naughton harbored little confidence that the supposed facts of the public report would stand up to weeks and months of scrutiny. But that was something he could not worry about at this point. What mattered solely now was ensuring the situation remained calm until two days hence, May 2.

Opening Day.

———————— ————————

NAUGHTON ENTERED THE OFFICE AND found Coyle pacing. "Fitton has demanded a meeting," his aide said.

"How do you know? Did he send a messenger?"

"I only wish. He's in the commissioner's suite right now, in the outer office."

"He's here?"

"He's here. He seems angry."

"Is he with Caffrey?"

"No, alone, other than his attendants."

"Do you know what he seeks?" he asked Coyle.

"No, neither does the Monystian. I can hazard some guesses."

"Please." Coyle was generally soft-spoken and gave a first impression of timidity, but Naughton knew the young aide was constantly evaluating, theorizing, calculating. It was a helpful trait, on which Naughton frequently relied.

"First, I suppose, he sees the report as bogus and wants to demand access to whatever real inquiry we have underway."

"That's certainly possible," Naughton agreed.

"Or perhaps he has new information that is not favorable to the Setheridge nation."

"Also possible."

"I've no doubt the commissioner can handle either discussion."

"No doubt."

"But I believe we should not allow this, sir," Coyle said. "Permitting team owners an audience with Lord Bart without sufficient notice sets a difficult precedent. If word gets around, they'll all be showing up, day and night."

Naughton smiled. Coyle, in some ways, was more vigilant than he. More protective of the old man. He had hired his aide five years earlier, after his original aide, Barnabas Waters, had abruptly quit. Coyle was young, then just 28, born after the declaration of the Eternal Ceasefire. Like so many younger adults now, he had known nothing but peace. Yet to his credit, he had dedicated his life to its preservation.

There was, though, one matter that had nagged Naughton when he considered the hiring: Coyle had never played baseball. It was not a large enough issue to change his decision to hire, but Naughton knew that Coyle's lack of an athletic background might later hinder his career.

But for now, though, the young man was a comfort. If his own attention and thoroughness to the Leagues were to slip momentarily, Naughton knew Coyle would be there to correct him. If he ever took a prolonged holiday from the post, perhaps between baseball seasons, he knew Coyle could handle the duties in his absence. And other than Amelia, Coyle was perhaps the only person in whom he shared questions, concerns, and doubts.

Coyle had, in just five years, become indispensable.

"I will go see Fitton," he told his anxious aide. "We'll see what this is about."

He found the Helderan owner in the parlor outside the commissioner's office, seated and studying the *Crenshaw City Statesman*, one of the leading Helderan broadsheets.

"Mr. Fitton, good morning. What is the purpose of your unannounced visit?"

The Warthogs' owner looked up from the paper. "Well, Andrew Naughton, you are certainly to the point."

"These times do not lend themselves to warm pleasantries, kind sir."

"Fine. I am here because I need to speak to the commissioner. Post haste."

"The commissioner is at his home. As you know, the doctors are closely monitoring him given the strain of the past few weeks. He is in attendance at the League Office only as needed. And his schedule, as you can imagine, does not easily accommodate spontaneous visits."

"I'm sure it does not." Fitton stood and looked down at Naughton; he was easily a head taller. Naughton imagined he was the type of man who tried to use that height to intimidate. "But I do know the commissioner's estate is just minutes away by carriage. I would be more than pleased to make that trip in order to see him."

Naughton took a deep breath. Lord Bart would not want him to refuse the request of a team owner, particularly a Helderan. But he needed to discern the nature of Fitton's message before agreeing. "I would be more than happy to make the request, but a messenger will have to be dispatched. A reply may not return for an hour."

"Ah, so your pneumatubes are broken? I do so despise when that happens."

"We are not in the habit of sending confidential League communiques by tube, Mr. Fitton. I'm sure you can understand."

"Then why don't we save that time by making the trip now? I will wait in the carriage while you go inside and ask."

"I have no way to guarantee that he'll be disposed toward this. Why don't we schedule a meeting next week? We could even meet in a more neutral spot, say, Skate River."

"This will not wait."

Now, thought Naughton, *here is the opening.*

"And what, prey tell, is so urgent?"

"Suffice it to say, Mr. Naughton, that if I cared to divulge it to you directly, I would have done so at the onset and spared us both this tortuous little dance. You'll get nothing from me. I need time with the commissioner. I need time alone. And I need it today."

"Then I must ask: in what capacity are you here?"

"Capacity?"

"Yes. Are you here as a representative of the executive of your sovereign nation, Willison Caffrey, or of your own volition?"

"I am here on my own. The executive has no knowledge of my presence." That was a crucial distinction: if Caffrey had dispatched Fitton rather than appear himself, it might hint to a bit of gamesmanship on Caffrey's part. But to have this younger, more combative owner here of his own accord was perhaps more problematic.

Naughton excused himself and repaired to an inner office with Coyle to review options. "What do you suggest?" he asked his aide.

"Keep him waiting. Make him wait all day, if need be. For now, I should travel to the commissioner's estate and consult with Lord Bart and his doctor."

"That's fine. Go now. I will bring Gill up to date and see if I can probe Fitton further."

As Coyle departed, Naughton snapped his fingers and Crandy was at his side, at attention. Naughton looked down and delivered a seldom-used command. "Full surveillance." The servohound barked in assent, then followed Naughton as he returned to the parlor. Fitton was in a whispering discussion with one of his aides, but ceased when they entered.

"Mr. Fitton, I have dispatched my aide to the commissioner's residence. He should return within an hour with a reply. In the meantime, I would imagine you and your party are quite hungry." He locked eyes with Fitton, hoping the Helderan would not spy Crandy as the hound sniffed the visitors' briefcases. "I have asked the commissary to prepare some suppers."

"That is quite welcome, sir," Fitton replied. "We trust that remaining in this comfortable parlor while we await the commissioner's response is satisfactory."

"Indeed." Naughton began to leave, and snapped his fingers for Crandy to follow.

"And I trust," said the Helderan, "that your mechanical hound gathered the impressions you sought." Naughton stopped in his tracks and glanced back at Fitton.

"Whatever do you mean?" said Naughton, feigning innocence.

"We are all friends here, Mr. Naughton," Fitton said, ignoring the question. "We all want the same thing, to preserve the peace. The Commissioner understands that. I only wish those closest to him did as well."

———————

AT HIS DESK ON HIS lower level office, Naughton picked at his mid-day dinner, a jackaloupe and potato stew. Crandy, back in low-power, rested on his side next to his chair. He rubbed the hound's belly with his foot as he ate.

Coyle had, moments earlier, returned with Lord Bart's answer: the commissioner would meet with Fitton in two hours, and would come to the League office rather than allow Fitton at the estate. Keeping the Helderan leader pacing two hours was certainly advantageous. Still, Naughton felt queasy and wished there'd be no meeting at all.

On the desk lay three thick folders: transcripts of interrogations conducted in the past two weeks with leaders of the three rebel groups that had led the Great Insurrection: the "Helderan Liberationists," "Helderan Freedom and Liberty" and the "Army of Islanders." During five decades of war, the groups were revered among their people, their fallen achieved the status of heroes, and scores of Helderan boys dreamed of joining their ranks. But after three decades of peace, their numbers were few, their funding minuscule, their voice in the Helderan nation nearly nonexistent. The monicker "the Usuals" stemmed from the colloquial — and derogatory — phrase 'the usual suspects,' but it was used so often that it now seemed a term of endearment, as a nickname for a bumbling uncle.

So Naughton hadn't even brought himself to read the full transcripts. Gill's summary was likely sufficient: "The leadership of the Usuals, to a man, offered inept and clearly transparent attempts to claim credit for the airship attack, claims that ironically only offer further proof of their inability to carry out such an operation. The membership of all three groups is aging and dysfunctional; indeed, most spend inordinate amounts of time arguing over rules, procedures, and credit for past achievements. While they bear some continued scrutiny, our security resources are clearly better spent by focusing in other directions."

But that left the search for suspects more unclear. The Monystian's network of contacts ran deep, but he had detected no odd shipments of materials by bus or ferry, nor any odd movements of cash among banks. It was a very large continent. It would be simple to evade detection.

So Naughton pushed the folders back, retrieved his cooling meal, and pondered over this looming meeting between Lord Bart and Fitton.

He reached into a cabinet and retrieved the dossier on Fitton that Coyle prepared when the Helderan bought the Warthogs. Born January 9, 1874; Fitton was, at 49, the youngest owner in either the SIP or ALE leagues. He had made his fortune through land speculation, focusing mainly on war-torn causeways that criss-crossed the northernmost portions of Heldera. A year after one such purchase, a new vein of the gas methane — used for fueling the steam motors upon which the Continent relied — was discovered on that land. It provided Fitton a tidy fortune when he sold it to the largest Helderan mining corporation. With that money, he bought land, land and more land. Huge swaths of the the countryside were gobbled up by Fitton holding companies in the northern tier. He followed that by spearheading major developments — markets, apartment buildings, theaters — in Crenshaw City. All by the time he was 40.

And then came Fitton's prize acquisition, made just two years ago: the Warthogs baseball club. It immediately made him one of the most powerful men in Heldera.

"We are all friends," Fitton had chided. Once there was a time when that could have even been true, at least among the Helderan and Setherian team owners. Cunningham had ensured that the original owners of both nations became wealthy enough to afford the teams, but not so wealthy as to be unswayed by their profits. This meant these owners were wedded to the massive revenues that the immediately popular baseball games brought. With this newfound wealth came an allegiance to the preservation of the Leagues and of the Eternal Ceasefire. Their support was ultimately rooted in self-preservation. *Nay, greed,* he thought. *The very foundation of the Leagues.*

But was it enough to maintain allegiance to Cunningham himself? Did some of the owners, in fact, see the old man as vulnerable, particularly in the wake of the airship crash? It was a given that some forces sought a return to warring; every citizen knew that. But before him now was a surprising possibility: there were forces about — perhaps this impertinent Fitton — that could seek an end to Cunningham's tenure even as they ensured the preservation of peace.

He saw three points of a triangle: the greedy ones, the warring ones and the ones who merely sought power. And he, as Special Assistant to the Commissioner of the Leagues of SIP and ALE, merely had the task of sorting out who was who.

"ALEXANDER FITTON!" THE OLD MAN greeted the Helderan owner with a steely smile. "You certainly are persistent, my aides tell me!" Cunningham made his way across the parlor to greet Fitton, clasping both his hands.

"Commissioner, trust me when I tell you there is no other course. The continent's safety compels me to seek this audience with you."

Cunningham studied the young owner, then settled onto a linen-upholstered couch and offered Fitton a seat as well.

The Helderan took stock of the others in the room — Naughton, Coyle, Gill, and Cunningham's attendant. "I need you in private, Lord Bart."

"I'm sorry, Sir Fitton—" Naughton began to protest.

"No—" Cunningham interrupted. "Gentlemen, please afford my guest his wish. I will summon you when we are ready." The others filed out obediently, but Naughton proceeded far more slowly, prompting the commissioner to admonish him. "Naughton, do get along now. My time is limited. Take the dog as well."

A half hour later, Fitton emerged from the parlor, and was brusk as he departed. Naughton followed him out to where his carriage awaited. "I do hope, Mr. Fitton, that you leave satisfied with the outcome of your talks with the commissioner?"

"Spare me, Naughton. You did everything you could to scuttle the session."

"Appointments with Lord Bart have never been extemporaneous, not even with the owners."

Fitton slipped on white gloves and adjusted his top hat, then leaned in toward him. "Naughton, I trust the commissioner appreciates your diligence," Fitton remarked. "I, however, don't enjoy having my valuable time expended by your recalcitrance."

"Then I do wish you a speedy journey back to Crenshaw City."

Fitton was about to recline into the plush red velvet carriage seat when he stood again and leaned over to Naughton in a whisper. "You should reconsider your propensity to alienate those Helderans who support your master. We are not the problem."

And with that, he was gone.

Back inside, Naughton dismissed the others, powered down Crandy, and returned to the commissioner's suite. The old man remained behind his desk, an enormous hand-made wooden structure, covered in a glossy lacquer, trimmed with brass caps at the corners. There was a time, years ago, when the desk fit him, but now Cunningham was dwarfed by it. He had swiveled his chair around to face out the window toward the carefully landscaped courtyard below.

"He wouldn't leave," Naughton offered. "I tried to get him to delay."

The Commissioner waved off the attempt at an apology. "Do not be concerned. It is good we met." Cunningham swung around, and Naughton saw for the first time that his face was drained of color. "They want power sharing."

It was the answer to the question Naughton had not yet even had the chance to voice: what had Fitton sought?

"They?"

"Fitton and the other Helderan owners. They want me to cede some authority over the leagues. He said there is growing unrest throughout their nation, particularly on their Island homeland, where distrust runs deepest. There are reports of rancor in some of the team clubhouses. There is a growing perception that the accident report was a sham and designed to assuage public relations. Worse yet, Fitton says there are some who claim that the findings were intentionally transparent so as to fuel anti-Helderan suspicions. And beyond all that, they feel that I, as a Setherian, have too long favored the Setheridge contingent of owners. He says they are tired of it."

Naughton lowered himself into a guest chair. "And they sense you are vulnerable."

"Exactly."

"What sort of power sharing?"

"He proposes that the leagues be run not by a single commissioner, but rather a board of five: two Helderan owners, two Setherians, and myself."

"You would control any split votes."

"Yes. He says I would retain ultimate control while giving the appearance of ceding power."

"And I'd imagine Fitton says this would calm the Helderan people."

"Precisely."

"And thus reduce the threat to the Ceasefire."

"Yes."

Naughton mulled Fitton's demand. It was not, he had to admit, unreasonable. "And what did you tell him?"

"I asked him if he was responsible for the airship disaster."

Naughton jumped upright. "What? You asked him—"

"Yes," Cunningham laughed broadly. "You should have seen his expression."

"And then?"

"He said the question was inappropriate, and he bid me an abrupt farewell."

Naughton swallowed. The old man's response was audacious and risky. The Helderans were clearly trying to capitalize on the tenuous situation, the threat to peace that rippled through the continent since the abortive 30th Anniversary Celebration. Opening Day was just two days away, and they were demanding changes that could further destabilize the Leagues. And old Lord Bart had essentially kicked the young owner on his posterior.

"You look tired, Commissioner. You should go home. Your doctor will be furious if you don't soon return."

Cunningham summoned his man to ready the carriage. "Yes, it would seem I have a lot of people mad at me of late, wouldn't you say, Naughton?" His tone was almost jovial, as though the old man was enjoying this.

"Yes, Commissioner. Quite a lot of people, indeed."

May 1

WIDMERTOWN

THE HURLERS KEPT TO THEMSELVES.

It was like that wherever Halloway had been: as a player, as a coach, and now, for the past seven years, as a manager. The hurlers were very much individualists, particularly the starters. That their playing time involved standing alone on the mound, tens of thousands of eyes upon them, was not a coincidence.

He hovered at the edge of the field and watched his own hurlers sprinting between bases. In the middle, his head turned down, was the Count, Ketter Asgar. Fans and columnists had rejoiced after Langford, the team general manager, traded

MICHAEL BARBATO-DUNN

for him in January. But after the deal was consummated, other managers privately offered Halloway curt descriptions, from "callous," to "belligerent," to "an enigma."

Now was the time, Halloway reasoned. Opening Day was one day away, and Asgar would be starting.

"Bring him in," he told the hurling coach, Gabriel Keating. Halloway went to wait in his office.

———————

Asgar was tall, probably was a good head and a half over Halloway. His forearms and biceps were broad and solid, he eyes seemed locked into a squint, and a shock of curly brown hair couldn't contain itself under the Squirrels cap. "Good day, Coach," he acknowledged as he entered Halloway's cramped office.

"Come on in, Ketter. Grab a chair."

"Gabe said you wanted to see me." Asgar fiddled with the brim of his cap. Removing it would have been the proper motion in this setting, a nod of respect, but Halloway resolved to ignore Asgar's failure to do so.

"We haven't had a chance to talk since you arrived here." Halloway offered a tentative grin. "It is good to have you aboard."

"Thank you, Coach. Though I can't imagine there isn't a single manager in the entire league who wouldn't say that."

Halloway grimaced at the Count's utter lack of modesty. He doubted it was an affectation; the hurler was overflowing with confidence and ego. But of course, he reminded himself, a player did not become an all-star hurler in the SIP League without vast amounts of both. "Are you ready for tomorrow?"

"Would you think I'm anything less than ready?"

"No. Of course not. Have you studied the charts on their batsmen?"

"I've been around this league, Coach. I know the strikers. They don't have any surprises."

"Perhaps. They do have three newcomers starting. Three. We didn't see two of them at all in spring training. Did you read up on them?"

The Count scowled and brushed wrinkles and lint from his uniform pants. "I suppose I have some homework to do."

"Yes, I'd say so."

The two sat in silence, staring at each other, then looking away.

In all his years in baseball, he had never so immediately despised a player, be it a star or a journeyman. But Halloway did not have to like his players, nor to be liked by them. Performance was all that mattered.

"Anything else, Coach?" Asgar offered finally.

"You tell me. Is there anything you care to discuss? Baseball, or otherwise?"

The hurler considered this briefly, then nodded. "As long as you ask, Coach, tell me: do you agree that the season should be played?"

"Yes. Absolutely. Don't you?"

"Thirty people died, and the League quickly laid this at the hands of the Helderans."

"What leads you to think that? You know the report found this was an accident, two mishaps happening simultaneously."

"Do you believe that, Coach?"

"Mine is not to analyze forensic reports, Ketter. Mine is to win ball games."

"It is widely held — even by some League staffers — that the report is flimsy and easily doubted."

"I believe that no matter what they put in the report, there would be people doubting it."

Asgar stood and began pacing. "You were a national hero, Coach. I know that. It is taught to us in school. Who knows if the Leagues would have succeeded had you not been willing to play for Setherians."

"Yes. But what those books don't teach you is how reviled I was by many. For weeks, for months."

The hurler cocked his head. "Reviled?"

"Yes. Name calling. Vandalism on my parents' house. Death threats."

"And did you report this?"

"No, Ketter. That would not have helped."

Asgar stood at the far wall of the dim office and studied the memorabilia that Halloway had hung: plaques, commemorations, awards. "They say your father died in the war."

"No, it was my grandfather. My father fought, but he returned."

"Grandfather?"

"Yes. And my great-grandfather before him."

Asgar repeated the words with incredulity. "Your great-grandfather?"

"Yes, he was one of the original insurgents, actually. He died in a mine explosion just before the war was formally declared."

"So... 80 years ago?"

"Closer to 90. I think he was 35. My grandfather died about 75 years ago, when my father was ten."

"Do you want their deaths to be in vain?"

Halloway's fists tightened on the wooden arms of the chair. He made it a point to exhale before answering. "Ketter, every day that the nation of Heldera continues to exist, their deaths are not in vain. And as far as I'm concerned, as long as the Leagues of SIP and ALE continue to exist, their deaths are not in vain."

"That is an extremely simplistic view."

"How so?" he replied.

"There is a school of thought within some Helderan political circles that is growing in popularity. It is the Kender Hypothesis, named for the professor at Leadland University who first postulated it."

Postulated? Halloway realized this was much more than a case of a malcontent star hurler. This was an erudite, articulate, and analytical malcontent star hurler. "Go on."

"The theory is frighteningly simple. The Setherians, realizing that the war could not be won, created these leagues of baseball to mollify the Helderan people, to lull them into complacency."

"Complacency?" Halloway wondered how he could extricate himself from this discussion. "We were granted our own nation, Ketter. Did you or your professor conveniently forget that? Bartholomew Cunningham did that — and I'm sure you know that convincing Setherians to give up control of nearly half of the continent was no small task."

"True, but that is a key part of the hypothesis. Kender suggested that after, oh, say 30 years or so, events would be staged to shatter the peace in a way that the Helderans were blamed. Setherians who claimed our people were unworthy of independence would cite those events as proof. And then we would be, once again, as we were for centuries, subjugated to second-rate status."

Halloway looked for his timepiece — 11:30 a.m. — and held it up to the hurler. "Sprints for strikers. I'm going to watch."

"Do you not see it? The theory supposes that even at 30 years, our independence was never meant to be anything more than temporary. Our independence was a sham, a carefully orchestrated sham. We were never meant to have it forever!"

"Ketter, honestly, that's a far-fetched theory. I highly doubt something so intricate as a 30-year ceasefire, and the creation of a new nation, could be concocted so as to trick an entire race of people. To say it was all a ruse is frankly absurd."

"Coach, Professor Albert Kender of Leadland University died 18 years ago. He wrote his hypothesis five years before that."

"So?"

"I'm telling you that in 1900 Kender, an esteemed academician, predicted that in three decades' time, a disaster would strike a Setherian location that would blamed on the Helderans. He predicted a disaster like the crash of the *Lady Crym* 23 years ago. And he predicted it would serve as the beginning of the end for the Helderan nation!"

Halloway stared at the hurler, mouth agape. Rarely did he come in contact with people caught up in the machination of power and politics. And when he did, they were certainly not young men in baseball uniforms.

Just one day before the start of the season the coach of the Widermertown Flying Squirrels found himself in his own office, dizzy, nauseous and at a loss for an adequate reply.

He dismissed Asgar with a brusk wave. "Go finish your stretching, Ketter. Get out there."

TREDGEMOND BUTTE

RONNELL FOUND THE SCATTAWAY DIFFICULT to enter. The publick house was a favorite of ballplayers, and clusters of young fans huddled near the entrance and sides, hoping to get a glimpse of members of the hometown Hounds, perhaps even the visiting Mules of Red Beach. Inside was more boisterous, and he pushed his way through the crush near the front of the bar, peering for familiar faces, or at least an open bar stool. Eventually, he chose the latter, back toward the kitchen, and a bartender who thankfully set him up immediately.

Tredgemond Butte was the only major city on a chilly sliver of a peninsula in the northwestern region of the continent. Though Ronnell had been national baseball columnist for 20 years, he had only visited the town and its ALE League affiliate twice. It was distant and inclement. But now, with the continent seemingly on the precipice of war, he presumed that Tredgemont Butte would be the perfect locale in which to spend Opening Day. The remote city could prove to be a true gauge of whether public opinion was still supportive of Commissioner Cunningham and his ever-loyal minions, and whether Lord Bart could survive this crisis.

Yet getting to 'the Butte,' as it was affectionately known, had meant hours of discomfort for Ronnell. The cable cars from Mt. Waylandtown only went as far north as Binney. From there he had endured seven hours of private carriage rides, with three stops to feed the horses. Ronnell spent most of the time trying to sleep, then stirring and damning himself for attempting the journey.

Yes, he could have taken an airship. That is how visiting teams and the occasional tourist arrived. A dirigible would have cut the entire journey in half. But Ronnell had long ago sworn off airships, despite their speed and modern amenities. What goes up cannot help but come down, went the old saying. He much preferred to be in full control of when he did come down, and that was one luxury the airships could not provide. The *Lady Crym* disaster had certainly solidified his resolve.

So he'd arrived now, one day before the opener, exhausted and stinking of the cigars and whiskey that had made the journey palatable. One day early: enough time to let a room and bathe.

Tredgemond Butte, like many of the ALE cities, had a population that was majority Amandean. They loved their ball, Ronnell mused as he surveyed the rollicking crowd, almost as much as they loved their drink. That, in fact, was the very point of the league: the Amandean League of Everyman. Amandeans made up only about 20 percent of the continent's population, but they constituted 75 percent of the ALE ticket buyers, and 95 percent of the patrons at the bars near the ballparks.

In fact, it was the desire of the Amandeans for baseball in the smaller cities that led to Cunningham's creation of the ALE. Ronnell remembered it well: the original plan had been for a single league with affiliates in the 16 major municipalities — eight in Setheridge and eight in the newly created nation of Heldera. The Setheridge Island Professional League of baseball. The SIP. Sixteen teams were enough, Lord Bart had reasoned; he didn't want empty seats in the ballparks. But within weeks of the formal announcement of the SIP came a clamor from the more rural areas that had had independent baseball squads in the years before and during the war. Cities with large Amandean populations, with names like Folgerly Bluff and LaValleyFord Prairie. And of course, the remote Tredgemond Butte. They wanted their own league.

The Amandean outcry had taken Cunningham by surprise, and yet in what proved to be a political master stroke, he embraced it. And so was born the Amandean League of Everyman, 20 teams, ten in each nation. The ALE: how fitting. A mug of beer in its logo.

Its creation — and the ways the Amandeans embraced it — helped ensure the immediate success of both leagues and of the ceasefire. Lord Bart was their hero.

Or so Ronnell believed; his memories of those days would always be hazy.

Vivian had left him by that point, and he had instead become intimate with the local bourbon each night after the games.

"Ollo, my old friend! Whatever brings you to these wretched parts? Surely not the weather!"

The columnist turned and saw Anders Mathis, hitting coach of the Hounds, squeezing his way over to where Ronnell sat. It was good to see a familiar face.

"Anders, I didn't think you still patronized publicks. I thought your drinking days were done."

"I only wish. Fretting over whether some of these youngsters can hit a breaking ball sends me back to the bar every time."

The two laughed, and Mathis signaled to the bartender for another of the same whiskey that Ronnell now cradled in his hands. No barstools were open, so he stood next to Ronnell and leaned his elbows on the bar. "I thought you never left your newsroom," he kidded.

"Ah, sometimes its good to get fresh air, especially lately."

"No doubt."

"How's your squad looking?"

Mathis had been hitting coach for the Hounds for the past six seasons, and they'd made the play-offs in all but the last year. Fans wondered if it was the beginning of a decline for the team. "I think we'll be back in the hunt," the coach predicted. "That's my answer on the record."

"Off the record?"

"I'm not so sure." The two laughed. "But honestly, Ronnell, why are you here?"

The newspaperman sighed. "Things are in chaos back home. No one knows what to think. Rumors are flying left and right. Cunningham has been ridiculously quiet — a couple of tepid statements and then he releases that insipid accident report, as though that's going to solve everything."

"But I saw your last column. You went easy on the old man. Just being a good friend?"

"You know Cunningham and I were never friends. We don't talk outside a news conference."

"Just being a good citizen, then?"

"I suppose. Its what Corcoran wanted."

Mathis peered at him with a raised eyebrow. "I doubt you let Corky dictate what you write. You went easy on Lord Bart, Ollo."

Ronnell swirled the liquor in his glass and said nothing.

The coach slapped him on his shoulder. "Oh, Ollo Ronnell. You're a bit soft at heart, beneath that grizzled scowl."

"I wrote what I did because it was the proper thing to do, Anders. We in the press occasionally can be responsible."

"And now you want to get as far away from Schawmount City as possible?"

"I want to find out what people — real people — are saying here. What better time than Opening Day? And what better place than the coldest damn place on the continent?"

He downed the last of his whiskey, far ahead of Mathis, and waved to the bartender for a second. For a time the two sat quietly, watching the other patrons, most of whom seemed to be university students and shift workers from the local steam plant. Ronnell knew there was also a backroom bar for players, usually Hounds, but occasionally those of visiting teams. Fans, coaches and especially reporters were barred. No matter. It was fine out here, in the main room. In the center section, a tradesman took out a fiddle and those near him struck up a traditional league melody.

A man on first, a man on third
They'll even up the score
We'll cheer our squad as they're driven in
And then we'll call for more

The young phenom who throws the heat
Will quickly win our hearts
The bench warmer who strikes a slam
Is honored in all parts

For in Setheridge, in Heldera,
There's an end to bloody strife
Lord Bart gave us the SIP and ALE
And baseball's in our life
Oh, baseball's in our life

The two turned back to the bar.

"So Grafton's really gone," Ronnell said.

"Hard to believe. But we'll survive."

Peter Grafton, one of the greatest starting hurlers in the history of either league, had retired at the end of the '22 season. He'd been with the Hounds his entire 23-year career, during which he compiled an astounding 419-149 record, with an earned run average below three. Even in his final year, at age 44, he'd been as strong as ever, tallying a 21-8 record.

"We expected him to just keep going," said Mathis. "He gave us no warning. Just walked in one day to the general manager and announced his retirement. Just like that." Mathis snapped his fingers. "I wish every star ended his career like Grafton. No farewell tour, no public posturing," said the coach.

"Just like when we retired," said the columnist. At this they both laughed. They'd played during the same period, roughly the first six seasons of the Leagues. Their paths, though, had never crossed: Mathis was a utility infielder for the Squirrels in the SIP League, while Ronnell put in strong seasons in the ALE as the first bagger for the Mudhens of Leadland.

Only later, in their second careers, did they come into contact. Mathis had first pursued coaching in '07, ten years after retiring as a player, when he was offered the position of striking coach for the Stone Crabs of Pear Falls. Six seasons later came a dubious opportunity: he was hired as manager of the Toads of Fanningana Falls, one of the league's most consistent losers, and the only team never to have qualified for the play-offs.

This was where Ronnell had met Mathis. He'd gone there to write about the futility of the Toads and their loyal fans. He still remembered his lead: "Fanningana Falls sits at the western base of the Red Tummlyn Mountains, and the post-war revitalization seems to have completely passed by this quiet town. Despite a lack of jobs and a flight of residents fleeing for bigger cities like Skate River and Kern, and despite a baseball team that each game seems to find new ways to lose, the residents of Faningana are Amandeans through and through. They love their parties, they love their drink, and they love their baseball. Quite simply, this trio keeps them going."

Ronnell knew Mathis loved managing but hated his time with the Toads. The constant losing tore at him. In '17, when the far more successful Hounds offered him the striking coach position, Mathis grabbed it and had been in Tredgemond Butte ever since. He was happily along for the ride: five first-place finishes, one Continental Series championship, and far less stress than if he'd continued managing losing clubs.

The bartender arrived with Ronnell's second drink and filled up Mathis's while he was there. Ronnell thought about stopping now — he wanted to get up early and see batting practice — but hell, it was just one drink.

The publick house was now more crowded than ever.

"What do you think he's doing?" asked Mathis.

"Grafton?"

"No, the old man. The commissioner. Cunningham. Around here, Ollo, I'm hearing rumblings that it is time for him to resign. To pass the mantle. Such talk would have been unthinkable two months ago. How will he defuse this?"

"I'm not sure, Anders. I'm not sure even he knows. But I have to find out."

"Well, for everyone's sake, I hope you're able to. This is all too blengin' scary."

It was now past midnight. Opening Day had arrived. Their glasses were empty, but neither man moved. The bartender was nowhere to be seen. The two simply watched the crowd, unsure what to do, whether to go. The fiddler fiddled, and the younger patrons raised mugs and sang on, clapping hands and stamping feet, their words reverberating through the dimly lit Scattaway and out into the suddenly cool night.

I saw my lady love today
A walkin' down the lane
I tipped my hat but passed her by
For I'm heading to the game!

And if our team should falter
As the boys race to the crown
We'll curse the fates and rue the day
But it'll never get us down!

For in Setheridge, in Heldera,
There's an end to bloody strife
Lord Bart gave us the SIP and ALE
And baseball's in our life
Oh, baseball's in our life
Yes - the Leagues of SIP and ALE are here
Now baseball is our life!

May 2

SKATE RIVER

A FERRY CARRIED THE COMMISSIONER AND his entourage across the width of the River Valencroft, due east of Shawmount City, then northeast through a small tributary that flowed into Jared Lake. The Mad Dogs' ballpark could be seen in the distance on the lake's eastern bank. Naughton watched it approach from the bow. "I am relieved we made it to this day," said Coyle, next to him.

"Indeed, Roderick."

Gulls overhead cawed, as if laughing at them. The ferry glided on, toward the Helderan shore, toward the Skate River ballpark. Toward Opening Day.

The tradition that the Skate River Mad Dogs host the first scheduled game of each season dated back to the inception of the Leagues. Naughton was unsure of its origin; he did not join the Leagues until a decade later. But he imagined that the scheduling was quite deliberate: Skate River was the Helderan city closest to the Setheridge border, and as such it allowed the commissioner and other dignitaries to make a symbolic foray from one nation to the other as each season began. An important statement, particularly in those first few years. Whoever had conceived the idea — perhaps it was Naughton's predecessor — deserved praise. Now, this year, never was the tradition more important.

He scratched Crandy's back and peered out over the ferry's stern. Opening day. It had always meant one thing: hope. Hope for a team's fortunes in the coming season. Hope for the arrival of a successful spring, then a summer of leisure. Even during the Great Insurrection, before the Ceasefire and the inception of the Leagues, there was opening day for the loosely organized ball clubs, amateur and semi-pro, that dotted the continent's landscape.

He'd loved the sport from the start, and had played every chance he had in pick-up games on the streets of Mount Jarviswell. It had occupied most of his childhood. There was little else.

Naughton had grown up knowing that both of his grandfathers had been killed in the Insurrection, fighting for the Setherian forces. His own father, Nicholas, had served for several years before Naughton was born, but was allowed to return home after the boy was born because the birth left Halley, his mother, in ill health and in need of constant care.

When he was eleven a neighbor came to retrieve him in the middle of the school day. The woman was solemn, as suddenly were his teachers, and Naughton knew his mother had died.

Except he was wrong. It was his father who was dead, succumbing to a heart seizure after an attack by Helderan insurgents on downtown Mount Jarviswell.

The paradox that his father survived actual combat but became a civilian casualty was not lost on Naughton, even at that age. He remembered, even to this day, an uncle arguing with city officials that Nicholas Naughton should be declared a wartime casualty. Arguing to no avail.

After that attack, with his mother still bedridden, he was mainly left to fend for himself. Halley's siblings, his aunts and uncles, came by often, but he was an only child and now nearly orphaned.

He was on his own, a fate not uncommon to youngsters after decades of war.

And while Naughton remained devoted to both his schooling and his mother, his free time was devoted to baseball. He was a decent striker and slick with the glove at the second bag, and what he lacked in talent he overcame with sheer enthusiasm. By this point, the Leagues of SIP and ALE had been in existence for a few years, and Naughton was occasionally scouted by coaches from a few of the Setherian professional clubs. Eventually, one of them, the Goodwyn Fork Hedgehogs in the ALE League, made him a league-minimum offer to come and play in the 1899 season, six years after inception. He had just turned 20.

While tempting, the offer posed a dilemma: his mother needed constant care, and although Goodwyn Fork was only three hours from his home, it was still too distant to allow him to stay at home. Nor could he afford to hire a full-time nurse. He turned down the offer and stayed to care for her. He took classes at Jarviswell University.

No other team ever made an offer. His baseball career was over before it had begun.

——————— ———————

THE GROUP SETTLED INTO VELVET seats in the owner's suite atop Jared Lake Stadium. Crandy nestled at Naughton's feet. The commissioner himself was seated between the owners of the two teams that were about to play. To his right was Harry Gander of the Mad Dogs, just 48 years old, who had inherited the team from his father, the late Darren Gander. To his left, Broadlun Clay of the Schawmount City Jackaloupes, a contemporary of the elder Gander, and the executive of the nation of Setheridge. Both had helped gather support for Cunningham and his bold idea at a time when few other prominent figures — Setherian or Helderan — were willing to do so. Cunningham had ensured that they were rewarded appropriately.

The three men held monoculars to their faces as the opening festivities began to unfold on the brilliant grass field below. A marching band offered a rousing rendition of the Helderan national anthem, followed by the Setherian anthem. Naughton knew that shortly the public address announcer would make mention of the commissioner's presence at the game. The thousands in attendance — and many more listening on audiocasters in publick houses — would cheer. Or so he hoped.

Whether Cunningham should make a speech had been subject of a brief debate. Should he offer words of comfort, and words of hope for a peaceful but competitive season? Ultimately, they decided against it. While the venue was different, a stadium speech by the old man would seem agonizingly reminiscent of the Anniversary Celebration tragedy. "The less said the better," Lady Lynam had cautioned. Though her presence still grated, Naughton admitted to himself that she occasionally offered sage advice.

Each of the teams that hosted an Opening Day game was responsible for security at the park. That was the only way — the resources of the leagues were not nearly so vast as to be able to handle that task at all the venues. Naughton had no doubt that the Mad Dogs' contingent could adequately protect the old man. Still, he was relieved there would be no speech, and thus no direct exposure to the crowds.

"May I join you?" Naughton looked up to find Preston Dronwell standing above him. Crandy immediately jerked his head upward and sniffed the man's pant leg. The servohound swiveled his ears front to back and front again, and then uttered a low growl.

"Crandy, stop," he admonished. "Preston is an old friend. Please, sir, have a seat."

"Old, am I, Naughton?" They laughed and shook hands. Crandy's eyes shifted side to side, and they remained on Dronwell as he settled back to his resting position.

Dronwell took the seat at Naughton's right and acknowledged Coyle. "Roderick, glad you could join us as well." He was a gaunt man, near Naughton's age but with a full beard overwhelmed by a wide mustache that curled to points at the edges of his mouth. "Naughton, your hound is certainly at heightened attention. I suppose the events of the last two months have prompted you to raise its surveillance capacity."

"I think Crandy understands—" Naughton caught himself. Amelia often admonished him for ascribing too much sentience to the device. "I think he is calibrated appropriately."

A waiter came by and offered Dronwell a cognac, but was waved off. "A fruitade, if you have it, will be fine."

Now the players on both clubs were being introduced, with rapturous cheers reserved for the hometown Mad Dogs, particularly the team's slugger, third bagger Jake Stratton. The likely Hall of Famer doffed his cap to acknowledge the cheers.

"How is Broadlun holding up?" Naughton asked. Preston Dronwell had been the special assistant to Broadlun Clay for 18 years, nearly as long as Naughton himself had served the commissioner. They had stood side by side at many festivities, many ribbon cuttings, many speeches. They knew the tensions and pressures each other faced.

"I must tell you Naughton, not well."

"Pray, tell more, Preston."

"Well, as you can no doubt imagine, Broadlun is hearing constantly from his fellow Setherian owners."

"Hearing what?"

"Andrew. Do you need *me* to spell it out? Here, of all places?"

Of course, he did not. Clay had undoubtedly heard a litany of issues: voluminous misgivings from the other owners over Cunningham's handling of the situation; skepticism about the League's official report on the crash of the *Lady Crym;* worry of the possibility of further attacks; and, most importantly, rumors of the possibility of Helderan complicity in the matter. "I'm sure Mr. Clay understands that whoever perpetrated the attack wants precisely this type of reaction among owners on both sides of the border."

"I understand that, Naughton. I have told him that, repeatedly. But he is the senior owner, he is the Executive of the Nation of Setheridge, and he is the statesman most viewed as having the ear of the commissioner. So I'm sure you and Lord Bart understand that Broadlun Clay can do little to qualm the fears of his fellow owners, however misguided they may be. And he likely can do little to repulse a growing call to take up arms."

A marching band on the field struck up a rousing piece played at each Skate River game, "Mad Dogs Lie Down for No One." Skate River's starter, the veteran

Marmaduke Conner, continued his warm-ups on the mound. Thousands in the upper stands scampered up narrow steps to take their seats. Cunningham and the two owners stood and applauded as the players took the field.

Naughton sighed and scratched at the nape of Crandy's neck. Everything Dronwell said was true. The continent was a tinderbox, and even the resumption of the beloved sport of baseball would do little to douse these embers.

"What is it Mr. Clay would have the commissioner do?" he asked after a time.

Dronwell paused before answering, then leaned in closely to whisper a reply. "Executive Clay has a simple message he is too polite to deliver directly, in this august setting. It is this: tell your beloved Commissioner Cunningham not to forget his roots."

"Is Executive Clay suggesting that as a native of Setheridge, the commissioner should somehow favor Setherians as he handles this crisis?"

Dronwell scowled and gathered his top hat. "You and the commissioner can interpret that message anyway you see fit. Suffice it to say, Executive Clay and the other Setherian owners are watching. Closely."

Naughton gritted his teeth and leaned in closer to the man. Crandy shifted his ears in renewed attention to the discussion. "Preston, please tell Executive Clay this: Bartholomew Cunningham is Commissioner of the Leagues of SIP and ALE. His allegiance is to no nation, no race. His allegiance is solely to the preservation of the Eternal Ceasefire, for the good of all."

Dronwell backed away, stood, and said nothing.

"You tell him that, Preston Dronwell. Or I will ask Lord Bart to tell that to Executive Clay directly. I trust you'd prefer the former."

"Indeed," said the man as he stood, put on his hat and turned to exit. "Enjoy the game, Andrew Naughton. I do so hope we have many more."

Crandy growled again, and below on the gleaming field the home base arbiter cried out two words that millions had, for weeks, yearned to hear.

"Play ball!"

TREDGEMOND BUTTE

RONNELL MADE HIS WAY OVER to Zephyr Field on the outskirts of Tredgemond Butte, still bleary eyed from the smoke and whiskey of the previous night at the Scattaway. The park was a beautiful sight, one of the prettiest in the ALE, and, though three decades old, the owners managed to keep it pristine. Bunting in burgundy and black — the Hounds' colors — hung above each section, snapping in the typically bitter Tredgemond breeze. The stands wrapped around the first and third base lines only at one level, then continued past the outfield wall, with a deep stretch of grass bisecting the furthest sections of the seating. Eight enormous poles, each affixed with arrays of gas-fed night lamps to illuminate the entire field for the evening games, hovered above the expectant crowd.

He'd missed batting practice, though that was no great loss. What he really wanted was some time to mix with the fans before the game got started. That would not be easy either, as all 9,100 tickets had been sold and the fans, mostly Amandeans, had quickly made their way to the seats. On anything but opening day, he could find a seat in some distant section without much effort. Today, though, every spot was claimed.

Instead the columnist crossed a corridor behind the seats nearest third base. Before the curve at the start of the outfield were two rows of high-topped bars, for overflow crowds. They were mostly empty at the moment, so Ronnell positioned himself midway on the front bar and waited for fans to arrive.

On the field below, the groundsmen tended to the grass and finished laying down foul lines in chalk. He'd long remembered the words of his first manager, Daniel "Soldier Boy" Aberman, who said a good groundskeeper could be worth four or five wins a year. And he was right: the crew could tailor the height of the outfield grass or the incline of the mound to meet the needs and the talents of the hometown players. Of course, every team did this, so he supposed it all balanced out.

Within short order the Hounds' faithful began milling in, lining up at the concessions, and finding their seats. Unlike the SIP League, where fans were referred to as patrons and arrived in formal attire, this game — and the ALE League as a whole — brought a tremendous mix, with some men in jackets, others in overalls; some even wore light cloth shirts and shorts trimmed above the knee. Ladies' dresses were colorful and casual, more suited to a picnic than a party. A few even chose skirts and sleeveless blouses. Youngsters were allowed to run freely through stands, some in costumes or face paint. If SIP games often were treated as society events at which fashion and gossip became underlying themes, then ALE games were neighborhood carousals at which frivolity and merriment were the orders of the day.

By the time the Mules' starting hurler, Harmon Andrews, was taking his final warm-ups and the arbiter was giving the home bag one last dusting, the standing-room bar area was crowded and boisterous. Some fans had arrived by cable car, but — as with most ALE League cities — many couldn't afford that and traveled by bus or on foot. Most had secured overflow tickets at the gate within the past hour, others had undoubtedly procured them through shady re-sellers or had sneaked in with the help of friendly security guards. Such was the way of the ALE League.

On his right appeared a broad-shouldered man, probably 50 or so, with pepper-gray hair that covered the collar, and the thin, up-turned nose and rosy cheeks of the Amandeans. Ronnell imagined the man was taking in the game after a shift in the farms or mines had ended. A longtime fan of the Hounds, he surmised, someone distanced from the politics of the day. The man took an empty bar stool next to him and nodded.

Ronnell grinned. Here would be his column.

The hawkers began arriving, and Ronnell signaled for a beer, then asked the man if he was ordering as well. "No thanks, have to get to work in a bit."

"Where's that?"

"Where's what?"

"Your job."

"Oh, across town. The steamworks."

"You?" the man asked.

"Just visiting. Just here for the game." He extended his hand. "Ollo Ronnell."

"Arbutus Chapp." The man stopped for a second as Ronnell's name sank in. "The columnist!" Ollo nodded. "Well, well." Then he called out to his friends, "Boys, we got ourselves a big name here." The others gathered around them to offer handshakes.

His cup of ale was passed down the row to him, and he passed payment forward, waving to the vendor to keep the change. Ale, locally made and quite bitter, was sold throughout the park, but no other alcohol was permitted. That, of course, didn't stop many from putting flasks in their inner jacket pockets.

Then the contest was underway. Andrews, the hurler, set down the top three in the Mules' line-up with just six pitches: a 1-0 fly-out to deep right, an 0-2 strike-out, and a first throw fly-out to shallow center. Chapp joined in the applause as his Hounds trotted back to the dugout for their first at-bat.

"You get to many of the games?" Ronnell asked.

"Most. Not much more to do really, in the Butte. What in the continent's name would bring you up this way?"

"Oh, I needed to get away from Schawmount, I suppose."

"I'd not blame you for that. We just read about the mess in the papers. I can't imagine being there."

Vendors continued their forays into the standing room section. They did well hawking fan favorites such as billy-bread rounds and fried jackaloupe strips, fare that was far less pricey than what was available at most SIP League stadiums. Ronnell saw that Chapp, like many here, had brought in his own food — permissible in the ALE, forbidden in the SIP. The steamsman unwrapped a large roasted turkey leg and began chewing away.

The game settled in, the innings wore on, and Chapp proved to be a quiet companion. Ronnell surmised that this was the man's ritual: attending with friends but keeping to himself, studying the nuances of the managers' decisions and shouting only when the arbiters muffed a close call. He wanted to press Chapp with more questions, to get a sense of the mindset of a random ALE League fan, but he sensed intuitively that further questions would only cause him to become even more reserved, or perhaps even to leave.

So for four innings they watched the field in silence. Both Andrews and the Mules' starter, Stewart Rocheford, had plowed through the line-ups in the first three innings. In the fourth came some runs: Andrews yielding a solo home run to the Mules' left fielder Peter Redwynne, and then Rocheford giving up two in the bottom of that frame after the Hounds strung together some hits.

Chapp was silent. Ronnell was patient.

The smokestacks of the fabric mills pronounced themselves in the skylines beyond the outfield seats. Ronnell knew that as a steamsman, Chapp worked below ground, in the plants on which every city and town now relied. Millions needed the steam to power the cable cars, the heating, the pneumatubes, the audiocasters, and even the meters that regulated the gas for cooking and lighting that fed every modern home. And, of course, the myriad other devices that post-war science had wrought, from portable ovens that toasted slices of bread to machines that brewed coffee and the damned mechascribes that populated every newsroom in the continent. The Great Insurrection had fueled the science of steam, and 30 years of peacetime saw its acceptance into every home and workplace. Only in the hinterlands, the less populated rural towns and villages, was the new technology slow to arrive.

And steam brought jobs to the cities: back-breaking, grueling jobs embraced by thousands of soldiers returning home at the start of the Ceasefire. Ronnell could easily imagine that Chapp had been one of them: a veteran, probably with a wife and young children, a small home, and the offer of a good paying job thousands of footlengths below the surface of the world.

In the steamworks.

Still, he held silent. Years of convincing people to talk had taught him the very simple truth: they opened up more readily when they were not being probed.

The next few innings proceeded quietly, workman-like, with the most cheering reserved for a fistfight in the bottom of the fifth, apparently some rowdies in the stands nearest third base. Such scrapes were all too common at ALE games, particularly in later innings as some got fairly drunk. Vendors rarely cut off beer sales to even the most inebriated fans. It was, after all, how the Amandeans — who made up the greatest contingent of the ALE League's fan base — preferred things.

The visiting squad tied the game in the top of the sixth, again thanks to the prolific Redwynne, one of the Mules' most dangerous strikers. He doubled to lead off the inning, and then scored when the Hounds' third bagger, the normally sure-handed Edward Dunson, let a routine grounder through his legs and out into left field. The sixth ended 2-2; it was proving to be a great season opener for the two squads.

"You don't ask many questions for a reporter, now, do you?"

Ronnell grinned. "You didn't seem to be in a talking mood."

Chapp nodded. "Right. I probably never am. My friends over there are, maybe you want to try them?"

"I'm fine here."

More silence. Ronnell knew he was close. He would be patient.

And then, as he had hoped, the man opened up.

"Have you ever gone below, Ollo Ronnell?"

"Below?"

"Yes, below. To a steam plant."

"No, Mr. Chapp. I actually never have."

Chapp took a deep breath. "Most people haven't. Most people have no idea what its like."

"I'm sure it's… it's difficult."

"Difficult, yes. And deadly. Did you know that?"

"Uh, I'm sorry, I guess…"

"Not many pay attention, no need to apologize. We lose about ten men a year down below. Just at our plant. Nearly one a month."

"How?"

"Every way you could could imagine. Explosions, usually. Fires. Stupidity. Carelessness. It's all down there. We turn rainwater into steam, Ollo Ronnell, but we do it on a massive scale."

Ronnell nodded, careful not to interrupt the man's reverie.

"Do you know why they build the steam plants below ground, Mr. Ronnell?"

"Call me Ollo, please. And I suppose I don't know. Because of the noise?"

"Maybe. Mainly, though, to save money. Far cheaper to capture and transport the rainwater. But being below ground only makes the work more dangerous."

"And it makes it less likely that the public learns of the accidents."

"Yes, and the companies are quick to buy the silence of the families."

"Is that so?"

The man nodded. "Besides, the public loves its steam, Ollo Ronnell. Modern life depends on it, and so there will always be these jobs, and men desperate enough to take them."

Out on the field, it was now the eighth inning, the score remained tied, and the crowd around them — fueled by ale — was cheering or moaning on every throw and swing.

"I don't really like this game of baseball, Ollo Ronnell. I'm probably one of the few."

"But you come anyway."

"Yes."

Ronnell knew he needn't prod. The answer was forthcoming.

"Croften Brittenham was his name, Ollo Ronnell. No one remembers him now. We grew up together, fought in the war together, even dated sisters for a time. And when the Ceasefire was declared, we became steamsmen together.

"And sure as the Valencroft flows south, he loved his baseball. He was never happier than when Lord Bart announced the Leagues. And he yelled with delight when they announced a team right here in the Butte. By that point we'd both married, both had young children, and on our days off we'd come down here for the games. If we had weekends off, we'd bring the young ones, but if our days off came mid-week, we'd come alone. Sit up here, in the overflow section.

"Crofty loved the little things of this game: the leisurely pace, the arc of the throws from the outfielders, the brilliant precision of a double play. I learned a lot from him, but the game never grabbed me the same. I thought Lord Bart's plan was a lot of bunk."

Then Chapp stopped. His lips quivered.

Ronnell knew he needed a slight bit of prodding to continue. He waited a minute, then said, "He died down there? Is that it, Arbutus Chapp? He died down below?"

The man nodded, his jaw shaking. "We'd been on the job just five years. The technology was so new, and the demand to expand was so great, the damned managers kept pushing. Kept cutting corners. It's safer now, but not by much."

"How old was he?"

"Twenty-nine. His boys were seven and four."

"And you were there, with him?"

Chapp nodded. "After the explosion the medics took a full half hour to get down to us, to get down below. By that point there was nothing to be done. I held his hand the whole time. Then, finally, the medics placed a sheet over him and I carried him up myself. Up to the surface. Up to daylight. Up to his family."

Ronnell swallowed and stared at his glass. He realized he had never spent time pondering the lives of steamsmen. He had traveled the continent for years and enjoyed the results of their labors, without once giving thought to them. He had walked over streets and in buildings without any recognition of what these men were doing far below the ground.

He looked up again. "So you keep coming to the games. In memory of your friend."

"Yes, sir. For all 25 years since Crofty died. I've missed seven or eight games, I believe, for weddings and such. A sick day, now and then. His wife remarried and moved away. No one around here even remembers him." The words were choked. Ronnell looked away.

Alas, a Hounds victory was not to be. The Mules got to Andrews in the top of the eighth for two runs. A double for backstop Simon Faramir. An intentional walk — Ronnell hated those — to first bagger Theodore Smyth. They advanced on a ground out, and then pinch batter Edgar Bruno came through with a double on Andrews's weakest throw, a change-up, up and in. Both runners scored, and 9,000 Hounds fans exhaled in disgust.

After that, Rocheford couldn't be touched. The Hounds went down quietly in both the eighth and the ninth, with the Mules' starter going the distance. Both Ronnell and Chapp stood as the dispirited Butte crowd began filing out of Zephyr Field.

"Here's a quote for you, Mr. Ronnell: the Hounds are going to win the division. Trust me. Tell that to your friend the commissioner."

"I will, sir. I will." He extended his right hand and they shook.

The man gathered his coat and began to leave. "Oh," he turned, remembering one more thing. "Thank Lord Bart for keeping the games going. We need it, desperately. You can quote me on that."

To this Ollo Ronnell simply nodded with a slight bow of his head. When he looked up, the man was gone.

And soon enough, the park was empty.

May 10

WIDMERTOWN

IN THE FIRST WEEK OF the season the Flying Squirrels of Widmertown jumped out to a 4-0 record by sweeping the Grizzlies of Red Tummlyn. The first two games were won by overwhelming margins, the second pair of games by a single run. But any potential cockiness on the part of his players was quickly erased in the next series, for they were swept handily by the Warthogs of Crenshaw City.

The throwing went south; the bats fell silent.

The swings of the game, Halloway mused.

Now, at 4-4, the Squirrels were to begin hosting a three-game series against the Screech Owls of Kern. The Owls were 6-2 and seemed to be matching the rampant predictions that they'd contend for the Helderan South Division title. After all, they'd won it in '18, '19 and '21.

For this game, Halloway decided to go outside his usual four-man rotation by giving the start to the middleman, Morris Treesparrow. The hurler was 28 and in his third season with the club. Last year he'd started four games and fared well, and Halloway had every intention of giving him a good dozen starts this year when his big four needed rest. This was, he knew, quite early in the season to be doing this, but he sensed it would prove helpful.

SIP and ALE teams normally rostered six hurlers; rarely was there a need for more. Four starters on each club formed the rotation and were expected to finish the games on most occasions. The only others would be relievers, expected to finish off the final inning or two, or to throw the entire game in those occasional instances when a starter was too hungover to even make it out to the mound. Treesparrow was one for the Squirrels; the closer Ryan Foreman the other.

Halloway knew that in recent years some teams had begun keeping track of the number of throws offered by starters in each game; often a hurler would top 150. He saw no need for such a tally, and had no doubt that the Squirrels' starting four — Asgar, Harald, Broughan, and Skelly — would all reach 250 innings thrown by season's end.

Barring injuries, of course. There was always the specter of injuries.

Across the field he spied Hendry Smallwood, the Owls' manager, and they acknowledged each other with a wave. Halloway didn't speak much before a game. He didn't like disrupting his routine. He would watch batting practice two hours before the first throw, then sit at his desk and eat a dish of bore stew while he pondered his line-up. He'd look at the opposing hurlers' record against his regulars, consider who was hurting, and study the past week's statistics. But he was a traditionalist, often relying more on intuition than a line score, and he cared little for the newer level of statistics that were recently in vogue among younger managers. Those numbers made his eyes glaze over.

Ultimately, his line-up varied little from night to night, particularly the top four in the order: Ambrose Goldwell, the fielder in center, would lead off; catcher Jeremy Minnocks followed, then the big, new free-agent first bagger, Gillighan Alley and, of course, Pyce Marsh, the great young fielder in right, to clean them off the bags.

Pyce Marsh: only 22 and already one of the premier batsmen in the SIP League. Sander Halloway pondered the boy: raw power, eye, and speed, encased in a lean frame. Years of productivity ahead of him. Not an ounce of ego either. At least not yet.

Back in '21, his freshman season, Marsh took a curveball, up and in, square to his jaw. Never once did he complain about the hit; some thought it had to have been an intentional, 'welcome to the league' shot from the Grizzlies. The boy took a few days off and when he returned, he never shied from anything thrown inside.

One time, one of the veterans spilled a post-game ale all over the clubhouse floor, and Marsh, without being asked, stooped down and wiped it up as though he were the attendant. One of the older guys, third bagger Lucius Cameron, pulled him aside and warned, "Don't ever do that again. The clubhouse boys clean up. You're a player. Act like it." Marsh had given him a quizzical look, but the message eventually got through. When that season was over, he was named winner of the coveted SIP League Newcomer of the Year award.

"Marsh!" the manager called out. "Get in."

The youngster, shagging balls in right, looked up at him, then lumbered toward the dugout.

Pyce Marsh, Halloway believed, could be destined for greatness, though, of course, he would never say it to the youngster.

Or, like other prospects he'd seen over the years, Marsh could become unraveled by his own slight failings, victimized by a fragile psyche, and then begin a long slide toward mediocrity.

MT. WAYLANDTOWN

"Tell me, did the commissioner dispatch you?" asked the columnist Ollo Ronnell.

"Not specifically, no," Naughton replied.

"Does he know we're meeting?"

"No."

"Fine. Now I know the context."

Their next round of drinks arrived, along with a steaming loaf of coal-black molasses bread. Naughton watched as Ronnell tore off a chunk and wiped it with melting butter. An odd thought came to him: *This man has no friends. The game is his life.*

"So how are the Amandeans, Ollo?" Naughton asked.

"Oh, they love their baseball as much as ever. They're turning out at every park. But you know that."

"I do. But I don't know their mood."

"Indeed. As go the Amandeans, so go the Leagues, as they say."

"Yes. And that's why you went all the way up to Tredgemond Butte last week?"

"Indeed. And why I was in Mount Jarviswell earlier this week, and why I was in Fanningana Falls Park last night."

"Good games?"

"It's all good, Naughton. It's baseball."

"Yet your columns seem focused on the anxiety of the fans, of the populace."

"Of course. I think you can safely say no one was fooled by that report of yours. What was Lord Bart thinking?"

Naughton looked to his right and left, then back to the scribe. "This is off the record, Ollo?"

"Yes, of course."

"It bought us time. We needed time."

"I assumed as much. And what did the commissioner think of my column the next day?"

"He was grateful of course, though a bit perplexed. We'd been skewered by everyone else, as you know."

"I know. I predicted as much."

"Why did you write that? Surely not to appease the old man?"

Ronnell leaned forward and scowled, agitated. "Why do you assume there was some hidden motive, Naughton?"

"Given the history between you two, I can't imagine you wanted to offer him a respite from unrelenting criticism."

"History?"

"You two don't like each other. Everyone is aware of that."

"It hasn't always been like that."

"Care to elaborate?"

The columnist scowled and returned to his meal. "Never mind."

For a time the two sat in silence. The mid-day crowd at the Redoubt was sparse. He'd chosen it for that reason, as most of Ronnell's colleagues were apt to gather for lunchtime libation at the newer publick house three blocks down, the Brown Brook.

"What else are you hearing?" he asked the scribe.

"I hear there's a young scientist in Kern scaring people with his steam toys. Is that legal, Naughton?"

"Actually, I have some League barristers looking into that very question as we speak. And that's off the record, not to be used."

"Hmm." Ronnell finished a bite of bread and wiped a cloth against his mouth. "This job has changed you, Andrew Naughton. I remember when the commissioner first brought you on. So thrilled you were. So idealistic. Now — now you see conspiracies in every corner."

"You're absolutely right. And sometimes I actually find them."

"Are you looking closely at the Magera, at Hood?"

Phangorious Hood. Millions of people across the whole of the continent knew the name. As the smoke had cleared at the end of the Insurrection, Hood had

risen to the top position within the secretive Magera power structure, from street operator to lieutenant to the undisputed leader. And over the ensuing 30 years, as peace prevailed over the continent, Hood had consolidated his power and his riches, exploiting the base instincts of the residents of both nations, appealing to their vices, stamping out threats from within, extorting the local mayors, and avoiding major disputes with the League. The press, always in need of catchy monikers, titled him the Commandant.

"We do not believe that Hood played a role," Naughton answered. "He has a vested interest in the preservation of the Ceasefire. A return to warring would only throw his operations into disarray."

"So you believe."

"So the commissioner believes."

"But yet you have been unable to find who caused that airship to crash."

"Rest assured, we are trying."

"And I would wager that the findings will not be made public."

Naughton surveyed the room again to ensure that the conversation was not being overheard. "That determination rests with the commissioner. You haven't answered my question, though: why did you write a column asking that all residents give Lord Bart the benefit of the doubt? You were expected to be the first calling for immediate change."

Ronnell held back on an answer for a moment as the waitress delivered their lunches — grouper and scallion casserole — and a steward refilled their water glasses. "I urged a benefit of the doubt for the commissioner because he deserved it. Simple as that. You don't wipe away more than three decades of peace because of one incident. My personal animus toward him should not blind me to that fact. That's what I told my readers. And frankly, for you to imply that I had some ulterior motive is insulting."

"It was not intended as such."

"Your intentions here, Naughton, don't matter. Only your words."

They both picked at their meals. Ronnell quaffed the last of his drink, and Naughton signaled to the waitress for another round.

"I need you to talk to him."

"We haven't spoken privately in years."

"How long?"

"Thirty, probably." The columnist smiled.

"He needs your counsel, Ollo. Now more than ever. And he's as prideful as they come."

"Always has been."

"Ollo, he needs your counsel because he is increasingly deaf to mine. He hears only Lady Lynam."

Ronnell looked up from his plate.

"Do you know her?" Naughton asked.

The newspaperman laughed as he wiped away remnants of the drink with his napkin. "Yes. I do. I did."

"Well, he hears only her counsel, and this is the worst possible moment in the continent's difficult history for a leader to be following a… a friend's advice."

Ronnell momentarily closed his eyes, a silent acknowledgment of the gravity of the situation.

"Will you?"

"Naughton, the three of us — Bartholomew, Vivian, and myself — go back many, many years. Trust me when I tell you that if she is at his side again, my attempt to seek him out will only worsen matters."

"Can you say why?"

"No. I cannot. I can only say that the rift between Bartholomew Cunningham and me goes beyond pride."

Naughton knew then that there would be no changing of the old striker's mind. Nor would he learn what lay behind Ronnell's resistance. He stared at Ronnell, who poked at his casserole with a grimace. "If you won't meet with him, I need your assurance that you will continue to write in a supportive manner."

"And why, daresay, would I ever give you such an assurance?"

"Because, as we've seen, your stance greatly influences scores of other writers. And because, as you said, he deserves it."

The columnist leaned back and picked some food out of his teeth, then re-lit the stump of his cigar. Then he stood, the roll of tollar weed dangling from his lower lip, and donned his jacket and hat. "Andrew Naughton, that is a request of a man either naïve or desperate, or some combination of both. I bid you good day."

"Ronnell—" But the old ballplayer turned and departed the musky publick house. Naughton shook his head and sighed. Not only had he failed to accomplish his goal, he may very well have exacerbated the matter.

Michael Barbato-Dunn

"WE DIDN'T GET A CHANCE to speak very much during spring training, Pyce. How are you feeling?"

"I'm good, coach. I'm good."

"And your folks?" Halloway fiddled with a pencil, twisting it in the fingers of his right hand. He remembered that the kid hailed from West Somerchester, the big port town on the Valencroft River. It was not uncommon for some of the younger players to be homesick. That would surprise outsiders who heard about it — how could an athlete brimming with confidence still need the security of his parents? Yet they were still, in so many ways, just children. Marsh was no exception.

"My folks came to the season opener, coach. They're good. But you know, they got to get home." The boy's father worked in an iron mill, and the success of their son did not yet obviate the need for the modicum of income that job provided. "Anything else you want to talk about, Coach?"

"Not really Pyce. Just want to make sure you're getting along."

"Coach, I didn't have nothing to do with it."

Halloway halted, confused. "With what?"

"With all that talk. Isn't that what you called me in about?"

Halloway cocked his head sideways. "I just want to know what's on your mind."

"I said, Coach, I didn't have nothing to do with it. All that talk — I wasn't any part of it."

"I didn't think you were." Now he was vamping, pretending to understand the boy's underlying topic. "But you can still talk to me about it."

"Well, Coach, I don't get on with all that political stuff. I don't quite understand it all, to be honest."

"Neither do I, Pyce. Neither do I." He feigned a smile, trying to put the youngster at ease. "But what was the talk?"

"Like I said, it didn't make a lot of sense to me. But some of the guys…." He hesitated, clearly worried that he shouldn't be betraying teammates.

"Go ahead, Pyce. No one will know we spoke."

The slugger fiddled with the brim of his cap and avoided Halloway's eyes. "Some of the guys don't think we should be playing. Some of them think that the Setherians are going to blame us Helderans for all those people dying."

"I know. That's a pretty common feeling right now, Pyce. Your teammates are not immune to believing that."

"What do you believe, Coach? You were the first Helderan to play for a Setherian team. But that was 30 years ago."

"Oh, I'm like you, Pyce. I don't really understand the politics of all this. But I do trust the commissioner to do the right thing, and if he thinks that the continent is better if we play this game of baseball right now, then that's enough for me."

The slugger nodded but was still ill at ease.

Halloway probed for more. "What else did they say?"

"They said it was probably a good idea if us Helderans fight back."

"Fight back? There's no fighting going on at all..."

"They used a word I'm not good with. Pre-temp...."

"Preemptively?"

"Yes, that's it. I wasn't sure what it meant so I looked it up. It means 'preventing something from happening.' They said Helderans should fight preemptively."

"Well, Pyce, that's just something a lot of Helderans are talking about right now. But it's just talk. There's been no fighting. People are scared and that's just the way they talk. I wouldn't worry about it. You just play your game; just focus on baseball. Don't let that talk get to you."

"I'll try."

"Good. Now go along. Batting practice in 30 minutes."

Pyce went to the door and turned back. "Thank you coach, but I still don't like it. There's no reason for ballplayers to be wanting to hurt fans."

Halloway froze. He wanted to think that he had heard Marsh wrong. But, of course, he hadn't. He tried not to show alarm, not to overreact. "They're planning on hurting fans?" He tried to sound calm.

"That's what some of them were saying. They said, 'That will send a message.' Coach, please don't ask me to tell you who. I don't want to be a rat. I've already said enough. But would they really do that?"

Sander Halloway's heart was racing. He struggled to hide any show of alarm.

"I hope not, Pyce. But like I said, you just focus on your game, and don't worry about the rest."

"I will try, Coach, but it's not easy." And with that, the future star, more child than man, grabbed his mitt and left.

Sander sat in silence for several minutes. He still needed to make out his line-

up card, and he had hoped to watch batting practice. Suddenly, all that seemed terribly unimportant.

Hurt fans?

His pencil snapped in two.

He knew the proper course was to immediately notify the League Security Office.

He knew that would destroy his team, ruin the season.

Hurt fans? What is going on in this world?

Sander Halloway stood and closed his notebook. He was dizzy.

He replaced the Flying Squirrels cap on his head, twisted it down and, with a resolute gait, went out to prepare for batting practice.

He would keep this quiet, at least for now.

June 7

SCHAWMOUNT CITY

THE DOCUMENT, 55 PAGES LONG, lay on Naughton's kitchen table. He had read it now, what— five, six times? He'd lost count.

Fifty-five pages on which the fate of the continent hung.

A courier dispatched by Gill had delivered it to his house just past midnight, slipped under the door. The movement of the envelope through the mail slot had alerted Crandy, who rushed from their bedroom to the front door. Naughton followed, and ordered the hound to carry it to him after sniffing it sufficiently.

At first he had returned to bed, Crandy following at his feet. He was relieved that the ruckus had not woken Amelia. He slipped the envelope under the pillow and tried to sleep. Two wakeful hours later, he returned downstairs to study the contents.

Now the sun had risen. He might have dozed off after several readings, right there in the chair. He wasn't sure. From the kitchen he could see dew glistening on the grass of the park across from their home. Normally, he would have ridden his bicycle to the office, but today, with the envelope in tow, that trip was simply too risky. He dispatched Crandy to hail a carriage. He would hold it under his vest during the trip.

He heard footsteps: Amelia. She'd risen to ready Jack and Isaac for their schooling and was startled to find him in the kitchen. "I thought you'd left. I thought you were already—" Then she spied the folder of papers on the table. She understood. "Oh. Is it bad?"

"It is not any worse than I had expected. But it only leads to more questions than are answered."

"The Monystian prepared this?"

"Yes."

She went to his chair and wrapped an arm around his shoulder. "And do you trust him?"

He looked up at her and smiled. "Its been three months since the airship crash, and I ask myself that about everyone, Amelia, not just the Monystian. Every single person."

She pulled over a chair to face him fully. "Don't let doubt overtake you, Andrew. Don't let it consume you." She kissed his forehead, then rose and went off to wake the boys.

<hr />

LADY VIVIAN PACKER LYNAM ARRIVED tardy, effusing apologies, sweeping into the room with the mock pleasantries that belied the seriousness of the situation.

"Naughton, you look quite tired. Surely you can delegate your duties a bit more," she suggested.

"Madam, thank you for your concern. We are all working feverishly to resolve this situation, and rest is, frankly, a bit of a luxury at this point."

Three months after the airship disaster, he had yet to accept her presence. During his 20 years in the service of the commissioner, Lady Lynam had been at Lord Bart's side only for social functions. It was well known that the two had long had an intimate relationship, yet they had never married and she lived on her own. In addition to her penthouse apartment in downtown Schawmount, she owned an equally luxurious unit in Kern, a mountain estate south of MacKaness, and a seaside cottage north of Boundymount Corner — all of which, according to rumor, had been acquired for her by Lord Bart. She traveled regularly and was a staple in the society circles of both nations. Cunningham had also been part of that for years, but as he aged he'd become somewhat reclusive.

Yet never had she been involved in political matters. Nor had she a say in decision making.

"Are we meeting before the commissioner arrives?" she asked. "I do so hope to see this report from the Monystian."

Naughton gritted his teeth. "Madam, the commissioner is due shortly. We will wait for him. Please stay in the conference room for now, and my secretary will bring you some tea."

Her lips pursed. "That would be lovely."

After she left, Coyle moved toward him and spoke in a whisper. "Your disdain is palpable."

"She shouldn't be seeing this report."

"I understand. But it is what the commissioner chooses."

"What we need right now is more control, not less. And she clearly is out of our control."

"Are you jealous?" Coyle asked.

He turned to the aide. "Please. Do you really think that of me? Do you really think this is about my hold on power?"

"No, of course not. But certainly others could see it that way."

Naughton nodded; the idea had not occurred to him. "I suppose."

"Regardless, if you insist on her removal it will only upset the old man. That could cause an even worse outcome."

"You're full of clarity this morning, Coyle."

"Isn't that why you have me here?"

———————

THEY GATHERED IN THE COMMISSIONER'S private meeting room. Naughton seated himself on the old man's right, while Lady Lynam took the chair to his left.

Security Chief Gill, standing, cleared his throat. "This report is for internal use only. All copies are to be destroyed once the commissioner has had a chance to review it and has decided on further courses of action." Lord Bart, at the head of the long oak meeting table, craned forward, as if he was surprised by this.

"The findings are thus: the airship crash, as we have long realized, was by no means an accident. Second, neither Setherian nor Helderan insurgent groups had any role. We believe it was a group of Amandeans."

Lady Lynam clasped a hand to her cheeks. "Amandeans?" she blurted. "Amandeans?"

"It would appear. Of the 30 fatalities, three were Amandeans with criminal histories: mostly minor crimes, but court records nonetheless. And they appear to have shared, at various times, an employer: a bookmaker from Red Mine named Hardwin Jellum. Mr. Jellum does not appear to have been among the other victims, and his whereabouts are not known to us."

Naughton had read the report at least ten times, so the surprise of an Amandean connection had dissipated. He studied the reactions of the others: Lady Lynam was scowling; the commissioner's countenance was unmoving.

Gill continued on. "Jellum is also Amandean, and is thought to be 62 years of age, with a good number of those years spent in prison. To answer what I'm sure will be your first question: it remains unclear to us why he planned this, or to what degree — if any — he was merely a conduit between the three thugs and other conspirators. Suffice it to say that my operatives — including associates who are not officially on the League payroll — have fanned out across the continent to find him."

At this, Cunningham spoke out. "What means will you use to locate him?"

Gill pondered the question a moment, and Naughton seized upon the pause to answer for him. "Sir, I'm sure you understand that the inspector's methods for obtaining information are focused on the greater good of preserving the Eternal Ceasefire. The specifics beyond that are best left unstated."

The old man nodded. "Yes, the greater good. I see."

"These three miscreants," said Gill, "were identified as Hones Dodd, Ring Newton, and Higs Fishbourne. It is believed that they arrived in Schawmount City the night before the Anniversary Celebration by cable car. They seem to have already procured tickets to the event; at least we have no knowledge of them actually purchasing admission on the day of." The Monystian paused again and studied his notes.

"Is there more, Inspector?" Lynam asked.

"Not of those three."

"And we don't know for certain they were involved in any conspiracy, correct? They may have been a trio of former felons who simply wanted to attend."

"Very true, madam. But unfortunately, following the trail of these three men is the best hope we have at the moment of solving the matter."

"Very well," said Lord Bart, rising to adjourn. "Keep us—"

"Sir," Naughton interjected. "There is one more item."

"Go on."

Gill resumed reading from his notes. "All inspections of the Airship *Lady Crym* prior to the flight were complete and normal. However, some material found in

the wreckage is not consistent with the technology of the craft. Remnants of a small device, scattered amid the charred seats of Section 351. It was impossible to determine whether the device had been originally attached to the airship or placed in the stadium."

"Pneumatic?" asked Coyle.

"Yes. But it is not of a type familiar to us. The condensers were microscopic. The clockworks as well. We know it is foreign to any known airship. The remains, though, are simply too charred and shattered to determine its use."

"Is there other forensic evidence?" Lord Bart asked.

"Much of the command compartment burned. We attempted to reconstruct the control panels, but it was fruitless."

"I have our best staff engineers studying the found material," Naughton added, "to see if we can possibly determine its function. We must proceed on the assumption that its purpose was to cause the crash, at least in some fashion."

Lady Lynam looked pale. "Could it have been… a weapon?"

"Madam, anything is possible. This seems to be a clear example of new science put to ill use," said Gill.

"And if a weapon, the miscreants could have… they could have used it to fire upon the airship."

"Indeed," Gill concluded. "It is possible. But ultimately we do not know what happened, and unless we find Jellum, we may never know."

She smiled, but still looked out of sorts. "I— I wasn't expecting this."

"What did you expect?" the commissioner asked.

"I'd assumed, I guess as so many do, that Helderan groups were involved."

"Now, Vivian. I'm sure many in the nation of Heldera would have guessed that Setherians were involved. And no one would have thought Amandeans." The Commissioner, 86 years old, for three decades the de facto leader of the continent, swiveled his chair away from them, toward the large window behind him. "Amandeans?" he mused. "Amandeans."

Then he swung back to the other four. "What do you recommend?"

This was Naughton's cue. "We have two options. First, we do nothing. The findings are destroyed; we five make no mention of it, even as we continue the clandestine search for Jellum. Alternately, we make the findings public, and acknowledge that, in fact, the initial report was fabricated in order to lessen tensions. That would increase our chances of locating this Jellum character, and perhaps lead to a very public trial. We would also face possible recriminations against the Amandean people by both Setherians and Helderans. All of that would be distasteful."

"Of course," added the commissioner, "we have at our disposal a third option."

"Please, Bartholomew," piped Lady Lynam, "it is one or the other." She nodded toward Naughton in assent.

The Commissioner offered her a wan smile. "Wrong, Vivian. The third option is quite apparent: we simply find a less distasteful culprit."

Naughton and the others looked askance at the old man.

"What are you talking about?" Lady Lynam pressed.

"The company that operated the airships, Skygear Dirigible Air Tours — it is my understanding that several of its ground employees are Setherian, others Helderan. We simply release new information that shows the group, acting together for some sort of financial motive, or perhaps a desire of retribution against their employer, took steps to cause the airship malfunction. And we have them all arrested!"

Cunningham stood and began flailing his arms. "The story really is ideal; it confirms suspicions in both nations that the disaster was not accidental, and yet the conspirators are not political. It defuses the intense blame and name-calling that has swept the continent. At the same time, it elaborates upon our initial report rather than render those findings moot. Third—"

"Stop!" Lady Lynam burst out. "Have you lost your mind, Bartholomew? Frame innocent people? Working men? Make them scapegoats for the murder of 30 other innocents? How can you even voice such a thought?" Her hands were shaking.

"Vivian, spare me your histrionics." He pointed directly at Naughton. "Our friend Andrew here understands the concept of the greater good. It has always been our overriding principle. The single most important factor here is the preservation of the peace."

"I don't need to be told that," she countered. Naughton could not recall hearing her using as combative a tone with the commissioner.

"And I'm sure, Vivian, that you don't need to be told how many hundreds, nay, thousands would die — perish! — if the peace crumbles at this juncture." Gill, who'd been standing the entire time, moved to his seat. Coyle shifted side to side and stared at his notes.

"This, then, is the balancing act we face," the old man continued. "Four or five innocents, arrested and put on trial, would likely be a small price to pay in order to achieve the greater good, to relieve the simmering tensions. They would, in a way, be heroes."

At this, finally, Vivian Packer Lynam stood and roared. "Bartholomew Cunningham! Did you not ask me to be part of your inner circle to provide counsel at this moment of crisis?"

The old man froze, then nodded sheepishly. "Yes, Vivian. I did."

"Then you will sit down now and listen to me, and you will come to your senses. The lives to be spared, you claim? What about the lives ruined by our latest fabrication? It is one thing to create a report that blames the crash on a malfunction of equipment. And I can see how it would be a proper choice to withhold the truth of Amandean complicity from the public. Either of those are, surely, as you say, for the greater good." She stood with hands clasped on the edge of the meeting table. "But we are about to cross a dangerous line when you are talking about framing innocents. Framing innocents! Bartholomew Cunningham, I have known you now for more than three decades, but I do not know the answer to this question: at what point did you lose your moral compass?"

There was silence. Naughton studied the commissioner, whose countenance had turned ashen, and he was unsure if the old man was struck by her condemnation of his morals or simply by the ferocity of her speech.

Finally, Lord Bart smiled and spoke. "Vivian, you haven't lost one bit of your tenacity. It's what I always loved about you."

"Oh, spare me your condescending nonsense, Bartholomew. These men here have work to do. Let them get on with it." She turned to Naughton himself. "We will choose your first option, Mr. Naughton. These findings are to be destroyed. They are not to leave this room. They are not to be spoken of. And you must find this Jellum thug, sooner rather than later. That is now our priority."

———

"So you see, Andrew, I can be of help to you."

Naughton had returned to his office after the tumultuous meeting and was startled to find Lady Lynam sitting in the guest chair perched in front of his desk. "Madam, I thought you had left."

She adjusted the large feathered hat and leaned forward. "I know you don't want me here. Your demeanor makes that quite clear."

He did not bother to feign arguing the point. "But the commissioner very much wants you here; so it shall be."

"But Andrew, you need me here."

"And why is that?"

"Do you even need to ask after that meeting we just had? You could not have dissuaded Lord Bart from his bizarre scheme on your own. Only I could have done that."

Naughton assessed the comment as he put down his notes and binders, then took a seat on a neighboring couch. "I suppose that is true."

"You need to understand the value of my presence at this difficult time. You, Naughton, need to want me here."

"Why?"

"Because I fear..." She paused, and clenched a handkerchief. "I fear he may be..."

Now Naughton leaned forward. "...losing his faculties?"

She nodded and blinked wet eyes.

He took a deep breath and then nodded. "You have been away."

"Yes. For two years."

"So now you see the changes?"

"I left because of the changes. But after the airship attack I realized he needed me back. As do you."

"Well, I share your concern, Lady Lynam. I've been worried about his condition for more than a year now. He goes off on tangents, makes sometimes wild speeches to no one in particular, and is more prone than ever to anger. But when you are around someone every day, as I am, and these changes are so gradual, it is easy to overlook them, to dismiss them." Naughton was surprised at his sudden willingness to divulge this to her.

"That is why I've come to you, Andrew. We cannot dismiss those changes any longer. We must take this into our own hands."

"In what way?"

"We — you and I together — must keep the League office functioning, ensure that Bartholomew has a public presence under controlled conditions, find the true source of the conspiracy, work to ease the political tensions. And quash these annoying rumblings from all sides that he should resign."

"Together."

"Yes. None of that will happen if you and I are not in concert. We must work together, or it all will fail."

He could not bring himself to respond. On the surface, she made perfect

sense: as he'd just seen, she was the one person who could truly tell Lord Bart when he was wrong. Yet her convenient reappearance after the airship disaster gnawed at him.

She sensed his hesitancy. "Let me tell you a little story about Bartholomew. He told me this himself, several times, but as far as I know he never mentioned it to anyone else. He was 23 years old when he left university and decided to travel across the continent. It was early 1870, and the war had dragged on for nearly 33 years. But Bartholomew wanted no part of the fighting. He wanted to be an entertainer, a singer and comedian. No one doubted there was a need for merriment, even in wartime. So without a bit of money to his name, he hopped cable cars and stowed away on carriage trucks, and made his way from his hometown, Bottom Brook, to the big city — Schawmount City."

"I've heard this, I believe."

"What you didn't hear was that the journey to Schawmount took about three years longer than he anticipated."

Naughton cocked his head.

"He was taken hostage. Helderan insurgents holed up in an enclave south of Goodwyn Fork grabbed him and three friends as they'd gallivanted down the road. Apparently, the rebels thought they were children of wealthy Setherians.

"Three years they were held, Andrew. He told me they weren't treated poorly, at all. The insurgents fed them, didn't beat them, even let them write and exercise. But one of the other prisoners, a childhood friend of Bartholomew's, couldn't bear the isolation, and one morning they found he had taken his own life."

Naughton swallowed.

She adjusted her scarf as a momentary distraction, then continued. "The captors, he said, felt bad, and they let the remaining three bury the boy just outside the perimeter of the enclave. And then … then they let them go! Just like that, after three years of captivity. And these rebels were, of course, well aware that once released Bartholomew and the others could inform Setherian forces of their whereabouts.

"So as they were freed, Bartholomew asked them why. Why did the Helderan insurgents risk the chance that they themselves would then be captured?"

"What did they say?"

"They were tired of the war, they told him. They were exhausted. They'd had enough. Just like the boy who took his life. Enough. Naughton, that is what drove Bartholomew Cunningham at first. Not some theoretical concept about the need for continental peace. Not the need for glory, for acclaim. And not, in those early days, by the need for power. He was simply haunted by that suicide, by the needlessness of the loss. And — most of all — by the willingness of the Helderans to spare him."

They sat in silence. Recounting the tale had left Lady Lynam short of breath, and Naughton felt as though he should comfort her, should hold her hand. He did not.

"And now, Lady Lynam, you believe he has lost sight of all that?"

Her fists clenched around the handkerchief, and she looked at him fully. "Yes, Andrew. He appears to have forgotten."

"Forgotten the friend who hung himself."

"Yes." She reached over and clasped his hands. The touch warmed him. "You need to trust me, Andrew. For both of our sakes."

Then she stood, gathered her belongings, and left his office.

June 9

West Somerchester

THEY RETURNED BY PRIVATE COACH, the most luxurious of the various ways baseball teams traveled. But the carriage swayed to and fro, rocking those who were attempting to sleep. In the back, some of the younger players swapped stories of girls, while one strummed a mandolin.

Halloway, sitting near the front, closed his eyes, trying to doze, but analyzing every bit of the just-concluded series: three losses to their fiercest rivals, the Rhinos of West Somerchester. Road trips would never be enjoyable to Halloway, but there was none more difficult, more fitful, than a return home after being swept by division foes. It was the sort of series that churned in his stomach days after its conclusion.

The Rhinos had won the Helderan South Division last year, only their third such title in the history of the league. Then, after their general manager traded for starting hurler Cornelius 'Eager Beaver' Blanchfield, many pundits predicted that the Rhinos would repeat their victory this season, with the Squirrels tabbed to finish a close second.

So now, as if to fulfill those prognostications, the Rhinos had mowed down Halloway's squad: on May 7th, a 4-3 loss, with a fielding error by backstop Jeremy Minnocks costing starter Ketter Asgar two of those runs; on the 8th, an 8-2 lopsided defeat that was over when West Somerchester's top strikers got to Benjy Harald in the seventh.

Worst of all was this night's concluding game: Phillip 'Bomber' Carson, the third man in the Rhinos' killer rotation, gave up just two runs over nine innings, with 11 strikeouts as well. Halloway's hurler, the promising youngster Cokely Broughan, yielded three, including an unfortunate two-run home run to a light-hitting utility infielder by the name of Raynard Stilb. One mistake, low and away, but right in Stilb's zone. It was enough for the Rhinos to complete the sweep.

If the Squirrels were to contend — and Halloway believed they would — games like those needed to be won.

Low and away, be damned.

The carriage, pulled by a team of six, crossed out of West Somerchester, a busy metropolis in the western portion of Heldera. The moon shone through his tiny window.

Truth was, he was more bothered by the Marsh matter. It had been nearly a month since the youngster had first mentioned the supposed threat to 'hurt fans.' The two had not spoken of the matter since. But in the interim he had witnessed two strange outbursts by the young slugger. First, not long after their meeting, Marsh had been ejected by an arbiter for arguing balls and strikes in the first inning of a game.

"What was that about?" he had asked Marsh in the dim tunnel between the dugout and the locker room, moments after the ejection.

"Coach, he wasn't calling them right. I am not going to take it."

"Marsh, you know damn well that he's testing you. He wants you to get angry. You cannot — I repeat, cannot — show up an arbiter, no matter how bad he is. That hurts you, sure. But worse, it hurts everyone else."

The boy cowered like a puppy. "I understand, Coach. I get it."

Then, just two weeks ago — another incident. Marsh was caught by teammates berating a teenage clubhouse attendant over some minor mistake. Other players threw him up against the locker and forced him to apologize. Halloway had stayed out of that one. It was not, after all, on the field, and it had been self-policed by the team.

But he kept watching, listening, because the possibility of wider unrest among players had him far more vexed than a three-game sweep by a division rival.

THE COACH ARRIVED SIX HOURS later at Hot Bear Bend, the port city on the continent closest to Widmertown on Heldera Island. They transfered quietly to the waiting ferry. It was past three in the morning, and most of the players scrambled inside the ferry, a private charter as well, to claim cots that had been laid out over two levels.

Archibald Ferns, the striking coach, stayed up on deck, leaning against the bulkhead, watching gulls squawking in the breeze as the boat pulled up anchor and edged out into the bay. "You're not going to try to sleep?" Ferns asked Halloway.

He shook his head. "Not after those games."

"We'll turn it around," the coach consoled. Ferns was 56, six years younger than Halloway but truly a veteran: this was his 19th season coaching. He'd been with four other clubs, most recently Kendall, before Halloway had hired him away just this past off-season.

"How many play-offs have you been to, Archie?"

"Just one, Coach. With the Screech Owls, way back in '07. That was it. Never found another winner since."

"But you won it all that year."

"Yes. Quite a parade in Kern we had. Of course, all the cheering was for the players. We coaches road a carriage near the back."

They laughed together. That's the way it always was. The coaches were bums if the team lost or nearly forgotten if they won.

Ferns had been given only one shot at managing: in '09, when he was hired by Gregorson to bring in an immediate winner for an impatient owner. He was then promptly fired at season's end when they finished third. He'd never had another opportunity to run a team since. Such were the pitfalls of managing.

Halloway wrapped his jacket against his chest as the bay winds whipped over the ferry's empty deck. He imagined everyone else save the sparse crew was sound asleep. "Archie, I'm going to tell you something that I need you to keep to yourself."

Ferns cocked his head to the right and offered a pensive expression. "Um... yes?"

"Marsh hasn't been himself of late. Have you noticed that?"

"You mean beyond getting tossed? I know he's been irritable. But I assume it will pass. He's still a boy."

Halloway shook his head. "Yes, but...." He hesitated. "He told me, a few weeks back, before he got ejected, that others on the team are plotting something."

"Plotting something?'

"His exact words were, 'There's no reason for ballplayers to be wanting to hurt fans.'"

Ferns looked stricken. "Hurting fans? Who was he talking about?"

"He wouldn't say, and I didn't press him. I assumed he had just overheard some idle talk. Dangerous idle talk, perhaps. But ultimately, just talk."

"And you don't believe that anymore?"

Halloway turned and faced his coach fully. "Deep down, in my gut, no, I don't. I think there's something to it."

"Why?"

"Looks. Stares. Whisperings that quiet when I enter the room. A group of players that stays clustered together, too much for their own good."

"Every clubhouse has that."

Overhead a gull cawed wildly, as if laughing at his uncertainty. "No, not like this."

"Sander — don't think I mean this critically, but isn't it possible you're becoming paranoid about this? You need more than whispers and stares to find a conspiracy — particularly among your own players!"

"There is more."

"Tell me."

"Back on May 1st, just before the season started, I had a long discussion with the Count."

Ferns glanced back to the middle portion of the ferry, as if checking to make sure no players were listening. "Do you believe he was the one talking about going after fans?"

"Archie, I have no proof. But I do know he is always at the center of that group of whispering players. I do know his reputation as a hothead. And his ego knows no bounds."

"So you called him in."

"Yes. And he veered off quickly from baseball talk to political stuff. Archie, did you ever hear of the Kender Hypothesis?"

"No."

"Neither had I until Asgar brought it up. And what he told me is that a

Professor Kender had many years ago predicted that the 30th anniversary of the SIP and ALE Leagues would be marred by an attack of some sort."

"Is that true?"

"After our meeting, I had one of the front office interns go check it out. You met him, Colter, that university student. He traveled to Leadland, where this Kender fellow supposedly taught."

Ferns now looked both alarmed and fascinated. "And..?"

"And he found that Kender did indeed exist, he did teach at Leadland, and his hypothesis can still be viewed at the Leadland University archives."

"Fine. So some academician made a prediction that seems farsighted. What does this have to do with Pyce Marsh and the supposed attacks on fans?"

"Colter explained to me, Archie, that Kender's hypothesis was more than that prediction — in the first years of the league, it became a huge conspiracy theory among Helderan insurgents. Kender claimed that Cunningham had pushed for Helderan independence, for a free Helderan state, as a 30-year ruse. He would preside over three decades of relative peace, a false independence, then stage a calamity that would be blamed on the Helderans. And Kender predicted that a short time later, Cunningham and the Setherians would then use this calamity as a convenient excuse to end Helderan sovereignty, to return the continent to one-nation rule."

"And your intern found all this?"

"What he found goes further: the Kender Hypothesis had been largely forgotten for years, but has more recently become the foundation of a growing insurgency in Heldera — a few anti-Setherian political groups are focused on the possibility of the commissioner retracting our independence."

"Lord Bart would never do such a thing. That alone would prompt immediate war."

Halloway leaned back, exhaled, and thumbed the brim of his uniform cap. He was in street clothes of course, but he kept the cap with him at all times. He found it comforting. "Agreed, Archie. I'd like to think he wouldn't."

Dawn had crept in by the time the team returned to the stadium. Twenty players, two coaches, one manager, one traveling secretary, one trainer, two ball-boys, two club-house boys: all were exhausted. Attendants threw their bags into their own private carriages for shorter trips to their homes.

It was early Sunday morning. Fortunately, Monday was an off-day, and the Tuesday game was scheduled in the evening, so they had nearly two days to recuperate.

Halloway noticed Ferns was hanging back, waiting for the others to leave. He had more to say.

"You were 32 when the Leagues began, Sander. I was 26. I had been on front lines for three years. I fought in the very same towns we now play ball in."

"As did I."

"I saw some pretty horrible things."

"As did I."

"And like you, Sander, I didn't understand a bit of it. It was all we knew. My father fought, yours did, all we knew was fighting. And along comes this crazy showman, Bart Cunningham, telling everyone to lay down their arms and play baseball instead! Baseball of all things. And everyone was just tired enough, sick of all the horrible things, to somehow go along with it."

"Yes, sir. Crazy."

"And it worked."

"For a time."

"Thanks to you, Sander. You were the first Helderan to play for a Setherian team. Cunningham had no guarantee that you or any other player would be willing to do that, and he certainly didn't know if the Leagues would succeed without that gesture."

"I suppose." Halloway fiddled with his carry bags.

"You have a duty to report this," Ferns said.

"I know."

"But it will destroy our season if it gets out."

"I know."

"And so that's why you wanted my opinion."

Halloway nodded. "Yes." But he realized there was no good answer, and it was probably unfair of him to have put Ferns in that position. He put his hand on the bench coach's shoulder. "Don't worry. You don't have to answer. I don't want you involved."

Ferns's carriage driver waited patiently nearby. He edged closer to Halloway. "You never asked to become a hero, a symbol. And I never could have done what you did. You and I, Sander, we weren't meant for politics. Or for conspiracies. We're just ball players."

Ferns began walking toward his carriage. "You can't have this on your shoulders, Sander. You've got take it up the ladder. Before something happens."

Halloway nodded. He'd known that was the right thing, from the start. He'd go to the general manager, Eldon Langford, in the morning.

"Go get some sleep, Archie. We'll see you Tuesday."

Ferns rode off. Halloway retrieved his bag from the coach. He couldn't stomach the thought of returning to his vacant apartment in the center of the city. Instead, he walked to the darkened ball park, unlocked an outer door, and made his way inside to his office near the clubhouse. There, the manager retrieved the small flask of whiskey in his lower desk drawer and lay down on the thin mattress of his wooden cot, never bothering even to light a lamp.

June 10

Mount Waylandtown

THE THIRD ROUND LED TO a fourth, and then to a fifth. His vision swirled, and he told himself he had to stop. He had a column to write.

Maybe, he thought, just one more. He waved his hand.

"Ollo." The bartender, who'd been chatting at the opposite end of the bar, walked down toward him. "Ollo, this is a lot, even for you."

"I know, Teddy." Tonight it had not been the local ale, but some pricey Leadland whiskey.

"I'm stopping you. For your own good."

"I know, Teddy."

"You want me to get you a carriage? You need to sleep this one off."

Ronnell slid a fourthweight across the wooden counter-top toward the man. "Keep the rest, Teddy. I have to go back and write."

"This late?"

"Corcoran's holding a spot for me."

"You'd better get to it, Ollo. He's probably fuming already."

Ronnell slipped his wallet back into his jacket and stared at his hands. He would have to use a mechascribe to write this piece. The newsroom now had the

newer ones, in which each key was spring-loaded, and thus easier on the hands. No matter, he still hated the contraptions. But his preferred method — writing longhand and then having a copy boy punch it in — was not an option now; the boys were probably long gone. The paper was probably complete save the two rightmost columns on the front page that Corcoran had reluctantly agreed to hold.

These hands used to swing a bat, he reminded himself.

He tried to remember what it felt like.

These hands…

He tried to remember what she felt like. What she looked like, that very first time.

He'd served as an infantryman, then captain, major and finally lieutenant for the Setherian Allied Forces. He'd laid mines on Helderan properties near the border. Mines that children might have stepped on. Mines that sometimes exploded prematurely and claimed the men who'd been planting them in the ground. Some of them, his friends.

After his discharge in 1884 — the 47th year of the Great Insurrection — he took up life as a journeyman ballplayer, playing for a series of teams in the independent leagues that dotted the Setherian countryside. He played for meals, slept in homes of generous fans, sometimes even with the families of the coaches or managers. It was a meager life, but for men who'd finished their service, it was a welcome respite from warring.

He had begun the season in Bottom Brook, a small town whose team was then called the Tridents. A slugging first baseman. The owners loved him, as did the fans. He was 27, and making a meager living playing the sport he loved. Playing it, in fact, quite well.

Ollo remembered the sight of her in the stands, sitting in a regal posture as if she owned the damned team. He'd made eye contact right there on opening day, and although other teammates had done the same, it was to Ollo that she returned the gaze. The other men moved on.

They were quickly inseparable, the oddest of couples. He, a scruffy ball-player, with no real job, no university degree. Vivian, by contrast, had earned a doctorate degree in philosophy at age 21, and had begun a career of teaching at the hallowed University of Schawmount. Quickly disillusioned with academia, she had resigned her position at age 25 to travel the countryside. That is how she came to be sitting in the stands that day in Bottom Brook. Traveling alone, she told him that first evening, just passing through.

Their relationship came to the chagrin of her parents, Mattheus and Marinda Lynam, prominent architects in Mount Waylandtown. Marinda was a talented designer, Matt more workmanlike, but together they established a continent-wide reputation as profoundly original designers, and their services were sought-after for residences of the wealthy. They, in turn, became wealthy.

"She is a difficult mother," Vivian had told him one evening as they lay together. "But she pushes me. She hates society, she hates male supplication, she hates women who are mere window dressing for successful men."

"Yet she doesn't want you with a ballplayer."

She laughed. "She'll warm up to you, Ollo Ronnell. You can't deny that most players are less than articulate."

This made him laugh. "True enough."

The two women had argued endlessly during the 18 months that she and Ollo were together. "He wants your money," the mother had insisted. "He offers you nothing."

"That is the great irony of Marinda," Vivian told him at one point. "She wants women to be independent, but bristles when *I* insist on being so."

Eighteen months. Ollo had told himself repeatedly during that time that it could not last. She would tire of his ways, she would move on.

But he'd never expected her departure to singe so savagely, so relentlessly, nor its pain to last for decades.

THE BARTENDER JOSTLED HIS SHOULDER to wake him. Ronnell grumbled a thanks, ambled out, then made his way east four blocks to the Chronicle's newsroom. Perriwinkle and Tomastin, two crime reporters, pecked away on their stories, then looked up and laughed as he entered. They knew what was coming.

"I'm holding the blengin' front page for you, Ollo," Corcoran shouted from across the room. "You've got precisely one hour to get it in or I'm putting her to bed." Ronnell waved him off and scowled, then settled in behind his desk and stared at the black metallic device. If only he could remember how to use the contraption.

He chewed vociferously on the soggy, unlit cigar. His head ached already. His stomach shifted and lurched. The morning would be rough.

Then Ollo Ronnell took a deep breath and activated two levers on the side of the device. Gears clicked into play, the box lurched and small streams of steam jetted out its sides.

And then, with trepidation, he began to type.

CHRONICLE EXCLUSIVE:
THE TRUE CAUSE OF THE *LADY CRYM* DISASTER

WHY THE COMMISSIONER MUST GO

By Ollo Ronnell, National Baseball Columnist

Your faithful reporter takes no pride in what I am about to write. We have obtained a copy of an internal investigation conducted by the Office of the Commissioner into the Lady Crym disaster, and its findings contradict the League's earlier report — a report widely suspected to be — and now proved to be — bogus.

The internal report, delivered to us by an unimpeachable source who requests anonymity, finds that a lifelong Amandean criminal figure by the name of Hardwin Jellum hired three compatriots to sabotage the fated ship. Jellum, according to our source, remains at large, and the other three — identified as Hones Dodd, Ring Newton and Higs Fishbourne — died in the stadium stands amid the crash. The report says investigators located remnants of a newfangled pneumatic device in the wreckage, and they believe this dastardly foursome used the object to fell the craft and murder dozens of innocents.

The report does not ascribe a motive to the Amandean clan; neither does it reveal who funded their horrible operation. Suffice it to say that many serious questions remain.

According to our source, Commissioner Cunningham opted to keep the study private so as to spare the continent incipient anti-Amandean sentiment among both Helderan and Setherian residents. He also

apparently sought to salvage the finances of the Leagues, given their reliance — particularly the ALE League — on Amandean fan support.

Loyal readers will recall that when the commissioner's initial report on the Lady Crym disaster was released on April 23rd, I opined that while the document looked questionable, our Commissioner deserved "the benefit of the doubt." Now, six weeks later, I regret that sentiment. The time when Lord Bart is deserving of any such benefit has passed. Let's look at his actions since that fateful crash:

—First, he refused to comment in public, and had his lackeys issue only a couple of bland statements on his behalf.

—Second, he needlessly delayed any announcement on whether the season would proceed, further heightening anxieties across the continent.

—Third, he issued a blatantly phony report claiming the crash was an accident, a report widely mocked and dismissed.

—Fourth, when this actual investigation was completed, he chose to keep it private despite its damning evidence.

Dear readers, this shameful list leaves little doubt that the time has arrived for new leadership. Who that should be, I won't begin to ponder. Lord Bart's 30-year grip on power has left the Commissioner's Office with a staff full of yes-men, panderers, none deserving of nor qualified for succession. The same is true of the 36 Setherian and Helderan team owners, who control all aspects of commerce, finance, politics, and justice in their respective cities, for they have been more than happy to accept the status quo while their pockets are lined with gold.

As I said at the onset, I take no pride in bringing you this news. I urge, I plead, for calm. Do not rush to take up arms. Let us wait to see if a new savior, a new Bartholomew Cunningham, can step up and prevent the Twin Nations from falling into another 50-year war. Otherwise, kind readers, the conspirators — whoever they may be — have won.

But this much is clear — Lord Bart must go.

———————————

CORCORAN HAD READ THE DOCUMENT three times over but didn't seem convinced. "Can I see the report?"

"No."

"Are you certain this is authentic?"

"Absolutely."

"Have you been drinking?"

"Absolutely."

"If you're wrong, Ollo, it'll mean both our jobs. I want to hold the column."

"If you hold it, Crom, another paper will likely have the report by tomorrow. My source wants it out."

"And do you realize what upheaval this will cause for the commissioner?"

"That's not my problem."

Corcoran activated a lever on his chair, glided in closer, then spoke in a whisper. "But it's mine, Ollo. Very much mine. The backlash against us by the Leagues if this story proves false could be considerable."

"I know that. But if we don't run with it, someone will."

"That's fine with me if this proves false."

"It won't prove false."

"Your source is good?"

"My source is the best. The very best."

The editor sighed and shook his head. Ronnell knew he'd won: Corcoran was still a reporter at heart, he wanted the story out. He certainly didn't want to get beat. "Very well, Ollo." The editor snatched the sheets and wheeled back to his own desk, muttering to himself.

Ronnell leaned back, closed his eyes, and gnawed further on the butt of the unlit cigar. Corcoran would now parse the column, word by word, and then bring it to the publisher for approval. From there it would go to the presses, tens of thousands of copies would be printed, and several of those copies would make their way to the headquarters of the Leagues, to be read by the esteemed Lord Bartholomew Cunningham.

And also by Ronnell's long-ago friend, Vivian Packer Lynam.

June 12

Widmertown

SANDER HALLOWAY STARED AT THE game's box score on his desk, but could not focus. The game had been another frustrating defeat: a 6-5 loss to the Monkeys. The Count, Ketter Asgar, lasted eight innings but was shaky throughout, giving up three runs through the first seven innings, then three more in the eighth.

He looked at the game log for that inning: single, a two-run home run, then a double and another single. He should have pulled Asgar after the home run. He had tossed nearly 130 throws by that point.

Halloway shook his head. He couldn't remember being as perplexed by his own decision making, or lack thereof. A double play to end the inning had saved them both.

Reporters were waiting outside with their usual post-game round of questions for him. He was surprised they had even bothered to cover the game given the events of the past two days: the *Chronicle's* release of the secret report on the airship crash, and the ensuing — and growing — calls for the commissioner's resignation. Yet there they waited, hungry for pithy quotes.

It nagged him: why had he left Asgar in? Was he afraid of confronting him? Was he afraid of what would be said?

And, of course, there was the other issue: he had put off informing Langford, the team general manager, about Marsh's accusations. He had found no convenient time in the three days since his conversation with Ferns. But he realized now that was mere rationalization — he was avoiding the matter. He sighed and placed the paperwork into the pile of the season's accumulated box scores.

Through the opaque glass of his office door Halloway noticed the scribes dashing away. And from the locker room, he heard a commotion.

Schawmount City

Naughton, came without Coyle, nor Gill. He came only with Crandy.

He came in trepidation.

In the past 48 hours, the situation had spun out of control. Starting with the publication of the report by Ronnell in the *Chronicle*, then to emergency meetings with the Setherian owners, to several impromptu protests outside the League headquarters, to a hurried private meeting with Willison Caffrey, the Helderan executive. To the escalating calls from all quarters for Lord Bart to step down.

And now, this. The worst.

Naughton had arrived at the estate moments before ten p.m. Cunningham's attendant had indicated that the old man was still awake. He was ushered into the ornate antechamber outside Lord Bart's bedroom suite. There was no immediate answer to his knock. So he tried again.

"Yes?" came the frail voice.

"Commissioner, it is Andrew Naughton. It is a matter of urgency."

The door opened. The old man was in his nightclothes, though all the lamps in his bedchamber were still well lit. Sheets were pulled back, and a book lay on the bed. Naughton wondered what it was titled. A drinking glass, now empty, sat on the nightstand. He wondered what it had held.

"Is there a matter that is *not* urgent?" the old man looked up at him with a weak smile.

"No, sir, I suppose at this stage, there is not."

"Have you found him, this Jellum character? Tell me you've found him."

"Sir, no. The search continues. But that is not what brings me here."

"Oh. Who wants my head now?"

Naughton maintained his grim countenance. There'd be no small talk. There'd be no levity.

"Your Excellency, it is my duty to report to you the unfortunate news that fighting has begun. We have seen the first instances of Helderan-Setherian clashes since the declaration of the Eternal Ceasefire three decades ago. We appear to be on the brink of war."

Widmertown

Halloway pushed his way back through the reporters, barking at them that the locker room was off limits. His coaches, Ferns and Keating, rushed toward the source of the commotion as well. They entered the locker room as a group, pushing the doors shut against the scribes.

Inside they found a tumultuous fist-fight involving, by Halloway's quick count, a dozen players. The other eight stood and jeered and catcalled. The coaching staff dove in, struggling to separate the warring sides. Several of the players had bloodied noses and cut lips; others seemed dazed, striking out at whoever came near them. The coaches peeled players away in a frenzy, screaming for order, demanding that the fighting cease.

Within minutes they came to the focal point of the frenzy: Ketter Asgar and Pyce Marsh, battering each other without let up.

Ferns was able to pull Asgar away, Keating clamped down on Marsh, and Halloway stood in the middle. "Damn you," he screamed in frustration. "Damn you all. What are you doing?" Then he remembered the reporters, still clustered outside the locker room outer door, probably with their ears pressed against the door, trying to make sense of the fracas.

Asgar had a puffy, bloodied cheek and a contusion across his forehead that already seemed to be turning black and blue. Marsh had several scrapes on his cheeks and a bloodied nose. He was cradling the elbow of his right arm with his left hand, apparently in pain.

Halloway pointed to both men. "I want you and you in my office after you clean yourselves up. The rest of you: shower, and get out of here. Wasn't losing tonight enough?" Then he lowered his voice but made sure all could hear him. "And I don't want any of you talking to those reporters. If they ask what happened, just say good-natured horseplay got out of hand. Do you understand me?"

A smattering of 'Yes, Coach' replies followed, and the players dispersed to the showers.

He turned to Ferns. "Tell the scribes the clubhouse is now closed. Tell them to write what they want. But we're not talking."

SCHAWMOUNT CITY

NAUGHTON READ FROM DETAILED NOTES that Coyle had prepared, based on dispatches gathered in the past three hours. Some portions he read verbatim, others he paraphrased. "The first incident came at about four p.m. near the northern tip of the Setherian-Helderan border, about 400 fieldlengths due west of Bereton Park. According to our information, a group of about 20 Helderan men stormed into the small Setherian border enclave of Ganger Gulch. The residents there only number about 230, and many of them are Amandean, and most of them fled immediately. So the active Setherian resistance was limited. We are unsure of the number of dead and wounded on either side, as gathering information is difficult that far north."

"Twenty men," the old man remarked. "Enough for a baseball team."

"The second incident took place an hour or so later, further south, and seems to have been prompted by a larger group of Setherian teenagers armed with bats and clubs. They stormed across the border to two small Helderan border towns, Dancer Bay and Crater Lake, both north of Skate River. It's unclear precisely how many teens were involved or from where they hailed. All we know is that there were casualties in both towns, that Helderan resistance was formidable. We do expect more information from both towns by morning."

The commissioner showed little reaction, but the tone of his voice was of sadness. "Is there more?"

"Yes, a third incident that was, as far as we know, the bloodiest. It took place in at least three coastal towns along the northern edge of the border area between West Somerchester and Kern, about an hour south of here. We believe those clashes are still ongoing and potentially involve a couple of hundred men from both nations. There are accounts of some brandishing axes and engaging in quite brutal fighting. Fortunately, we have no accounts — at least yet — of women or children being harmed."

"At least yet," Cunningham repeated, as if in a trance.

"Yes, sir. At least yet."

WIDMERTOWN

HALLOWAY'S HEART WAS STILL POUNDING, his hands still shaking, as he called the two players in to his office. By this point the trainer had attended to both. Marsh seemed to have gotten the worst of the fisticuffs, with the bruised right elbow. Halloway hoped the outfielder would not have to be taken off of the active roster. Watching the way Marsh cradled the elbow with his left hand, Halloway was not so sure.

"So who wants to start?" he asked them both.

The two looked at each other. Asgar, the veteran, began. "Coach, I will apologize if I brought any disrespect upon this team. Your budding little star, here," he pointed to Marsh, "seems to think he's in a position to comment on my performance tonight."

Halloway suddenly found himself breathing a bit easier. Given his earlier conversations with them, he had assumed that the fight was prompted by the larger political issues that were weighing on everyone. He turned to Marsh. "Pyce, is that correct? Were you questioning the Count's performance?"

"Coach, I merely asked if his earned run average was ever going to get below four."

Halloway rolled his eyes. He didn't blame Asgar for trying to pummel the youngster. "Well that's a pretty stupid thing to say, now, don't you think, Pyce?"

"Why, sir?"

"Why? Do you want him questioning why you lifted a lazy fly-out in the ninth inning with the tying run on first base? Do you find him asking you that?"

"Sir, if he did, that would be within his right."

"No. You're wrong. We are all professionals here. And the assumption, first and foremost, is that we are all, at every moment, trying our best. And if the results are less than satisfactory — as they were tonight for everyone, including myself — then openly questioning our motivation is uncalled for. It is disrespectful. Do you understand that, young man?" He stressed the word 'young.'

Marsh sat silently for a moment, and Halloway found his lack of immediate response aggravating. "Marsh!"

"Sir, I don't think Mr. Asgar here is a particularly good influence on this team."

Asgar started to rise, as if to reach for the boy's throat, but Halloway shouted him down. So this was about more than the game, then. Now it would be more difficult to defuse.

"That's not yours to decide. That's what I'm here for."

Asgar looked at Halloway and pointed to the striker. "Do you see what nonsense I've had to listen to since spring training?"

"Count, stay out of this for a moment," the manager chided, but Marsh, resilient, shot right back.

"Ketter, you want me to have to explain it all to him? What you've been talking about?"

Asgar pursed his lips. "I don't know what you're talking about, kid."

"You most certainly do."

"Enough!" Halloway shouted. He was fed up. Exhausted by it all. It was time to be out with it all. "Count, I'm not deaf."

Asgar grimaced in confusion. "I have no idea what you mean."

"What I mean? You and others have been plotting something. I don't need

young Mr. Marsh here to tell me that. I have ears. My coaches have ears. We know what's going on."

The hurler bit down on his lower lip and stared at the two of them. "I'll talk to you, Coach, but I want him out of here."

"Fine." Halloway pointed at the slugger. "Get out, Pyce. That elbow had best be healed by tomorrow night."

Marsh glowered at Asgar and stormed out. Now it was just the two: the manager and the veteran.

"Proceed, Ketter. Tell me what you want to say."

Schawmount City

THE OLD MAN ASKED NO further questions of Naughton. He rose and went over to the bar in the sitting room and poured what appeared to be a Tredgemond Butte vodka. He did not offer one to Naughton.

"I suppose, Andrew, you agree with so many others that it is time for me to step down?"

"Sir, I long ago pledged allegiance to you and to your office."

He returned to his chair with his drink, hobbling slightly, the glass shaking in his hand. "Ah, Naughton, yes. Your allegiance. But that isn't what I asked you. I asked your opinion."

This was a crucial moment. Handled properly, he could assuage the old man while still laying the groundwork for an orderly transition. But — transition to what? That was the most difficult part. Fitton and the other Helderans were already sending messengers by the hour, demanding updates and meetings with the commissioner. The Setherian owners, including key allies, were only slightly less persistent. All of them were more polite than the separatist groups now gathering outside League Headquarters, chanting for the commissioner's head, their numbers growing by the hour. And layered on all that were the dozens of journalists from all the SIP and ALE League cities now flocking to Schawmount City to cover the burgeoning crisis.

Naughton weighed his words carefully. "Sir. Thirty years is a long time to preside over two nations. Particularly when neither likes the other. You've saved hundreds of thousands of lives. History will, of course, look kindly on you no matter what you do."

The old man scowled. "But what you're trying to say, that you're far too polite to say, is that history may not judge me kindly if I cling to power too long."

"Sir, yes. That is what I mean to say."

"But of course, determining what is 'too long' is a subjective thing."

"Well, history is subjective."

"No, young man. History is factual. Only those who interpret it are subjective." The volume of Lord Bart's voice was steadily increasing. *Best to back off a bit.*

"Commissioner, you spoke days ago of the greater good. There are great many who believe that what is needed now for the greater good is leadership in which all the races of the continent have confidence."

"And are you so certain that the confidence the people have of me has eroded? How do you know? Are you basing that on the noisy complaints of owners trying to take advantage of the situation to promote themselves? Of the provocateurs who clamor on our front lawn at this very moment?"

Now the old man's tone was turning belligerent, and Naughton feared the moment was slipping away. "Sir, you misunderstand. I only mean that in weighing your options, you should not fail to take into account—"

"What *you* have failed to take into account, Andrew Gilpin Naughton, is the will of the people. Not the noisy miscreants who seek power for their own personal gain. But the people — the true people of the continent. Setherian, Helderan, Amadean, Rebular, Monystian: the people! They know what is best. They know that I, and I alone, brought peace to the continent!"

Naughton sagged in his seat, nauseous. The old man would go nowhere. The opportunity for an easy transition was already lost.

"So you tell those ungrateful owners that they owe their great fortunes to me, that they are the ones who are suffering diminishing support — and if they care to cling on to their little fiefdoms, they'd better hope that I, Bartholomew Cunningham, remain as commissioner!" The old man became more animated with each exclamation. "The greater good! You dare tell me about the greater good? I know for a fact that peace will not endure if there is to be a transition…"

At this point Naughton stopped listening. He fiddled with the brass clasp on his jacket. He yearned for the companionship of Crandy, left waiting at the doors of the estate. He yearned to be cradled in Amelia's sweet arms. And more than anything he yearned to be far from Schawmount City, far from the league offices, far from this odd little man, the combative, belligerent Commissioner of the Leagues of SIP and ALE.

"Did you look into the Kender Hypothesis?" Asgar asked his manager.

"As a matter of fact, I did," Halloway replied. "A fascinating bit of history."

"Is that all you see it as?"

"No. I see it as a pretty astounding coincidence."

"Coincidence? That's awfully naïve, Coach."

"How so?"

Asgar leaned forward. "Because what has played out in the Commissioner's Office in the past two days merely shows that Kender's theory was correct beyond just the prediction of an incident on or about the 30th Anniversary Celebration. What we've seen is that Cunningham and the other Setherians are setting the stage for reclamation of our country. They will use this crisis as an excuse to deprive us of our independence. Nothing in that hypothesis has been proved wrong yet. How can you write it off as a simple coincidence?"

"I'm not a political scientist, Ketter, and neither are you. We're ballplayers. That's all we do. Leave it to the politicians to resolve this."

"But coach, you didn't do that 30 years ago when you uttered your famous speech and went to play for a Setherian owner. You were making a political statement then. You were not just leaving it to the politicians."

Halloway gritted his teeth. "I didn't plan that speech; I didn't ask to be thrust into that position. The Griffins drafted me, and so I announced my intention to play for them."

"You did more than that. What were your words? We had to memorize them in grade school. 'For nothing less will ensure that this newborn peace becomes eternal,' I believe it was."

"That's enough! I was not being political. My actions became politicized, and that is very different."

"I'm not raising my voice, Coach. Why are you?"

"Because I'm frustrated, Ketter."

"As you should be. It is the politicians who created the mess. It was the failure of the Helderan leadership 30 years ago to heed the skeptics like Kender. They fell prey to the plotting of Cunningham and the Setherians."

Halloway heaved a sigh. "They were willing, simply, to believe in peace. They weren't duped. They were promised a homeland; they were given half the continent."

"All of which," Asgar countered, "was land won during the Insurrection."

"They were promised Helderan sovereignty. They were given — we were given — a nation of our own."

"Under a clever ruse to wrest it from us 30 years later."

"We'll get nowhere with this, Count. I'm exhausted from your grade-school antics in the locker room. Marsh was out of line, but I demand that you and the other veterans act your status. You need to set an example—"

"You're changing the subject, Coach. You wanted to know what I was saying in the club house."

"Yes."

"I said perhaps it is time to lay down our bats and gloves, perhaps it is time to put aside this silly little game of baseball. Perhaps it is time to take up arms in defense of our homeland."

The words hung thickly in the space between them.

"And that is when Marsh questioned your pitching?"

"Yes."

Sander Halloway leaned back, raised his arms behind his head and closed his eyes. He'd had enough. "Ketter Asgar, if you want to go fight in a war, you should leave this clubhouse now. Or if you want to hurl for the Widmertown Flying Squirrels, you can show up tomorrow, like everyone else, for practice at two hours past the noon. Think about it."

"And what is your preference, Coach?"

"Ketter Asgar, my preference is that we win a blengin' championship this season, and that you are part of it. I need you here in order to win. But I need you to be a member of the team in every respect, not just by your uniform and the logo on your cap. And that means keeping politics out of the locker room."

The Count scowled, then settled his Squirrels cap back onto his head and stood to leave. "As you wish, Coach."

SCHAWMOUNT CITY

THE OLD MAN HAD QUIETED down and was merely rocking back and forth, muttering to himself. Naughton gathered his papers and bid the commissioner goodnight.

He nodded to the overnight attendant and made his way out through the outer waiting room, with its walls lined with Lord Bart's gifts and plaques. The paintings of the formative days of the Leagues. Awards honoring his lifetime of peacemaking.

Michael Barbato-Dunn

Even some framed letters from schoolchildren — now likely adults — announcing their love for the leagues and for him. In the center of the furthest wall hung a replica of the actual Eternal Ceasefire proclamation. Three names: Cunningham, the Setherian military leader Jackson Scowden, and the Helderan separatist leader Ellswerth Crackel. Three signatures. The document was lengthy and detailed. The paper was frayed at the edges, cracking in some places. Naughton read to himself the phrase that every schoolchild memorized. "Whereas it is the desire of every man and woman to live in peace," it pronounced, "we proclaim a lying down of arms, a cessation of animosity, and an end to hostilities. We proclaim a Ceasefire that, with the firm resolve of every inhabitant, shall be nothing less than Eternal."

Outside, Crandy stood and wagged as Naughton emerged from the estate, and the two entered the waiting carriage. He leaned in to the front cab and roused the sleeping driver. The man cracked at his whip and the two horses began a steady trot. Naughton, though, heard two other sets of hoofs and, as they pulled away, noticed that a second carriage was heading toward the front of the estate.

He thought of ordering his driver to stop, but discretion, as well as exhaustion, held him back. Instead, he craned his head out of the side window of the cab and leaned backward as far as he could. At the entrance to the house, lit by four gas lamps, the other carriage had indeed stopped, and a lanky figure in the draping black cloak emerged. The man stepped toward the house, then turned back and looked out into the darkness.

Naughton squinted, trying to make out the face, then sunk back into the plush back seat of the carriage. Crandy, sensing his anxiety, uttered a low cry.

Lord Bartholomew Cunningham, at 11 in the evening, at his greatest moment of crisis, was being visited by the strange scientist, Dr. Iphonious Henry.

the Pnuemorg

June 13

THE OLD MAN INSISTED ON speaking from the podium alone. That was fine with Naughton. He watched from one of the balcony boxes that lined the upper perimeter of the League auditorium. His chest felt tight; he was thirsty. He stroked Crandy, resting at his side.

Across the auditorium, he spied Enoch Gill, peering down at the crowd that had gathered. Undoubtedly, the security chief had officers posted in street clothes throughout the packed seats at the mezzanine level. Though this was a controlled crowd, invitation only, the risk level was great, greater even than back in March when the sabotage of the airship sent the entire continent careening toward chaos.

Greater, because chaos has now arrived.

Only owners certain to be loyal to the commissioner had been invited — 12 in all were asked to hurry to Schawmount City for the hastily planned event. Of those, six had come. That only half were willing to lend public support was an ominous sign. Broadlun Clay, the Setherian Executive, had not even responded.

Most of those filling the auditorium constituted the true intended audience: dozens of scribes from the restive press. Naughton had already informed them of the ground rules: the commissioner would make a speech, the transcript of which was to be carried verbatim in all newspapers, alongside the newspapers' own reportage. Several had grumbled openly at the requirement, but he rebutted that it was a matter of public service. Audiocasters were rarely available in the villages and hamlets, and the populace needed to read Lord Bart's words unfiltered.

After the speech, Cunningham would take a few questions from the scribes.

Naughton had not seen the speech. As with his 30th Anniversary Celebration remarks, Cunningham had sought no suggestions, no critique. The stakes were enormous, Naughton knew. The old man needed to demonstrate that he was of sound mind, of clear judgment.

"Watching from afar today, Andrew?"

He turned. Vivian Packer Lynam, a linen scarf wrapped around a full-length, brass-ornamented suit jacket, brushed past the servohound and settled in next to him.

"One can only do so much, Lady Lynam."

"Please use 'Vivian.' Formalities are a hindrance at times like these."

"Vivian."

"I know you suggested to Bartholomew that he resign."

"He told you?"

"Yes. I met with him this morning. He had risen hours earlier to write the speech."

"I never actually asked him to step down, I merely—"

"Stop, Naughton. There is no need to be defensive. It was a good thing you did."

He stopped, eyes wide. "G— good thing? Why? It only served to set him off."

Lynam pursed her lips, as if debating how to answer.

"Why was it a good thing?" he repeated.

Her eyes, hazel with brown lashes, peered away, avoiding him. "One day I hope to tell you, Andrew."

The answer was unsettling, but he moved on. "Do you know what he's going to say, Lady Vivian? Have you seen the speech?"

"He's a wonderful speech maker, Andrew. You know that. His words heal wounds."

"He'll need a great many words, then."

The commissioner stepped out from the side of the stage, walked with his cane to the podium, and adjusted his glasses. The reporters' low rumble of chatting faded as they offered attention.

"Gentlemen and ladies, of course, we appreciate you coming on short notice. As per the directions you have already received, we are asking as a matter of public service that my comments be printed verbatim in your publications. We are near a state of war, and I trust that your publishers realize the gravity of the situation. Whatever you choose to say alongside my comments, of course, is at your discretion. But give your readers the opportunity to read my words as spoken.

"Yesterday was a grave and horrendous day in the history of the Twin Nations. We have seen the first incidents of Setherian versus Helderan violence since the end of the Great Insurrection. To those who were wounded, I give my condolences. To those who perpetuated these acts, I can do nothing but repeat the words I spoke

32 years ago, when I first proposed the creation of the SIP and ALE Leagues and an end to the warring.

"What I said at the time, and what I say to you now, is quite simple: the gods have given us so many gifts: the ability to speak, to create, to love, to build. But we are also endowed with the ability to hate and to fight. None of this can be eradicated. None of this will ever go away.

"We are full of hate! We are full of anger! We all feel somehow wronged! And nothing can change that. But viewed from that perspective, the choice is actually a simple one: we give ourselves over to those baser instincts, or we channel them into productive means.

"Thirty-two years ago I proposed one productive way — the centuries-old children's sport of baseball. A stick and a ball. Some rules and some teams. Winners and losers, and for the losers, a chance at redemption the following year.

"Thirty-two years ago I proposed that we fill our lives with that competition — beating swords into bats. And to the credit of nearly every adult at that time, it was a proposition that was accepted. A year later came the Ceasefire, a year after that, the inaugural season."

The Commissioner paused to catch his breath. Naughton, perplexed as he was, could not help but admit the words were just right for the occasion. Bring the people back to the time when peace had arrived. Remind them of the reasons for the Leagues.

"Why was this accepted? It was not that Helderans and Setherians had sudden faith in me, in my leadership. Most didn't know who I was. They accepted it simply because—" Cunningham leaned forward for effect "—they were tired of war. Not just physically tired, though there was that. They were emotionally tired of living with the constant threat of violence in their own cities, their own neighborhoods. On their own doorsteps. Tired of the caskets of their sons and neighbor's sons coming back. Tired of the amputations, the civilian deaths, the friendly fire. The mines.

"And now we have youngsters who don't remember a bit of that. Of course they don't. They weren't born when the Insurrection was concluded. All they know, they learned in history class. It is all too easy, then, to take up arms.

"So let me say this to anyone under 30 years old who has the temerity to want to see a return to warring: talk to your parents, if they survived. Talk to your grandparents, if they survived. If not, talk to older neighbors or relatives who remember.

"Or talk to me. I will personally welcome any person who wants to discuss this to meet with me at League Headquarters. All I ask is that you lay your weapons at my doorstep, never to be retrieved.

"Our fore-bearers nearly destroyed the continent over a matter that was vital — the Independence of the Helderan people — but a matter that could — no, should — have been settled peacefully. Fortunately, the continent has recovered. Our economies are growing, population is rising, and the Leagues of the SIP and ALE continue to enrapture millions of fans each year.

"The continent — both the mainland and Heldera Island — is a gift for which we all are responsible. It is all we have!

"I beseech you: do not be the generation that destroys the gift that is our world."

———————

THE OLD MAN WAS DONE. He gathered the papers quietly and stood at the podium, waiting for questions. At first, though, there was only silence. He wondered if the old man had somehow won over this most difficult of audiences: a group of cynical scribes.

Finally, one of the reporters raised a hand: Blakeford Gash of the *Blue Square Noble Daily*. "Mr. Commissioner, are you serious about your offer to meet personally with insurgents?"

"Absolutely."

"And what if your offices are overrun with them? How will you manage?"

Cunningham grinned. "I will be here; I will talk, as long as they want to talk. I will manage."

Another reporter, Rowland Warde, the longtime baseball columnist for the *Tillbrookson Bluff Register Times,* followed. "Commissioner, what is your response to those who say you have bungled this entire matter since the crash of the Airship *Lady Crym*, and that it is high time for you to step down?"

Naughton leaned forward.

Lord Bart paused, grinned, and took off his glasses. "You know, that idea doesn't come just from my opponents. Some of my very own advisers have suggested that I hand over power." Naughton and Lady Lynam exchanged glances. "And of course, some of you in the press are quick to call for that. My response is no."

That single word, 'no,' immediately dispelled the seemingly positive mood that had settled in on the assembled press corps. They began shouting follow-up questions to the point where no single voice could be discerned. Cunningham waited until the din subsided.

"If you will allow me to finish. I am convinced that this would be the worst possible time to step down. Of course, that day will come. I cannot say when that will be. But what I can tell you is this: the Office of the Commissioner has presided over a three decade-long ceasefire. Now, at the very moment when that peace is most threatened, is the least appropriate time to leave. No one would doubt that a leadership vacuum at this point will only lead to a further degradation of the situation. Thus, I will stay. When relations between the Twin Nations are normalized — and I hope that will be very soon — I give you my word that at that point, we will begin proper planning for the next stage. For now, though, what is needed is stability.

"Gentlemen of the press, I urge you to put that in your headlines. What is needed now, more than anything, is stability. That is what I will give you."

The reporters filed out, pushing past one another. Their faces bore the stress of the deadlines they now had to meet, but none of the countenances was of skepticism. Naughton sensed all the beat reporters had readily accepted the old man's stance. Cunningham, ever the showman, ever the promoter, ever the politician, had again worked his magic.

A handful of columnists, with less need to rush, moved to the front as the commissioner stepped off the riser to engage in what Naughton assumed was simply conversational banter, small talk. Perhaps even about baseball. The handful of Setherian owners in attendance huddled amongst themselves, uncertain whether they'd want to be seen publicly congratulating the commissioner.

"Masterful," remarked Lynam.

"You wrote that," declared Naughton, still staring straight ahead.

"I helped."

"You're propping him up."

"What is the alternative?"

"Succession."

"And to whom? Another Setherian? Or is there some neutral leader out there who would please everyone?"

"You yourself said before it was a good thing I suggested to him that he step down."

"Yes."

"I don't understand."

"Andrew, I don't think he should resign, not now. But I do believe he needed to see that even someone as loyal as you feels it is a reasonable concept."

Naughton sighed. "So he'd understand the severity of the situation."

"Yes."

"Now what?"

Vivian Packer Lynam stood and wrapped the scarf tightly around her shoulders, then looked out at the emptying auditorium. "Now, Andrew Naughton, you need to decide whether you are with the commissioner still, or are not."

He gasped ever so slightly. "And if I'm not?"

She patted him on his shoulder. "Then you should leave."

June 14

CRENSHAW CITY

ALLOWAY PLODDED ACROSS THE FIELD to the hurler's mound. For road games such as this, he always toured the infield of the opposition park. He looked for irregularities, potential problems. Groundskeepers were not above that, he knew. Even his own. A slight dip in the right side of the mound, for example, could easily throw a left-hander off. Perhaps just for the first inning, but sometimes that was enough to spell defeat. Tonight he found no problems.

On this field, at least.

Wilddon Field, home to the Crenshaw City Warthogs, was one of the newer parks in the SIP League, and one deserving of the very modern moniker 'stadium.' It boasted the latest in technological theatrics, and from the top of the mound Halloway could see the gleaming scoreboard high above right field, with hundreds, perhaps thousands of gas lamps. He'd heard they were controlled by a massive clockwork calculating engine far below the stadium. A single person sitting in an enclosed box at the other side of the oblong park — behind and far above home base — could activate a board of switches and remotely control the messages that appeared on the scoreboard. Scores from around the league, statistics of the current batter, suggestions for the fans to cheer — even advertisements and league messages: all scrolled seamlessly across the board during games. Halloway had little doubt that soon enough all the SIP League parks — whose owners were generally flush with profits — would have them installed. *It is a wonder.*

The strikers would be out soon enough for batting practice, but for now he had the field to himself. He peered across to the home bag, envisioning his own batsmen with their nervous ticks and mannerisms: the incessant practice swings, the rising and lowering of shoulders and legs, the crouches and bends, the twitching of their bats. All part of the ebb and flow of the game, of the thousands of small moments that escape many fans.

It had been three days since the cross-border attacks, two days since the commissioner's rousing speech. Somehow, all the games of both leagues had managed to be played. Attendance was down, Halloway had heard, but not terribly so. Fans were still paying to see baseball. Perhaps this storm could be weathered.

It is a wonder.

"HELLO SANDER."

Back in the visiting manager's cramped office, he found Langford waiting for him. He was surprised, for the Squirrels general manager had not been on the team carriage.

Halloway had yet to tell Langford about the accusations leveled against Asgar by Marsh. The recent road games, the outbreak of fighting, the questions of whether the season would be put on hold: all became convenient excuses to avoid explaining the messy matter to his superior.

Perhaps, with Langford's appearance, the moment had been chosen for him.

The general manager stood and began pacing. "I've been informed by the League that two investigators are to arrive in several hours to question us about last week's fisticuffs."

"What?"

"They're to arrive at 4 pm."

Sander Halloway sat behind his desk and fumbled with the still-blank line-up card. Nausea engulfed the pit of his stomach. "I— I don't understand. The Ceasefire is crumbling, the future of this season, let alone the Leagues, suddenly is in doubt, and the League is worried about some punches thrown in a locker room?"

Langford nodded. "Apparently, it is precisely for those reasons that the commissioner's office wants to learn what happened. Caffrey tells me that they are concerned about incipient violence in the clubhouses, particularly between

Setherian and Helderan players. It is one of several indicators they are using to gauge whether the season can continue."

"And they'll question me?"

"Yes, and me. Anything you need to tell me?"

Halloway took a deep breath. He'd dreaded this moment of confession, had procrastinated on initiating it. Yet now he welcomed revealing the truth: the ugly matters involving Marsh and the Count had been bothering him for weeks now, as if they were eating away inside him. "Actually, Eldon, I've been meaning to tell—"

Langford leaned over, five thumblengths from his face. "I said is there anything you *need* to tell me?"

The manager lurched back, perplexed. "I was about to—"

"*Need,* Sander. I'm sure we both know there are certain matters that are best left inside the confines of the clubhouse."

In that moment Halloway understood: Eldon Langford feared his own interrogation by the authorities, and wanted to be able to properly, honestly, claim ignorance.

He doesn't want to know anything.

The general manager rose and brushed wrinkles from his linen slacks. "Who's starting tonight?"

"Um, uh… tonight. Uh, Harald."

"At least the weather should be clear; no chance of rain." Langford examined the tips of his fingernails. "Fine night for baseball. Hope the fans turn out. Anyway, I'll send a messenger when the League folks arrive."

With that, he was gone.

Halloway sat and stared at the empty line-up card. He felt dizzy. He reached down into one of his travel bags. Far in the back sat a flask filled with bourbon. He rarely touched it, usually only after a difficult loss. Now he took three long swigs.

———

THE INVESTIGATORS ARRIVED AN HOUR later. They were curt and expressionless, and wide in girth. Sharp and Mackle were their names.

"How long have you worked for the league?" he asked as they placed two carry cases on his desk.

"We don't," said the one called Sharp. "We're private detectives here in Crenshaw City. We pick up quick contracts from the League on occasion."

Mackle poked a toothpick into his gums. "The League doesn't have that kind

of manpower. They hire out for routine stuff like this. They have jobbers in every city."

"Routine," Halloway repeated.

Without comment, the slightly smaller one, Mackle, fiddled with a lock on the handle of the larger case and snapped it open. From inside he removed a lacquered wooden box. A variety of switches and knobs were inlaid on the cover, and three exhaust tubes protruded from the back. Brass fittings covered eight corners of the object. On its front was a chrome receptacle. Mackle fiddled momentarily with the settings of the knobs, and the device vibrated, its knobs lit, and puffs of steam emanated from the rear.

"A falsehood detector?" Halloway asked.

"The actual name is 'Pneumatic Veracity Extractor,'" the one named Sharp said. "Don't be alarmed. This is a standard procedure. It speeds the interrogation."

"Does the Office of the commissioner sanction this?"

"Indeed, coach. They insist on it."

Sharp then produced from his own briefcase a lengthy tube and attached one end to the receptacle on the box's front. The other end terminated in four smaller tubes with clips. "If you'll please roll up your sleeves."

Halloway complied. His mouth felt dry. Mackle leaned forward and clipped two of the tubes to Halloway's thumbs, so that a small metallic pressure plate bore down on the center of his palms. The other two were clipped to the brim of his ballcap, with the plates angled in against his temples. The rumbling of the box accelerated.

Sharp picked up a clipboard and quill. "Let us begin. This shan't take long." Halloway felt dizzy but nodded.

"Your full name."

"Sander Raymond Halloway."

"Residence?"

"5 Courtland Way, Apartment 11, in Widmertown."

"Married?"

"No."

"Been married?"

"Yes. Twice."

"Why did your marriages end?"

"What does this have to do with the incident? Why is this necessary?"

"Coach, we're just calibrating the Extractor. We need a baseline for the results. Just bear with us, and we'll be finished soon enough."

He took a deep breath. "My marriages ended for the same reasons that most marriages of baseball players and coaches end. We're never home. We are on the road constantly. Half the year, or more. Its not conducive to a long marriage."

"Very well." Sharp studied a small glass display on the top of the contraption and wrote down some notes. "Now, as to this incident. What day and time did it happen?"

Over the next 20 minutes Halloway provided a detailed account of the fracas involving Marsh and the Count. Never at any point did the investigators probe beyond the surface. Never did they seem concerned about the motivations of the two belligerents. They took it only as what it seemed to be: two hot-headed players, one a veteran, the other a rising star, in a minor squabble. They never asked how he'd dealt with the matter beyond separating the two, nor what the players had said to him.

And never at any point did Halloway offer that information.

"Since the fight, have the two had further difficulties?" Sharp asked.

He chose his words with care. "They keep their distance."

The investigator seemed satisfied and made some additional notes. "Very well. I believe that's sufficient. Sorry to have bothered you, Coach."

Mackle removed the tubular attachments, deactivated the device, placed it away, then picked at his teeth and stared out at the field. "Who's hurling tonight?"

"Harald," Halloway replied.

"Nah, I mean for the Warthogs. I was thinking of picking up tickets..." His voice trailed off in a manner that made clear he'd be pleased if Halloway suddenly handed him two for tonight's game.

"Fawcett is going for the 'hogs," he replied, pretending to be oblivious to the man's hints.

"Yeah, well. Fine. Sharp, are we done here?"

"Yes, we're done. Pleasure meeting you, Coach Halloway. You're still a hero in my house, for what you did as a player, even if you do coach the Squirrels!" The investigators laughed.

Mackle leaned over and extended a hand. "Good luck this year coach. Just not too much luck!" The two chortled further, then gathered up the equipment to leave.

"Excuse me, gentlemen."

They turned.

"Are you also questioning Asgar? Marsh?"

Sharp shook his head and threw the toothpick on the floor. "No, not necessary. Fights happen. The commissioner's office will be satisfied with your account."

DANIEL FAWCETT, A 30-YEAR-OLD HURLER who was already having a rough season, failed miserably against Halloway's Squirrels that night. He gave up two runs in the first frame and four more in the second, and while he settled down after that for a bit, those six runs were enough for Benny Harald to coast to an easy victory. It proved to be a quiet affair, and most Warthog fans were gone by the seventh inning.

But the win was not enough to wash away the unsettling conversations of the afternoon. This day had been his best chance to lay out his concerns about Asgar, first with Langford, and then with the investigators. But in both instances he had held back. He'd made no mention of Asgar's talk of political upheaval and the Kender professor's convoluted theories, nor of Marsh's claim of teammates plotting to hurt fans.

He had said not a word. Even with the damned lie detector connected to him, he hadn't volunteered the full story. He thought about his famous speech at the Inaugural Draft, eloquently accepting the offer to play for Setherians, and he wondered where that courage had come from. He thought about his two wives: Kiara, who'd been starstruck that a ballplayer showed her attention, but was ultimately consumed by imagined jealousies during his long road trips. She left him after two years.

Then, Ruth. Dear Ruthie. Their marriage had lasted far longer, eight years, and he still wished it had not ended. Unlike Kiara, she did not begrudge how baseball took him from her for long periods of time. In fact, she'd loved the sport itself, the pure essence of the competition, and she understood its strategies and nuances. And he knew Ruth had never been enamored of his fame or success. She seemed to look upon him, to understand him, not as a ballplayer, but simply as a man. Halloway wasn't sure he could even do that himself.

But she wanted children, a family, and he had no interest. The game, he told her, was simply too consuming. So one August day, during a team road trip, Ruthie moved out, leaving the apartment bare except his baseball memorabilia and a terse note.

He had to get to the locker room. The beat writers were waiting for a few perfunctory quotes. They'd ask about the game, the substitutions he'd made, the performance of Harald. They'd ask broader questions as well, about the team's chances for holding down the division and qualifying for the play-offs. He reached into his carry bag for another swig from the thin flask.

In an hour, they'd board the ferry for the overnight ride south on Tummlyn Bay, back to Heldera Island and their homes in Widmertown. Halloway imagined that he'd sneak a few more swigs during the trip.

Langford didn't want to know. Neither did the investigators. Likely, neither did the team owner, Caffrey. Nor the League Office.

I'm on my own, he realized. *The continent has become a tinderbox, so for this I'm on my own.*

June 15

WIDMERTOWN

ULLO RONNELL STOOD AT THE fore bulkhead of the ferry taking him from Hot Bear Bend to Widmertown. Gulls swooped past, diving into the bay for their dinners. The sun, masked by a blanket of white clouds, hung high behind him. It was late afternoon, and the ferry was due in by 4 p.m. He had arranged for a carriage to take him to the ballpark, but beyond that, nothing was set. He'd simply appear and then ask questions.

The smell of the seawater, the salt in the air, the cooling breeze that bounced off the waves: all felt invigorating. Of course, the smooth whiskey sours brought to him by the pneumatic half-waiter helped as well.

Ronnell had read about the fisticuffs in the clubhouse of the Flying Squirrels a week ago in the *Widmertown Herald-Leader*. The paper's baseball beat writer, Obediah Noone, had reported that the entire clubhouse had been involved, but that it had seemed to have originated with two players, the veteran Ketter "the Count" Asgar and the former Newcomer of the Year award winner, Pyce Marsh.

That prompted Ronnell to call his best contacts within the organization. None wanted to speak on the record, which was not unexpected. What they all said, off the record, was that Squirrels manager Sander Halloway was doing his best to contain clubhouse animosity, and that the team had actually seemed to feed off the adrenaline of the fight: they'd won five of their next six games and now sat firmly atop the Helderan South Division standings. But one of his sources, Lucius Cameron, their longtime third bagger, had mentioned something peculiar. It was this, more than the fistfight itself, that prompted Ronnell to travel to Widmertown.

Cameron believed the fight to have been political in nature.

Political. Perhaps, thought the columnist, that should not have been odd. After all, the entire continent was embroiled in a political crisis. The ceasefire had momentarily crumbled, only to be resuscitated by Lord Bart. Why should ballplayers be immune? The Squirrels were very much a Helderan team; all of the key players, including Asgar and Marsh, were of Helderan descent. Yet none, to his knowledge, had ever been active politically.

In the Widmertown press, the controversy over the fisticuffs had been quickly overshadowed by the three incidents of low-level Setherian and Helderan clashes that had erupted along the border that very same day, the first true fighting since the declaration of the Eternal Ceasefire. The papers, understandably, were entirely focused on the insurgent violence; a momentary fistfight seemed of little consequence.

Also, the team was winning. Nothing douses the flames of a controversy, Ronnell knew, like a string of victories. Conversely, of course, nothing so readily inflames otherwise minor dust-ups like losing.

So when Ronnell had told his editor that he would be traveling to Widmertown to check out the squad and the division, the fistfight never even crossed Corcoran's mind. Ronnell didn't bother to bring it up. The less said the better. Corcoran and the publisher, Bennet Rinkins, probably assumed he simply needed to get away after publishing the *Lady Crym* report; that perhaps he felt some degree of guilt that the story had prompted an outbreak of violence.

None of that was the case. He smelled something amiss in Widmertown. His gut told him a story was to be found there. And he had every intention of finding it.

——————— ———————

THE SHIP PULLED UP TO the Widmertown docks with an abrupt thunk of hull against pier, jolting Ronnell's bowler off his head and onto the wet deck. He cursed the pilot under his breath, shook water off the hat, and made his way down the dock to the waiting carriage. At the very least, he thought, tonight's game would be a feisty one, pitting the Flying Squirrels against another contender, the Bereton Park Hammerheads. The 'heads had won the Continental Series last year and were expected to be back when this October came around.

On the dock he found the hired driver, and a half-hour later Ronnell arrived at Catalinaside Stadium. He had not arranged any meetings in advance nor even bothered to notify the club administrator of his arrival, as would have been common courtesy. It was not so much that he sought to be discourteous — there was no reason to anger the officials of any club — but Ronnell wanted to surprise team officials so they had no opportunity to prepare a coordinated response.

His first stop would be the manager himself, Sander Halloway. Ronnell knew him only in passing, despite Halloway's crucial and unexpected role in the formation of the Leagues: the first Helderan to play for a Setherian team. After that momentous decision, Halloway had gone on to a fairly productive if unspectacular playing career, and Ronnell had at times wondered if the enormity of his fame had weighed him down on the field.

Still, after retirement, Halloway developed a solid reputation as both a bench coach and, for the past seven years, as the Squirrels manager. He had terrific baseball acumen, always had his players schooled in the raw fundamentals, and managed to avoid — until now — clubhouse histrionics. That was part of why this incident was perplexing. Halloway, to Ronnell's knowledge, kept his players firmly in line.

The manager's office was deep in the bowels of the stadium, down a tiny, dingy corridor from the locker room. Ronnell rapped on the door and received no response. Then he made his way up into the tunnel that led to the park itself, and there, engrossed in watching batting practice with his coaches, was Halloway.

"Sander, long time." The columnist extended his hand.

Halloway at first said nothing and gave the handshake offer a quizzical look. After a few awkward seconds the manager reciprocated, but then asked, "Don't you know batting practice is closed to reporters?"

"I'm sorry, Coach. I just was hoping we'd have a few minutes to talk before game time. Its a 7:05 start time, is it not?"

"Yes."

"When should I come back?"

Halloway scowled and looked back at his bench coach, Ferns. "Does the front office know you're here?"

Ronnell did his best to play naïve. "Front office? Not sure. I told my editor I was coming to see the team. I assume he notified your people."

"If he did, no one told me."

"I'm sorry for that."

"What is it you're here for?" Ronnell was disappointed at Halloway's degree of suspicion; he'd been hoping to catch him with his guard down. That would clearly not be the case.

"I'm here to see your club play."

"Fine." Halloway stood up, towering over him. "Mr. Ronnell, I know you're quite the popular columnist in many parts. But I make it a point not to play favorites with members of the press. You will get no particular access that other reporters, especially the local guys, don't have. So come back at 5:30, in one hour. That's my pre-game session with reporters. You are free to join in."

Ronnell was not about to give up so readily. Trying to squeeze in a question in the middle of a free-for-all with other reporters would not work at all.

"Give me one minute, Sander. Alone."

The manager looked to his coaches, Ferns and Keating, then nodded. Ronnell followed as Halloway rose and made his way down the dugout steps, into the clubhouse and his miniscule office.

"I'm here about the fistfight, Coach. Pure and simple. I'd like ten minutes of your time, alone. Either now or after the game, either is fine with me. But I would imagine that you have no desire to discuss the matter in front of the rest of the press gang. My early arrival is actually helpful to you."

"Mr. Ronnell, I have no idea what you're talking about. What fight?"

Ronnell grinned. Clever guy, Halloway. "Coach, you know full well what I'm talking about. The fisticuffs in the locker room one week ago tonight. It was in the morning paper the next day, though obviously buried amid reports of the border clashes. Surely you read the Widmertown paper, Coach."

"I have only one response to you, sir: I am not aware of any fist fight. There was a minor altercation among a few players last week, but to my knowledge no blows landed. Just some horseplay that got out of hand. The matter has been dealt with and totally rectified. And what happens in the clubhouse—"

"Stays in the clubhouse. Yes, so I've heard, Coach." Ronnell chewed on the moist end of his cigar.

For a moment the two held silent, simply staring at one another.

Finally, the manager broke the silence. "Is there anything else I can help you with at this point, Mr. Ronnell?"

"No, apparently not." He grabbed his bowler and moved to the door. "Good luck to your team tonight, Sander."

"Thanks. But next time you need to talk, go through proper channels. You know the routine."

"Of course. My apologies."

Ronnell opened the door that led to the vacant, darkened clubhouse, then turned back for one last comment to the Squirrels' manager. "Sander, you've got it all bottled up inside. I can see that. Whatever it is, I can see it's consuming you."

Halloway looked to his right and left, as if someone had whispered a secret. Ronnell knew he'd hit the mark. "Don't keep it in," he continued, "it's not going to do you any good."

"Rest assured, Mr. Ronnell," the manager shot back, his voice peppered with disdain, "if I ever do need someone in whom to confide, it certainly won't be the columnist who nearly brought the nation back to war."

Ronnell did not reply, but quickly flipped one of his business cards onto the manager's desk. Earlier he had scrawled on its back the name of the Widmertown hotel at which he was staying.

He turned and left, but Halloway, the crafty old ballplayer, was quick enough to flip the card back at him before the door closed. "Keep it."

SCHAWMOUNT CITY

TWO DAY'S WORTH OF NEWSPAPERS, collected from across the breadth of the continent, lay piled on the kitchen table at his home. Broadsheets and tabloids. Setherian and Helderan. Two day's worth of reportage, analysis, and commentary on the old man's plea to the Twin Nations. Naughton spread them out to survey the headlines.

Amelia came down the steps. He must have woken her when he returned just past eleven in evening. Her thin, reddish-brown hair was tied in a bun. She wore a thick down robe and crossed her arms against her chest to ward off the morning chill. Crandy, who'd been laying near his feet, wagged and nudged her as she entered.

"What is it, love?" She petted the hound and kissed Naughton on his forehead. "Why don't you come to bed?"

He shook his head. "I'm fine. It's just... it is remarkable." He held up several editions. *Stability Needed, Pleads Commissioner* read one. *Lay Down Your Arms* said another. "This is precisely what Cunningham had asked. They followed the old man willingly."

"That is his talent," she said. "He's had that from the start. People follow him." She went to the stove and lit a flame, then filled a kettle with water. "So the old man will survive this crisis."

"Apparently so. Not been a single violent clash has been reported since his speech. No further outbreaks. The Ceasefire is teetering but holding. The entire schedule of the SIP and ALE Leagues goes on, not a single game missed, and attendance seems as strong as ever."

"This Jellum character, the one named in the report—"

He shook his head. "Still unaccounted for."

"What about the Magera? Isn't it likely that they're involved?"

He smiled at her perseverance. "You're full of theories, just like me."

"I'm quite serious, Andrew. Hood could very well—"

"Amelia, Lord Bart and Phangorious Hood have long had a mutual understanding. The Leagues leave the Magera alone, and indeed provide several key sources of revenue. In return, Hood and his minions are duty-bound to avoid an activity that would threaten the Ceasefire."

"And what is to stop Hood, given sufficient enticement, from breaking that agreement?"

"Honoring promises is the Magera way. It may seem a contradiction, but they have their blood oath, and part of the oath is allegiance to vows, even as the activities in which they engage are illicit."

She cringed. "I know of the blood oath. It's horrendous." The Magera oath was administered during a brief, bizarre ceremony involving, among other things, the amputation of the ring finger of the initiate.

"Horrendous, but binding. They are criminals, but they are good to their word, which is perhaps more than we can say about many law-abiding citizens."

"I suppose." She reached over and took his hand. "I still cannot believe you asked Lord Bart to step down."

"I merely suggested the idea."

"And it set him off."

He closed his eyes at the mention of that scene. "It was… disturbing."

She stood and retrieved two empty mugs for the tea. "And now this curious, wondrous thing: an elderly man, with the sheer force of his words, seems to have again convinced a teeming, desperate continent — two nations, millions of people — to step back from the brink of war."

"Yes. And in doing so, he consolidated, at least for now, his own power."

She leaned toward him and covered his hands with hers. "So tell me, Andrew Naughton, if the situation is defused, if the peoples seem content, why is your forehead knotted in worry?'

He smiled. She knew him too well. "Well, for one, the old man was quick to issue a completely falsified accident report and ordered the actual investigation to remain private."

"Which led to Ronnell's publication of the probe."

"Yes."

"So if he'd simply released it from the start, without attempting to convince the Twin Nations of false excuses, we might have been spared the outbreak of clashes."

"Yes, I daresay. And…" His voice trailed off.

"What?"

"He wanted to arrest three innocent men to further divert attention."

She leaned back, mouth agape. "You never told me that."

"Fortunately, Lady Lynam thought better of it, and convinced him not to. And… and he is increasingly belligerent and prone to spells of ranting."

"Lady Lynam? I imagined they were in lock step."

"I cannot tell. At least yet. I cannot say if her motivations run counter to his. All I know is she had left him for two years, and now miraculously re-appears as this crisis descended."

Amelia pulled out the previous day's *Chronicle* from the stack. Even the national baseball daily had taken up the cause: *Commish to Youthful Insurgents: 'Talk to Your Parents,'* its headline read.

"And what has your dear friend Ollo Ronnell written?"

"Not a word."

"What?"

"Since the commissioner's speech, his column has not appeared. If fact, he has not written a word since he published the report of our internal crash investigation."

"Do you think he's been sacked? Forced out?"

"No. Rinkins couldn't afford that." Rinkins, the publisher, knew that a good reason for the *Chronicle's* steady sales was the acerbic writing of Ronnell, who had become, over the years, an icon in his own right. The scribe would never be ousted.

"After the leaked report was published, I sent a communique in the commissioner's name, demanding Ronnell's appearance before Lord Bart. I need to find how he obtained the report."

"Will he appear?"

"The editors said he had left for Widmertown hours earlier. They feigned ignorance over when he'd return."

"Convenient."

"Yes."

"So now?"

"The commissioner will call in Rinkins himself to reiterate our displeasure with Ronnell. Lord Bart will tell him we need certainty that Ronnell's next column won't be inflammatory."

Amelia looked askance. "Might not that backfire?"

"How so?"

"If the publisher not only ignores your request but chooses to report it, the citizenry learns that we are trying to manage press coverage, to sway public opinion."

"Unlikely. Rinkins publishes a continental daily devoted primarily to baseball. He has a vested interest in the Leagues continuing. I doubt he would go that far."

Her countenance made clear she was unconvinced. "Except — perhaps he is among those who has a vested interest in a return to warring."

Naughton considered her idea. "Well, a war certainly would sell newspapers."

She sat back. "Yes it would."

The kettle came to a boil.

Before turning in, he checked on Jack and Isaac, hoping to leave them with quiet kisses on their foreheads. Jack's sleep was deep but Isaac, the younger boy, woke and grinned when he recognized his father. "Daddy!"

"Shhhh. Isaac. I didn't want to wake you. Go back to sleep."

"I have to go to school."

"Not until the morning. It's still nighttime."

The six year old shook his head. "I have a question."

Naughton sat on the bedside and held his son's hand. Isaac was ever the inquisitive one. "Yes, you always do. Go ahead."

"Randy, who is in my class, says there are other countries we don't know about."

"There may be. I've told you before, much of our world is not known. We know only our continent. Sometimes adventurers have gone out, by boat, by airship."

At this, Isaac's eyes brightened. "And they didn't come back?"

"Yes. So far, none has come back."

"Why?"

"No one knows."

"Did they get eaten by monsters?"

Naughton smiled. "No. I'm sure they didn't get eaten by monsters."

"Then what happened?"

"We don't know, Isaac. Explorers have tried for years and years. But boats and airships and balloons are not ideal for long trips over the oceans. Perhaps they ran out of food, or ran out of the gas that keeps the airships afloat. Or, they ran into storms. It could be anything. We have never heard back, so we do not know. Now you need to get back to sleep."

"They could have been eaten by a monster! They could have!"

"No, Isaac. There are no monsters. But I'm sure that one day we will have an answer. One day someone will invent an airship that does not rely on the special gas. A ship with some sort of motor. A ship that will be able to return."

"Would it use steam?"

"I don't know."

"Like a cable car? Only in the air?"

"I said, I don't know. Perhaps one day." Naughton reached down and pulled the sheet over his son's arms. "Now, please, try to—"

"Daddy, just one more question."

Naughton laughed and Isaac grinned in return. "Go ahead."

"If there *are* other continents, do they play baseball there?"

He stood, smiled at the boy, and swallowed. "I hope so, Isaac. I certainly hope so."

"Randy says baseball started in a land called Merrica thousands of years ago, before the kitty-casm."

"Cataclysm. The Wide Cataclysm."

"Yes! The kitty-casm!"

"That's just a myth, Isaac. A legend. No one really knows how baseball started. Now, I need to go." Naughton stood, kissed the boy's forehead again, and went to the bedroom door.

"Daddy, one more question."

"Yes, Isaac."

"Are you sure there are no monsters?"

"Yes. I'm absolutely sure. There are no monsters, Isaac. Now, please, try to sleep."

June 16

WIDMERTOWN

A COURIER ARRIVED EARLY AT RONNELL's hotel room with word that the Helderan Executive, Willison Caffrey, would have a major announcement in the afternoon, and would be joined by other Helderan owners.

The columnist was grim as he read the note. He had been prepared to check out after breakfast and board the ferry back to the mainland; this would force him to change his itinerary and stay longer on this suffocating island. Moreover, he was still frustrated at his inability to wrest any sort of story out of the Flying Squirrels coach about that team's clubhouse scuffle.

But the courier had been dispatched by his editor at the *Chronicle*, so clearly the newspaper expected him to be at the announcement and file a piece posthaste. Ronnell sighed. Some days he felt he was getting too old for traipsing across the Twin Nations in search of headlines. But at least he'd be coming home with a story that justified the trip.

He unpacked his bags, then made his way down to the hotel lobby to inform the concierge that he'd be staying at least one, possibly two more nights. Next, it was to the publick house, the oddly named Brown Cloud Down, where haggard waitresses greeted him warmly, the coffee was bitter enough for his liking, and the cook served a decent potato-and-egg mash.

What could Caffrey be doing? he wondered, settling into a window seat. Most likely, he surmised, the Helderans would attempt to ratchet up pressure on Cunningham to yield power, or resign. *What's next for this godforsaken continent?*

He ordered a whiskey to follow the coffee.

IN THE MORNING, AS NAUGHTON was about to leave, Amelia pushed the stack of newspapers toward him. "Take these away. I don't want them in the house."

He nodded. There was no need for blaring headlines greeting the boys at breakfast. "I will try not to be late."

She snorted. Amelia had learned long ago it was a hollow though oft-repeated promise. "Just be safe." She hugged him and opened the door. "And keep our boys safe."

A carriage awaited him, and as he and Crandy stepped inside, he caught his reflection in the door's window. The image was that of a stranger: deep creases under his eyes, necktie askew, complexion gaunt. It was just four days ago that he had tried to prod the old man into resigning. Now here he was — propping up the old man by trying to skew the newspapers on Lord Bart's behalf.

He settled in to the seat. *I'm back*, he thought. *I'm back in the fold. How did I so quickly revert?*

Perhaps this should not have been a surprise. He'd been with the old man 20 years, and it seemed like no time at all. His path to becoming the Special Assistant to the Commissioner felt effortless, natural. Fated.

He had taken a job at a local accounting firm after finishing University, and was quickly promoted to office manager. He lived at home, caring for his mother and playing baseball for a small amateur team on weekends. At night he'd attended the games of the hometown Mount Jarviswell St. Bernards at Irismore Park. In 1903 the All-Star Game of the ALE League was scheduled at the park, and the team, in advance of the event, wanted to hire a professional manager for planning. Friends cajoled him to apply, and two weeks later he was the St. Bernards' Special Events Planner.

Naughton expanded the All-Star Game from a single-day affair, with nothing more than a day game and a celebratory dinner for League officials afterward, to a three-day event, with a festival featuring some of the players on day one, the home-run derby on day two, and the game itself on day three. The weekend proved a rousing success, selling out the park and drawing rave reviews. The event immediately became a tradition with both the ALE and SIP Leagues.

Two weeks later, Naughton was summoned to League headquarters in Schawmount City. Lord Bart's top aide was retiring, and the commissioner was looking for a younger man to replace him. Someone with great operational and managerial skills, but with a strong flair for promotion and public relations. Someone who could manage crises.

He had been 24, young for a position of such stature, and many around him were skeptical. But the commissioner, for some reason, seemed to trust him implicitly.

The old man believed in him.

So Naughton had pledged devotion not just to a job, but to the man himself. And to the cause: preserving the Leagues and the peace.

WIDMERTOWN

THE WIND SLAPPED AGAINST HIS overcoat as Ronnell made his way to the Flying Squirrels' corporate office, where Caffrey's announcement would take place. Carriages rushed passed, splashing mud puddles in his direction, but Ronnell was pleased to be walking. It helped to ease the discomfort of his back, which had tightened the moment his departure was delayed.

A horse-drawn cab pulled up to him and a door opened. "Come in, Ollo, you're too old to be out in this." It was Galahad Berry, baseball beat writer for the *Leadland Leader*, covering the Mudhens of the ALE League. Next to him were two other reporters he didn't recognize. He waved them off. "Gally, when you get to be my age, you'd better be walking." The three in the cab laughed and pulled off.

He hated feeling old. The wind and cold crept into his bones each morning, but he knew much of the ache was from the wear and tear of his playing days. Some mornings when he woke, his knees would barely bend. The remnants of too many slides into second. Too many swings at throws in the dirt. Too many dives for balls stroked up the middle.

Too many nights of sleeplessness over a simple idea, taken from him.

It had come to him 35 years ago, late at night, after a Trident victory over the MacKaness team, known at the time as the Mountaineers. Bottom Brook was situated just off Farigswall Bay, and in the summer evenings the eastward breeze brought them a break from the humidity and the smell of fishing trawlers off the coast.

They laid together in her apartment above a clothier, listening to blasts of mortar fire in the distance. The war itself rarely appeared first-hand in Bottom Brook; for that, he was thankful. But its sounds were never far.

Ronnell remembered her voice that night, soothing as a silk blanket. "Put it aside," she had told him, "it will never end."

He hadn't been sure if she was talking about that night's game, or of the mortar fire. It didn't matter. The two merged together. He had approached an at-bat as methodically as he'd approached the laying of mines: preparation was essential, calm at the moment. The blast of a fastball against the meat of the bat: sometimes it split the wood along a thin seam and the ball repelled down the length of the bat, striking it repeatedly. Some games, he wondered: at the very moment of a hit, was a child stepping on a mine?

Ollo Ronnell, laying in the dark all those years ago with Vivian Packer Lynam curved against him, had shuddered. And then came the thought that changed everything. He blurted it out without concern for its consequences, without any sense that the idea could even possibly take hold. "We should put down our guns and take up balls and bats. We should have a bi-national league."

Vivian lifted her head from his shoulder and peered at him quizzically. "What are you talking about?"

"Its simple. We are approaching five decades of war. Everyone is exhausted and the leaders have lost sight of the very reasons war began. The Setherian and Helderan peoples would form a professional baseball league that will span the continent and Heldera Island as well. We would lay out our aggressions on the ball field, not the battlefield."

She suddenly sat up on her elbows and studied him. "A continental baseball league?"

"Yes, Setherians versus Helderans."

"Instead of a great war," she replied, as if thinking out loud, "hundreds of bloodless little wars."

He peered back at Vivian. Though they'd met only a year earlier, every bit of her was completely familiar, as if their time together had spanned decades: the way she maintained the society-driven stiff back when entertaining, only to slouch the minute others left, the way her laughter began as a boisterous guffaw and then trailed off each time to a giggle, the way she pursed her lips seconds before erupting in anger, the way she sighed loudly and her gaze became distant when deep in thought.

As she was doing at that very moment.

"Little wars," she whispered.

He pulled her against him.

Later, in his office, Naughton dropped the newspapers onto the growing pile on the floor, then collapsed into the swivel chair behind his desk and stroked Crandy. A slight knock came to his door, prompting the servohound to rear up and utter a low growl. "Shh, boy. It's fine. Yes?"

Security Chief Gill entered. "Sir, my sources report—"

Naughton jumped up. "More fighting?"

"No, sir, thankfully. The border region, north to south, remains quiet. But my sources tell me that the Helderan Executive Caffrey and several other owners plan an announcement of some sort."

"When?"

"In two hours, apparently. In Widmertown. I have dispatched two agents for covert fact-finding. But the scribes have been summoned, so we should fairly quickly have press accounts of the proceedings."

"Have they formally notified the League?"

"No."

"So we must feign ignorance?"

The inspector pondered the question. "No. My source will not be betrayed if you or the commissioner were to reach out to Caffrey now to demand a briefing. Invitations have been issued to the press, so they should not be surprised that we quickly came to learn of it."

"Fine. Tell Coyle to 'tube a query to Caffrey's men. Demand information, now."

"Will that be all, sir?"

Naughton took a deep breath. "No."

"Sir?"

"Sit down, Enoch."

The Monystian pondered the request for a second, then adjusted his uniform vest and reclined into a nearby chair.

"You've been quite dutiful in your short time here."

"I take my responsibilities seriously."

"And you withhold comment."

"Except when asked."

"I haven't done much asking since this disastrous time began, Enoch. That is my failing."

"I am here to ensure security. I was not hired to provide advice."

"Except when asked."

"Yes, sir," replied Gill. "But you did not hire me, the commissioner did. You did not want me here. And now as you harbor doubts about Lord Bart's veracity, you naturally have doubts about my arrival. That is a good thing."

"Good?"

"Sir, it is my very job to look upon everything with suspicion. Everything. So far be it from me to question someone in your position doing the very same. I would actually be quite bothered if you were not suspicious of me."

The man makes too much damn sense. "I—"

"You are confused." The Monsytian spoke without a hint of criticism or condescension, as if he was merely declaring a known fact.

"Yes."

"You have spent nearly two decades successfully balancing multiple forces to achieve success — peace and stability for the millions, prosperity for the owners, longevity and acclaim for the commissioner. And you did all that by subtly controlling all those various forces."

"Go on."

"But now, in an instant, everything seems out of control: the peace is shattered, the owners are fractured, the commissioner is—"

"—is not stable."

"Yes. You are struggling because you don't know who to trust."

Naughton's lips felt dry, his throat parched. Could others see through him so readily? Or was this only the case of a man who excelled at perception, at clarity. "So tell me, Enoch Gill. Tell me the solution."

The Monystian leaned forward and his dreadlocks swung over the front of his shoulders. "It is actually quite simple."

"Simple?"

"Yes. You're so focused on the Helderans, on the press, even on the commissioner himself, that you're refusing to see what all signs so clearly point to."

"And that would be...?"

"That would be the connection between all of what has transpired and the scientist from Kern, Dr. Henry."

"Iphonious Henry? What of him?"

"That is what you need to find out. Think about it: Dr. Henry, within days of a monstrous attack during the Anniversary Celebration, demonstrates publicly

a device that could have caused it! Has that not occurred to you? He might claim coincidence. And what of his late night visit to the commissioner, just hours after the first widespread border violence in 30 years breaks out? Is that also a coincidence?"

"You know of the visit?"

"Would you not expect me to have the commissioner's residence monitored day and night? Of course I know. I know you personally attended Henry's lecture in Kern, and then chose not to deliver to the commissioner a detailed account of the evening."

"I—"

"You don't have to explain. That was your decision. But yes, I know of all this. And what of money?"

"What money?"

"What is the source of money for Henry's research? Do we know that? It's doubtful that Kern University itself is funding it; many of his colleagues in Kern are apparently quite jealous of the attention he is now getting. And the Scientificka leadership is, to a man, said to be suspicious and concerned about him. He ignored their request for a hearing. So does he have other benefactors, perhaps? Helderan team owners? Who, sir, is paying his bills?"

"But…" Naughton sighed deeply as he grasped the Monystian's larger point. He'd pushed the Henry matter aside as nothing more than a sideshow to the larger crisis that wracked the Twin Nations, when the strange scientist could easily be, as Gill said, the root of it all. "I see. It's been right in front of me, and I haven't been watching."

"I have."

"And?"

"You need to go talk to this Iphonious Henry. Not me, not Coyle. You. After Caffrey's announcement, go."

WIDMERTOWN

A BLOCK AWAY FROM THE Flying Squirrels' offices, 10 minutes before the scheduled start of the Helderans' mysterious announcement, Ollo Ronnell chided himself for not accepting Gally's offer of the ride. He was tired. Perhaps, after this crisis eased, the time would come to take a rest. Let the younger ones chase the future crises.

A Helderan League administrative assistant greeted him at the door and ushered him into the already cramped board room. Ronnell positioned himself in the back, behind three newspaper artists. He would be pleased not to be noticed.

Within minutes, four Helderan owners paraded in.

Caffrey, the national executive and owner of the Squirrels, led the pack, followed by his longtime ally, Hammerheads owner Carroll Massey, nearing 70 but spry as ever. Next came two of the newer owners, Morren Godwyn of the West Somerchester Rhinos and Dr. Granville Chanley of the last-place Gregorson Monkeys. Chanley was among the younger owners, only 53 as best as Ronnell could recall, and he was known as a bit of a loner. His appearance here only heightened Ronnell's unease about the whole scene.

They stood in silence behind the empty chair at the top of the varnished conference table at the room's center. Ronnell mulled the mix: two of the old guard, two of the new. *This will prove interesting indeed.*

Caffrey, burly yet short for a Helderan, settled into the front chair, adjusted his notes, and cleared his throat. The others whispered amongst themselves and consulted notes. The crowd quieted.

"Gentlemen," Caffrey began, twisting his mustache, "I will spare the pleasantries of thanking you for coming such a distance on such short notice. Suffice it to say, the events of the past four months have been distressing to both nations of our great continent. But particularly so for the noble people of the Nation of Heldera. And I speak not only of the race of Helderans, but the minority races that also populate our nation — the Amandeans, the Rebular, the Monystians. We have, over the past 30 years, developed a national pride that is now distinctly threatened by the turmoil of this 30th anniversary season of the Leagues of SIP and ALE."

Ronnell scribbled into his worn notepad. "When our Helderan forefathers agreed to the Eternal Ceasefire," Caffrey continued, "it was an exceedingly complex matter. The terms ran several hundred pages, barristers on both sides of the conflict negotiated for endless hours, days, and weeks. But the truth is that the matter was a simple one. It could be boiled down to one word: trust." He paused, letting the word resonate.

"Trust. After 50 years of warring, the Helderan peoples agreed to do the most difficult and courageous thing imaginable: place their trust in the one man proposing the Ceasefire and the creation of the Twin Leagues: our commissioner, Lord Bartholomew Cunningham. We thought that he had, over time, proved to be worthy of that trust. After all — the peace, and Helderan autonomy, prevailed.

"So I speak now directly to Commissioner Cunningham himself, and I have

faith that the reporters gathered here will faithfully relay my thoughts to him. Commissioner, the peoples of the Great Nation of Heldera agreed to many things in signing the Eternal Ceasefire. But we never agreed that you would rule in perpetuity. Nor that you would have sole authority to determine your successor. Nor — and this is perhaps most important — that your successor would necessarily be, like you, a Setherian.

"In short, Commissioner, while our trust in you seemed boundless, it was not then nor is it now limitless. The time has come for an end to trust. The time has come for skepticism. The time has come for change."

At this the other reporters in the crowded boardroom shifted in their seats; a few began to stand. The moment when they would learn the ambitious Helderan's true plans had finally come.

"So today," Caffrey resumed, "I announce simply that I am stepping down as executive of our nation, effective immediately. Henceforth, our proud peoples are to be governed by a new voice, a younger man who will lead Heldera into a new era." Gasps cascaded around the meeting room.

The elder leader by this point was sweating profusely. He turned slightly to the trio to his left, then faced the crowd of shocked reporters. "Gentlemen, I give you the new Executive of the Sovereign Nation of Heldera, the owner of the Crenshaw City Warthogs — Alexander Fitton!"

A side door behind the riser opened and out strode Fitton, immaculate in top hat and silk coat with burgundy lapels and matching kerchief. He grasped Caffrey's hand in a congratulatory shake, then looked out at the audience. A cacophony of shouted questions and expressions of shock enveloped him. His back was arched, as if in a regal pose. His teeth shone amid his broad grin. He made a slight adjustment to the tilt of his top hat and flicked a speck of lint from a pant leg.

In the back of the room, Ronnell shifted in his seat, then folded his notebook without writing a further word. He stood, his back throbbing from the walk from the hotel. He'd summon a carriage for the return.

Besides, there was no time to walk back. He had a column to pen. For the world had shifted, quite abruptly indeed, and he needed to wax eloquent about the change.

June 20

The University of Kern

THE RIDE TO KERN LASTED three hours by private carriage, so Naughton used the journey for routine League business: reviewing team reports. He relished the chore's normalcy.

Naughton tapped the empty portion of the bench seat and Crandy jumped up from the carriage floor, then curled in next to him as he unwrapped the documents. They were sent by courier each day by League operatives in all 36 of the SIP and ALE cities and towns, and included attendance totals, and gross revenues of the gate, concessions, and the like. The reports also featured a summary of each game and resulting issues, including disputes between teams and the arbiters, and anything else out of the ordinary.

Coyle was usually assigned to forage through them and condense the findings into a single summary for him. After the airship disaster, Naughton had begun asking for the full reports as well. Part of that was to be thorough — as detail-oriented as his assistant was, something key could be easily missed. Secondly, the reports undoubtedly would convey a tone, an intangible voice, that could not be easily summarized. He flipped through the most recent weeks' worth of documents.

This stack proved fairly dry reading until one report caught his attention, concerning the Widmertown Flying Squirrels. It included the transcript of the questioning of manager Sander Halloway, concerning a fistfight that had broken out June 12th between one of their hurlers, Ketter Asgar, and striker Pyce Marsh. Asgar had a reputation as an instigator, prone to speaking his own mind. A clubhouse cancer, some managers believed. On the other hand Marsh, Newcomer of the Year winner in the Helderan Division two years ago, was only 22 and likely to become one of the stars of the Leagues.

The Squirrels' manager, the famed Sander Halloway, had been interviewed about the matter, and it seemed like a perfunctory dust-up. But the operative, Charles Sharp, noted that on the 18th — just two days ago — Marsh had been ejected from a game in the first inning for arguing balls and strikes. It struck him as odd. He looked up the arbiter's name: Frederick Darnell. He was one of the best. It was not necessarily odd that a player argues, but usually it comes late in a close game, when it matters. Players knew they did not do themselves or their team any favors by arguing after routine at-bats. Early in games, players had more subtle ways to make their points to the umpire, through dark stares or kicking dirt. Marsh had been around long enough to know this, so something must have particularly bothered him.

But not even the rarity of a first-inning ejection would have risen to the level of noteworthy were it not for Sharp's final comment: 'Marsh later requested a leave of absence for personal reasons, which was refused.' Was there a personal matter that could escalate? Naughton circled the comment, as a reminder to discuss it later with Coyle, and perhaps directly with the team's general manager, Eldon Langford.

Then, he stopped himself. *What am I thinking?* The fate of the entire continent swung precariously, the situation was by no means resolved, and every day meant trying to bring citizens of both nations a sense of calm. Matters like Marsh and the Squirrels would have to fall by the wayside. He scratched behind Crandy's ear, then turned to the next team's report.

———————————

THE UNIVERSITY OF KERN OFFERED a sweeping entrance: a gate of dark cherry oak and brass appointments, a uniformed guard, a beautifully landscaped campus. His carriage driver asked the guard for specific direction to the *House Scientificka,* and within minutes Naughton was ushered into a nondescript outer office. An attendant offered a liquor, which he refused, and a carbonated water, which he accepted. After ten minutes, Iphonious Henry came out to greet him.

"Mr. Naughton, I do appreciate you coming to my office. I trust I didn't keep you waiting too long."

"Not at all. A welcome bit of quiet after a bumpy carriage ride."

"Yes, the roads leading to Kern are quite in need of some upkeep. But I daresay the city is too cash-strapped to deal with it. Perhaps the League Office could offer its resources."

"I appreciate the suggestion."

"Ah, I'm sure. But you didn't ask to come to talk about road paving. How can I help you?"

Naughton peered around to ensure that Henry had no assistants within hearing distance. "Dr. Henry, when last we met you'd managed to frighten the entire Opera House audience with your beam device. Now we know — the entire continent knows — that a device of unknown origin and purpose was found amid the wreckage of the *Lady Crym.*"

"Yes, I did read about that. Most curious."

"Then you failed to appear before the Association of Scientificka's governing board, as you'd been asked."

"I told you that evening I would not. I am a man of my word. I have no time for Northgood and his bureaucratic buffoons."

"You were observed visiting the commissioner at his estate on June 12th, at the very outbreak of fighting eight days ago."

"Yes, he summoned me after reading your report of my lecture. Were you not aware of that?"

"I never gave him my report. He never saw it."

"Don't be so certain."

Naughton adjusted his tie and moved on. "Dr. Henry: was that your device found in the wreckage?"

Henry leaned back and smoothed the ends of his mustache. "I resent your implication. Do you think I would be so foolhardy as to demonstrate my beam device if I, in fact, had involvement in the demolition of the airship? Why would I draw attention to myself? Nay, Mr. Naughton, my public unveiling of that technology is perhaps the clearest proof that I bear no culpability."

Naughton sat without response, without expression.

"You remain unconvinced," said Henry. "I have a suggestion. Come back with me now. I would like show you my research facility. I daresay you'll find it thought-provoking."

———————————

HENRY AND AN AIDE LED Naughton back to a smaller inner room, then through an armored door with multiple locks, then up a flight of steps. Crandy followed, hunched as if on prowl.

They were now at the mezzanine level, walking down a narrow corridor lined with gas lamps. At its end, a quick turn right, and then they entered a cavernous room that would quickly cure any claustrophobia. The vaulted ceiling rose three stories high, lit by four ornate chandeliers reminiscent of the Opera House where they'd first met. Metallic and leather tubing, ducts, and conduits crisscrossed in a maze across the length of the ceiling. Within the chamber were six lengthy examining tables, arranged in a two-by-three pattern, and on each table lay an array of odd mechanical equipment and what appeared to be chemical apparatus. Four or five assistants in gray smocks worked silently, independently. The rhythmic rumbling of steam machines, probably beneath the flooring, echoed throughout. The room smelled mildly of — Naughton wasn't certain — perhaps sulfur, with a touch of methane.

So this is it. The laboratory of Dr. Iphonious Henry.

Crandy rose on alert, perched as if ready to pounce, and uttered a barely audible growl. Naughton caught his breath, then asked in a halting voice, "The commissioner would not look kindly on this."

"And is that why you sought this meeting with me, Andrew? May I call you Andrew?"

"Yes, that's fine."

"Please rest assured: I don't have any desire to skirt the law, to work in hiding. This is for the good of the continent."

"The good of the continent."

"Yes, absolutely."

"And what precisely is 'this'?"

Henry smirked. "This is the hatching ground for great advances in pneumatics! Our continent loves its steam! I have focused on the science of transporting steam in microscopic ways to create advanced mechanizations."

"Mechanizations?"

"Worry not, Andrew. All of this falls well within the precepts of accepted research as dictated by the League. I merely have over time managed to procure quite a few interesting objects that aid in my research. In fact this—" Henry swept his right arm across the view of the laboratory, "is the logical extension of the science our modern world already relies upon. All of this, Andrew, is inevitable."

———————————

THE COMPLETE TOUR OF EACH of the six tables took a full hour. Naughton followed behind Henry and listened with little comment to the doctor's detailed explanations. Much of the science was beyond him. Two tables contained mechanical devices that displayed what Henry said were refinements of servohound autonomic technology. "I've borrowed ideas. I've borrowed research. And I've processed them in ways no one else has even imagined."

Two other tables, with flasks and beakers and an array of measuring devices, focused on chemical compounds and pneumatic reactions. The final two were more medical in nature, with scalpels, lancets, drills, and forceps. To the direct right of this table stood a vertical, rectangular black box.

"I am particularly proud of this," beamed Henry. "I call it the Scanner Biopneumatic. Simply, it allows one to see inside the human body. Calistas, come over here." One of the assistants put down his clipboard and stood directly behind the box. It covered the entirety of his torso. Henry activated four knobs on the side of the box, pulled several more brass levers, and Naughton could see a series of thin, gas-fed tubes illuminate in green. The device reverberated throughout the room, and Crandy began barking.

Naughton felt his heart stop. The front of the box lit up, and a black-and-white, moving image appeared: a skeleton, but alive. Organs: heart, lungs. Bones, encased in the shadow of the man's trunk. "Is this a trick?" he called out above the din.

"Anything but," the doctor responded. "Calistas, walk away." The assistant retreated from behind the box and Naughton saw the skeleton and organs move correspondingly.

Henry released the levers and tubes and the device lost its power. He grinned. "Do you need anything, Naughton? A chair? A drink? You look pale."

Naughton waved away the offer, and caught his breath. "Dr. Henry, if this doesn't violate the letter of League restrictions on Scientificka, it clearly violates the spirit."

"Do call me Iphonious, Andrew. No need for formalities. Before you attempt to shut my work down, I urge you to consider the implications of what I have here, for the continent and for the Leagues. For the commissioner."

"Why did you choose to show me this?"

"I will answer that with another question, Andrew. Why did you go out of your way, during a very intense week, to attend my lecture? Why do you seek me out today, when the wretched border violence must surely be occupying your energies?"

The two stared at each other. A stalemate of sorts. Naughton had come expecting to engage in a theoretical, political debate. Instead... this! "What exactly are you trying to do?"

"I can answer, if you will allow me, with one more demonstration."

Naughton ran his tongue over the edges of his parched lips, then nodded.

"Calistas, go get her."

The assistant retreated into a side room. Minutes passed. The two stood without comment. Naughton glowered. Crandy lowered into a crouch and paced toward the scanner device, sniffing its base. Gathering information.

The door opened, and Calistas re-entered. At his side: another servohound. Crandy moved toward it. This hound was brown, with a torso the size of Crandy's but slightly shorter legs.

"Sally, come!" Henry commanded.

The other hound obeyed, running excitedly toward the doctor, tail wagging. Like Crandy, her limbs were metallic and hinged, with the outline of steam-powered ligaments and gear-driven joints visible beneath thin metal sheeting. The tail was a tubular strip of pliant steel, articulated at several points.

But unlike Crandy, Sally had the outward appearance of a canine, with fur across her back where Crandy had steel, and with natural pads clearly visible on all four limbs. And the gait: Naughton observed that the creature's bounding gallop was clearly a marked improvement over Crandy's, whose prancing bore the rigid stamp of automation.

Crandy trotted over and sniffed at Sally's behind. The hound paid her counterpart no mind. She greeted her master, then turned about to stare at Naughton. He leaned down and offered his outstretched palm for the device to sniff.

The dog's nose on his hand was wet and cold. Her tongue briefly emerged and licked his skin, and Naughton felt… warmth! He reached forward and grabbed the device's jaw; inside her mouth, a drooping, red cheek interior, four rows of teeth, and a quivering esophagus clearly visible at the back of the throat. And the eyes, bright, darting about, far from the dull black rotating dots that passed for eyes on Crandy.

It is… real.

Naughton stood firmly and looked directly at the doctor. "What have you done?" he pressed.

"If this shocks you, I apologize, sir. It was not my intent."

"I ask you again, before I have you arrested: what have you done?"

"This, Naughton, is simply the natural outgrowth of the very technology that allows you to have your beloved hound. I have successfully taken an actual Labrador — wounded, maimed by an abusive owner, slated to be euthanized — and given her new life."

Naughton jumped back. "Is this beast or machine, Henry?"

"I prefer the term pneumorg: a pneumatic organism. You see, among my research over the past three years has been adaptation of the pneumatic technology that the League adopted for use ten years ago for automota. As you know, servohounds were an expansion, on a limited basis, of research by the famed Dr. Cepheus Colla, back in the earliest days of the Eternal Ceasefire. Dr. Colla created what are generally referred to today as logic circuits: tiny boards with tinier tubes that carry steam in assorted patterns. These patterns, Colla found, could be deployed in a way that small amounts of steam could actually perform rudimentary calculations."

"This much all school children know. Tell me what you've done."

"Fine. A decade ago the servohounds were the ultimate enhancement of the Colla tubes. The logic boards were so advanced, they could essentially mimic the thinking of a trainable dog. The rest, the actual physical structure of the hound, was by comparison relatively easy to mimic. And so, we had a thinking machine, disguised as an animal.

"What I have done, Andrew, is follow the utmost precepts of Scientificka to take those developments to their logical extreme. I have found a way to synthesize servohound technology into a living being. The development took three years and much painstaking testing."

Naughton looked down at the creature. She sat calmly, staring up at him, wagging her tail. Her tongue drooped. Her eyes shone. "She lives?"

"Yes. Sally lives, unlike the collection of programmable gears and tubes you call Crandy."

Then Naughton watched as Sally ran off, across the laboratory and into the back room. She emerged moments later with a leather rope in her mouth. She crouched with her front down, rear end in the air, tail arcing like a metronome, eyes fixated on Crandy, whose tail wagged in response.

And then the two hounds began to play.

July 2

WIDMERTOWN

THE NEWLY APPOINTED EXECUTIVE OF the Sovereign Nation of Heldera, his Excellency Alexander Fitton II, was coming to see a ball game.

That announcement had been dispatched to Halloway by one of Langford's assistants. Langford himself had been noticeably absent from the clubhouse since the League investigators had visited on June 15th, and had not spoken directly to Halloway since. The general manager likely feared losing his job if clubhouse tensions erupted, so he wanted to be able to plausibly deny knowledge of the matter should it worsen.

So be it. Halloway was resolved to live with that reality. But now, this: the eyes of the continent would be upon his Squirrels as they hosted the Warthogs of Crenshaw City for an evening game. Fitton — who owned the Warthogs — would not only be in attendance but was expected to meet with reporters.

It was now four hours before the first throw. Batting practice complete, Halloway strode into the locker room. Around a folding table sat six players, Asgar among them, pitching cards in a game of Terrace. Coins and bills lay strewn across the table. The Count had thrown the night before, and his right arm was still wrapped in ice and toweling. He'd keep it that way for another day or so. Others were chatting, reading magazines, and working oil into the creases of their fielding mitts. In the far corner sat Marsh, hovering over his equipment, staring as if in a reverie.

"Gentlemen," Halloway called out. Those who hadn't already noticed his arrival straightened up. "As you are probably aware, the Helderan owners have chosen a new executive to lead our nation, the Warthogs owner, Fitton. He has decided to attend tonight's game.

"I want to say that I am extremely proud how all of you," he paused and stared straight at Asgar, who was thumbing a deck of cards, "*all* of you have managed to avoid being distracted by the events of the past few weeks. Yet while we will be proud to welcome our new executive to Catalinaside Stadium, it is, of course, another potential distraction from our game. I trust that you will do your best to remain focused on our contest tonight."

He turned to leave when one of the players called out, "Coach?" Swinging back to the players, he saw it was, of course, Asgar, and he did his best to avoid an obvious grimace.

"Yes, Count?"

"Coach, don't you think it's inappropriate telling us that we need to ignore political matters?"

"Inappropriate? Not at all. We are being paid to play baseball. Other matters are not our concern."

"With all due respect, Coach, if our forefathers had that attitude, we Helderans would still be without our own nation."

Others stirred and murmured, clearly surprised by the boldness of Asgar's talk. The coaches, curious, walked out from their separate changing area. Halloway knew that with the entire team watching, he could not back down from the hurler's challenging words.

The room was silent. Asgar stood.

Halloway stepped forward and cocked his head to the left.

Asgar stepped forward as well.

The two men were two footlengths apart. Halloway looked directly at the Count. "Ketter, my great grandfather and my grandfather both died in the Insurrection. Both left widows as they fought for Helderan independence. So I do not need you, or anyone in this room, reminding me of what they were fighting for. Do you understand?"

Asgar inched back slightly and looked down at the ground. "Yes," he mumbled.

"What?"

"Yes, Coach. I understand."

"Fine," Halloway continued now looking across the entire club house. "I will say it again: our job here is to play baseball. The rest is out of our control. So tonight, when the newest Helderan leader sits down in the stands, and watches us take the field — make me proud. Make him proud! Play to win, and don't concern yourself with the rest."

A few whispered, "Yes, sir," and then others agreed more loudly, and a few even clapped.

Later, back in his office, his hands shaking, forehead drenched in sweat, Halloway vomited into a trash can, and hoped no one in the locker room could hear his heaving.

THE ENTOURAGE OF THE NEW executive arrived at six o'clock, an hour before game time.

Halloway watched from a distance. The group was on the field, behind the batting cage. Fitton shook hands with fans, greeted the arbiters, then cast an admiring look toward the field as the players warmed up. Advisers surrounded him, pointing to various players and then whispering to their new leader.

He wore a silk vest, buttoned snugly against his slim torso, but in the warm sun he had left it to an aide to carry his jacket and bowler. He had donned Warthogs cap that had been offered by a ball-boy; it looked odd amid his otherwise formal

MICHAEL BARBATO-DUNN

attire. Brown muttonchops converged at his bushy mustache. *He's a youngster,* thought Halloway, *younger than me. Trying to look much older.*

Halloway spied a gaggle of reporters rushing toward the executive. He motioned to Ferns. "Call the boys. Get them into the clubhouse." Ferns whistled to the players now running sprints in the outfield. Once they were inside, Halloway walked to the batting cage, barely 30 footlengths from Alexander Fitton's first news conference as Executive. A front row seat.

"Gentlemen, for now I have but a brief statement," the executive began. "I would like to thank my fellow Helderan owners for their confidence in me that I should lead our people at this difficult time. I want the millions of residents of our anxious nation to know that we have plans to retain our sovereignty despite rampant fears that it is about to be wrested from us. I urge every one of us to stand down, to lay down any arms, and to perish any thought of inciting violence. Give me a modicum of time, and I vow that I will, in due course, reward your confidence.

"That I am delivering this message here, on a field of players, balls, and bats, of fans by the thousands, is obviously intentional. Let the games go on. Let the sport flourish. Let the Ceasefire remain eternal.

"So I proudly announce the formation of a new political party: Peace First. Its name signals our intentions." Hands shot up and a flurry of questions erupted from the assembled newspapermen, but Fitton waved them to cease. "The platform of Peace First is to maintain the sanctity of the Eternal Ceasefire, unless otherwise provoked."

Halloway noted Fitton's sleight-of-hand with the phrase "unless otherwise provoked." A simple, three-word caveat that could very well be used later to justify a return to warring.

Fitton continued. "This party is truly an amalgam of the long-standing yet fractured political groups that have dotted the landscape of Heldera for 30 years. It is time for us to come together in the face of this threat. Peace First is a unified party — we speak as one.

"So I tell you this: while all of the owners here have had — or attempted to have — private, constructive conversations with Commissioner Cunningham since the attack, none of us have seen our concerns treated with respect. That will now end. Today I am here to demand that the Leagues of SIP and ALE convene a peace conference, in one month's time, with representatives of both leagues, of both nations, and of all the races of the continent. The conference will serve as an opportunity for all parties to air their grievances. Then, together, we can recommit ourselves to the Eternal Ceasefire, and to the Leagues of SIP and ALE."

Fitton put down his notes, smoothed his lapel, and paused as if to relish the moment. "And now I will be happy to take your questions."

The press corps erupted, but one scribe — a youngster, Halloway didn't recognize him — managed to shout the others down with his question. "Mr. Fitton—"

"Executive Fitton," the Helderan corrected.

"Executive Fitton, sir. What if the commissioner refuses?"

"Young man, that is a very astute question. I am sure it is one your editor will want answered. Alas, it is a hypothetical, and I care not to deal with those. I have issued our demand. The ball, as they say, is now firmly in the commissioner's mitt."

Then, another question: "Executive Fitton, will anything less than partial control of the commissioner's office satisfy you?"

"Well, the question is not whether power sharing would satisfy me, but whether it would satisfy the people of Heldera. Suffice it to say that at this point in time we have announced only our primary goal — the continuation of the Eternal Ceasefire. How that is attained, and what form of leadership the Leagues have going forward, is, of course, subject to negotiation. Thus, the necessity of a peace conference."

Only then did Halloway notice Ollo Ronnell standing in the back of the throng of reporters, hat askew, chewing on the end of his unlit cigar. He grimaced, still disgusted over Ronnell's attempt to uncover details of the locker room fistfight. The columnist was past his prime, full of ego and lacking in talent, and Halloway hoped the *Chronicle* would soon insist on his retirement.

"Why, Ollo Ronnell," Fitton called out at that very instant, as if he also had just spied the columnist. "Mr. Ronnell, you're awfully quiet today. Have you no questions?"

"Actually, Mr. Executive," Ronnell replied, adding in the slightest tinge of sarcasm as he uttered the new title, "I do."

The others — murmuring, squirming, and scribbling — quickly hushed, knowing this question might reveal the perspective of the one columnist who could sway thousands of readers.

"Go ahead."

"This is not a hypothetical, Mr. Executive, nor is it a question of terms yet to

be negotiated. I simply want to know: did you and your Helderan compatriots plan the crash of the Airship *Lady Crym*?"

The question struck those on the field like a lightning bolt. Only Ollo Ronnell would have had the standing to implicitly accuse Fitton of a criminal act. Halloway moved a few steps closer.

Fitton himself seemed unmoved. "Another excellent question, sir. And also one that is on the minds of many. And this one I can certainly answer directly."

At this point the new leader of the Helderan people leaned forward and stared directly at Ollo Ronnell. "The answer is no. I say this without hesitation to all the peoples of our troubled continent. We did not direct, nor were any even remotely involved in, that despicable act."

And then Fitton himself added a trace of sarcasm to his final comment. "And I only hope that in the months ahead, the great commissioner Bartholomew Cunningham is able to put that question, once and for all, behind us."

July 3

SCHAWMOUNT CITY

THE MEETING WOULD BE ATOP the elephant.

Naughton learned of this only when he, Coyle, and Gill arrived at the commissioner's estate. They had been summoned to discuss the ascension of Alexander Fitton as Executive of Heldera.

"The elephant?" he asked Cunningham's butler in the entranceway.

"Yes, sir. The elephant. They are in the carriage that encompasses the mechaderm's upper torso. He'll lower stairs for you to climb in."

"They?"

"The Commissioner, sir, is joined by Lady Lynam."

The trio was escorted through the estate's foyer, then out onto a back patio. An enormous terraced lawn lay beyond, immaculate in its landscaping, with sculpted shrubbery and brilliant gardens. In the furthest and largest terrace stood Lord Bart's elephant.

Gill and Coyle, who had never seen the device before, gasped in unison. And

with good reason: the structure was easily 50 footlengths in height, and enormous in girth. Naughton had viewed it in past visits, though only from a distance.

"What is it?" asked Coyle.

"That, gentlemen," Naughton explained, "is Nellie. One of the primary attractions of the Publick Circle, Lord Bart's traveling troupe during the war. Apparently the crowds were enraptured, for at one time it actually moved. Slowly, but it did move. They'd wait in line for hours for a ten-minute ride."

"How old is it? It's a relic," said Gill.

"I'm not sure. He retired his troupe at the inception of the Ceasefire, and I'd imagine he'd had it in use for at least a decade before that."

Bartholomew Cunningham had, by the late 1870s, made himself into a minor celebrity simply by hosting a series of popular theatrical events throughout the continent, even in the midst of the war. First he presented an escape artist, the Magnificent Tobor, who would have himself chained upside down, dunked into a tank, and then would miraculously appear a tense 10 minutes later fully clothed, dry, and devoid of shackles.

Next came Cunningham's traveling theatrical group, "The Revelers," offering comedy and song, much of it considered to be a shade risqué for the more rural regions of the continent. That reputation only enhanced their popularity.

Then, in 1881, at age 33, Cunningham created a bigger attraction: "The Daring, Death-Defying Publick Circle." It was an odd name and an odd idea but, like his earlier endeavors, it quickly caught favor. Lord Bart had recruited a strange assortment of peculiarities from across the continent: a man who put his legs behind his ears and walked on his hands, an Amandean hermaphrodite, a Monsytian woman taller and stronger than most men, and a gaunt Rebularan who sang love ballads in a falsetto. Cunningham hired daredevils who crossed above the theater on a tight wire, balancing themselves only with a long, wobbling pole. He displayed trained jackaloupes and foxhounds that performed choreographed dances together. He claimed to employ a man with three legs, who hid in the shadows of the stage and who prompted gasps of outrage from the audience when the spotlight found him. But Lilly was Lord Bart's greatest triumph: a mechanical elephant, four times the size of an actual elephant and able to traverse the distance of a town's main street.

The Publick Circle, with Nellie in tow, traveled for five years across the continent and back, in the midst of the warring. The troupe avoided a few of the most war-torn areas. But Cunningham otherwise did not shirk away from the trouble spots, so that every corner of the continent, from Boundymount Corner to Crenshaw City, and even Heldera Island, was able to experience the Publick Circle. In small towns and large, Cunningham would rope off the publick square, transforming it into not one circle but three, with quickly-constructed bleacher seats and handsome admission fees.

The Publick Circle's success was overwhelming, for it brought residents a desperately needed dose of levity and also a fragment of hope. The response transformed Bartholomew Cunningham: he became, finally, an extremely famous man. And an astute one: he learned first-hand the curative power of entertainment.

"Nellie helped make him rich," Naughton whispered to the others. "The Continent had never seen anything like it."

They walked down three levels of terrace steps toward the hulking edifice. Naughton doubted that it could move anymore. The massive steel hinges of the legs and trunk, visible through large gaps in the elephant's wooden exterior, were encased in rust. At this point perhaps sculpture was a more appropriate term than mechaderm.

The trunk sloped downward from the motionless head in an arc, its tip touching the grass at their feet. In its interior they could spy the primitive pneumatics — interwoven tubing that fed dozens of small condensers, mounted across and perpendicular to the tubes themselves. Fifty-year-old technology.

They craned their necks upward. The elephant's ears, large sections of leather sewn together like a quilt, flapped lightly in the breeze. Its eyes were black beads, lifeless. Large sections of wood, painted gray to mimic hide, encompassed the unhinged areas of its torso and legs. The elephant's back was a cabin, ornate as that on a yacht, with brass fittings amid deep mahogany walls and railings. While Naughton saw cracks and dirt on the painted wood closest to him, on the legs and trunk, the cabin sparkled in the sunlight.

"Hello! Naughton! We're up here!" They found Lord Bart waving from the porch on the near side. Lady Lynam hovered behind him. "Bring your men, I'll drop the stairs!"

Minutes, later the commissioner, gleaming, welcomed them into the cabin. "Welcome to my Nellie, gentlemen. She is as regal as ever."

Naughton and the others nodded, and bowed slightly to Lady Lynam, who acknowledged their formality with a slight nod and pursed lips. They gathered around a small oak table mounted into the floorboards, offering seating for six. At the far end of the cabin, toward the elephant's head, a small set of steps led up to the cockpit within the head. Inside that small room was a leather chair facing a modest window, and below that, an array of levers and switches that once made the mechaderm mobile. Lifelike.

"We had wonderful times in this beautiful creature," said the old man, staring out at the grounds of his estate. The glass was without a hint of dust, as was the entire cabin. It was clear to Naughton that, even if the pneumatics and mechanics of Nellie were no longer functioning, Lord Bart had his staff regularly maintain the cabin. "Even in the midst of the war, they were wonderful times."

Naughton cleared his throat, hoping to break the old man's reverie. When the old man turned back, Naughton began.

"The purpose of this meeting is to determine our next course of action. Specifically, whether to agree to Executive Fitton's demand for a peace conference. Commissioner, it is the staff's recommendation that you reject such a gathering. There are several reasons—"

Lady Lynam interrupted. "Unfortunately, Bartholomew, we may have little choice. The adroit moves of the new Helderan leader seem to have forced our hand."

Naughton offered a quick rebuttal. "We feel a conference will only ascribe greater credibility to Fitton. It will only enhance the perception of his standing among the people of both nations."

She shook her head. "Andrew, I'm afraid any opportunity to reduce his credibility has long since passed. The Helderans, at least for the moment, seem united behind him. He is young, magnetic, articulate, and forceful. The elders among the Helderans view Fitton as a tremendous new force for their cause. A rallying point, if you will."

The commissioner looked away, seemingly considering the two positions, then announced his decision. "Lady Lynam is right. Our best bet at this point is to stage this silly conference, yet manipulate its framework to our advantage, and hope to stay one step ahead of the upstart." The old man looked away. "Have you caught the Amandean, Jellum, yet? What is taking so long?"

"It is a large continent, Commissioner," Naughton replied. "We will not rest until he is found. But... I must say that I strongly—"

"I know you disagree on this, Andrew. But my decision on the peace conference is final. Just don't allow this Jellum character to disrupt the event, as he appears to have done back in March."

Naughton slumped back and grimaced. Coyle picked up his notes and read

from them. "Commissioner, in anticipation of your decision, I have prepared a schedule. The conference will convene in West Somerchester, site of the 30th Anniversary Season All-Star Game. The owners will gather on August 4th, the final day of baseball before the three-day All-Star break. That day will consist merely of a formal ceremony to convene the gathering. Day Two, August 5th, will consist of substantive meetings that will be closed to the public and the press. The owners, led jointly by Fitton and the commissioner, will hold a series of meetings in small groups, and then, ideally, the full body of ownership by day's end."

"Excellent," replied Lord Bart.

Naughton felt a line of perspiration on his forehead. He had not directed Coyle to draw up such a plan, even as a contingency, nor had he been aware of it. "May I ask, Commissioner, to what end?" Though Naughton posed the question to Lord Bart, he stared directly at Coyle.

"To what end?" asked the old man.

"Yes. What would we achieve?"

Lady Lynam interjected. "The ostensible goal, the stated goal, would be to either revise the original Proclamation of an Eternal Ceasefire, or to create an entirely new one. But our true goal — never to be stated — is simple appeasement, without any actual concessions."

Naughton could hold his anger no longer. "Blasphemy! The Eternal Ceasefire is exactly that — eternal! To revise it is to undercut its very essence."

Lord Bart reached his hand out across the table to calm him. "Unfortunately, Andrew, we have little choice here. What we need to do is craft revisions to the Proclamation that will appease them without ceding one bit. A show, if you will."

"They'll see through it. As they did the falsified report on the crash—"

"No, Andrew. This youngster Fitton will go along. I believe he implicitly understands formal power sharing will never work. And I surmise that his goal is more immediate, and limited: to shore up his newfound position as leader of the Helderans."

Naughton tried to follow the reasoning. "So you would craft a deal with him?"

"Yes. Exactly. A deal."

Gill jumped in. "But sir, would not a deal need to be reached before the conference? What if he stonewalls?"

The Commissioner nodded. "A true concern, yes. There's no telling. I will make entreaties toward him between now and August 4th. For the moment, though, we have to give him everything he wants that is of little substance. And if that means the opening ceremony of the peace conference finds me standing side by side with Fitton, so be it. That's symbolic but ultimately meaningless." The give-and-take with the old man was taking on a difficult edge, and he saw a pensive furrow rise across Cunningham's forehead.

"Sir, I am not optimistic about this upstart's willingness to accept the meager bones we may throw his way. He will want something of substance. Much as your strategy is appealing, I doubt it will suffice." Naughton hoped his tone was neither scolding nor condescending.

Cunningham pursed his lips then rose from the chair. He placed the tips of the fingers of both hands on the edge of the conference table. "Naughton, I invited you here to provide advice."

"I am doing so."

"Rejecting courses of action is all well and good, my friend. But do you have any alternatives? That is the sort of advice I need."

Naughton shot a furtive glance toward Gill, and knew that the inspector too feared the discussion was veering out of control. He too started to rise. "Commissioner, I do not mean to offend—"

"Stop, Naughton!" the old man shouted. "I asked you a question. Do you have any actual advice for me?"

Naughton bit down on his bottom lip, sighed, then stood and gathered his things. "Yes, Commissioner, I have advice. You should just tell this blengin' Fitton fellow there will be no silly peace conference. Tell him you're busy running two leagues. Tell him you're busy overseeing a vast continent, as you've done for the past 30 years. In other words, sir, just tell him 'no.'"

Lady Lynam stood and pointed at him. "How dare you speak to him thusly! My dear Bartholomew deserves no such disrespect."

"Sit down, Vivian," the commissioner ordered.

"But—"

"Sit down, I tell you. Andrew is as loyal an aide as I could ever hope to find. I don't take his frustrations personally."

She retreated to her seat, clasped the sides of her vest together against her chest and turned away. The old man grabbed his cane, stood and shuffled at a deliberate pace toward the porch of the mechaderm's cabin. He looked out at the immaculate lawn and spoke in a whisper. "But, I am resolute. Prepare for the peace conference, as Coyle outlined."

Naughton bit down on his lower lip. "Very well, sir."

"Oh. Also, see what can be done to get Nellie moving again."

"Sir?"

"I'd forgotten how wonderful she is. I've let her fall into ill health. See what can be done."

Naughton cast a stern look at Lynam, who avoided it. "Yes, sir. We will see."

Gill extended the collapsible wooden stairs at the far side of the cabin and the trio made their way down the elephant's side.

Naughton, the last of the three to exit, could hear the old man muttering as they departed: "Nellie. My sweet Nellie. I have failed you."

As they walked across the plush lawn, Naughton looked back at the massive device. The black bead of its left eye glistened in the sunlight, and for a moment it seemed as if the elephant was winking at him.

AFTER THE GROUP RETURNED TO the league headquarters, Naughton went directly to Coyle's office. "You prepared that plan without my knowledge."

"I thought I had told you."

"No. You did not. And whether I was aware or not, Roderick, I never asked for such planning."

"I apologize, sir. But I was simply trying to be prepared."

"Prepared?"

"Yes, for the possibility that the commissioner would want to proceed with the conference."

"Oh."

"Sir, you have always asked me to be prepared. You have said it is the key to your own longevity in your difficult post."

"Indeed, Roddy. I have."

"I thought I had told you."

Naughton steadied himself against the aide's desk. Exhaustion crept through his back and arms. "Very well. I suppose, then, I should thank you."

Coyle grinned, the smile stretched wide as if in glee. "You're very welcome, sir."

HOURS LATER, NAUGHTON WATCHED FROM his office window as dusk fell across Schawmount City and the League's hundreds of employees filtered out of the building. He leaned back in his chair and clasped his hands, rubbing the palms in a steady rhythm.

Coyle? Does my own aide have ambitions?

On the rear wall of Naughton's office, 18 audiocaster speakers were mounted, six across, three high. They allowed him, at any moment, to listen to the commentary of the games in both Leagues as they were being played — the same commentary now being heard in the plazas and publick houses across the continent. Four games were in progress at this moment, and he kept the volume of those speakers up fully. The voices of the announcers merged into an unintelligible collage. Crandy, sitting nearby, cocked his head as if trying to understand the words.

When Gill arrived, Naughton adjusted the speakers so the din was louder. The building was nearly empty, but he needed to ensure that no one else could hear.

"I need your discretion again, Enoch," he told the security chief.

"Of course, sir."

"I objected to your hiring, but I have come to understand you can be trusted."

"My allegiance is to the commissioner, as is yours, sir."

"Then I hope you will understand when I ask this of you. I need a full report on Lady Lynam."

"Lady Lynam?" The Monystian stammered. "Vi- Vivian Packer Lynam? But wh—"

Naughton waved him off. "Please do so. No questions."

The inspector nodded, though with a despondent gaze. Naughton understood the Monystian's reaction: Vivian Packer Lynam had been there at the very founding of the Leagues, at the formation of the Ceasefire. She'd been at Cunningham's side throughout. She was, to this day, nearly as revered as the old man himself.

"You will need to be discreet, of course. You will need to use outside investigators. Your most trusted."

"Yes, sir."

"No one in the League Office is to know."

"Yes. I understand."

"Including Mr. Coyle." Gill shot another glance of surprise, then departed.

Crandy looked up at him, tail swishing. The miniature flexors that controlled his artificial countenance seemed to mimic Gill's expression. But the servohound wagged and flipped onto his back, enticing Naughton to scratch his belly. He readily complied.

July 17th

ARLY IN THE SEASON, STUDYING the Squirrels' entire schedule, Halloway had circled July 17th. It marked the start of a three-game series in which his squad would host the Rhinos of West Somerchester, and he predicted they would be pivotal games. Now that day had arrived, and Halloway smiled at the notation on the calendar that spread across his desk. He'd been prescient, for the Squirrels now held just a single game lead over the second-place Rhinos in the Helderan South Division.

He stood in the home-team dugout, arms crossed, alongside Gabe Keating. The pair watched the Rhino's starter, the venerable Cornelius Blanchfield, warming up on the mound an hour before the game.

Blanchfield, at 36, was one of the oldest hurlers in either league, and he seemed to have lost only a touch of his fastball to age. He wore a small patch of a beard, a strip of hair from the lower lip down to the base of his chin, and he carried a chip on his shoulder from years of not being taken seriously in the game. He had come into the league with only a modicum of talent, perceived as disposable. Now, though, the ruddy-faced, lanky hurler was midway through his 15th major league season, and he had transformed himself into one of the most reliable starters in the league. Fifteen years: few lasted that long, particularly hurlers. Halloway imagined Blanchfield would just continue on.

His own starter, George "Larry" Skelly, now back tossing in the Squirrels' bullpen, could very well be the next Blanchfield. His first season with the Squirrels, '19, had been disastrous: 0-3, with an earned run average that topped seven. But in each of the succeeding seasons Skelly had steadily improved to the point where now, at 26, he was emerging as the club's ace. It was all finesse; his fastball was so slow it barely skirted past a bat. Yet he had three other solid throws: curveball, slider, and change-up, and all four emerged from his left hand with the same movement, leaving strikers guessing and gasping.

Halloway felt a tap on his shoulder. "Excuse me." Behind him stood a small, older man with a traditional blue, horn-rimmed cap that designated a licensed courier. "I have a communique for Coach Halloway."

"That's me." He opened the envelope. The letter bore the embossed letterhead of the Commissioner's Office and was addressed to him. He read aloud to Keating. "Please inform your players that the League is proceeding with the All-Star Game despite the unsettled political situation. And please present our congratulations to the Flying Squirrels' two representatives in the game: Ketter Asgar and Pyce Marsh. We trust they will be proud to display the silver and gray as the Helderan teams do symbolic battle with their counterparts in Setheridge."

He tried masking a grimace. Pyce and the Count: the very two whose pairing he most feared.

Keating nudged his elbow and pointed upward. An airship droned over Catalinaside Stadium. Halloway cringed. "I thought airships were prohibited over ballparks now," said the hurling coach.

"They are." The Commissioner's Office, immediately after the 30th Anniversary Celebration disaster, had expressly banned any airships before, during, or after games.

"Whose is it?"

Halloway scowled. "Take a close look." Keating squinted as they both mouthed the three words bannered across both sides of the slow-moving craft: "Heldera. For Helderans."

"Fitton."

"Yes," replied Halloway. "He's blatantly flouting the dictates of the commissioner."

"Why? Cunningham agreed to the peace conference. Why would Fitton agitate?"

"Because he can."

"Oh. Oh my."

"Yes, exactly."

Blanchfield finished his warm up with a nasty slider that flew into the strike zone, then dropped straight to the dirt. The catcher missed it entirely and the ball skittled back to where Halloway and Keating were standing. Halloway threw it back and tipped his cap toward the veteran hurler. Blanchfield returned the acknowledgment with a wave. *Good guy, wish we had him.* Then all four looked up as the shadow of the airship enveloped the field.

"Good game today," Langford offered. "Skelly looked sharp."

While Halloway's own office was in the stadium's bowels, Langford's was at

mid-level, buried back behind the kiosks of the concessionaires and merchandisers. The general manager cleared a chair of paperwork and offered it to him.

"That he was. I could have left him longer, but with that kind of lead, there's no need. I'd rather keep him fresh."

"What's his innings projection at this point?"

Innings counts: it was a relatively new concept for the leagues of the SIP and ALE. Teams routinely kept to a four-man rotation, and it was not unheard for starters to hurl upward of 250 or more innings per season. Lately, some of the general managers wanted the young starters coddled with strict innings limits, Langford increasingly so. Halloway abhorred the concept, but found he had no choice but to defer to the general manager's predilections. "I hope to keep him under 200. He went 191 last year."

Get to the point, he chided himself. *Now is the time.*

A deep breath, and then: "Eldon, I'm concerned about the Count."

"Ketter?"

"Yes."

"Why? His innings count seems fine."

"No, about his... his, um, reliability."

Langford cocked his heads sideways in confusion.

"On the mound?"

"No, off. Off the field."

"How so?"

"He is, uh..." Another breath. "Over the course of the season he has expressed to me strongly held beliefs about the need for Helderan autonomy."

"Yes. So? Many of us do. As do many Setherians. What of it?"

"I know you preferred I handle the aftermath of the fistfight myself. But Eldon, perhaps I should have come to you then. That fight between the Count and the Kid was about politics, not baseball."

"Excuse me?"

"Politics."

"Are you certain?"

"Yes. I grilled them both afterward. Separately."

"And?"

"And Marsh said that Asgar was talking about... about hurting fans."

"Hurting—" Langford lurched forward from behind his cluttered desk. *"Hurting* fans?"

Halloway nodded. "Yes. But the boy offered no more details than that. No specifics."

The general manager drummed his fingers on the wooden desk and stared intently out the window behind Halloway. Dusk had arrived, the game was complete, and the ballpark had long since emptied. Langford spoke in a hushed tone, as if worried he'd be overheard. "You should have come to me immediately. Why the hell didn't you—"

"I tried. You cut me off."

"What are you talking about?"

"After the fistfight. You made clear to me that you did not want to hear it."

"Sander, I don't know what you're talking about."

The manager stopped short of escalating the exchange. There was no point. Langford, he knew, would merely continue to feign ignorance.

Eldon Langford stood and walked toward the window. It faced out to a large dusty dirt lot that just hours ago held hundreds of horse carriages. He was 65 years old and had served as a general manager of teams in both the SIP and ALE Leagues for 28 years — an amazing run. First in Powlet Creek Summit in the ALE, then his first SIP stop — five seasons running the Binney Foxes. Next to Blue Square, Red Tummlyn and, finally, hired in '16 by Squirrels owner Willison Caffrey to run the prized franchise in Widmertown.

Halloway had been the team's striking coach at the time, and the two struck up what had seemed to be a strong friendship, so much so that a year later Langford promoted him to manager.

Only twice during that 28-year span did any of Langford's teams make the play-offs, and never had he been to the Continental Series. Nothing to show for the years of late-night worrying, deadline trading, and contentious contract negotiations.

Halloway watched the general manager at the window. This season could end Eldon Langford's personal drought. Approaching the All-Star Break, the squad had a solid five-game lead in the always-competitive Helderan South Division. Their rotation of four hurlers was dominant. The offense was balanced and productive. They lead the league in many statistical categories. Though no one but scribes would deign to say this aloud, the 1923 Widmertown Flying Squirrels had the distinct air of champions.

But a championship was threatened by the burgeoning turmoil — both within the clubhouse and across the continent.

The general manager turned back to face him. "So the two of them — the two of them *alone* — will be traveling to and appearing in the All-Star Game."

"Unfortunately, yes."

"And if anything were to happen, it would likely be at the very game. The owners will be in attendance, the peace conference will be underway, and fans of both nations will be listening on the audiocasters."

"I suppose we must notify the league," Halloway offered.

"We can't. Not now."

Halloway grimaced. "But—"

"We're in contention. We're likely to qualify for the play-offs. We can't endanger that."

"But—"

"You've put me in a difficult spot, Sander. Two months ago it would have been far simpler."

"I'm sorry, sir."

"Yes, Sander. So am I."

Langford sat back down and ran his hands over the blotter that covered his desktop. Halloway could see that the August page was festooned with scribbled notes — dollar figures, names, reminders. The minutia of running a ball club.

"You will go to the All-Star Game," the general manager proclaimed after a few silent minutes. "You will accompany our two players. And for the whole of those three days, you will never take your eyes off Ketter Asgar."

July 23

Schawmount City

"WE NEED TO FIND JELLUM."

"'Tis no easy task."

"That is quite evident."

"But I think this may help."

The Monystian inspector sat directly across from Naughton, holding a stack of binders, each of which seemed to hold hundreds of pages.

"What is it, Enoch?"

"This," said Gill, "is the trail that I believe will take us to your evasive suspect."

The security chief grimaced as he hoisted the pile directly onto Naughton's already cluttered desk. "But I will need several hours to explain it to you. It is quite complex."

Naughton nodded. Exhaustion had enveloped him hours ago. Amelia, no doubt, had long since given up hope that he'd return home for a late dinner. A few more hours would not matter.

It was past 10 in the evening. Though most of his staff had been working long hours to prepare for the peace conference, Naughton believed everyone had gone. The building, usually a frenzy of activity, was dark and desolate. Crandy sat perched at the door, ready to offer an early warning if someone should approach.

"It starts," said the inspector, "with Lady Vivian Packer Lynam. Three weeks ago you asked that I investigate her."

"Yes."

"I think your misgivings are not without substance."

"In what sense?"

"That's the problem. I can't say precisely. She disappears from view for long periods of time. Even my best operatives have trouble tracking her without losing cover."

"And Lord Bart continues to give her access?"

"Absolutely. That is perhaps the only sustained period when we are able to observe her whereabouts. She has apartments in both Kern and Schawmount City. Yet there are many times when she is in neither place."

"And that is what bothers you?"

"In part. There is a secretive quality to all of her dealings. She is quite popular in the social circles, both Setherian and Helderan, yet no one quite knows her. We certainly don't."

"Indeed."

"So I began trying to examine her sources of income. I knew the League paid her a stipend; Cunningham had apparently insisted on that years back, on the notion that she was one of his personal advisers. And that money is still allocated in the League budget, a nominal amount."

"Yes. I have long been aware of those payments. Some might object to it in principle, but no one could argue that it is excessive."

"But I did an exhaustive review of miscellaneous league expenditures in the past year, and found four other payments to Lady Lynam — substantial ones."

"Substantial?"

"Yes, on the order of six figures each."

"Precisely how much?"

"Seven million yore in the last 12 months."

"Seven million?" The alarm in Naughton's voice escalated.

"But there is more, sir. Other suspicious payments were made."

"To whom?"

"To a series of holding companies in Heldera. I have not yet had the chance to determine the true ownership of those companies. I have, though, traced them to other sham corporations."

"And those amounts?" Naughton by this point was almost afraid to hear the answers.

"More than 20 million yore over the course of the past year."

Naughton swallowed. "That can't be."

"It is, and how this was accomplished is quite ingenious." said Gill. He flipped open the first of the binders and began turning pages. "Let me show you."

———————————

SPECKS OF SUNLIGHT GLITTERED THROUGH the blinds of his office by the time the Monystian was complete. The proof, though detailed and often arcane, was irrefutable. League money was being funneled through a chain of little-known and most likely bogus corporations. Dozens of payments made over the past two years, most of it channeled through eight sham businesses, each of which was related to one of the three holding companies.

"This is money laundering."

"Yes, sir. Pure and simple," Gill replied.

Nausea overcame him. Naughton was, among so many other things, responsible for the finances of the Commissioner's Office. Yes, there was a position of Director of League Monies, but he had seen three accountants come and go within the past four years, and the position was currently unfilled. Moreover, the Commissioner's Office was ostensibly a non-profit operation, existing only to maintain overall function of both leagues, and its costs were borne equally among all the SIP and ALE team owners. And while those owners ostensibly would review those accountings, in reality the teams were so profitable that no owner — not even those from Heldera — had bothered to raise questions, let alone demand an external audit.

"And you cannot yet ascertain who carried this out?"

"No. Until you allow me to openly question other League employees, including those in the Department of League Monies, I will be unable to tell."

"And we cannot do that, at least not now, because it would reveal our own suspicions—"

"And alert those who are complicit. Including, potentially, Lady Lynam. And sir, keep in mind there might be more. It took my best men three weeks to trace through this, and yet several branches of the trail remain unresolved. Given more time, we might uncover additional convoluted paths."

"Do any of the paths thus far link to Phangorious Hood? To the Magera?"

"That's difficult to determine," the Inspector replied. "It is hard to imagine that Hood doesn't have his hands in some part of this. But I've yet to ascertain a specific, tangible connection. If he is involved, he's been quite crafty."

The two sat silently for several minutes. Naughton felt his hands tremble, his back stiffen. Thirst overwhelmed him. A particular type of thirst. He reached into the lowest of three drawers. Deep in the back was a barely touched bottle of Helderan whiskey. He had no glasses, and so motioned the bottle toward Gill as an invitation to drink.

"No, thank you, sir. I'm on duty."

"No, you're not. You need to go get some sleep. One shot."

The Monystian shook his head, the dark dreadlocks cascading at his shoulders. He was resolute.

So Naughton opened the cap and indulged. It was top-shelf whiskey, distilled in the Helderan city of Pear Falls, and it flowed down his throat like a salve. Another drink, and he closed his eyes.

Until now, he had viewed the chaos of the past four months as the result of circumstances beyond his control. He was not so self-critical to fault himself for the airship crash and the emergence of Alexander Fitton. But this— this was entirely within his control and he had failed miserably: money laundering, right under his own nose.

"I am glad you're here, Enoch Gill."

"I hope that is the case, Andrew Naughton. For I, like you, want this league to survive."

A third drink from the bottle, and then he sat upright. "Go ahead, Gill. Ask your questions."

"Sir?"

"I know that any good investigator uncovering this sort of money trail would start at the top. And you are obviously not starting with the commissioner. So start with me. Ask your questions."

"There's no need."

"Why?"

"You are beyond reproach, Andrew Naughton. I don't need to pepper you with questions to know that. But then…" His voice trailed off, and he looked away.

"Then what?"

"I have no such faith in your own assistant."

Gill's eyes told him the rest. *Coyle.*

A well of anger rose up like a squall. "Damn it!" With a single motion he stood, lurched forward and shoved the stack of black binders, the damnable evidence, off the desk. Some binders flew against the wall, the clasps that held their contents snapping open, dozens of sheets cascading into the air and then floating, almost peacefully, to the ground.

Gill did not flinch.

Naughton collapsed into his chair and spoke softly. "I give you… I give you permission to interrogate Roderick Coyle."

The security chief stood and began gathering the papers from the floor. "We will conduct that questioning together, sir. He must understand that I am doing it with your knowledge and assent."

"Fine."

"But there is more."

"More? Isn't the possibility that Coyle himself has been part of a vast conspiracy enough?"

Gill, like most Monystians, was a good seven footlengths tall, and now as he rose from his crouched position his figure seemed to blot out the illumination of the room's two gas lamps, casting a shadow fully across the now-emptied desk.

"Before we question your assistant, sir, you need to go directly to the person who is most capable of orchestrating this sordid financial dance."

They looked directly at one another. There was no need for Gill to speak the name. Naughton understood.

"I will go," he told the Inspector. "After the All-Star Game. After the damnable peace conference."

"No, sir. This cannot wait."

"But I need this time to—"

"We have no time, sir."

Crandy, who had remained at alert at the doorway throughout the hours of Gill's briefing, looked at his master. Naughton sighed and wiped his brow. "Very well. I will leave tomorrow morning. We will deal with Coyle when I return."

"And these, sir?" Gill held out the stack of binders. The evidence. The money trail.

"Lock them in your vault. Take your investigators off the matter until I return."

"Indeed, sir."

The security chief turned and retreated to the hallway, binders in hand. When the door closed, Naughton leaned back in the chair, scratched the scruff of Crandy's neck, and finished the remainder of the soothing whiskey.

July 25

In transit

THERE WAS NO SIMPLE WAY to get to Gregorson from Schawmount City. That was probably for the better.

Naughton could have gone by airship, certainly, but that method was far too public. He could not risk being noticed.

Instead, Gill had plotted a convoluted itinerary, and Naughton traveled by a series of obtuse connections involving hired carriages, cable cars, and public buses. Every detail of the trip — the arrival and departure times, the route numbers, the addresses, the contacts — had to be memorized; Naughton left the paperwork behind lest it somehow fall into the wrong hands. He carried nothing save a change of clothes.

He set out before dawn, traveling from Schawmount southwest to Finchenland and then to Tillbrookson Bluff. His route then swung south again and east, to the most southern tip of the nation of Setheridge in New Ungerapolis. A ferry carried him across the Valencroft River, docking in LaValleyford Prairie, where he had stayed the night, finally, to get some rest.

Now he was on the final leg, riding in the bumpy coach of a cable car that made an early morning run to Gregorson. He was dressed in a working man's dark overalls, with a broad dark cap that masked his eyes. He had not shaved since the planning had begun, and a nearly full beard encased his jawline and cheeks. If he happened upon any reporters, or even Helderan officials, he doubted he could be recognized.

He sat between two heavyset women in gray working dresses. One snored loudly and he felt her weight shift against him. The woman on the other side, perhaps an acquaintance, found his discomfort amusing and struggled to suppress a laugh. But he dare not speak to her; she might recognize his non-native accent, his educated diction. He could easily be revealed as someone other than what his garb implied: a Helderan laborer commuting to a factory shift.

The hour-long ride ended with a discomforting lurch, and the sleeping woman jerked awake, prompting her friend to explode in laughter. "Ah, Crelly," she cried, "you ought to try sleeping at home instead of on strangers."

With that, both women laughed, and Naughton could do nothing but acknowledge them with a polite grin. "You don't say much," said the one-time sleeper, now studying his face. "I haven't seen you riding here before, have I?"

He shook his head.

"Do you talk?"

He pondered a response, then decided to feign confusion by simply shrugging. "Crelly," called the other. "We got here a shy boy or a mute!"

"Or both!" The two erupted in another round of guffaws.

The next stop, thankfully, was his, and he tipped his hat to both ladies and gathered his bag. Out into the sunlight he stepped, onto the streets of Gregorson.

It was a bustling city teeming with factory-bound workers and effusive merchants. One of the oldest cities on the continent, and set in its ways. The muddied streets and crumbling red brick storefronts were testaments to that.

He walked for a good half hour. Men with dusty leather jackets and caps pulled to eye level hurried down the roads, passing heavyset women in gray smocks dragging empty shopping carts. Small groups huddled near the entrances of alleyways, playing games of chance and warming their hands near kettle fires. Rusty servohounds scurried in the alleyways, and a few could seen chasing equally decrepit half-butlers and wait-tables, all long abandoned by owners too uncaring to deprogram the devices. The air was gray and had a mildly rancid odor. The streets broke open in spots and steam spewed out in bursts.

During the Insurrection, the city had been the primary manufacturing base for the Helderan war effort, but though its economy thrived, the city itself never seemed to benefit. Most profits were easily retained by the small group of metal barons, including Doctor Granville Chanley, who would go on to become owner of Gregorson's SIP League team, the Monkeys. The natives of the city, the tens of thousands throughout the southern region, those who suffered through the five decades of warring, never saw a doubleweight of that money. So now the streets were lined not with gravel and cobblestones, but filth and refuse.

Eventually, Naughton made his way to the port section of the city, a series of wooden wharfs and docks where the waters of the Aspil Sea slapped up against the fishing boats. Here his memorization of the street plan would be most tested, for he continued at a steady pace through a series of small alleys that seemed to spring out of nowhere. Right, then left, then left again, and another right. At one point — the alley seemingly vacant — he took a moment to lean against a dusty wall. It was partly to catch his breath, partly to be certain no one had followed him.

He waited a solid two minutes. He did not hear a sound. He stepped forward and began to walk— then abruptly stopped. Listening. All was still quiet. He suddenly swung around 180 degrees. No movement.

He was almost there.

Two more alleys, then a quick set of steps to a storefront below grade. A pawn shop, seemingly long shuttered. This was the place, he knew.

Naughton checked his timepiece and realized he was an hour early. No matter. He had arrived, and his task was at hand. He sat down on the lowest step, virtually out of sight from any passerby. And he waited.

———————— ————————

THIRTY MINUTES LATER HE HEARD steps inside the dingy storefront, and a lamp was lit. It had begun to rain, and above him a torn awning pooled water, releasing a steady drip near his head.

A pair of eyes peered out from behind a lace curtain, and then the door popped open a touch.

He gave his name and was ushered inside.

The greeter was, like most Rebular, thick armed and broad shouldered. He was young, perhaps 22 or so, and substantial in height, with a pale, yellow complexion and black locks that flowed over his shoulder. He clasped the end of some sort of weapon under his black linen cloak. He motioned to Naughton to sit on a bare wooden stool, and then watched him from atop a taller stool without comment.

More time passed, and the two avoided each other's gaze. The waiting felt tortuous.

Finally a newcomer entered. "I trust your journey was without incident?"

Naughton stood and extended his hand. "Yes, sir. Without incident and, to the best of my knowledge, without notice."

"Very well," said Phangorious Hood. "Let us repair to my office."

The guard stood close by as the Magera leader led him to a back room. Inside, Naughton found a sparsely decorated chamber, with threadbare drapes blotting out the light. The chairs at least offered more comfort than the stools of the waiting room.

"I'm sure you could use some food and drink," Hood offered. "I will have my staff prepare us a meal, and then we can talk."

Naughton demurred. "My utmost apologies, Mr. Hood. League business dictates that my stay be brief, and I'd prefer we get to the matter at hand." He knew the Magera admired tact and efficiency, so he had no worries that Hood would take offense.

"At least let them bring us a drink, to toast to the health of the Twin Nations."

"That would be most welcome."

Naughton studied the man — a craggy lined forehead, narrow and widely separated green eyes with no lashes, a broad nose and pale lips. Like most Rebular, he had straight, dark hair that flowed down to the middle of his back. Four rings — two on each hand — glittered even in the dim light, illuminating long nails. A diamond pierced his right nostril. While millions knew his name, few in either country would recognize his face. He remained out of sight — a cipher, an enigma. His anonymity no doubt helped account for his longevity, and certainly increased his mythical status across the continent.

Phangorious Hood: the name was synonymous with the Magera. Leaders of most cities and towns loathed the sort of low-level crime in which the Magera specialized: numbers games, fencing of stolen goods, counterfeiting, high-interest loans, gambling and the like. But they also knew that the stability of Hood's leadership brought order to those activities. So long as Phangorious Hood remained, the sidewalks would stay relatively clear of blood. And he was able to capitalize on that fear in a very real way; the financial tributes he demanded of city leaders were seen as payments toward peace.

Hood leaned forward, smiled broadly and offered Naughton a small glass of Rebular gin.

"To the peace," he toasted.

"To the peace," Naughton responded, and their glasses touched.

"Commandant, Commissioner Cunningham sends his most heartfelt appreciation for this meeting."

"Please, Mr. Naughton. Surely you know that 'Commandant' is a title created by the press. It is not one I adopt, nor is it one I care for."

"My apologies. No offense was intended."

"No matter."

Naughton swallowed. "Sir, as you know this is a most difficult time. Suspicions between the Setherian and Helderan peoples are greater than ever in the wake of the airship crash. The incident is playing on the pervasive fears of Setherians that the Helderans plan another uprising, that they seek control over the entire continent. The Helderans, meanwhile, fear that the crash will be used as an excuse by the Setherians to strip their nation of its sovereignty and return their race to its second-class status."

Hood took it all in and nodded slowly. "All this I've heard. I don't envy you, Andrew Naughton. You do face a veritable tinderbox."

"Yes."

"So you come to us."

"Well, Mr. Hood, I'm sure you are concerned about the matter as well. A return to continental strife would do your business no good."

"Perhaps." The Magera leader grinned and leaned back, studying his lengthy nails. "A wartime economy can be strong indeed, particularly for enterprises such as mine."

Naughton weighed his words carefully. "The commissioner, as you know, sir, has always been quite willing to afford you a great degree of latitude over the past many years."

"And for that, Lord Bart has always had my gratitude."

"It would be mutually beneficial, then, if you could assist us at this time to stave off a more precarious situation."

The Magera leader poured another shot glass full of the gin, downed it without flinching, and then glared at Naughton. "Get to the point, sir. What is the assistance that the commissioner seeks?"

"Of course. Stated simply: we have isolated a series of significant payments from League offices through a matrix of what are likely to be bogus corporations."

Hood twisted at a lock of his flowing hair. "And you come to accuse me of orchestrating it?"

"It bears the hallmarks of the Magera, sir."

"And the airship crash? Are you here to blame me for that as well?"

"There are many who openly speculate that the Magera were involved."

"And what do you tell them?"

"I tell them that the Magera would lose too much if the Ceasefire collapsed. Dare I say its fortunes — and, of course, your personal fortunes — have flourished in peacetime."

"An astute observation."

"I only hope for both our sakes that it proves accurate, Phangorious Hood."

"You have my assurance. I am too old, too set in my ways, to start upsetting all that I've worked to build — even if a war economy might ultimately prove more lucrative."

Hood looked over at two aides who hovered in the corner of the dark room nearest the door, then nodded. Naughton watched the duo retreat through the doorway to the outer room.

Hood looked at Naughton's empty glass and raised the bottle toward him. Naughton nodded.

"To prosperity," Hood offered as a second toast.

"To peace," Naughton countered.

They drank and Hood laughed. "Thankfully, Naughton, the two are not mutually exclusive."

"In fact, ideally they are inclusive."

"So then how can I help you?"

"I need you to find Hardwin Jellum. I need to find him and unravel this ungodly mess."

"Have not your own security officials been able to find this varmint? I thought you had that Monystian, what was his name—"

"Gill. Inspector Enoch Gill."

"Yes, Gill. Hasn't he been able to locate the conspirators?"

"Unfortunately, no."

"Because…?"

"Because he and his staff must abide by traditional, dare we say legal, means of investigation. And those means have thus far proved fruitless."

"Ah. What a shame."

"And we recognize that your staff has means of extracting information without being bound by those restrictions. In addition, we have little faith that locating

Jellum through traditional means could be kept from the ever-prying eyes of the press."

"Ah, yes, those persistent reporters. Couldn't Lord Bart just lock them all up?"

"I only wish."

"And what makes you think I am able to help you?"

Oh, I am so tired of this, Naughton thought. *Must everyone engage in endless gamesmanship?* But he kept the frustration to himself. Control was vital. "Mr. Hood, it has been a grueling several months. I need you to find Hardwin Jellum. We both know you have that capacity. We both know I would not turn to you if I was not in dire need. There is a complicated conspiracy amid all the posturing, the grandstanding. I need to unravel it."

Phangorious Hood rose and went to the small window, pulled back the gray curtain and studied the grayer sky outside the narrow window. The chilled rain continued to fall on Gregorson City, and Naughton imagined later he'd be returning across muddier streets. He wondered if his shoes and pants would survive the journey home.

"You realize, Andrew, that such an endeavor carries great risk. Both in terms of manpower… and risk to my own reputation."

Naughton said nothing but arched an eyebrow. The idea of Hood being worried about his reputation seemed preposterous. People feared him.

"In fact, I could face a downturn in my various sources of income should it become known that I'm working at the behest of the League."

"Oh. I see."

"So I need to know precisely, Mr. Naughton, how the commissioner would intend to show his appreciation."

This is where he extracts his price. "What would you consider fair compensation?"

"Hmm." Hood furrowed his brow in mock consideration. "Well, for one, there is the little matter of the ferry."

"The ferry?"

"The Valencroft River Ferry. It strikes me that the League runs it quite inefficiently."

"Oh?"

"Yes. I've never quite understood why League employees must staff it."

Naughton was tired, and he saw no need to partake in this particular dance. Gill had predicted that Hood's price would be control of a substantial business operation. The ferry line, which crisscrossed the river with routes among ten cities, from McKinmond Lakes in the north to New Ungeropolis in south, was precisely that. "It's yours."

Hood smiled. "And perhaps privatization of the lift operation at Tillbrookson Bluff—"

Naughton waved him off. "That will remain in League control." He stood and reached for his overcoat. There would be no more bargaining. "Mr. Hood, the League has its All-Star Break in 10 days, at which point a supposed peace conference will convene. We need answers, and soon. What should I tell the commissioner when he asks for a date of delivery of your findings?"

The Magera leader rose as well. "I will need three weeks. If I can get this done sooner, so be it. I doubt this will take longer."

"Two weeks and the ferry route is yours, Hood."

Hood grinned, revealing several gold caps on his teeth. "So it shall be."

Naughton extended his hand and allowed himself one moment of informality. "Your gin is quite the elixir, Phangorious Hood. I trust that you find that a profitable operation as well?"

Hood accepted the handshake. "Indeed. In fact, your Setherian brothers in Schawmount City are among my greatest customers."

"Of that I have no doubt."

The guards returned to the room to escort him out. Their hands still clasped, Naughton leaned toward Hood so the minions would not hear. "I need Jellum alive, Hood. Dead does me no good."

The Magera leader grinned. "Dead does very few people any good, Andrew Naughton."

Naughton released the handshake and made his way up to the outer office, then through the nondescript front door of the equally nondescript storefront. On the stoop he readied himself to navigate the port city's decrepit streets, and as he turned he heard from below a wave of laughter. A bellowing, rapturous laughter.

He shuddered and moved on.

———

His return to Schawmount City involved a route just as circuitous and exhausting. It was past midnight of the following night when he arrived in the city limits; past one by the time he made it home. Amelia and the boys, of course, were asleep, but like so many times before, his wife awoke when he entered.

"My god." She was aghast to see his condition: unkempt, greasy hair, a beard

that had only gotten more foreboding during the trip, reddened eyes, a jacket ragged with dust and pants muddied to the knee.

"Yes. I know."

Amelia sat him down, kissed his forehead, and ordered him to change. When he returned she wrapped him in a robe and grabbed the piles of clothes. "I drew a bath."

Naughton moved slowly to the washroom and settled in to the warm, sudsy water that filled the tub. Part of him hoped she'd come in, as he missed her terribly. But he also needed quiet. Desperately.

Eventually, he emerged, clean but exhausted. Amelia had already returned to bed but was not asleep, and he settled in next to her, soaking in the smell of her hair. She rested her head on his shoulder and studied his hands. "Can you tell me about the trip?"

"No. No, I can't."

She pulled back. His wife worried constantly, he knew, about every aspect of his job, about the boys. But her level of anxiety, like so many, had escalated greatly in the wake of the airship crash. He stroked her fine hair and stumbled for some soothing words. "My heartkind, it is better this way. It is better that you not know."

She scowled in the darkened room. "Don't let our boys down, Andrew Naughton. They depend on you too much. Don't get yourself into something that has no good outcome."

"I won't," he promised. But as he drifted off into sleep he wondered if in fact he already had.

August 4

West Somerchester

THE 36 OWNERS OF THE Leagues of SIP and ALE arrived for the peace conference within the space of two hours. Naughton spied their carriages proceeding past Rebaley Field — home park of West Somerchester Rhinos, where the All-Star Game would be staged in just two days — to the Cotillion Plaza Hotel, five blocks away.

He watched the parade of gilded carriages from a slit of a window in a

narrow office at the ballpark. The room had been loaned to him by the Rhino's general manager, Newton Langstaff. Coyle remained at the hotel, to assist the commissioner during the lengthy greetings. Naughton imagined the tortuous arrivals of the owners. The Setherians, as was their nature, would go through a show of pleasantries and mock affection. The Helderans would remain dour and grim.

Naughton sighed. It would be a long three days, and he was already exhausted. At least Gill was there, watching over all, including Coyle himself.

When all the carriages had passed the field, he returned to his planning. The opening ceremony — in the Cotillion ballroom — would feature three speakers, Lord Bart, thankfully, not among them. First would be the Rhino's owner, Morren Godwyn, speaking as host. Neutrally, Naughton hoped.

Next, speaking for the Setherians, would be the Lizards' owner Benedict Cheesley. Naughton fretted; he had requested an advance copy of Cheesley's remarks, but none had been forthcoming. True, Cheesley was usually reliable, but this was too important an event not to review the comments ahead of time. Every word would be parsed and dissected by both the press and the Helderans. He made a notation on his agenda.

Speaking third would be the newly anointed Helderan Executive, the man who had insisted on this conference, Alexander Fitton. Naughton had not even bothered asking for that speech in advance.

A messenger knocked and stepped in. The borrowed office was really not much bigger than a supply closet, and the boy wedged his way between the door and a file cabinet to hand Naughton a small card with a handwritten note.

Fitton wanted to meet him in one hour, at the Valencroft Inn, a small hotel on the docks of West Somerchester, far from the Cotillion and the hordes of reporters.

———————

Halloway traveled by ferry to the mainland, disembarking at the port at Hot Bear Bend and then hopping on a cable car to West Somerchester. He passed the time studying notes and scouring broadsheets tossed aside by other passengers. But it was difficult to concentrate.

Asgar and Marsh were already in West Somerchester, though according to the team's traveling secretary, the two players had traveled separately. Even better, the secretary had arranged it so they would not share a room. That the two stars would not be in close quarters came as an immense relief.

The cable car station in West Somerchester was overflowing with commuters and tourists, and Halloway doffed his hat to ladies and the elderly as he made his way through the crowd. West Somerchester Station served a host of southern Helderan cities: Kern, Hot Bear Bend, Buck Falls Heights, LaValleyford Prairie and, further south, near the tip of the mainland, Gregorson. It was equally a gateway to Setherian cities, with links by tram over the Valencroft River to New Ungeropolis, Red Mine, Tillbrookson Bluff, Finchenland, and northeast of that, Schawmount City.

At the station's west side he passed through a high, arched entranceway leading to the streets. Halloway scowled; no cabs were in sight. So he began to walk; the Brigand Arms Hotel, where he was staying, was a good half hour away, even at a brisk pace.

A typical West Somerchester breeze, warm yet biting, washed over him. The sidewalks were nearly as crowded as the station: Kern may have been the titular capital of Heldera, but West Somerchester was its economic and social hub. Its office buildings stood grand and tall, some reaching ten stories. Residents never found themselves in want of shopping and fine foods. And now, with the All-Star Game approaching, the city gleamed as scores of visitors arrived from all regions of the continent.

In the eastern sky he saw the broad and towering range of the Pargerveron Mountains, the peaks encased in clouds. He'd climbed them once, as a child of 12. The memory made him shudder.

It was 1873. The Helderan forces had already claimed much of the southern region, and the ruling military council began encouraging families to leave the security of Heldera Island for this newly held portion of the mainland. Few went. Few trusted that it was safe. But his father, Blanton Halloway, by then a retired and decorated ex-lieutenant, had insisted on doing so as a show of support to his former generals, as a statement to unwilling friends and neighbors that Helderans needed to quickly embrace this land as their own.

So that August, Blanton bundled up Sander and his younger brother, Stepp, for hiking and climbing in the war torn mainland. Their mother Bryana agreed to join them only when it became clear that Blanton would neither come to his senses and stay home nor leave the children home with her.

This was 50 years ago. A full 20 years before the ceasefire. Making their way to Culbertson, the small town at the base of the primary mountain trail, took five days. They slept in small inns along the way. He still remembered overhearing his

MICHAEL BARBATO-DUNN

parents, arguing in hushed tones after he and his brother were to have fallen asleep. His mother had wanted to turn back. "All this," she had pleaded, "all this for five nights in the mountains? Risking our sons lives? Is this worth it?"

"Bryanna. Someone needs to set the example. The Insurrection isn't fought just by soldiers. It is fought by families. Helderan families. Families who were and are willing to make some sacrifices—"

"Spare me your platitudes, Blanton Halloway. All that matters to me are those boys and you. Do you know how I worried when you were away fighting? Did I tell you how every report of casualties that filtered back to the Island made me want to vomit because I feared your name would be among the dead? I have paid a price for your years of warring. I do not want to be paying a larger price."

Then, silence. Halloway remembered hearing the door to the cabin closing and someone leaving for a time. He imagined it had been his father, but he was never quite sure. Two days and two towns later, a mortar shell exploded five streets from where they'd let a room. That settled the dispute; she'd have no more of it. They would not press on. The journey was over, and they returned home safely.

After that his father became distant and was frequently away from home. It seemed that his parents barely spoke. Only when the two brothers started playing baseball, and began to excel at the sport, did Blanton re-emerge. By then Halloway didn't care.

He now traipsed through the heart of the city, crossing several streets before reaching Handelson Plaza, where he would lunch. Carriages meandered over cobblestones, and he dodged puddles and horse droppings. Up the block, across the length of the plaza, he spied that annoying columnist for the *Chronicle*, Ollo Ronnell, the one who had come snooping around six weeks ago after the Asgar-Marsh fisticuffs. Again, his gut tightened. He hoped Ronnell would focus on grander things than the fistfight.

Of course, if Ketter Asgar indeed planned to a disruption, Ronnell would have plenty to write about.

Halloway turned a corner and shot one last glance back at the mountain range. In the many years since the aborted journey, he had traveled his parents' route repeatedly, as a player, then a coach, then a manager. Had it been foolhardy for his father to insist on that journey? Or was he guilty of nothing more than the courage of his convictions?

Even now, Halloway was uncertain.

GILL ACCOMPANIED NAUGHTON TO THE meeting. Fitton, in tuxedo and top hat, dismissed his own voluminous entourage, telling Naughton that he wanted the two of them to speak alone. Gill, ever suspicious, was not pleased, but Naughton waved him off, and the door to the hotel room closed.

"Andrew," the Helderan leader said, removing his white gloves and revealing several large rings, "May I call you Andrew?"

"Of course."

"I thought we should meet, Andrew, because you and I are in similar situations. We are both ultimately just deputies to a 30-year-old power structure, a structure that your employer seeks to preserve and that the peoples of both nations seem willing to let continue. So we can, I believe, help each other."

Help each other. The words surged through him. They felt like a lifeline. *Help each other.* He had not, until that moment, fully realized how lost he felt. "Yes, sir. Go on."

"Call me Alex. I understand your dilemma."

"Dilemma?" He feigned confusion, but dilemma was precisely the right word to describe his situation.

"Andrew, I have followed your career for many years, since long before I assumed ownership of the Warthogs. Your loyalty to the Leagues has been nothing short of exemplary."

"Thank you."

"Notice I said 'to the Leagues.' I didn't say 'to the commissioner.'"

"So noted."

"For many people there is no difference. Perhaps for you there is no difference. And for many years, the priorities of the Leagues and the priorities of Lord Bartholomew have been one and the same." The Helderan leaned over to emphasize his point. "But we both know that's no longer the case."

"How do you mean?"

"I know your loyalty to Lord Bart has always been a given. It is part of the very fiber of your being. You have devoted your career, your life, to his continued success. And now for the very first time, you are uncertain of his judgment, his veracity, dare I say his sanity. You are confused. You are perplexed."

Naughton, lips tight, said nothing.

"And you are starting to realize that ensuring peace on the continent does

 MICHAEL BARBATO-DUNN

not necessarily mean ensuring the continued reign of the great peacemaker, Bartholomew Cunningham."

Fitton stopped, waiting for Naughton to offer assent, but Naughton gave none.

"Here's what you are thinking, Andrew: you know that the Twin Nations still harbor those who would prefer a return to fighting. But the greater majority wants a continuation of peace, and they don't know of any way to see the peace other than through the revered Lord Bart."

Again, a pause. "Fine," Andrew offered. "I accept what you have said so far. I admit this is how I feel. What of it?"

"Here is what I came to tell you, Andrew. To tell *you*: the real impediment to having the commissioner step down is not the commissioner."

Naughton cocked his head.

"It is the lack of a good alternative. That is the missing part of the equation. There are no other viable leaders. That is how he was able to readily convince those who staged the border clashes to lay down their arms in June. It is how he maintains strong support throughout both nations despite all the recent bungling.

"That, Andrew, is part of Lord Bart's brilliance. For the past 30 years he has sufficiently identified and defused all potential opposition. Most of those who would seek to succeed him have been easily satiated by the bones he threw them, be it team ownership, franchise agreements, trade deals, lucrative positions. He determines who might pose a threat, determines their price, and buys them. The result is that there is no one who can readily step forward."

Naughton clenched his fists. "Except you?"

Fitton smiled broadly. "With your help, of course, Andrew."

"And what makes you believe you would gain support among Setherians? You are not only Helderan, but you are, with all due respect, little known."

"Because I *am* little known. I am one of the youngest and newest owners. I have no history with the Insurrection. I have no familial ties with those Helderans who first waged war 80 years ago. And many of the Setherian owners understand that the only way to spare the continent another five-decade war is that the next commissioner be a Helderan national."

Naughton maintained a scowl of skepticism. "The owners, perhaps. But the Setherian people are not ready for that, I can assure you."

The Helderan stood and began pacing across the room. "Andrew, have you heard of the Kender Hypothesis?"

"Yes, I'm somewhat aware of it. Some Leadland professor years ago is said to have predicted the airship crash. Talk of it fills the publick houses, I'm sure."

"Yes. In the wake of the airship crash, a good number of people in both nations are hailing him as some great prophet."

"So what of it? He made a series of predictions and one of them proved correct. Even a stopped timepiece—"

"—is correct twice a day, yes, I'm familiar with that. But whether the theory has merit is irrelevant. What matters is that enough people believe it. Kender's theory is that Lord Bart would create a crisis to use as an excuse for rescinding Helderan independence. There are now a good number of people throughout my nation who firmly ascribe to that theory. And only one thing will convince them otherwise." He raised his right index finger and pounded its tip on the table for emphasis. "One thing."

Andrew completed the thought. "An orderly succession to a Helderan owner."

"Yes. Only that will persuade the already skeptical nation that their independence is, even at 30 years, not a temporary ruse."

"And only that," Andrew continued, "will avoid another war."

"Yes. Only that. And only you, Andrew, are in the position to navigate these difficult waters, to convince the old man that the time has come to step down and pass to me control of the Leagues."

The door opened. It was Gill, and he looked toward Naughton.

"Sir, the commissioner has summoned you."

———————

Ollo Ronnell sat at an outdoor cafe on the Handleson Plaza in downtown West Somerchester, sipping a mid-day tonic. The carriage traffic on the eastern end of the plaza was slow moving as hundreds streamed into town. He had booked his room at the Cotillion months ago, when the only reason to be here this week was simply an All-Star Game. Now, with the peace conference suddenly scheduled just prior to the exhibition, the city's grandest hotel was sold out, as were lesser hotels in the city proper, and word was that some reporters were forced to book rooms in the countryside, a good hour-long ride from downtown.

The tonic did little to settle his unease, nor did his cigar. He couldn't recall the last time he'd written a column entirely about baseball, devoid of politics. More than anything that had transpired over the past five months, this saddened him.

Michael Barbato-Dunn

The issues that had engulfed his work and the distance they had taken him from the joy of the sport were, he thought, remarkable. And telling.

So now the upstart Fitton had his peace conference, his chance to claim the continental stage, and there was no telling what he would do. The rumors were rampant, floating through West Somerchester in every hotel bar and publick house: Fitton would threaten war, he would mobilize troops, he would demand complete control of the league. Or, at the very least, he would simply withdraw all Helderan teams from both the SIP and ALE Leagues.

Whether any of it was true, Ronnell hadn't a clue. His sources within the commissioner's office had been unavailable, and those close to Fitton were too afraid even to speak off the record. His attempts to arrange a private session with Fitton also proved fruitless. The new Helderan Executive had not made any public appearances nor granted any interviews since Cunningham had agreed to the conference. He couldn't recall a time when the unfounded rumors so greatly outweighed actual insight into the situation.

Of course, that dearth of facts needn't stop him from writing a piece. That was the dirty little secret about newspaper columnists: they could dash out a column time and again with pure speculation, without talking to a soul. He could do this right now, in fact. But what value did that have? He wanted insight. He had none. He'd simply be guessing, along with everyone else. His stomach churned.

There was one thing of which he was certain: that his attendance at the peace conference greatly increased the likelihood that he would cross paths with Vivian Lynam.

Ronnell crushed the butt end of his cigar into an ash tray, laid a crisp fourthweight on the table, more than enough to cover the bill, replaced his fedora, and made his way up the Plaza toward the hotel. The conference would formally convene in about three hours.

Four blocks later, he stopped in mid-stride. A carriage rounded the corner, toward the Cotillion, and Ronnell spied the face of its occupant. He considered running toward the vehicle to confirm his suspicion.

Instead he froze, mouth slightly agape, and watched as the carriage made its way past the ballpark, toward the hotel, toward the conference that would supposedly bring renewed peace to the Twin Nations, carrying — Ronnell was certain — the famed and feared Magera leader, Phangorious Hood.

———————————

Naughton chose to walk to the hotel, despite the acrid humidity that wafted through West Somerchester. The city sat on the east side — the Helderan side — of the Valencroft River. Yet it also sat on the western end of the Pargerveron Mountain range that stretched across the width of the southern portion of Heldera. As such, the city had two battling climates, and it was not uncommon to become — as Naughton was now — both sweaty and chilled during a single walk. He gripped the lapels of his suit jacket and pressed them to his chest. Crandy trotted alongside him, pleased to have an outing.

It was in the Cotillion's appropriately named 'Commissioner's Suite' that Bartholomew Cunningham was holding court. The old man's primary physician, Morgan Vinge, hovered nearby with two nurses. Lord Bart shooed them out of the parlor with a scowl as Naughton entered and sat down. The servohound lay down at his master's feet, feigning a nap but remaining at high alert.

"Andrew," the old man began. "How long have you been with me?"

"It will be 20 years in a few months."

"Yes. I thought it would be about that. Two decades, and most of the time you've been quietly in the background."

Naughton held silent, unsure where Cunningham was taking the conversation. His collar felt tight.

"Andrew, it was nearly two months ago that you suggested I step down. I greeted that with my usual obstinacy."

At this they both laughed. "I expected nothing less," Naughton said.

"Yes. I know." The old man stood from the plush parlor room sofa and made his way to the east-facing window, where the sun warmed a patch of the carpeting. "You have great patience with me, Andrew Naughton. Don't think I don't recognize that."

"Commissioner, I appreciate your concern. But time is pressing, and I very much need—"

"Oh, stop, Andrew. This peace conference will not work. You know that. The Helderans are unified, and actually my only surprise is that it has taken them this this long to achieve that. Thirty years, Andrew! Do you realize what we accomplished? Three solid decades without a single death attributed to the animosity between the two races."

"What *you* accomplished, sir. I merely accompanied you part of the way."

"But now 30 people have died in the airship crash, we've had border skirmishes — actual warring! — and we still remain unsure if Fitton or one of the other Helderans, or even one of our Setherian friends, was the true culprit."

"Commissioner, I need—"

"Hear me out, damn it! These events have been tumultuous. They have unified the Helderans. They have taken their toll on all the races of the continent. And they even prompted my most loyal assistant to suggest that I step down."

By this point the old man was looking not at him but out the window that faced the hotel's immense courtyard. Naughton saw no way to leave or even to interject. The Commissioner of the Leagues of the SIP and ALE, on the cusp of the meeting of league owners, was lost in an angry reverie.

"Step down! Resign!" Lord Bart swung back to face him and shook his right fist. "Never! And with good reason! To end a war — I did that! To shape an entire world — I did that!" Now the old man was flailing his arms around and stamping his feet. "To create an Eternal Ceasefire — I did that! No one can take that away from me!"

Naughton swallowed hard, then leaned down and whispered to Crandy. The servohound crawled behind the couch and pushed open the door to the anteroom. "And now this little scrap of a man, this Fitton — a boy! a child! — deigns to believe I'm simply going to hand over the reins of power. To him? To the Helderans? He is too young to understand the sacrifices of his fathers, the sacrifices of my generation! My sacrifices!"

The Commissioner moved toward him and pointed his finger. "And you! Do you think I don't understand what you're planning? You claim to be loyal, yet you ever so gently try to push me out the door? To walk away from all I have built? Who are you to decide that, you little… boy! You should be—"

The doctor, two nurses and two house aides rushed in, surrounding him quickly and administering a sedative through a syringe. Crandy followed behind, and Naughton offered the hound a nod of praise.

The medicine's effect was speedy. The commissioner slumped back on the couch and began singing to himself.

Met a Skate River girl who lived 'round the bay
Lucy sang for her dinner and slept in the hay
I fancied her dancing and chased her all day
Where's my Skate River girl who's changing my ways?

Naughton shuddered. The peace conference would begin in less than four hours, and Cunningham had gone in one moment from combative and belligerent — bad enough — to delirious and incoherent. Dr. Vinge looked toward

Naughton and signaled with two fingers: in two minutes the commissioner would be asleep. Naughton acknowledged the signal with a slight nod. Vinge's aides laid the old man on a couch as his singing continued.

That Skate River girl she had little to say
The sun shone in her hair when the sky wasn't gray
She picked flowers in fields and ran back the long way
I married her down at the chapel in May

In the anteroom, with Crandy hovering at his feet, Naughton asked the doctor for an assessment. "I administered a mild elixir. It should wear off in about two hours. He'll probably have a slight headache, but otherwise should be no worse for wear."

"Have you seen these episodes before?"

"Yes."

"Often?"

Vinge twirled one end of his long mustache and pondered the question. "Often is a relative term, sir."

"Don't be difficult. How often?"

"Two or three such episodes a month would not be above the norm."

"How long has this been taking place?"

"The first such episodes were reported to me by house staff approximately three years ago."

"And you didn't tell me?"

"The commissioner is my patient, and he expects and shall receive confidentiality. You are not kin, Mr. Naughton."

"He has no kin. Not even Lady Lynam has legal ties."

"True, not even Lady Lynam."

"Dr. Vinge, it is on your patient's health that the fate of the continent hinges. It is to that concern that you and I both owe allegiance. So from this point forward you are to report to me on every aspect of your patient's health, as if I was his son. Do you understand?"

"I suppose."

"*Do* you understand, Dr. Vinge? Because if not, we can very easily find another general practitioner who would no doubt relish the prospect of being paid handsomely to care for one single patient. So *do* you understand?"

Vinge bit down on his lower lip. "Yes, sir."

With that the doctor departed, trying to mask his scowl, and returned to the parlor to care for Lord Bart. Naughton wiped his eyes, then left the suite, Crandy at his side, as the haunting singing trailed off in the distance.

But come Friday my Lucy was absent all day
I waited 'til dusk, then searched this and that way
Found her dress all in tatters and cried out her name
For a mine got her down near Framingham Bay
Oh, mercy me
Mercy me
Where's that Skate River girl who's changing my ways?
Where's my Skate River girl who is changing my ways?

August 5

WEST SOMERCHESTER

NAUGHTON WATCHED AS WORKMEN ATTACHED league banners to the curtain behind the riser in the Cotillion ballroom. The SIP logo was red and gray, with a baseball at its center, placed over a baseball diamond and covered by the three letters of the league's acronym. Given the propensity of Amandeans to imbibe during the games, the ALE logo was appropriately more festive, with the acronym in white letters over a bright blue background, a baseball below the name, and a frosted mug of ale atop it. The familiarity of their designs was comforting.

Beyond that, the ballroom was bedecked with bright bunting and banners. Coyle had seen to careful and equal distribution of the Helderan national colors of blue and white alongside the Setherian red and gray; such was the level of diplomatic detail required here. A long riser had been positioned in front of the chamber, a podium at the center, and six chairs on either side of it. The bulk of the ballroom was filled with rows of long tables in front of plush wooden chairs. It was enough seating for 200 — the 36 owners of both leagues, aides, league staffers and, of course, the barristers. The negotiators.

Naughton clenched his fists as he spotted Coyle on the riser, adjusting seats and checking schedules. He had not interrogated his assistant about Gill's discovery of apparent money laundering, and he remained unsure if that was even the best course of action. If Coyle was traitorous, if he was in the employ of outside forces, a direct confrontation might risk any opportunity to uncover the true culprits.

For now he would wait, and watch Coyle every possible moment.

The aide stepped down from the riser and waved to Naughton with a broad smile. Such was his constant demeanor: ceaselessly upbeat. Naughton had long found that positive mood a welcome contrast to his own tendency to brood and worry. Their temperaments complemented one another. *Soon enough, he may very well be gone.*

Coyle appeared at his side. "Sir, I believe we are set. The owners are to begin arriving in approximately 30 minutes. The opening remarks begin with Godwyn at noontime, to be followed by Cheesley and Fitton. The press will be allowed in for that portion, and once the speeches are complete, the reporters and any other guests will be escorted from the ballroom. Inspector Gill has supplemented his stable of guards with some temporary hires."

Naughton glanced around to make sure no one was within listening distance. He abhorred talking about security issues in public, but there was no time to retreat to a meeting room. "Will that be sufficient?"

"You can ask Gill yourself. He will have guards at all the doors of the ballroom's front entrance. The key issue will be the side entrances that lead to the hotel kitchen. Guards will be there as well, but it's possible we'll have a dozen or so waiters moving through constantly."

"Have the waiters been vetted?"

"As much as possible. I have also advised Gill to seal the doors if the proceedings…" Coyle struggled for an appropriate word.

"Break down?"

"Yes, break down."

Naughton sat down at one of the tables and looked at his sheaf of notes. *Break down.* There was no way to ward against it. Both the politics and the emotions of the moment were too volatile to lessen the chances of an outright collapse of the conference. The real issue would be how to mask it from the public. Would Fitton provoke a failure that — if made known to the populace of the continent — could very well lead to full-scale warfare? Would he dare?

"The room will be sealed," Naughton announced to Coyle.

"Sir?"

"After the opening remarks, the room will be sealed for the duration of the discussions. We cannot risk leaks to the press. This may very well get ugly, and I don't care to be reading quotes of it in the Chronicle tomorrow or the next day."

"The waiters?"

"I don't trust the vetting. We'll have a buffet set up. The guests will serve themselves."

Coyle stared directly at Naughton and was silent for a lengthy moment.

"Yes, Coyle?"

"Nothing, sir. The room will be sealed."

The aide turned and walked off toward the kitchen to deliver the change of plans. As Naughton watched, he realized that despite their years together, he had never fully felt at ease around Coyle. He had always assumed that it was his aide's youth or that he had never played baseball. That he was with the League not for the love of the game, or devotion to the peace, but rather the pursuit of fortune.

But perhaps he had simply intuited a more insidious trait: the man might be corrupt.

———————————————

OLLO RONNELL PEERED INTO THE ballroom and surveyed the layout. He spotted Cunningham's chief assistant, Andrew Naughton, off in the corner, huddled with the man's own assistant, Roderick Coyle. He considered walking over to press both men for some backroom insight, but then thought better of it. Neither would risk being seen chatting with him in so public a venue before the start of the proceedings.

He turned away from the ballroom and made his way to the location most likely to yield a better sense of what was about to transpire: the hotel bar, to the left of the lobby and past the Cotillion's restaurant. One half hour before the peace conference was to convene, Ronnell wasn't certain if he'd find anyone inside.

But the room was bustling. Cigar smoke wafted above the crowd, distributed by ceiling fans and illuminated by the gas lamps. The din was overwhelming. For a moment he considered leaving and grabbing an early seat in the ballroom. But then he spied a too-familiar face: the Fisher Cats owner Clement Sands, sitting by himself at the far end of the bar. Ronnell caught his eye and waved, and Sands signaled an invitation to join him.

"How is New Ungeropolis treating you, Clem?"

"This is off the record, Ollo." The two laughed. "I know well enough not to start spouting off to a reporter less than an hour before the start of the first peace conference in three decades."

"I'm just hoping you'll be spouting off *after the end of the conference.*"

"Well, that could come sooner than you think. And that's off the record!" They laughed again.

Ronnell waved off the bartender. Though he relished the thought of a brandy, the ceremony would start shortly, and he knew he must remain clear-headed. "But do tell, Clem. You've a better sense of how the other Setherian owners are feeling than most. Are they willing to throw Fitton a concession or two?"

"Off the record?"

"Yes, damn it! Off the record."

"There's a pretty deep divide. The older owners are resistant, and firmly behind maintaining Lord Bart's tenure. The younger ones, the ones who came to own their teams through inheritance or new money, are adamant that only by appeasing Fitton will the Helderans stand down."

"Fine, I see that. But what do they think will appease Fitton?"

"That, Ollo, is the most difficult of questions. How do the younger Setherian owners satisfy Fitton and yet gain the support of the old-line faction?"

"Any ideas?"

The Fisher Cats' owner sipped the last vestiges of his drink. Clement Sands was only 49, younger by 13 years than Ronnell himself, so it would have been easy for him to align himself with the other youthful owners. Indeed, he very well could have gathered support for his own ascendancy to prominence among that faction. But Ronnell knew that, despite his age, Sands was far more inclined to support the old guard. He had inherited the Cats from his father, Tyler Sands, who had been among those most instrumental in coalescing support for Lord Bart's grand plan more than 30 years ago. The elder Sands was, in that sense, one of the founding fathers of the SIP and ALE Leagues. Ronnell presumed that Clement felt to offer anything less than full support for Cunningham at this juncture would be to betray his father's legacy.

The Setherian owner finally answered the newspaperman's question. "There is no good answer to this, Ollo Ronnell. Just as there was no good answer 80 years ago, when the Helderan rebel forces first ignited the Great Insurrection."

"No good answer," Ronnell repeated.

"None, Ollo." Sands shook his head, then threw a doubleweight on the bar and rose to leave. "The only person to ever devise one was His Excellency Bartholomew

Cunningham, when he conceived his idea of using baseball as a way to end the incessant warring."

"His idea," Ronnell repeated. His craving for a drink intensified.

"Yes, of course, Lord Bart's idea. But it may prove to have a limited life span." Ronnell turned away.

Sands's hometown, New Ungeropolis, was the southernmost Setherian city, and the mindset, Ronnell knew, was often far different than in the chillier climes of the central and northern lands. It was, very much, a beach town, a leisure town. The Fisher Cats were a terrible team — they had finished last in the Setheridge South Division for three of the last four years, had never won a Continental Series and, in fact, had not even made the play-offs since '09. Yet the residents loved the team with a passion that dwarfed the fanaticism of any city across the whole of the continent. The Setherians of New Unergopolis had little taste for ugly matters.

Such as war.

Such as politics.

And Ronnell sensed that Clement Sands's appreciation of that mindset was what shaped his approach, perhaps even more so than the long shadow of his father. "So we should be pleased the Ceasefire held for even this long?" the columnist asked.

Sands stood and retrieved his overcoat and folio. "Indeed. It has been foolhardy to expect that a silly little sport could stave off our warring nature forever. I shall see you at the peace conference, Ollo Ronnell." He stressed the word 'peace,' drenching it in sarcasm. "Best not be late."

——————————— ———————————

Naughton raised his right hand slightly and signaled to staffers in the front of the room. Then: fanfare from four buglers ceased conversations and prompted a smattering of polite applause. On the riser in front of the ballroom four men entered, announced one at a time by Coyle, who stood off to the side.

"Ladies and Gentlemen, the commissioner, Lord Batholomew Cunningham, hereby proclaims the opening of the Conference for the Continuation of the Peace!"

First the host, Morren Godwyn, owner of the Rhinos, took the stage to polite applause from both halves of the ballroom. Then came the Setherian representative, the Lizards' owner, Benedict Cheesley, greeted by a smattering of clapping from the Setherian side. Next, Alexander Fitton himself. His fellow Helderan owners rose to deliver a tumultuous ovation. Reporters seated in a bullpen area off to the far right of the riser scribbled furiously on their pads. Fitton himself waved and smiled.

"Gentlemen and ladies," Coyle announced, "I present the Founder and Commissioner of the Setheridge Island Professional League of Baseball and of the Amandean League of Everyman, prescriber of the Eternal Ceasefire, his Esteemed Excellency, the Honorable Bartholomew J. H. Cunningham the Fifth!"

If there was a single moment at which Naughton knew the peace conference was ill-fated, it was this: as Cunningham, aided by two bodyguards, trudged up a small flight of steps to the riser, the room was utterly silent. That the Helderans failed to offer polite applause, a modicum of respect, was disappointing. That the Setherians also remained mute as Cunningham laboriously made his way to his seat was simply painful.

Does it end this quickly? Naughton wondered. Save a world, a continent, two nations, five races, countless millions — and yet a leader can quickly, unceremoniously, be shown the door. He knew the time had come. But still it felt brutal.

Coyle, usually imperturbable, also seemed thrown by the response. He was to serve as the announcer throughout the proceedings, and now he fumbled for words. "The Continental, uh, yes. Um. Yes. The Continental Peace Conference hereby convenes. The honor of hosting this august assemblage, uh, body, should go, that is, does go to the owner of the West Somerchester Rhinos, our host, the Esteemed and Honorable Morren Godwyn."

Godwyn, seated to the far left, rose to the podium and began what Naughton hoped would be a brief address. Crandy peered up from his customary 'dozing' position, cocking his metallic head right and then left, then sniffing the air.

"What is it, boy?" Naughton whispered.

Crandy's artificial eyes were cosmetic only; Naughton knew that the pneumatic sensors placed at the inset of his ears delivered to his primary processors the equivalent of sight. Yet the eyes often seemed to speak to him, to emote, and this moment was no different. Naughton could tell something — if indeed this was possible for a device made hard of metal and intricate pneumatics — was bothering the hound.

Perhaps he was simply projecting on his hound his own growing sense of foreboding. His own exhaustion. But it seemed as if Crandy was, simply, sad.

Ronnell knew that he, along with the rest of the assembled press, would be ushered out of the ballroom once the opening speeches were complete. He was determined to find a way back in. He had no desire to craft a column based solely on the vague platitudes that would undoubtedly be offered up in these initial remarks. His colleagues would be satisfied, and would fill their stories with these meaningless morsels, then call it a day.

Indeed, there were days when that would suffice for Ronnell himself. But not today. Not at this point.

On the stage, Morren Godwyn droned on, offering a stream of platitudes from amid his drooping mustache. "I can't begin to tell you how proud we in West Somerchester are to bear witness to the historic events that are about to unfold…"

It was hard to stay focused. Ronnell remembered that Godwyn had been one of the first of the Helderans to commit to the new league, and for that Cunningham had always been appreciative. Having Godwyn host the peace conference was fortuitous for Lord Bart, because the owner was trusted by the Setherians yet accepted by the new guard of younger Helderan owners.

"…and in closing, we know the fair winds of change need not harbor ill tidings, and they might capture the goodness that is found in the rapture of hope, and foment the deeds of our forefathers…." Goodness, Ronnell thought, the man was soporific. Indeed, many of the owners shifted in their chairs and checked their timepieces. He imagined a headline for his paper: *Peace Conference Collapses Amid Boredom.*

Eventually, Godwyn finished and the proceedings gave way to the Setherian representative, the Lizards owner Benedict Cheesley, strangely dressed without a tie and in a jacket that seemed to have been folded over and crushed into a suitcase.

"Peace is an imperfect thing," Cheesley opined, and Ronnell knew they were about to be subjected to a speech as replete with trite aphorisms as Godwyn's. *Peace Conference Collapses Amid Boredom and Bad Fashion* came his imagined headline revision.

"…but peace cannot be placed on a shelf like a trophy. Rather it must be tended to, like a fragile garden, to be nurtured and watered and given sunlight…."

This is getting painful. At this rate reporters would not have to be evicted from the room when the speeches were complete, for they'd rush out on their own volition.

"…for though we hail from different cities across this wide and beautiful continent, and though we are of different races and different ancestries, we can never forget that we are all one people…" Ronnell was certain that last preposterous comment would have prompted hisses and booing if the owners had not long since stopped paying attention. *Peace Conference Collapses Amid Utter Apathy.*

Ronnell took notice of Lord Bart, seated on the stage behind Godwyn. Cunningham's countenance was strangely blank. He did not applaud, he did not smile, he did not grimace.

The columnist leaned forward and peered. It was odd. The commissioner was usually quite animated in public, and indeed fidgety when forced to sit for long periods of time. Now, it was as though he was not even listening, not present in the moment.

It was as though he had been drugged.

———————

THE SPEECHES WORE ON. NAUGHTON watched from the far side of the room, behind a silk curtain that served as a backdrop. He paced side to side. His hands fidgeted. He checked his timepiece repeatedly.

A reporter once asked Naughton what he viewed as essential to the successful operation of the Leagues of SIP and ALE. He'd thought long about an answer. Eventually, it came to him. The key, more than anything else, was leaving nothing to chance, was being certain how events would play out. Achieving as close to 100% absolute certainty was always his goal.

Of course, he often never came close. The 30th Anniversary Celebration — planned for months, derailed in minutes — was the most horrific case in point. And now this — an absurd peace conference. Naughton couldn't even begin to gauge the overall level of uncertainty that it brought. He wanted League events scripted as much as possible for public consumption.

But at this conference there was no script, at least not on the Helderan side, and for days his stomach had borne the brunt of the ensuing anxiety.

The curtain rustled a bit, and he realized that Preston Dronwell, aide to the Setherian Executive Clay, was approaching. They had not seen each since opening day, on the commissioner's ferry to Skate River.

"Preston, I hope the speeches are not too draining for you."

"Boredom, we can deal with. Concessions, not so much."

Naughton raised his eyebrows. "Is this a message from Executive Clay?"

"Indeed. We'll countenance no substantive compromises. That stands for Executive Clay and the majority of Setherian owners. And we resent the agenda

for this conference being established without so much as a single consultation with our office."

"Do tell me, Preston. How then do we satisfy this new Helderan leader? Would a new top hat and box of chocolate bon-bons be sufficient?"

"Spare me your sarcasm. I warned you back in May that the needs of the Setherians must be upheld. We expect that of the commissioner."

Dronwell turned to leave. Out of the corner of his eye Naughton could see Clay's Helderan counterpart, Alexander Fitton, walking to the podium for the third and final opening speech.

Naughton grabbed Dronwell by the elbow. "Preston, do listen to this one speech. It may change your perspective."

"Don't worry, Andrew. I wouldn't miss this for a no-hitter." The Setherian aide turned with a scowl and returned to the chamber.

Fitton, on the stage, alone at the podium, carried a single page of notes. He wore a simple day jacket and red bow tie, attire more casual than most of the tuxedo-clad older owners. On his lapel he wore a small gold button, the insignia of his new political party, Peace First. He clasped his hands on either side of the podium and peered out into the crowd. "I am proud of all of us here. Because we are here. Because we are meeting in one room and talking, and not — as so many of our ancestors did — simply studying each other from opposing sides of a battlefield.

"But I am most decidedly not proud of my own people. The Helderan people." Ronnell watched as the other Helderan owners, almost in unison, sat upright. They clearly had no idea where Fitton was taking this; self-criticism was the last tack they'd expected from their new executive. The entire room fell to a hush. Hurried, whispered conversations ceased. Fitton stood erect at the podium. "The people of the Nation of Heldera have, for the past 30 years, been far too willing to forget the atrocities committed on them by the people of Setheridge. Far too willing to forgive the decades of oppression. Far too willing to accept the bald lies of the League and the Nation of Setheridge that we truly are autonomous."

Naughton's mouth opened slightly. The Setherian owners began jeering; the Helderan owners shouted in support as if at some religious revival. Even the reporters seemed frantic, as if uncertain whether to flee for their safety. The unrelenting boredom of the first two speeches had, in a single instant, given way to utter pandemonium.

But Fitton was not finished. "I would like to read you something." The room quieted. "It was written 30 years ago by the late Albert Kender, a sociologist at that wonderful Helderan institution, the University of Leadland. He wrote: 'We Helderans need to focus on the fact that this Bartholomew Cunningham is a showman, and a Setherian. I've little doubt that the ceasefire is a sham, that our sovereignty is a ruse. I predict that at some point in the future, perhaps in three decades, when the people of Heldera have long since been lulled into complacency, Cunningham and his Setherian conspirators will stage a calamity, a disaster of some sort. I hypothesize that the showman and his ilk will cleverly blame Heldera for that catastrophe, offering the Setherians an opportune moment to rescind our supposed independence.'"

Fitton looked up from his papers. "I daresay Professor Kender seems to be prophetic. We now have our calamity. The Office of the Commissioner has already concocted differing accounts of the airship crash, and still has yet to apprehend the supposed culprit.

"Let me now say this clearly. As Executive of the Sovereign Nation of Heldera, I hereby demand an amendment to the Proclamation of an Eternal Ceasefire, one that guarantees a very simple but much needed provision: the next Commissioner of the Leagues of SIP and ALE will be a Helderan.

"And I assure you now that if we do not get that promise, that guarantee, we will declare war on the Nation of Setheridge."

August 6

West Somerchester

"COULD IT BACKFIRE?"

The question was whispered to Naughton as he stood in line at an open-air food vendor off to the east of Handelson Plaza. He had taken refuge here to clear his mind after the tumultuous events of the previous day, but even here he was accosted. There was no relief.

He turned. It was the wretched columnist, Ollo Ronnell.

"Oh, Ronnell. Did you follow me here?"

"I spotted you here. I was breaking the fast at the cafe at the end of the plaza and saw you. We haven't spoken in a while, Andrew Naughton."

"No. And now is not the time. This is too public," Naughton protested.

"No, actually, it's fine. If anyone sees us they'll think only that it is precisely what it is: a journalist talking to a League official."

"'Journalist' may be a stretch, Ollo."

"Spare me, Naughton. I do more actual reporting than most of the daily writers."

"What do you want?"

"You know what I want."

Damned scribe. Damned unrelenting newspaperman. Naughton gritted his teeth and replied in a hushed tone, "I still am not sure why I didn't seek to have you banned after you published our investigation of the airship crash…"

"Just doing my job, Andrew, as you do yours. You have no monopoly on loyalty and devotion."

"It nearly incited the next insurrection, and it still very well may. Perhaps your devotion should be more to the Eternal Ceasefire than to that rag of a newspaper."

"Ah, so I should have left the report on my nightstand for bedtime reading? Why keep the public informed? They do have those inconvenient traits, free thought and free will."

Naughton shook his head in disgust. "I suppose you're not going to tell me who provided the report to you?"

"You suppose correctly. But do tell me: what happened in the session after Fitton's speech? After they removed the press and locked the doors?"

Naughton glanced in both directions, ensuring that no one could overhear them. He weighed his answer. "This is off the record."

"Yes. For use in a story, but unattributed."

"Fine."

"What happened?"

Naughton adjusted the collar of his overcoat and then looked to the ground. "What happened was that Executive Fitton tried continuing his speech amid catcalls and jeers from the Setherian owners and staff."

Ronnell swallowed. "So I've heard. And then?"

"Then, scuffling. Name calling. I thought they'd come to blows, but Gill's men separated the most violent in the crowd."

"And what did the commissioner do throughout this?"

"He watched."

"Watched? Just sat and watched?"

"No comment."

"Naughton, I saw Lord Bart on that stage. He was in a stupor. You have to tell me. Is he lucid? Is he coherent?"

Naughton gritted his teeth. Ronnell certainly knew how to bear down to the essence of a matter. "I don't know. After yesterday's session, his doctor prescribed immediate rest. He will not likely be present at today's final closed-door meetings. If they even take place. I haven't been able to see him."

"His absence will certainly be duly noted by both sides."

"They are already aware."

"Oh, I see," said Ronnell. "And Fitton's response?"

"You'd have to ask Fitton."

"Off the record."

"I wasn't there, but I'm told he was not surprised."

"Anyway, Naughton, you never answered my original question."

"Which was?"

"Could it backfire?"

"You mean Fitton's gamble?"

"Yes."

"Of course it could."

"But he's a gambler," the scribe said.

"He certainly is."

"And what comes next?"

"The All-Star Game. You know that."

"That's not what I mean, Naughton. What comes next for Fitton? For Lord Bart?"

Naughton turned fully to face the columnist. He was a good footlength taller, yet Ronnell managed to carry himself with an imposing stature. "A good number of Setherian owners are refusing now to take part. They consider Fitton's ultimatum to be unacceptable. They won't talk."

"Will any of them do so?"

"Yes. The younger owners are willing to. Those who were mere children at the inception of the Leagues."

"And the commissioner?"

Naughton paused before answering. Why was he divulging all this? Would it suit his purposes to have this in the *Chronicle*, even unattributed? Of course, he reminded himself, Ronnell was likely to learn all of this from other sources regardless. "Lord Bart is, shall we say, not particularly amenable to even continuing discussions with Fitton. The Helderan's demand was, in his view, a serious breach."

"Then what are you going to do?"

Naughton thought for a second. "I will tell you, but you cannot use the answer in your story, even unattributed."

"Very well."

"We are trying to arrange a private meeting between the two men. It is by no means certain. Both need convincing."

"You would need the upstart Fitton to be somewhat deferential, or a direct meeting could worsen the situation."

"Yes, that is the risk. That is why you are not to report this. Sniff around. Stake out the meeting if you can determine its time and location. I won't help you there. But don't tell your editors, colleagues and, of course, your many readers about this."

"And after the meeting?"

"What we do and say publicly after the meeting depends, of course, on whether it happens and how it resolves."

The two paused briefly as they spied two of the All-Star hurlers, Phillip "Bomber" Carson of the Rhinos and the Flying Squirrels' ace Ketter "Count" Asgar, further down the plaza, staggering and singing.

The old scribe turned back to him. "I suppose you wish that drunken All-Stars were the commissioner's biggest problem."

"There was a time not so very long ago when it would have been."

"Now events are out of control, Naughton. Fitton, calling for this peace conference, demanding Helderan succession, talking of war. Lord Bart, unable to control the crush of reactions, in a medicated stupor. And the Commandant stalking about here and there."

"Excuse me?" Naughton tried to control the alarm in his voice.

"Hood. Phangorious Hood. You know the man, of course. Would probably own a team or two if his profits weren't so ill-gotten." Ronnell laughed.

"Quiet! Damn it, Ollo. If you ever hope for further surreptitious help from me, you'd better learn a bit of discretion. Now what about Hood?"

"He's here. In town. I saw him arrive two days ago. I assumed you knew. Aren't your intelligence agents scurrying about looking for precisely that sort of information?"

"Get out of here, Ronnell. Leave me be. I don't even know why I help you."

"You do know, Naughton."

"Oh? Why is that?"

"Because one day you are going to need *my* help, and that day may be fast approaching."

The scribe tapped his top hat, bowed slightly, and walked away at a labored pace. The vendor stirred a steaming pot of hot oat bran and looked up, but Naughton's appetite had vanished.

———————————

WITHOUT HIS UNIFORM, WITHOUT CLEATS, Halloway sat in the stands of Rebaley Field, where the fans would gather for the All-Star Game in just 36 hours. It felt odd not be out on the field. Some of the coaches taking part in the game recognized him in the distance and yelled, jokingly, for him to join him. He waved back and smiled.

The grass glistened as the westward sun reflected on the dew. A good number of Helderan All-Stars were in the infield, shagging grounders. There was Lyle Bentley, the Grizzlies' 24-year-old first bagger, only a rookie but already one of the top Helderan sluggers this season. There was Geoffrey Trent, the Hammerheads' third bagger, at 26 an astronomical talent as batsman and fielder. And of course, behind the home bag, taking soft lobs from the batting practice hurler, was the veteran Mad Dogs' catcher Edwin Celeron. Halloway would be thrilled to have any of them in a Squirrels uniform.

Beyond that group, near the opposite dugout, was Pyce Marsh, swinging a pair of bats as though they were one. This was his first time as an All-Star; though he'd won Newcomer of the Year in '21, he had not been chosen for the mid-season exhibition until now.

The youngster swung freely, repeatedly, and seemed to be oblivious to Halloway's stare. *It's fine if he notices me. I want him to know I'm here.*

He had come out this early not just to watch Marsh and Asgar, but to see whether batting practice might have been canceled given the events of the previous day.

Word of the acrimony at the start of the peace conference had quickly filtered out of the Cotillion to the publick houses, plazas, and private clubs. And then to the newspapers: according to the *Chronicle*, which he'd picked up outside the park, the new Helderan leader Fitton wanted to succeed Lord Bart, and threatened war if

MICHAEL BARBATO-DUNN

he was not promised that. It was, in Halloway's view, nothing short of astounding. Terrifying.

Out on the field the players laughed amongst themselves, casually tossing the leather balls as they shared ribald jokes. Marsh, though, remained apart, standing near the third bag, taking swings with a fungo bat. The thin lines of his lips were shut, his countenance firm, stoic. After a few minutes a bullpen catcher swaggered out and offered to throw to him.

Halloway knew Marsh would stay out practicing as long as he was able, long after the others returned to the clubhouse to change into their street clothes. Most saw the All-Star Game as an opportunity to relax mid-season while earning some extra cash. Marsh was focused only on the day ahead, and likely saw no distinction between this and a regular season game, or even the ninth game of the Continental Series.

Halloway's stomach churned and he adjusted the belt of his pants. He had gobbled down lunch — a plate of jackaloupe loaf — at a small eatery near the Cotillion. The discussion among the locals at the counter was solely about the peace conference. Not a word about baseball, of course. Not a word about the All-Star Game. The Helderan Executive's words possibly foretold a tremendous change, some had said. The tacit understanding that had guided continental relations for the past three decades had been unceremoniously shoved off the table with one bold, dangerous sentence.

Now he spied the Count making his way from the home dugout to the bullpen. He wasn't sure if Asgar knew he'd be coming; there'd be no reason to formally notify him. The two had barely spoken in the weeks since the clubhouse fight. Most of his words to the hurler were uttered on those occasions when he came out to the mound to relieve him. Asgar would hand him the ball with overt irritation but say nothing.

"Coach. What brings you to the park this fine morning?" Asgar had spied him.

"Came to watch, Ketter. I hear there's a game tomorrow."

"Yes, sir. Should be a good one. I think the Helderans are going to skewer some Setherian egos."

"Could very well." They laughed.

Asgar chewed on a wad of gum in his left cheek and stared at Halloway, flicking his ball repeatedly into the base of his well-worn glove. "What are you worried about, Coach?"

He had to give Ketter Asgar this much: the hurler got right to the point. He decided to respond just as directly. "I am worried about you, Count."

"Why is that?"

Halloway stood and stepped down three rows, so he didn't have to shout. He had no idea if reporters were around, and he certainly didn't want other players or coaches hearing.

"You know damn well why. Because you may very well be up to something. You may very well be planning something. Something that would hurt the reputation of our club, of our city. Or of the Leagues."

Asgar's chewing accelerated. "Now why would you think that?"

"Well, I've got a long list of reasons, Ketter. And I've relayed those reasons to the general manager, and that's why he sent me here. You can deny such plans until we're both exhausted; that's all well and good. But I want you to remember that I am watching you on the field. And I certainly will be watching you off the field."

Halloway realized his hands were shaking and he clasped them behind his back. He waited for the hurler to respond, but none came. Asgar merely scowled, flicked the ball once again into the crook of his glove, then turned and made his way to the bullpen for some warm-ups.

The manager of the Widmertown Flying Squirrels fell back into the stadium seat behind him, waiting to catch his breath, waiting for his hands to calm, waiting for his anxiety to ease. He had not planned to deliver a verbal warning — after all, his presence alone was enough to serve as that caution.

But it was done; the words had been spoken. Halloway hoped that would be the end of it.

———————————

THE OAK SIDES OF THE hotel's chamber clock vibrated as its chimes signaled five past noon. Naughton had hoped to find a few hours to return to Schawmount to see Amelia and the boys, but arranging the meeting between Lord Bart and Fitton had chipped away at the afternoon. He would ask a staffer to deliver flowers and candy. And yet another apology.

As if on cue Fitton entered, escorted by Coyle and accompanied by his own assistant, a gaunt young man by the name Droonan. They had been ushered in through the employees' stairwell so as not to draw attention from the dozens milling about the lobby.

Naughton rose and bowed slightly to the Helderan, dismissed the two others and commanded the tray-topped half-butler to bring some port and two glasses.

"We could have been spared all this if you had accepted my earlier offer to work with me, rather than against," Fitton chided.

"You vastly overstate my ability to influence the commissioner, Executive Fitton," Naughton replied.

"You're simply being modest, Andrew. Regardless, now we face this difficult game of brinkmanship."

"A game of your choosing."

"We have all made decisions that have brought us to this place."

Coyle opened the door and stepped back in, announcing the commissioner. Cunningham entered, looking spryer than he had in quite some time, and Naughton wondered if this newfound vigor was medicinally induced.

Fitton extended his hand. Cunningham looked at it, and then at the Helderan, and then sat down without reciprocating. Fitton awkwardly retracted his arm. If this was a game of brinkmanship, the old man had just scored an opening point.

"Mr. Fitton. How old were you when the Eternal Ceasefire was declared?" Lord Bart began.

"*Executive* Fitton. And I was 17, Commissioner."

"And do you have any clear understanding of what a monumental task it was that we achieved? And when I say 'we' I mean Setherians *and* Helderans."

"With all due respect, Commissioner, I don't need a history lecture."

"This is not from history books, Mr. Fitton. This is from sociology books. What I'm talking about is the nature of our very being."

Fitton cocked his head. Naughton shifted as well. He had little confidence the old man was going to remain lucid.

"Do you know that in all beings it is easier to smile than to frown? But the reverse is true when it comes to matters of war and peace, Mr. Fitton. It is easier to take up arms, to do battle, than to negotiate peacefully."

"I am here to negotiate, sir."

"I am not talking about now. I am not talking about you. I am talking about what my generation — including your parents and grandparents — accomplished three decades ago. We went against our very nature and agreed to lay down arms. We turned away from what would have been the easy decision — to simply keep fighting. And do you know how we were able to do this, Mr. Executive?" Cunningham's use of the Helderan's newfound title was tinged with sarcasm.

"Through your personal intercession, Commissioner."

"Yes, but that is not what I mean. We — the Setherians and Helderans, as well as the Amandeans, the Monystians, and the Rebular — we were able to enact the Ceasefire because we went against our very nature and agreed to trust one another. Trust, Mr. Fitton. It is the single most difficult thing that any of us can do. Have you tried it?"

Fitton leaned back in his chair and gripped the table with both of his hands, as if summoning the nerve to respond.

"Commissioner, my people have given you 30 years of trust. But even that difficult-to-summon quality has its limits, and you must understand, sir, that we have reached ours."

Silence. Deadening, uncomfortable silence. The two men stared at one another. Naughton thought of suggesting a break, a cooling off, but in fact he wanted this to run its course. Downstairs, Setherian and Helderan owners were keeping the press and onlookers occupied, and Naughton only hoped that charade of a meeting had not yet devolved into fisticuffs. But here, in front of him, was the true moment, the decisive moment, and he saw no reason to intercede.

Finally, Bartholomew Cunningham spoke. "Executive Fitton, do you want to be known as the man who returned the continent to war?"

"War is not my objective, sir."

"And what is?"

"Autonomy for the people of Heldera. True autonomy. Not the pretense of autonomy that you and your Setherian brethren have so carefully concocted."

"That is nonsensical, Mr. Executive. Your people have autonomy, evidenced by the mere fact that they have chosen you as their executive. Did the Leagues intercede when you were chosen? No. Did the Setherians intercede? No. If ability to choose your own leader is not autonomy, then I don't know what is."

Naughton sensed Fitton's ire rising. "You don't know what is? Have you deluded yourself into believing your own rhetoric? Into thinking that the nationhood granted us is anything more than a showpiece? Yes, the old professor Kender assessed you and your plan precisely. And we Helderans are not so stupid as to fall for this any longer."

The old man reddened. "We gave you half the continent. Do you know how hard that was for Setherians to accept? Do you know how many Setherians wanted me lynched for proposing that the continent be cut in half — literally? And you seem to think that is nothing but a sham?"

"Commissioner, what looks nice on a map has little bearing on reality. The Helderan people had known nothing but second-class status, and then five decades of fruitless war to achieve equity. So when you and your conniving Setherian cohorts offered half of a map, my people were all too grateful. And we didn't bother to insist on true freedom—"

"You don't—"

"Don't interrupt me, Commissioner!" Fitton stood and pointed at the old man. Naughton started to intercede but Cunningham waved him off.

"Go on, then."

"Sir, do you know who Uriah Coale was?"

"That name is not familiar."

"No, I don't suppose it would be. Uriah Coale was my maternal great-grandfather. He was 87 years old when you and your colleagues crafted the terms of the Eternal Ceasefire. Uriah Coale was 87 and was still working. Working to earn a meager living. Working for Setherians. He had done so his entire adult life, like most males of Helderan descent. Seventy years of work."

"And what of him?" said the old man.

"He worked in Schawmount City, Mr. Commissioner. He was in four different households during those 70 years. He cleaned the stables. At 21 he cleaned the stables. At 41 he cleaned the stables. At 61 he cleaned the stables and — imagine this — at 81 he cleaned the stables. Do you know what that was like, Mr. Commissioner?"

"I can only imagine."

"Yes. I'm sure you spent a lot of time imaging the lives of Helderans," Fitton snapped. "I'm done here. I've had enough. The peace conference is over. There is no point in continuing."

Fitton rose and gathered his hat and papers. Naughton began to protest the abrupt departure, but again Cunningham signaled him to desist. The Helderan leader opened the door to leave, but then turned and offered one final comment.

"By the way, Commissioner, I just recalled the address of Uriah Cole's last employer. It was 9301 Charcross Boulevard, in downtown Schawmount City. He died there. While cleaning the stables. They found his body, face down, in the horse dung."

With that, the Helderan was gone.

Naughton waited a moment and then asked, "Do you recognize the address?"

"Yes, I do, Andrew," replied the Commissioner of the Leagues of the SIP and ALE, exhaling long and loudly. "It was mine."

August 7

WEST SOMERCHESTER

NAUGHTON GLANCED AT HIS TIMEPIECE. Seven o'clock. The 30th All-Star Game of the Setheridge Independent Professional League of Baseball was to begin in just eight hours.

He made his through the plaza near the Cotillion, buffeted by a stiff river breeze. Down some steps, off the southern end of the plaza, he glanced around. Morning diners dotted the outdoor tables, but none familiar, and none paid him any mind. He seemed to be in the clear.

With Crandy trailing at his heels, Naughton crossed three streets, then turned left and hailed a carriage. The destination was probably walkable, but time was of the essence.

Inside, he gave the driver the address, then looked over the text of the release that would be going out to reporters shortly. He had drafted it immediately after word that Fitton had returned to Crenshaw City following the difficult meeting with Lord Bart.

PEACE CONFERENCE TO BE HELD IN ABEYANCE

(West Somerchester, August 7, 1923) — His Excellency Bartholomew Cunningham, Commissioner of the Leagues of SIP and ALE, today announced that the Conference for the Continuation of the Peace, held concurrent with the SIP League's annual All-Star Game festivities, will be suspended until the end of the season.

"The issues before us are weighty," said the commissioner. "They are not ones that can be dealt with in a few short days, or even weeks. It is best to focus for now on our beautiful pastime, the game of baseball, and leave the political discussions to the off-season."

Helderan Executive Alexander Fitton, who had originally proposed the Conference, agreed with the decision. "Let us continue, as our fathers and their fathers have done, to channel our efforts into successful baseball. Other matters can wait until the cold winter months. I look forward to seeing the Helderans triumph in the All-Star Game!"

No firm date has yet been set for the resumption of the conference. The commissioner will not answer further questions about it until the resumption of the regular season.

───────────────────

HE FOLDED THE PAPER BACK into his jacket pocket. Crandy lay at his feet on the floor of the cab, seemingly dozing. The fabricated Fitton quote especially pleased him. Let the obnoxious Helderan come back screaming at him.

Gill said Fitton had urged other Helderan owners to remain, telling them that the All-Star Game should go on, that the season should continue, and that he would have more to say about his plans at a later date.

Some of the Helderans in fact did stay for the festivities. For many of the owners, the All-Star Game was a perfect occasion to socialize, make business contacts, and imbibe. In that sense, Fitton's departure was a relief. It would shift attention, at least for a time, back to the game. And Naughton hoped it would make it more difficult for the press to focus on the failure of the conference. Instead, they'd report simply a respite.

The docks of West Somerchester were hidden behind winding narrow streets and ramshackle storefronts. He had been told to meet at the eleventh pier past the one at which the large schooner *Brendlehide* was moored. He counted each pier as it passed by the cab's window, and then, at the tenth, called out to the driver to stop. Crandy lifted his head, stretched, and rose, following his master out of the cab.

Gulls squealed overhead, as if laughing, and Crandy emitted a very low growl in annoyance. "It's fine, boy," he said, petting the servohound's upper back. "That's how they sing."

The two sloshed through puddles across the uneven street. The entire district reeked of gutted fish. Naughton surveyed the ship docked at the eleventh pier. It was a nondescript fishing vessel, about 70 footlengths from bow to stern, enough room for a crew of four. On its side was painted the name *Wave of Sands*, though the paint was chipped and worn and Naughton was unsure if that was, in fact, the full name.

A wooden plank led to the deck. He saw no one above deck, and cautiously began making his way across. "Wait here," Naughton commanded Crandy. But the servohound responded with a bark, apparently fearing the setting was unsafe, and not wanting his master to proceed unaccompanied. Naughton looked back at the boat, then at the dog, and revised his decision. "Very well. Follow. But stay above deck while I go below." The hound wagged his tail.

The *Wave* swayed slightly as they boarded, and Naughton grabbed a railing to keep his bearings. A small set of steps led down to the interior of the cabin. For a minute he hesitated. Crandy immediately sensed his indecision and whined. "Stay." Naughton held up his hand, palm toward the hound. "Stay up here."

Below, three men sat at a wooden table surrounded by benches that were nailed to the narrow walls. The cabin was lit only by a single gas lamp suspended on one of the walls. Their faces were in darkness.

"Mr. Naughton. We're glad you found your way," said Phangorious Hood. "It is a pleasure to see you again." From above, Crandy's whine grew louder in response to Hood's voice.

"Mr. Hood. Thank you for heeding my request to come. Though I do wish you'd have been a bit more discreet."

"Excuse me?"

"It seems none other than Ollo Ronnell happen to notice you arriving in town the other day. Your carriage passed him by."

"Perceptive, he is. He told you this?"

"Yes. Fortunately he is more focused at the moment on the failure of the peace conference than to ask more questions about you."

"And you feigned surprise, I hope." Hood leaned back, running a rough file across his long nails.

"Of course. But I'd appreciate that when our meeting is done, you depart West Somerchester with a bit less prominence. Now, my time is limited. Let's get on with this."

"Fine. I will introduce my acquaintances, but first — there is a little matter of, uh, shall we say, the arrangements."

Yes, Naughton thought. The arrangements. He produced an envelope and handed it directly to the Magera leader. "You'll find the documents inside meet your specifications." The envelope contained deeds to three properties in different parts of Helderan territory that had long been held by the League. All were either vacant or abandoned properties, but for each the land alone was worth a considerable sum.

Now they belonged to Phangorious Hood. Such was the price of peace.

"Very well. I trust there is no need to examine them," Hood replied. Then he spoke to his two companions: "Gentlemen, allow me to introduce the second most powerful man on the continent, Andrew Gilpen Naughton, Special Assistant to the Commissioner."

"Hood, you overstate my influence once again."

"Ah, Naughton. You've made a career of false modesty. It has served you well."

"If it had served me well, sir, I wouldn't find myself meeting you here."

"True enough." The Magera leader's laugh boomed through the dingy cabin, and from above Naughton heard Crandy emit a short yelp. "Naughton, we are more than happy to lend any assistance to the commissioner at his time of need. You know we in the Magera have nothing but the highest regard for him."

"And I'm sure those properties I just handed you only bolstered that regard."

The underworld leader scowled. "Let's get on with it. Ask your questions. I have limited patience, and we plan to depart this godforsaken town as soon as our business is complete. These are my long-time associates, C. T. Muldoon and Silas Pounds." A heavyset, bearded man with the distinctive broad nose of the Rebular nodded first, then a craggy older man with bent hands — years of fistfights, no doubt — pointed in acknowledgment. Both bore the distinctive disfigurement of the Magera: the missing ring finger, severed in the initiation ceremony.

"Muldoon is my chief associate in matters dealing with the Amandean people. And Pounds here *is* Amandean. Perhaps the highest ranking Amandean ever in my organization."

Naughton nodded back. *The proverbial Magera braintrust.*

"Gentlemen," Hood continued, "Mr. Naughton has just paid handsomely for a few moments of your time. But he expects your candor, and your discretion. There is to be no word of this meeting even to others with whom we are associated."

"Understood," said Muldoon, clearly the higher ranking of the two.

Naughton began. "Gentlemen. As I understand it, you are familiar with Hardwin Jellum?"

Muldoon replied, "Yes. He is well known in several smaller Helderan towns as a spreader."

"Spreader?"

"He ran the local numbers networks. Mainly in Powlet Creek Summit, Fanningana Falls and, for a time, further north in Folgerley Bluff. He apparently would overstay his welcome after a few years and then move on to another town."

"And the Magera? Don't you oversee the numbers operations?"

"Only in the larger cities," Hood interjected, "those with teams in the SIP League. The ALE towns are dominated by the Amandeans, and we are simply happy to let the locals control such activities. Sometimes we do expect a cut. But usually not, so long as they leave more lucrative operations to our exclusivity."

"But this Jellum," said Naughton, "was spotted back in June on a Helderan ship heading for Murrichswell Cove, on the Island of Heldera. My operatives were, unfortunately, unable to locate him after that."

The three Magera now glanced anxiously at one another. The one named Pounds, heretofore silent, now replied. "Mr. Naughton, it is our understanding that the one named Jellum never arrived in Murrichswell."

"Never arrived?"

"Never. It was a ruse. He was apparently never on the ship. We had our own operatives stationed at the port when it arrived. It was clear he'd never been there."

"Then where is he?"

"We don't know."

"Is he alive?"

"Again, we simply don't know."

Naughton threw his hands up in exasperation. He'd just paid a tremendous amount of money to be told that no one can find this mysterious bookmaker. "Is that it? He just disappears? Into the ether?"

"I'm afraid so," Hood said.

"Phangorious, you couldn't have just told me that from the start? That you had nothing? Simply to extort some additional holdings out of the League?"

"First of all, Naughton, we are a business operation. Never forget that. Secondly, do not assume we have nothing."

"What do you have?"

"We have information. Our specialty. I dare say your Monsytian friend Gill, the so-called security expert, never quite managed to find this out himself. Or if he did, he never managed to inform you."

"Go on."

"We learned that the three Amandean miscreants killed in the stadium stands by the falling airship had worked together in the past."

"We're already aware of that."

"But are you aware that the trio served as nightside dockworkers in Kern for a small company called Drewel Coastal Lanes?" asked Muldoon.

Naughton shook his head. "No. I was not."

Hood interjected. "We in the Magera have a vested interest in knowing every shipping company in every port city. And we had never heard of a Drewel Coast Lanes of Kern either."

"So you looked further…"

"…we looked further," said Muldoon. "And we found it was incorporated as an arm of the University of Kern, ostensibly to facilitate the shipping of laboratory equipment and supplies for the many members of the Scientificka who reside there."

"Lab equipment?"

"Yes. And other — material. So it seems that Drewel is a legitimate shipping entity, but small enough so that we knew nothing of them. And this Drewel saw fit to employ the three suspects later killed in the crash of the *Airship Lady Crym*."

"So how is that related to the Leagues?"

"Tangentially, it seems. The Drewel company was incorporated, as I said. And those incorporation papers could be found quite easily here in West Somerchester. You could have found them yourself." Muldoon tossed a sheath of papers in Naughton's direction. "Have a look, my friend. You'll see the board of directors of this firm numbers only two people — one is the Scientificka member with whom you're recently acquainted."

"Iphonious Henry."

"Yes."

"And the other?"

"Right there, on the first page, Mr. Naughton. There's the name."

Naughton read the sheet, scowled, then rose.

"Have you gotten your money's worth, Mr. Naughton?" Hood asked.

"Yes, Commandant. Yes, I have."

"As I said, Andrew, we are a business operation. We strive to have satisfied customers." Hood stood and extended his hand. The other two leaned back in their chairs and smirked.

Naughton ignored the offer of a handshake, donned his hat and climbed out of the cabin. Crandy, waiting and vigilant, tail at attention, howled when he appeared.

"Come here, boy. I'm fine." He tapped his thigh and the hound was at his side, and two stepped off of the eleventh pier, then hurried out of the steamy harbor.

HIGH CUMULUS CLOUDS DOTTED THE skies, pushed by the eastward breeze. A marching band from a local school paraded across the outfield, drums pounding, trumpets blaring. Thousands clapped in rhythm in anticipation of the game's start, including those seated near Halloway. Throughout the cavernous park, children played penny-whistles in unison. On the infield, around the perimeter of the hurler's mound, the costumed mascots of the 16 SIP League teams danced and mimicked hurlers and strikers.

Halloway had secured an aisle seat, thankfully. As he would be watching the All-Star Game alone, he cared not to be crowded between loud revelers. On either side of the bullpen, the starting hurlers for each team were warming up. The gloom that had enveloped him since his journey here, and particularly since his conversation with Asgar, lifted slightly. At least there was baseball to be played.

On his lap sat the morning edition of the *Chronicle,* with a blaring headline on the commissioner's suspension of the peace conference and Fitton's departure. He glanced at the story but then folded the broadsheet, tucking it into a crevice below the arm of the chair. He had no appetite for reading about the turmoil. His own immediate concern was enough for the moment.

Out on the field, more pomp and circumstance. A choir from West Somerchester college sang the Helderan national anthem, and then, to lesser applause, its Setherian counterpart. Halloway wondered if the students in the choir had any sense of the greater political forces that were playing out as the game unfolded.

And then: the opening throw, a ceremonial event, usually only for play-off games. The tinny voice of the public address announcer echoed throughout the stadium, proclaiming the arrival of the special guests: "Ladies and Gentlemen, we direct your attention to the hurler's mound. Taking the mound are two of the greatest players to ever wear a West Somerchester uniform: slugger Robert Egrid and hurler Arlan Harrelson!"

The crowd cheered and an organist played a fanfare. Egrid and Harrelson waved to the fans as they strode to the mound, each cupping a white baseball in his hands. They were apt choices: they had played for the Rhinos their entire careers, dating back to the very inception of the Leagues in 1893. Best as Halloway could recall, Egrid retired with 370 home runs and 970 RBI, astronomical figures. Harrelson, just 21 when the League came to be, managed to have even greater longevity: 198 wins over 18 seasons. His elbow had given way just two shy of the magical 200 mark.

That Egrid and Harrelson weren't likely to ever see the Hall of Fame didn't matter to the Rhinos faithful. The two were loved. They'd never even left West Somerchester after retiring; they were revered in the city and probably never needed to pay for a beer. Now they stood side by side on the mound and simultaneously tossed out balls to a couple of grade school boys, again to wild cheers. After the throws, they walked off joking and laughing, then signed the balls for the League to later display.

It was a symbolic moment given the political tumult that surrounded the All-Star Game: a Setherian and a Helderan who could have met on a battlefield instead had been teammates since the very founding of the SIP and ALE Leagues. And they were still together, still friends.

Halloway allowed himself a moment of pride: for it was his decision to play in Setheridge all those years ago that had allowed that friendship to occur, had allowed the Leagues to succeed. He had traveled across the border and played for the Setherians.

He looked around the crowded ball park. He had no doubt that behind home base, in the luxury sections, sat the very politicians who had been stirring up the tensions. He wondered if they recognized the significance of Egrid and Harrelson, walking off the mound as compatriots.

But perhaps, after 30 years, such noble sentiments had simply gone out of fashion.

———————————

AT FIRST OLLO RONNELL WATCHED the All-Star Game from the press box, where the beat writers congregated to both take notes and drink, more so the latter. But by the second inning he tired of their weak witticisms and left, to be closer to the field and away from the forced frivolity of his colleagues.

The stump of his cigar was worn and soggy. He considered tossing it aside and finding a new one, but he was too tired to bother. He made his way down the three flights of wooden steps that connected the press box to the bleacher seats, then snaked his way through the crowd to a lower concourse.

Eventually, he found his way to an unobstructed vantage point off the first-base line. On the mound, the Helderan All-Star hurler, the Rhinos' Phillip "Bomber" Carson, was whipping balls that teased at the edges of the strike zone. The strikers were flummoxed. Even the Jackaloupes' second bagger Zachary Quinn, with the highest batting average and on-base percentage in the entire league, shook his head after striking out. The ballpark had 44,000 seats, and most were filled by Rhinos fans who would have been perfectly content to see Carson hurl the entire game.

The crowd was boisterous. He saw fans singing and dancing in the aisles, and Ronnell supposed that their revelry had begun on the way to game or in the large area outside Rebaley where the carriages would be parked. Perhaps even the horses were drunk.

So rowdy you'd think this was an ALE game.

Yet foreboding gnawed at him like a dull headache. He bit down on the cigar, then threw it to the ground.

Ronnell flashed his press badge and spotted a vacant seat. Off to the left, behind the home bag, was the commissioner's box, framed by bunting and banners. It held maybe two dozen people, and Ronnell imagined that most of them were sponsors of the advertising that brought abundant revenue to the League coffers. In the front row was Lord Bart, staring straight ahead. His gaze, like at the conference two days earlier, was vacant.

To the right of Lord Bart sat Godwyn, the Rhinos' owner and formal host of the All-Star Game, his silver-gray top hat obstructing the view of those behind him. On the left, the Jackaloupes' owner and Setherian Executive Broadlun Clay, pensive and brooding. Behind them, sitting with arched back in a full-length, sequined gown and towering sun hat, was Vivian.

Her gaze was the antithesis of Lord Bart's; it darted in all directions as the game proceeded, as if she were a member of League Security. She likely was worried; this was Cunningham's first appearance in a stadium since the disastrous 30th Anniversary Celebration back in March.

Ronnell sighed. He could not deny that her devotion to Cunningham had been absolute and unwavering over three decades. He supposed that should have somehow eased the pain. It did not.

They didn't speak for years after she'd betrayed him. She had claimed his idea as her own, and then she fled into the arms of the famed showman, Bartholomew

Cunningham, the promoter of all things strange and wondrous. And Lord Bart, in turn, seized on the idea with a forcefulness that left no room for failure. A forcefulness that carried Vivian, and the entire continent, along.

And over the ensuing years he had spent idle hours wondering whether she had left him for Cunningham, or for the idea. For the revolution it brought. Ronnell didn't know which was worse.

Now a flask was being passed down the aisle, filled no doubt with whiskey. This was a covert tradition of sorts at ALE games. The man to his immediate right took a swig and passed it to him, and he complied, drinking a bit and then handing it to the man on his left. Technically, he was on duty and should not be partaking, but it would have been considered insulting to refuse. The flask might even eventually encircle the stadium, by which point it would have been refilled and emptied ten times over. The shot warmed him at first, then settled in the pit of his stomach with a jolt. Probably MacKaness whiskey, he guessed, straight from the heart of Setheridge.

The drink worked wonders, at least briefly. It revived his energy and lifted his mood.

On the field, the fourth inning had arrived, and the Setherian team had offered up its third All-Star hurler: the Terriers' veteran Gerald Jones. At 33, Jones had long since lost his fastball, but he — like many pitchers who learn to endure — had developed a crafty repertoire of throws that relied entirely on finesse: sinker, slider, change-up. He now faced the heart of the Helderan All-Star line-up: the Warthogs' slugging short-bagger Archibald Crane, hitting .317 with loads of power, then the Hammerheads' third-bagger Geoffrey Trent, only 26 and already a star in the making, then the former Newcomer of the Year, Pyce Marsh of the Flying Squirrels, four years younger than Trent and yet also slated for stardom.

With players like this, Ronnell knew, the Leagues had a promising future. Soon there would be an entire league — indeed, both leagues — made up of players who were born after the start of the Ceasefire. Players for whom the Great Insurrection was only something in the history books. A league of players who'd grown up shagging grounders and honing fastballs without the incessant clatter of mortar fire in the background.

Crane struck out, and then Jones got Trent to chase a nasty sinker. Trent's bat made weak contact and the ball dribbled easily back to Jones, who threw to the first bag. With two outs and no one on the paths, Marsh, a Helderan All-Star favorite, stepped to the home bag amid boisterous cheers. Jones rejected two of his catcher's signals, then nodded at the third and delivered a change-up that dipped down but somehow rose straight up as it entered the strike zone. A beautiful throw.

But the boy's stroke was fast, his bat connected squarely, and the thousands filling the stadium rose to their feet as the ball lofted over the right field wall.

Helderan All-Stars 1, Setherians 0.

Ronnell looked again at the VIP section and saw the Helderan owners applauding and hugging each other, while their Setherian counterparts shook their heads and grinned; all seemed to be enjoying the moment. They seemed almost as one.

Perhaps the Twin Nations could survive this crisis, he thought. Then he focused on Cunningham, also at his feet, though still stoic and expressionless.

Ronnell hoped the traveling flask would soon find its way back to him.

Naughton situated himself in the last row of the VIP section, and Crandy nestled against the legs of the stadium seat. Rebaley Field was full, with latecomers standing, the crowd loud and enthusiastic. Amid the political acrimony, the relief was palpable. Naughton even detected flasks being passed around, an old ALE League custom, but rarely seen in the SIP.

That the All-Star Game was being played — after the border clashes, after the Helderan demands, after the futile peace conference — was astonishing. So for the moment he allowed himself to relax, to trust that Gill's security plan was sufficient. At least no dirigibles flew overhead.

The riskier moment was still to come, for the commissioner intended to make a speech during the traditional break between the top and bottom of the sixth inning. Naughton had asked Cunningham's physician, Dr. Vinge, to discreetly administer a mild narcotic prior to the start of the game. The drug, the doctor had assured him, would guard against any breakdown of the old man's demeanor of the sort that they had witnessed privately. Yet its effects should not otherwise be discernible. Still, the old man would be very exposed during his remarks.

In the bottom of the fourth the young Squirrels slugger Marsh broke the scoreless tie with a home run that rocketed out of the stadium like a firework. Cunningham rose during the wild Helderan applause, as did the owners of both nations surrounding him. Naughton feared that fans would take note of the old man's inanimate demeanor.

Gill approached from behind and knelt down at his side. "The organist knows,"

he whispered. "He'll stay up there." Naughton had arranged to have the organist ready during the commissioner's speech. One of Gill's top men would stay in the organist's box high atop the ball field; if at any point the old man were to become incoherent, or rambling or, worse yet, belligerent, the musician would immediately launch into the West Somerchester team anthem, "Rally the Rhinos." Naughton was confident that song would immediately result in cheering and singing from hometown fans, and thus would sufficiently cover up Cunningham's display to all but those seated closest to him. Perhaps even the press might not notice.

It was wishful thinking, but it was the best contingency he could devise.

The inspector departed, and Crandy stirred. The hound had seemed uneasy since the start of the game, a demeanor that Naughton attributed to being in a stadium for the first time since the airship crash, and to general apprehension about the precarious nature of the event. The servohound may have been an amalgam of metals and pneumatics, yet Naughton ascribed to Crandy a level of perception akin to an actual canine.

Or perhaps he was just imagining.

Now the fourth inning was complete; Gerald Jones had settled down after giving up the home run to Marsh and made quick work of the next striker, the Rhinos catcher Asher Perryman. Then the Helderan Manager, 'Squint' Gendel of the Hammerheads, further riled up the hometown crowd by inserting the Rhinos' hurler Derrek Gerren to face the heart of Setherian order. The game was close, just 1-0, the crowd still reveling in the spectacle in the bright sun and soothing breeze, in the athleticism of all the young stars on both squads.

Naughton noticed Vivian Lynam staring at him. He nodded, tipped his hat, and smiled. She turned back to the game, chattering with the owners seated around her, basking in the attention and the excitement of the moment. *A survivor, she is,* Naughton thought. He remembered Gill's words from the security briefing two weeks ago. "She is quite popular in the social circles, both Setherian and Helderan, yet no one quite knows her."

His new information, the information given him just a day earlier by Hood, was the proof Naughton had been seeking for months: Lady Lynam's complicity. She served on the board of directors of a firm that had received surreptitious League funding, a company that harbored the accomplices of the airship disaster.

In a few days' time, when the All-Star Game was complete, when the final festivities were exhausted, when the owners and players and reporters had dispersed to all corners of the continent, when he and the commissioner returned to

Schawmount City — finally then he and Gill would call in for questioning Vivian Packer Lynam, Roderick Coyle, and Iphonious Henry.

And he would finally learn the truth.

<hr>

BY THE SIXTH INNING HALLOWAY had been lulled into a soothing stupor by the gaiety and enthusiasm that enveloped Rebaley Field. The 44,000 fans were making the most of the occasion, shouting before each throw, voicing disdain at the arbiter's calls, indulging in the endless food and drink sold by concessionaires, and also enjoying drinks smuggled in, hidden in coat-pocket flasks and passed around the stands. No league officials, nor any of the local West Somerchester police, would object. After the tumult of the past few months, the people deserved it.

Then he sat up: Gendel, the Helderan All-Stars manager, was bringing in Asgar to hurl the top of the sixth. Halloway studied the Count warming up on the mound. Nothing seemed amiss: Asgar went through the warm-up routines that Halloway knew so well. Asgar tossed the rosin bag in his left hand, his throwing hand, dropped it to the ground, swiped some gravel from the mound with his right foot, and then, with clear deliberation, lifted his head and stared straight at Halloway.

The two locked eyes. Halloway offered the slightest of nods. Asgar replied in kind. Only when the hurler looked away did Halloway realize his own hands were clenched around the arms of the seat. He exhaled.

First up against the Count was Tyler Porter of the Fighting Camels, 36 years old and still a perennial All-Star. With the count at one ball and two strikes, Asgar induced Porter to swing at his weakest throw, the slider. The left fielder popped up weakly to center. Next came the Jackaloupes' second bagger, the switch-hitting Zachary Quinn, who had struck out earlier against Carson. A foul for a strike, next a swinging strike, and then with an advantageous 0-2 count, Asgar opted to get fancy, throwing three straight pitches at the corners of the strike zone, all called for balls.

The count was full; the Count was angry, perhaps at the arbiter, perhaps at himself. The sixth and final hurl of Quinn's at-bat was the purest of fastballs, straight down the heart of the strike zone, a throw which, if struck by the bat, would have produced a run as quickly as Pyce Marsh's earlier shot. But Quinn had

MICHAEL BARBATO-DUNN

no chance. His swing was one of the fastest in the League, but it wasn't fast enough, and Halloway wished there was some sort of clockwork device that could measure the actual speed of a hurler's pitches, for this throw would tests its limits.

Strike three. Quinn slammed his bat on the bag and stormed back to the dugout.

Then Asgar had no more desire to get fancy. The third and final striker of the Setherian inning, the Terriers' short-bagger Oliver Freeland, was offered a crafty breaking ball. He accepted and flied out to left field. Asgar had escaped, and with brilliance. Halloway knew that with the Helderan All-Star roster still replete with starting pitching, the Count was unlikely to return to the seventh.

Halloway watched as Asgar walked off the mound. Strangely, the hurler moved not toward his dugout but away from it, toward the home bag.

He saw the commissioner making his way to a small podium for his traditional sixth-inning respite comments.

He saw Asgar, facing the VIP section, quickening his pace in that direction.

Toward Lord Bart.

Oh my. Halloway gasped, rose to his feet and lurched toward the railing that separated the seats from the field, only to catch his foot on a handbag left in the aisle.

"Stop him!" he cried out as he tumbled down the steps.

——————— ———————

RONNELL FELL INTO A STUPOR. Perhaps it was the refreshing gaiety that enveloped Rebaley Field by mid-game. Perhaps it was the simple fact that good baseball was being played, that the League's best talent — crusty veterans and younger phenoms — were putting on quite a show. Or the simple fact that the nations, at least for the moment, had avoided a return to warring.

Or perhaps it was the flask of some godforsaken concoction that had been making its way around the seats of his section now three, four, maybe even five times. As it approached, Ronnell resolved to refuse, but each time his willpower weakened as it was handed to him.

No matter. He felt good. In fact it was the first time in quite a while that his chronically aching back did not bother him.

The Helderan All-Stars made quick work of the Setherians in the top of the sixth: one, two, three quick outs, with Ketter Asgar showing why he was a perennial participant in the exhibition. The Count had been with the Red Tummlyn Grizzlies in the Helderan North Division his entire career before being traded to the Flying Squirrels. The change of uniform clearly had not affected him.

But Ronnell never really liked the guy. A bit odd. Reports over the years of ignoring team curfews, of frequenting less than savory establishments during road trips, of arrogant behavior toward rookies. And then there was this clubhouse fistfight in which Asgar was apparently involved. Still, he'd been a winner with Red Tummlyn, and at 29 still had good stuff remaining in his left arm.

Ronnell heard a shout. Someone seated several sections off to his right and a good ten rows back had yelled "Stop him!" Ronnell looked up to see who had exclaimed, but the man had tripped, and was now falling down the narrow aisle of stadium steps. The columnist then looked back to the field, and realized Asgar was walking not to the dugout but toward the VIP section, where Cunningham, Lady Lynam, and most of the owners were sitting. The Count's gait escalated from a deliberate pace to a brisk trot.

The VIP section. The owners. The commissioner.

Vivian.

What is Asgar doing?

Ronnell jumped up from his seat, unsure if others in those brief seconds had picked up Asgar's change in direction. Most fans were focused on the direction of the shout, of the fallen fan. They were misdirected. What about the security forces? Could they intercede?

He leaped over the railing and onto the field, landing about 30 footlengths behind the right fielder.

And with aging legs and troublesome back, still whoozy with whiskey, the ballplayer-turned-columnist began to sprint.

NAUGHTON HAD NOT PAID CLOSE attention to the flurry of line-up changes for either club and hadn't realized the Helderan squad had a new hurler in the top of the sixth, Ketter Asgar.

By the time he did notice, the Count notched two quick outs against Porter and Quinn. This meant the All-Star Game was moments from the point Naughton most dreaded: Lord Bart's traditional State of the Leagues speech. The wooden gate in front of the VIP section would be opened, Cunningham would step out onto the field, technicians would drag their bulky amplification system to the mound, and the commissioner of the Leagues of SIP and Ale would address tens of thousands of fans.

And he had no idea what the old man would say.

The third batsman for the Setherians was Freeland of the Terriers. The short-bagger stepped toward the striker's box, took a few cuts in the air, played with the dirt at home, and then positioned himself for the Count's throw. Asgar went right after the fellow with high heat down the middle. Freeland took a weak hack, managing a lazy fly out to left field. Inning over. The sixth-inning respite, and Cunningham's speech, was about to begin. Naughton swallowed.

Even before the Helderan squad left the field, attendants began helping the commissioner to his feet, and stadium boys jumped up to open the gate and lay down a small flight of wooden steps. Naughton felt his gut tighten, and Crandy, at the side of his seat, whisked his tail and whined, sensing his heightened tension.

What could the old man say? That all was well? That the issues were resolved? That the first half of the 30th anniversary season was simply a bad nightmare, and we could all move on? Naughton guessed that Cunningham's speech was about to be all of those things — and that he would likely tread dangerously close to further antagonizing not just the Helderan owners, and Fitton indirectly, but even the mostly inebriated Helderan fans who had boisterously cheered and swayed throughout the first half of the game.

Naughton wondered: would they get infuriated? Would they storm the field?

Cunningham, an attendant on each arm, was now gingerly moving down three steps that had been placed between the open gate of the VIP section and the grass field directly behind the home bag. The moment seemed to slow. Naughton's heart pounded like the marching band's drums.

He heard a shout and jumped from his seat. Ketter Asgar was trotting not toward the Helderan All-Stars' dugout but toward the commissioner, his throwing arm outstretched, as if to shake his hand. Then, more oddly, he saw the columnist Ollo Ronnell on the field, running toward Asgar. He heard gasps from the crowd, then screams of the frightened and confused.

In that instant, he remembered the report he'd read about the fistfight in the Flying Squirrels' locker room involving Asgar. *An instigator, a clubhouse cancer.*

Then he understood: Asgar was trying to reach Lord Bart.

Ronnell was trying to stop Asgar.

Without hesitation Naughton looked down at Crandy and in a sharp voice commanded: "Asgar!"

And the hound leapt forward.

SANDER HALLOWAY FELT HIMSELF TUMBLING. Tumbling amid the screams.

The moments of the fall stretched on without end, seconds seeming as if hours. He felt distanced from his body. He could see himself careening down the flight of narrow stairs that formed an aisle between rows of seats. He could see fans watching as he tripped, as his body flew slightly up and then rolled downward, plunging. Some reached out to try to stop his fall, others flinched back and shouted.

The fall became shrouded in fog. He thought about Asgar, about Marsh, about his second wife, Ruthie. He thought about his first at-bat in the major leagues, how his heart had throbbed so mercilessly that he vomited in the locker-room after that inning. He thought about his first victory as a manager, and how that wondrous satisfaction lasted only until the following day's defeat. He thought about his father, convinced more in the sanctity of the cause than of the competence of the insurgency's leadership. He thought about dying.

Eventually he came to rest at the bottom of the section, against a wooden gate that separated the fan seating from the grassy area near the home team bullpen. He saw in his daze four or five men standing over him, some wanting to pull him to his feet, others insisting that he needed to lay still until a doctor was summoned. And then the men seemed to shift their gaze in unison, upward and off toward something in the distance.

They are watching the traitorous Count, he thought. *I should have stopped him when I could have.*

And then all was black.

OLLO RONNELL'S RIGHT KNEE GAVE way just as he was within four footlengths of Asgar. He slipped to the grass, the hurler still out of reach. A searing pain shot through the leg, as if a needle had been inserted.

Stop him.

He pulled himself up slightly with his arms. Asgar, striding forcefully still toward the commissioner, was now further out of reach. Ronnell could see Lord Bart, being escorted down the stairs, grinning broadly, apparently welcoming a chance to meet the All-Star hurler, oblivious to the potential threat that Asgar posed.

"Bartholomew!" he cried out.

"Bartholomew—" He collapsed, the pain of the knee now cascading throughout his entire lower body. *Bartholomew.* Prostrate on the field, not far from the first base line, Ollo Ronnell sobbed and shuddered. He could no longer see what was happening, could no longer lift his head. But in those seconds before he fully lost consciousness, he heard the jarring sound of a hound growling.

THE PATH OF THE SERVOHOUND was efficient. Crandy veered left, right, right again, through the legs of owners and guests and dignitaries and hangers-on. The micro-pneumatic condensers that regulated his movement had calculated the route, adjusting nearly instantly as the limbs of the humans shifted. His gait was a gallop, front paws bounding forwards as the hind legs pushed off the concrete steps. Right, left, left again, even through the tunnel of one man's legs.

His growl was distinct, pronounced.

Naughton took all this in: Crandy, rushing forward to save the commissioner. The entire VIP section, standing in alarm. The Commissioner, reaching to receive the outstretched hand of the hurler, Ketter Asgar. Ronnell, collapsing in a heap footlengths away, as if felled by mortar fire. Lady Lynam, throwing her hands over her mouth to stifle a scream, then rushing forward as well. Enoch Gill and his cadre of security guards, appearing out of nowhere and converging as quickly as the hound on the entire scene.

Cunningham. Asgar. Ronnell. Gill. Lynam. Crandy. All moving as if propelled by fate, by destiny, by unseen forces, all toward the precise same spot: a small patch of grass behind the home bag, on a field designed for the game of baseball, in a teaming city by a flowing river that fed into an endless ocean that surrounded the continent of millions of people struggling for an eternity to simply live among one another, even as he himself was frozen in place.

And then the servohound leaped into the air and landed not on Asgar but the commissioner, the old man, the beloved and brilliant Bartholomew Cunningham. Lord Bart.

"Crandy!" he screamed, and he too propelled forward, rushing to stop the hound, to retract his command. "Crandy — no!"

Gill was first upon the convergence of the commissioner, the hurler, and the hound. He barreled his thick Monystian body into Asgar, whose left hand was still extended toward Cunningham, pushing the player to the ground and shoving his right foot on his neck. Crandy, springing like a jackaloupe, attached his front paws to the Lord Bart's back and legs, knocking the commissioner forward and down to the grass.

Naughton scrambled too quickly to see the first bites. He covered the short distance from his seat to the front of the VIP box in just seconds, but he was not fast enough. Crandy tore at the old man's side, then the thighs and calves of both legs.

"Crandy—halt!" came Naughton's final pleading. He was now at the gate leading to the field, and in desperation he leapt forward to grab the crazed servohound.

Then time seemed to halt on its axis, as if he were floating gently toward the wretched scene. The hound looked up him, a bloodied piece of Cunningham's pant leg in his mouth, and stared directly at his master. The eyes, once so full of worry and concern, were vacant. There was no recognition. There was no love.

Then the device — for it was clearly no longer his Crandy — was gone. A musket shot traveled through its body, sending metallic sheeting and pneumatic tubing, condensers, and conduits exploding into the air.

Crandy. My Crandy.

Naughton landed in a patch of the cool grass, green and lush, manicured and sculpted for the game of baseball, a sport loved by so many.

And thousands of tiny remnants of his hound rained down upon him.

August 10

NAUGHTON SQUINTED IN THE DIM light, as if that would somehow allow him to see the dank cell better. Only a slim beam crept in from an opaque window high above him.

He appeared to be in a wing of the jail house that was sparsely populated. The cell held four thin cots but was empty of other prisoners. At least he had been able to sleep.

Not well, of course. Fitful. But sleep did come.

Between the darkness and restlessness, he'd lost track of the days since the attack. Now, lying on the cot closest to the light shaft, he guessed that this was the third day. Three days without contact with anyone other than Helderan investigators and guards bearing food. No visits, no messengers. No contact with Gill. No contact with Amelia.

Amelia. Dear, sweet Amelia. *Does she even know I'm imprisoned?*

The smell of the cell was as discomfiting as the lack of light: the odor was of stale urine and the corpses of rats. His nausea had finally eased by the second day. And though they'd fed him, the smell and the circumstance left him with little appetite.

Oh, Amelia. He prayed she wouldn't worry. But of course she would. He prayed the boys were not distraught.

But of course they were.

The events of the horrendous attack on the commissioner were framed in his mind as a scene captured in an engraving: the hurler Asgar, unaccountably moving toward and reaching for the old man; Ronnell in the distance, running toward Cunningham and then crumbling to the ground; Crandy, launching onto the commissioner's back, teeth bared, then shattered by the musket blast into shards of tubing and wiring too numerous to count, the hound's essence obliterated in a single shot.

And then: several guards surrounding him immediately, whisking him away without question or command. Frozen in memory was that instant in which they grabbed him, the instant in which he ceased to be a free man.

"Get yourself up." A guard now stood at the cell's door, fumbling with a ring of keys. "You've got a visitor."

Behind the guard came a balding man who Naughton guessed to be another Helderan investigator. So far there'd been four. They had each asked him to repeat in excruciating detail the circumstances of the attack as he saw them. Perhaps they were hoping to trip him up, to catch inconsistencies. But he had told the same story each time, and he had no doubt that this time he'd do the same. He had his images. His engravings.

But it was not an investigator. "Patrick Steggles, with the West Somerchester Office of Public Barristers." He extended his hand in formal greeting.

Naughton returned the shake. "Public Barristers? I thought you only represent the indigent."

"Yes, we do. But for some reason unknown to myself, the executive of our nation has commanded my office to dispatch to you free legal counsel. He does not want it said that you were deprived of representation."

"Fitton?"

"Yes, Executive Fitton."

"I have been deprived of representation since I was taken here. I have not been allowed to contact anyone. I have no idea if my wife even knows…"

"She knows." The man's tone was enough. Naughton sensed immediately: his imprisonment was known throughout the continent. How could it not? Cunningham was severely injured, if not—

"The commissioner?"

"He survived. The Leagues aren't saying more than that."

Naughton gasped for breath. He was not ready to hear such a statement. *The Leagues! I speak for the Leagues!* He shook his head and wiped moisture from the corners of his eyes. More so than the confines of an odorous cell, the revelation was jolting: he was — for the first time in two decades — outside the Leagues of the SIP and ALE, looking in.

Steggles opened his valise and withdrew a sheath of elegantly handwritten papers. "Mr. Naughton, no formal charges have been filed against you, and under continental law you can only be held five days. Two remain."

So, there it was, his answer. It had indeed been three days since the All-Star Game.

"And will there be charges?"

"I do not know. That is a decision for the West Somerchester Minister of Justice and, ultimately of course, for the executive."

"Fitton."

"Yes."

"What will they do?"

Steggles looked down at the papers and seemed to consider the question, but then proceeded without answering.

"I need you to tell me what you know. I need to understand why the servohound went after the commissioner rather than the hurler Asgar." The barrister's eyes bore in on him. The look was not accusatory, but neither was it sympathetic.

"Yes. Certainly. As I've stated repeatedly to the investigators, upon hearing the Squirrels' coach shouting, I commanded Crandy to go after Asgar—"

"What did exactly did you say to it?" said Steggles in an accusatory tone.

Naughton did not appreciate the interruption. But he knew he was not in a position to protest. "I said precisely one word: 'Asgar.'"

"Would that have been enough for the hound to know—"

"Yes, it would have been enough." Now he was doing the interrupting.

"Yet he attacked the commissioner."

"Yes."

"Why?"

"I do not know."

"Do you have a theory?"

Naughton took a deep breath. "There are clearly three possibilities. I can eliminate two of them. The first is that Crandy mistook the commissioner for the hurler as he charged forward. I do not believe that for a second. Crandy's existence, first and foremost, is — was — predicated on protecting the commissioner. He was aware, at every single moment, of the commissioner's whereabouts and status. Mistaking Cunningham for another — particularly another who he had been ordered to attack — is simply not, in my view, possible.

"The second possibility, of course, is one that I'm sure is being whispered about the lounge halls and publick houses throughout the continent: that I commanded the servohound to attack the commissioner. I do not know what more I can say in denial.

"The third possibility, of course, is sabotage, perhaps by the very conspirators who perpetrated the crash of the Airship *Lady Crym*. It is entirely possible, given that the hound was damaged and repaired in the wake of the crash, that he was stealthily programmed at an appropriate time to attack the commissioner."

Naughton's defiant demeanor crumbled a bit. He covered his eyes with his hands and lowered his head. "It is all I can think of. I cannot see any other possibility other than sabotage." His voice choked. Both Crandy and Cunningham — lost in the same instant. He had tried subjugating the pain now for days. But now he could do little as it rushed up and overwhelmed him.

Oh, Crandy. Naughton felt an ache throughout his chest. Crandy had been reprogrammed. Crandy was gone.

The two sat without speaking as he composed himself. After several minutes, Naughton wiped his eyes and looked up.

"Very well," said the barrister. "These papers represent sworn statements of most of those in the VIP section at the time of the attack. "Your story is fully corroborated by their accounts."

"What does that mean?"

"It means that any prosecution of you would have to focus on matters that go beyond the incident itself. Matters that are clearly confidential to the Office of the Commissioner and are outside the jurisdiction of the Helderan Executive."

"Therefore…?"

"Therefore, I don't see at this point how you could be charged, let alone tried."

Naughton felt his mood lift slightly. "So I'd be released?"

The barrister nodded. "Unless—"

"Unless?"

"Unless the Office of the Commissioner decided it is in its interest that you be prosecuted."

"What? Why would the commissioner want me prosecuted? That makes no sense!"

Steggles twisted the end of his mustache and considered the question. "I am not a politician, Mr. Naughton. Nor a bureaucrat. Merely a barrister. But I can certainly suppose a scenario in which the commissioner does so as a gesture of goodwill to Fitton. Or conversely, to make life more difficult for Fitton. There are multiple possibilities, and while they may not make sense, very little about this entire affair does."

"When will we know?"

"Likely by the morrow. Absent any charges, I will not allow you to be held

much more beyond that. Though if they do decide to file, your stay here will be quite indefinite."

Naughton cocked his head. "Wouldn't I be released? On my own recognizance? On bail?"

The barrister peered down over the rim of his thin spectacles. "Given the circumstances, that would not be a given."

"My stay here could be lengthy?"

Naughton sunk back on the cot and stared up at the shaft of sunlight, which was now waning in the late afternoon. *Am I about to become a sacrificial pawn?*

Steggles stood and gathered up the papers, then donned his overjacket and top hat.

"Sir?" Naughton asked plaintively.

The man turned back to him as the guard opened the steel door. "Mr. Naughton, I suggest your greatest concern now is not how many weeks you'd be jailed before a trial, but rather how many years you could be imprisoned after one."

WIDMERTOWN

SANDER HALLOWAY HAD BEEN GIVEN an indefinite leave of absence from the Flying Squirrels to convalesce from his fall at the All-Star Game. Now that the season had resumed, Archie Ferns, his striking coach, was running the team in his stead.

Ferns was a close friend and Halloway knew he could be trusted to adhere to Halloway's own vision for the team. But he'd heard not a word from him, not by visit nor even a 'tubed communique, and he suspected that the coach was distancing himself from Halloway.

He had sustained multiple contusions in the fall down the steps, and briefly lost consciousness. The hospital stay lasted three nights, and then he returned by carriage to his rented apartment in Widmertown. His back ached, his head throbbed, and the doctors said there was little to do but rest. They were not certain why he had lost consciousness, but they feared a concussion.

This convalescence was in fact the most prolonged time he'd spent in the depressing rental. Each night he heard yelling from the family that lived above him. Each day the shouting of street vendors pierced the walls.

On the morning of August 10th he wandered out to a nearby publick house to break the fast and peruse the *Widmertown Herald-Leader*. The Flying Squirrels beat reporter, Obediah Noone, had a long piece and Halloway settled into a corner booth.

Noone was usually a succinct writer, but this story rambled, as if he was torn about the topic on which to focus: the continued winning ways of the club, the tumult surrounding Halloway's absence or the effects on the League of the continuing political crisis. Noone had touched on all three, but the article seemed to go nowhere. *Perhaps that reflects how fans are feeling.*

Separate from the front-page sports coverage were stories on the crisis itself: the commissioner gravely injured, tensions between the two nations, the entire season in doubt. When his food arrived, he put the paper down. He had little desire to read more.

HALLOWAY WOKE IN THE MIDDLE of the night, sweating. He remembered only slivers of the dream: tumbling down the steps of the stadium. He lay in the bed, panting for breath, trying to recall more, but as he tried it only slipped further away.

He sat up, reached over to the nightstand and lit the lamp. The room seemed more pallid than during the day. He lay back and studied the figures cast by the lamp on the walls and ceilings. The bedpost's shadow was ominous, leering down at him like a mocking nemesis.

Is this what I have to look forward to when I'm done? he wondered. *An empty room, with shadows as my companions?*

He'd known all along managing would be a solitary life: weeks and months on the road, little loyalty from the owners who employed you, nor from the players who claimed the glory. Yet this was what he had to show for his 20 years of coaching: two failed marriages, no children, an apartment that would certainly never become a home. And a team that likely distrusted him now, a team now being run by someone else.

Someone else. It rankled him. He felt his mood shifting from anxiety to anger.

It's my team.

The bedpost shadow glowered at him, as if mocking his predicament.

Halloway rose, shuffled to the bathroom and drew a bath. While the water warmed, he stared in the small mirror that he used to shave.

I need to get back to my team. I need to talk to Asgar.

Then the mirror fogged over.

 MICHAEL BARBATO-DUNN

A knock on the door woke Ronnell. It was likely a hotel attendant bringing breakfast.

"Leave it at the door," he shouted. The person must have complied, for he heard nothing further.

The intense pain in Ollo Ronnell's right knee had dissipated only slightly since the incident. The doctor who had tended to him at the stadium had prescribed a tonic, refusing his request for a narcotic, and the bitter liquid had done so little that Ronnell, in a pique, had thrown it in the trash. He would manage the pain on his own.

The doctor had also ordered him to stay off his feet for a week, but was well aware even as he spoke the words that Ronnell had no intention of doing so. It was damn hard to even chew on a cigar, let alone smoke one, when he had to get around on crutches. There was the option of a steamchair, like that used by his editor Crom Corcoran, but that would have been logistically difficult, not to mention depressing. So crutches it was. He'd left them propped against the nightstand.

Corcoran had contacted him by courier the evening of the incident, ordering him to immediately pen a first-hand account of the affair. He had remained holed up in his room at the Cotillion and wrote it in longhand, working sporadically amid the pain. Only yesterday was the piece complete, much to Corcoran's chagrin, and a messenger came to retrieve it. Then he had slept.

Now it was morning, three days after the horrible events. His stomach churned in hunger, but the thought of making his way to the door for whatever food had been left seemed too much to bear. The crutches rested upright against the side of the bed, and with his right hand Ronnell grabbed one and used it to pull open the curtains behind him. Warm sunlight flooded in. The throbbing continued. He closed his eyes and slept again.

Another knock woke him two hours later.

"Go away, damn it!" Ronnell had never been a morning person, and with this wrecked knee disrupting his sleep, he'd much prefer to stay in bed until noon.

Another knock. "Mr. Ronnell?" It was likely a message from Corcoran. He muttered more profanities under his breath, then rose from the bed, propping one of the crutches into his right armpit to balance himself as he threw on his robe.

Another knock. "I'm coming, by god!"

He kept his right leg bent at the knee as he hopped on the crutch across the length of the room and opened the door.

It was an attendant, a young boy with a frightened expression. Behind him stood a stiff, slender man, his top hat nestled under his arm, his expression bemused.

"I'm so sorry, Mr. Ronnell, sir," groveled the attendant. "I told him you weren't taking guests. I told him he should simply leave his calling card—"

Ronnell shook his head. "That's fine. I know him." He retrieved a halfweight coin from his robe pocket and gave it to the boy, who muttered numerous thanks and scampered out of sight.

The visitor reached down and picked up the breakfast tray and stack of newspapers that had been left by the earlier attendant. "May I?" he asked Ronnell.

"Do I have a choice?" The question was rhetorical. He turned and Alexander Fitton followed him inside.

<hr />

The hotel room was small but had a bay window with a tea table and two chairs. Fitton placed the tray on the table, and the two men settled in.

Ronnell lifted the domed lid covering his breakfast plate, and scowled at the now-cold array of fried eggs and boar sausage. "So do tell," he asked, "Why does the Executive of the Nation of Heldera seek out a lowly baseball columnist?"

Fitton laughed. "I've heard you called many things, Ollo. But never 'lowly.'"

"You just haven't been around long enough." He poured some tea and offered it to Fitton, who waved him off. "How did you know I was here?"

"Finding the location of associates is never a problem for a national executive. The better question to me would have been: does anyone know we are meeting?"

"Fine. Does anyone know we are meeting?"

"I doubt it. No one beyond my own top advisers."

Ronnell pushed away the tray and swallowed half a cup of the lukewarm tea in a single gulp. Then he pulled the stack of the morning's newspapers toward him. On top was his own, the *Chronicle*, emblazoned with multiple stories about the incident and its aftermath. And the centerpiece of the front page, of course, was his column. He couldn't even recall what he'd written.

Fitton grabbed it and read the beginning from Ronnell's piece aloud. "'I was trying to save the life of Commissioner Bartholomew Cunningham. Unfortunately, I failed. And so did the Twin Nations.' Certainly dramatic enough, Ollo."

Ronnell snatched the paper back and scanned the rest of the piece. Hopefully,

the copy desk had given it a good once over. "It was a dramatic moment, Executive Fitton. You'd know that if you had been there."

"If I'd been there, it might not have happened."

"How so?" asked the columnist.

Fitton ran his fingers through his thick oiled hair and smirked. "Just a hunch."

"That is a provocative answer if there ever was one. By the way, is this on or off the record?"

"Off, Ollo. I'm not here. Do you understand?"

"Yes."

"So why do you blame the Helderans for what transpired, Ollo?"

"What makes you say that? I said both nations failed to save Cunningham. Now he's dead, or soon will be. I didn't single out the Helderans."

"Spare me your word-parsing. You and I both know that the subtext of your column is to blame those who sought political change in the past few months. And that dart is aimed squarely at the Helderans. Squarely at me."

"There is more than enough blame to go around. The Setherian owners did little to quell the crisis. They could have done so."

"How?" asked Fitton.

"For one, by being willing to talk honestly about an orderly succession. There are few things that are certain about the entire situation, but one of them is that Bartholomew Cunningham was not going to live forever, even if never attacked. A succession plan was needed, and the Setherians remained in denial. Second of all, the argument that the Helderans — you — have been espousing makes perfect sense."

"And that is?"

"That the surest way to prove to the Helderan people that their independence is genuine is by giving them at least partial control of the Leagues."

"Ah, yes. That would be our argument."

"So both sides are at fault. Hell, even the Amandeans can be faulted. The Rebular. The Monystians."

"And the press?"

Ronnell laughed. "Yes, especially the press."

Fitton sighed. "We can help each other, you know. I can give you information on what is taking place on this side of the river. Information that any of your competitors would be happy to have."

The throbbing of Ronnell's right knee, which had eased significantly after he downed the tea, returned swiftly. "And what do you need in return, Mr. Fitton?"

"Please call me Alex, Ollo."

"Alex, fine."

"First, I need to know who is truly in charge at the Commissioner's Office with Cunningham in such a dire condition. His man Naughton, as you know, remains in Helderan custody. Who is left? The other faceless bureaucrats? That Monystian security man? His paramour, Lady Lynam? The old guard of Setherian owners?"

Ronnell remained silent. He had not been aware that Naughton, Lord Bart's longtime Special Assistant, had been jailed. *Is Vivian in charge?*

"I need to know," Fitton continued, "who will step in, even temporarily. Secondly, I need to know what is planned. I need to have a clear sense of what short-term measures are coming."

"Surely you understand, I don't work for the Leagues. I have never been given inside access."

"But your many contacts within the Leagues, particularly the owners and team general managers on the Setherian side, constitute what is probably one of the most pervasive intelligence networks outside of the Magera."

"You flatter me, Alex. But you exaggerate."

"No I don't, and you know it." The Helderan leader rose and cleared his throat. "I want you to think about expanding our relationship. It can be mutually beneficial."

Ronnell nodded, then stared back at the breakfast plate. He was hungry now, and would probably succumb once the Helderan left.

"Here's one thing I will give you for your next column. Consider it a sample of what cooperation can bring."

"Again, is this off the record?"

"This is off the record, but you are free to use it in your charming little broadsheet, attributed to a top-ranking Helderan official."

"Fine. Go on."

"You can say that the Helderan owners, out of deference to the commissioner, remain committed to doing nothing until season's end. But at that point — regardless of the health of the commissioner — we will press our claims for Helderan autonomy. We will no longer be subjugated."

"The Helderans have had autonomy for 30 years."

"Hah!" the Helderan mocked. "You sound like your old friend Cunningham."

"What makes you so certain we were friends?" Now the throbbing was unrelenting. Ronnell wanted the man out. He wanted to eat, and then to sleep.

Fitton turned, replaced the top hat, and made his way to the hotel room door. "Thank you for your time, Ollo. I hope your knee recovers."

Ronnell, now furious, rose, placing full weight on his healthy left leg, and balancing himself against the tea table.

"Mr. Fitton, you best tread lightly. You don't want to be known as the man who returned the continent to another five decades of war."

The Helderan's rebuttal was swift. "If that happens, to paraphrase a certain newspaper columnist, there will be more than enough blame to go around."

And then he was gone.

August 11

WEST SOMERCHESTER

NAUGHTON AWOKE TO MORE SOUNDS, clanging and rattling mixed with footsteps. The shaft of sunlight was gone, and he had no idea how long he'd been sleeping. The cell's rancid odor struck him again, and he wondered how long it would be before he was accustomed to it.

Were all prisons on the continent so deplorable? They were controlled by local municipalities, not by the League Offices. Naughton wondered how many inmates became sickened by the conditions and whether the illnesses were of a serious nature. He vowed to investigate once he returned to his—

He stopped himself. The barrister's message had been quite clear. He needed to change his perspective drastically. He needed to stop thinking in terms of the life he had long assumed would be permanent.

The guard clattered in to announce another visitor, but this time it was a familiar and welcome face: Enoch Gill.

The security chief settled onto the same cot that the barrister had used. He eyed the guard, who stood within listening distance, and then glanced back at Naughton with a narrow gaze. Naughton understood the message: they'd have to watch their words, and assume that everything being said would be overheard and repeated to investigators.

Perhaps even to Fitton.

"I'm surprised they allowed you to visit."

"Lady Lynam appealed to Fitton."

"Lady Lynam?"

"Yes. To the best of my knowledge, she has become the de facto Commissioner."

Naughton studied Gill's expression intently. There was more, and he knew that the inspector was hesitant to say it with the guard so close. *She has taken charge. She, who is complicit.* The thought shook him. He'd been days away from having her and Coyle interrogated over the information that Hood had supplied. He should not have waited.

"And the commissioner?" he asked.

Gill averted his eyes from him, focusing instead on the mildewed floor of the cell. "The Commissioner, I am told, is battling to survive."

"Will he?"

"That is unclear. He is to be transported in a day or so back to Schawmount City."

"And what of the Leagues?"

"The games continue. It was Lady Lynam's first pronouncement. She handled it, I must say, masterfully. Only the first two days of the post-All Star Game schedule were canceled, and those games will be made up by the various teams in both Leagues over the course of the season. She insisted that this is what Lord Bart desires."

"Is that accurate?"

Gill dropped his voice to a whisper. "Unfortunately, I have no idea. I have been precluded from direct contact with the commissioner or his physicians."

Naughton rubbed his eyes, weary from the days of squinting. He longed to leave the cell. He longed to breathe clean air. He found himself in that instant wishing the broad-shouldered Monystian would simply overpower the guard, and all other guards throughout the jailhouse, and whisk him back to the safety of the League Offices.

He forced himself to end the reverie. He needed to hear fully from Gill without the monitoring of the guard.

"Five minutes," yelled the guard, responding to their sudden silence.

He started coughing. Violently. Loudly. Gill grasped the plan and called out: "He needs water. He cannot tolerate the mildew and fungus that is rampant in this cell."

The guard peered in, clearly doubtful at the tale, but then shook his head in disdain and disappeared down the hallway.

When the footsteps dimmed, Gill leaned toward him and whispered.

"They do not trust me."

"They?"

"Lady Lynam and Coyle. Together. They have fully seized control. The Setherian owners do not seem to know, or if they do, they acquiesce to the woman. Regardless, I am being removed from the discussion, from the decision making."

Naughton paused and gasped for a breath. The claustrophobia that he'd experienced since the start of the incarceration welled up in his stomach and chest. "What are they going to do?"

But there was no time for an answer. The guard returned with a small cup of water. "So your coughing has stopped, eh?" he sneered. "I'm thinking it's time for your guest to leave."

Gill nodded to the guard and then glanced back toward Naughton and stared.

Then he departed. Naughton reached down to stroke the fur of Crandy, the companion who had so long been at his side, and found only air.

August 12

In transit

THE CARRIAGE TRUDGED THROUGH THE countryside leading to the city, its wheels clanking on the uneven roadways. The horses hung their heads as they trotted.

Hundreds lined the paths. Some waved as the procession passed, others cried. Some held signs. "Our Brave Commissioner" was the message on one. "You Sacrificed for Us," said another. A third said, simply, "Thank you."

They loved him, thought Ronnell, watching out the small window of his own carriage, which had paused at the roadside. *Even 30 years later, they loved him so.* He had already begun thinking of Cunningham in the past tense. He would be gone, soon enough.

It was five days after the servohound's attack, and the people of the Twin Nations had paused from their routines. The Commissioner of the Leagues of SIP and ALE was being transported by ferry and carriage back to Schawmount City. Back to his estate. A team of four doctors and six nurses attended to him. The entire journey would take at least four hours. As such, the procession was funereal in tone.

It is a matter of time. Ronnell sighed. *At some point soon, he will succumb.*

Then there would be a bi-national funeral. Thousands upon thousands would turn out. A stadium would not be enough to hold the mourners.

Ronnell had been in the midst of checking out of the Cotillion hotel in West Somerchester when Lady Lynam's messenger had arrived. She asked that he meet her at league headquarters back in Schawmount City. *Dearest Ollo, we need you in this time of crisis.* The note gave no hint as to the agenda. He'd thought briefly of refusing.

First: Fitton wanting him to provide intelligence. Now Vivian, the apparent interim commissioner, seeking — seeking something from him. None of this was good. He was a newspaperman. His obligation was to his readers.

But she had asked for him. She said she needed him.

The ferry from West Somerchester had disembarked in Finchenland, due south of Schawmount City. A series of small lakes and tributaries separated those two cities, so the procession had no choice but to head northwest first, then around the lakes and east to Cunningham's home. At this deliberate pace, this portion of the trip would take two hours.

It was, appropriately, a gray day. Out the window he could see the Schawmount Lakes in the distance, shrouded in a low-lying fog. The crowds at this juncture had thinned, but not dispersed. Children had been hoisted atop their fathers' shoulders for a clear view. Some waved as they passed. Other simply stood and watched, perhaps morbidly curious. Some cried.

His carriage hit a crevice in the road, throwing him to his right. Pain shot from the damaged knee to his hip. He grimaced, but resisted crying out.

Fitton and the recalcitrant Helderans had already backed off. So said his own column, appearing in the latest *Chronicle*; a copy rested now on his lap. A clever young man, this Fitton. He knew there was nothing to be gained by being aggressive at this point, particularly with Cunningham so close to death. One misstep, one clear overreaching of his grand ambitions, and he would be viewed on both sides of the border as a crass opportunist.

Is Fitton the one who should lead? Ronnell wondered. *If preserving the peace is paramount, is this Helderan the one to achieve that?* A transition to Helderan leadership of the Leagues seemed the only peaceful option. Yet if it turned out that Fitton was complicit in the airship attacks, the resulting war would dwarf the Great Insurrection. The questions gnawed at him, more aggravating than the ache of his leg.

The procession traveled on in the fog, slowly and quietly. Mournfully.

West Somerchester

After Gill's visit, Naughton resolved to keep better track of the days. He found a small crack in the masonry of the wall and pulled off a tiny piece. It fortuitously snapped away so that its end formed a point. On a bit of the wall beneath the cot that he used each night he scratched five marks, one for each night he'd slept here.

He looked at the result, and wondered: would his marks one day fill the entire wall?

Eventually, he slept.

In the morning Naughton immediately knew something was amiss: the guards woke him, as they had the previous days, but the meal they delivered was comparatively sumptuous: a steaming bowl of oats, some grapes, and a crusty end of a loaf of brown bread. Even hot water with lemon.

The two guards watched him as he ate, one with a sneer, the other bemused. When he finished, they removed his tray and commanded him to follow them.

Down the dim hallway they trod, then through a series of maze-like turns, finally arriving at what appeared to be a sealed, windowless meeting room. Naughton imagined it was designed for inmates to meet with their attorneys, though his own counselor had been brought to his cell. Then a more grim prospect occurred to him: the room was used for interrogations. Violent, forceful interrogations. His gut tightened.

They seated him at a rectangular table in the room's center. Three gas lamps hung from the walls. "Wait here," said one guard, while the other simply sneered.

He closed his eyes and leaned back. He found himself imagining he was in his home, on his couch, Amelia sleeping soundly against him. The boys upstairs, dreaming perhaps of their own ball games. A simple scene, one that days ago was easily attainable, yet was now horribly out of reach. He shuddered and opened his moistened eyes.

After 30 or so minutes the door opened, and in walked the Executive of the Nation of Heldera, Alexander Fitton.

"Naughton, I'm sorry to see you under such dire circumstances. I trust my people have been treating you well." The two guards scowled at him, uncertain of how he'd respond, but Fitton waved them out of the room before he could answer.

"I have no complaints about the conditions, Mr. Executive. I am, though, not pleased that I have been held without charges, and that three days elapsed before I could consult with legal counsel, that I was not given representation of my own choosing, and that I have not been permitted contact with my employer or my wife—"

"Naughton, Naughton, Naughton. All in due time."

"There is little time here. The fate of the continent is precarious. And you know full well that your own nation's laws necessitate formal charges by today if you insist on continuing to hold me."

"Which I do not."

Naughton stopped. "Excuse me?"

"I'm here to free you. You may go. We will not be charging you. You will not be held any longer. Goodbye."

"Can you explain?"

"There is little to explain. I have known you, I have dealt with you, I have observed you from afar. As have the other Helderan owners. Your conduct and your devotion to the Leagues — nay, to the commissioner — is beyond reproach. I don't need any witnesses or forensic evidence to tell me you were not responsible for the wretched attack on Lord Bart. I have legal advisers who believe otherwise, who want charges filed. I have political advisers, who want a trial to increase leverage for our demands. I will not do so, much to their chagrin. I will not make you a victim of convenience."

Naughton exhaled. In one fell swoop, an enormously problematic situation for him was resolved. "I suppose I owe you my thanks."

"That is not necessary."

"What then is necessary?"

"Pardon me?" asked the executive. Fitton rubbed his mustache with his right hand and awaited a reply.

He's just a boy, Naughton thought. Without the facial hair, without his baritone voice, Fitton's youth would be painfully apparent. He probably would have failed to gain support for the executorship. *So much in this world is about appearance.*

But he is just a boy, and probably quite a scared one.

"Surely you are not releasing me simply out of the goodness of your heart, Mr.

Executive. You have determined that, politically, my release is advantageous. So what is it that you seek?"

Fitton smiled. "Andrew, I appreciate the degree to which you ascribe my actions as purely strategic. Besides, do you assume the Commissioner's Office will have you back? Do you assume that upon your release, you would be in a position of power once again? Because I certainly don't."

Naughton felt dizzy and steadied himself against the table.

Fitton's action now made sense: he would be free, but without position, without status. He would no longer be Special Assistant to the Commissioner. With the commissioner still ailing, still possibly near death, the public would never stomach his return to the post.

His career was lost, and he was about to become a pariah in his own land.

And this outcome was clearly the best thing for Fitton: the executive would be spared having to press charges and being accused of staging a politically motivated trial. Yet at the same time he was ensuring that Naughton was removed from any decision-making position, thus prolonging the leadership vacuum in the commissioner's Office.

It was, Naughton knew, a masterstroke. "Well played, Mr. Fitton."

The young man nodded. "Andrew, just eight days ago I suggested we help each other. You were quite too full of your deep-rooted Setherian self-righteousness to see the value of that offer. Suffice it to say, had you agreed we would now be having a far different conversation, in a far different location."

Fitton then stood, summoned the guards to re-open the door, bade Naughton a cursory farewell, and hastily exited.

The guards left as well.

The door remained open.

Naughton pondered the scene with foreboding. He was now free to go.

But to where?

WIDMERTOWN

HALLOWAY FOUND HER WAITING IN a circular booth in the rear of the restaurant.

"Ruthie." They exchanged tentative kisses on the cheek. A curving bench surrounded the table rather than individual seats, so Halloway needed to calculate how close to sit near her. Too far would seem aloof, too close would be presumptive.

"Are you recovering?" she asked. "I was worried."

"I'm fine. My back is quite sore, but you remember I've always had bad aches since my playing days. This is nothing new."

Her cheeks sagged slightly and strands of gray were now woven through her fine reddish-brown hair, but otherwise she was simply as he remembered her: a full face, high cheek bones, deep almond eyes.

"I'm sure you're understating things, Sander. Can you tell me what happened?"

He shook his head. "It's internal. Team stuff. Things went awry. I didn't handle it well."

"Obviously." She laughed, but he scowled.

Ruth was the one who had suggested they meet. Halloway hadn't spoken to her in seven years, since shortly after the divorce was finalized and he came to the house to retrieve the last of his belongings. In the past week she had seen his name in the accounts of the All-Star Game fracas and 'tubed a message that she wanted to check on him. She still lived in Widmertown. He didn't know if she had met someone else. He wasn't going to ask.

Their divorce had come shortly after he'd been elevated from Squirrels striking coach to manager, and the juxtaposition of the two events was stark: a professional accomplishment, a personal failure.

"How are you doing, Ruthie?"

"Fine. Though worried. Everyone's worried. We don't need another war. Have you spoken to anyone?" The fine upward curve of the edges of her lips when she spoke: he realized he missed it.

"What about?" he asked.

"What happened, of course. At the All-Star Game."

"Yes. Investigators have questioned me at length."

"That's not what I mean. I know you, Sander Halloway. I know you're keeping all of this inside."

He stared at her, then looked away. He swallowed. She knew him too well, even after all these years.

"Tell me."

The waitress, with immaculate timing, delivered their drinks. He had ordered a brandy, and the glass had never been more welcome.

"Tell me," she repeated.

"I don't know what to say."

She reached out and took his hand. "I'm hear to listen."

Only then did he notice the ring on her left hand. "What is his name?"

"Tom," she replied. "Thomas Creffeld. He's an apothecary. He is also divorced, with three children. They stay with us on weekends."

"Ah. So you're a mother."

"Yes. In a way." She strained to smile and looked down. "Now tell me what happened."

Halloway finished the drink in its entirety and told her everything: from the initial concerns about Asgar, to the locker room fistfight, to Marsh's report of Asgar plotting to hurt fans, to Langford's astute ability to distance himself from the mess. To his own bungled attempt at stopping Asgar from reaching the commissioner.

"Might you be charged?"

"No, I've been notified that I'm cleared. Investigators from the Commissioner's Office, heading up the formal probe, questioned me at the hospital. At this point, at least officially, I am not a suspect in any way."

"That must have been difficult."

"They stood at my bedside at the hospital and questioned me for three hours, over the objections of my doctors. And they asked the obvious question: 'Why didn't you simply go to league officials with your concerns about Asgar?'"

"What did you say?"

"I told them it was decided that we would handle the matter internally."

"Is that correct?"

"Yes. Langford wanted the matter to go away. To vanish."

"Because?"

"Oh, Ruth, surely you know why."

She finished her own drink, then signaled to the waitress for a second round. "I can venture a guess: he feared that escalating the matter would disrupt what looks more and more to be a championship season."

Halloway nodded. "You never miss a thing. Never did."

"Oh, you boys and your ballgames. The winning becomes more important than anything." Her tone was scolding.

"Please, Ruth. This is my last chance. We're in first place, and we're playing well despite everything."

"What do you mean, your last chance? You're only 62. Plenty manage beyond that—"

"No. You know Caffrey is impatient and prone to replacing managers who could not place their teams in the play-offs."

"Like most owners."

"Well, I've been managing for seven seasons and have only one play-off appearance to show for it, back in '20."

"I know all this. I still follow your team. I still read about you in the newspapers."

The second round of drinks arrived. He looked around the darkened restaurant and relished the bite of the brandy. It had been a glorious season, 1920. They had run away with the division. Congratulations abounded. As did free meals, drinks and winks from ladies at various establishments. The joy of that accomplishment lasted a single week, for the Squirrels were eliminated in the SIP League Continental Series rather handily by a Setherian behemoth — the Terriers of McKilligan.

That loss was still painful, for they had not even been competitive in the final round. The club's bats fell silent, as if in awe of battling for the championship, as if making it to the finals was enough. That was followed in '21 by an even more hurtful second place finish, six games behind the Screech Owls, and then a third place finish just this past season, seven games back of the Rhinos.

Yes, first-, second- and third-place finishes in three seasons, nowhere but down, and it was widely assumed that anything short of a return to first this year would cost Halloway his job. But now they were back atop the division. If they could hang on for one more month, he'd have his second post-season appearance. Maybe even have a chance for redemption against the Terriers.

Halloway closed his eyes and allowed himself to be satisfied, to block out the horrible events of the past week. But it was difficult. Small tears emerged. "I don't know how I can possibly go back."

"What do you mean?"

"I'm not sure I can face the players. They know I suspected Asgar was going to harm the commissioner. They know that my shouting from the stands incited the tumult that led the servohound to attack the commissioner."

"Don't blame yourself, Sander. You did what you thought was right. You have nothing of which to be ashamed."

He shook his head. "Ruthie, this is not just another job. I'm not an office manager. I run a baseball club. I need to be able to lead."

"Sander Halloway, when did you become so wracked with self-pity? You were never like this when we were together. You were a star, a national hero. And you were always so—"

"Full of myself?"

She laughed. "Yes. That is an excellent way to phrase it. You were full of yourself. Where did that go?"

He stared down at his hands and rubbed his fingers along the crevices of the wood table-top. *She always could see through the muddle.* The drink was empty again. He looked up to find the waitress, to signal for another, but realized Ruth had stood and wrapped her shoulders with a shawl.

"I have to leave now, Sander. I'm sorry for what's happened."

"Ruthie—" He began to protest, to urge her to stay.

"No, Sander. I must go. I will tell you though, if you stay away from your team much longer, you might as well resign. The boys deserve to know who is leading them. If it's not you, then they deserve someone else."

He watched her stride toward the front door, then pause and turn back.

"Go back to them, Sander. That's your life. It's all you have. Go back and be their leader."

In transit

It was all very strange. The cell door remained wide open. No guards were in sight. Naughton walked into the dim corridor, skeptical, fearful this was some sort of trick.

It was not. The Executive of the Nation of Heldera had given him his freedom; it was as simple as that. He took a deep breath, arched his chest outward and strode down the corridor toward the exit. Most of the cells that he passed were empty. The few other prisoners in this wing were sleeping, paying him no mind, oblivious that their country's leader had just visited.

Within minutes he was at the intake room, where he was met by the two guards who'd been on duty since the night before. They scowled at him, and the one who appeared to be the superior pointed to a pile of clothing on the counter — his clothes, the ones he'd been wearing when he was seized, what he'd been wearing four days ago when the commissioner was attacked.

"You can change in there," the guard barked, pointing to a lavatory. "The Executive has a carriage waiting for you."

When he emerged, mercifully freed of his prison uniform, he looked to the guards. "Do you need me to sign anything?" he asked in a neutral tone.

"Sign anything?" came the elder guard's reply, in a mocking voice. "You were never even here." And then he laughed.

An enclosed wooden carriage, driven by a single horse, waited outside. The driver tipped his top hat and waited for his direction. "Sir?"

"Schawmount City, please," he asked.

"I can travel only as far as the border."

"That is fine. I will take the ferry to Finchenland."

He settled into the back of the cab. The ride to the ferry took only 30 minutes, he knew, and if carriages were for hire on the other side of the river, he estimated he could actually be back to Schawmount City slightly more than three hours.

The seat in the cab was wooden, bereft of padding. Yet being able to look out the window at the passing countryside felt luxurious. He felt hungry, and considered asking the driver to stop for some fruit, but thought the better of it. Best to get back as soon as he was able.

At the dock he learned the previous ferry had left minutes earlier, and the next would not be for another hour. About a dozen other people were already waiting in line for tickets. Such was his relief at being freed that only now, standing in line, did he realize he had no money. He had been carrying none during the All-Star Game ceremony; there would have been no need. His wallet was tucked away in his overcoat, hanging in the closet of his makeshift office at the ballpark in West Somerchester.

Naughton pondered the predicament for several seconds when a man approached. "Mr. Naughton?"

"Do I know you?"

"Now you do. I am Bradwell Cummings, Chief Inspector of the Detective Division of the Municipal Police Authority of West Somerchester. I have been dispatched by Executive Fitton to ensure your departure from the Nation of Heldera."

"Good of him to be so concerned."

"Not concern, sir. He wishes to be rid of you as soon as possible."

"That may prove difficult, as I find now that I am without my wallet."

"Yes. I am aware of that." Cummings reached into his leather sidebag and withdrew a package. Your overcoat, your wallet, your other belongings. You will find them untouched. We are keeping your notes that were left in the office."

"Those are property of the Office of the Commissioner. The Executive surely knows he has no jurisdiction over that."

As his voice lifted, several others standing near them took notice. They moved

away from the line, and found a relatively secluded bench that overlooked the River Valencroft.

"I will repeat," Naughton told the man, "materials belonging to the Office of the Commissioner are solely held by the Leagues, and the Executive is directed to return them to us immediately."

"Under whose authority, may I ask?" said the Helderan.

"Under the authority vested in me by the commissioner."

"Ah, I see." The detective leaned back against the wooden slats that formed the back of the bench and smirked. "And what makes you think you retain that authority?"

Naughton paused and swallowed. "I— I have been Special Assistant to the Commissioner for 20 years, and have not been notified otherwise."

"Assume what you will, sir." The man rose to leave. "Assumptions are the facts of the foolhardy. But here's one of my own that you may very well consider." Naughton cocked his head. "I would assume that you not only have lost your position, but that you are a wanted man in your own homeland, as you are generally thought to be responsible for the attack on your nation's much-loved Bartholomew Cunningham."

The arriving ferry could finally be seen in the distance. Cummings walked toward his own waiting carriage and called out. "So cast aside your assumptions, Andrew Gilpin Naughton. You are about to learn first-hand the duplicitous nature of the Office of the Commissioner."

With that he was gone.

Naughton spent a few minutes composing himself, and then went back to purchase a ticket for the ferry that would take him back to his homeland, the nation of Setheridge.

Schawmount City

Decades ago, when he first started playing professional baseball, Ollo Ronnell realized the best way to overcome anxiety was to expel it.

Most of his teammates believed that anxiety was to be quashed, covered over. The palpitations of the heart, the quickening of the pulse, the sweat on the brow: all to be masked, subjugated, subsumed. But he knew the solution was to channel it outward, and he did this by focusing wholly on an object that would absorb the intensity of the emotion.

In most cases, it was as simple as smashing a wooden bat against a thrown ball.

Now though, waiting in the ornate sitting room outside the Office of the Commissioner, Ronnell had neither bat nor ball. So anxiety cascaded over him in waves, washing over nausea and the continued pain in his wretched knee.

He had not spoken privately to Vivian Packer Lynam in 30 years. To face her now, under such difficult and bizarre circumstances, added unaccountable levels to his angst. He closed his eyes and imagined himself taking swings.

Then she arrived. "Ollo. Dear, Ollo."

He stood slowly and offered his hand in a formal greeting, but she leaned upward and embraced him, pressing the side of her head against his shoulder. He wondered if she would cry. He placed his arms around her, applying little pressure lest their bodies come too close.

They remained together in this awkward hug for a long few seconds. Then she turned and without a word brought him into the inner sanctum of Bartholomew Cunningham's private office.

To his surprise, she settled into the leather swivel chair behind Cunningham's desk, her composure quickly regained. *His desk,* he mused. *She fits behind it quite naturally.* And he wondered suddenly if he was meeting with the next Commissioner of the Leagues of SIP and ALE. It was a prospect he had not truly considered.

"Thank you, Ollo, for coming," she told him,

"How is he?" Ronnell asked as he lowered himself onto a linen-upholstered settee.

"We are about to get an update."

"We?"

"Yes, you and I. It is not for publication, of course. But I need your guidance now, and I know, Ollo, that your devotion to the Eternal Ceasefire takes precedence over your career. And over age-old hurts." They locked eyes. An acknowledgment of her betrayals: it was probably as close to an apology as she would ever utter.

"Some hurts don't ease over time, Vivian."

She folded her hands, pursed her lips, and looked away. "I know that, Ollo. There hasn't been a day since I left you that I haven't thought about what I did to you."

"That I doubt, Vivian. You think about only yourself. That is very much the extent of it."

She rose from the desk and moved to the window that overlooked the courtyard at the center of the complex. "If you feel the need to express your anger to me, go ahead. I will endure it, because I need your help. If that is what it takes to have you at my side now, then please proceed."

"What makes you think I'm angry?"

"Ollo, you've been angry for years. Decades."

"And only now, when you're desperate, are you willing to hear it?"

She closed her eyes and nodded. "Yes, Ollo. Only now."

He pounded his palm on the desk. "I introduced you to him, for god's sake!"

She remained transfixed on the courtyard view, unmoved by his outburst. "I know."

"You took my idea! And he took you!"

Without hesitation she retreated from the window, walked to his side and leaned over, enveloping her arms around his sagging shoulders. "You may think me cold and calculating. You would be right. But I know you loved me, Ollo," she whispered. "I have always known."

He nodded, his breath heaving, his hands shaking. Her smell was, as ever, intoxicating.

After a few moments she released him, then settled in next to him on the settee. He took a deep breath and turned to her. "Why do you need me now?"

"I cannot do this alone, dear Ollo. It is that simple. And there is no one else. I have not left Bartholomew's side since the attack. Five days hospitalized in West Somerchester, then the difficult journey back to Schawmount City. This meeting is the first time I have left him. In ten minutes I am to meet with the League's remaining executive staff for an update. I ask that you take part in the discussions, that you offer your thoughts freely, and that you help guide the Leagues, and the Twin Nations, back to a safe haven."

"I am a reporter, Vivian. A columnist. You know that."

"Oh, believe me, we are aware of that every time the *Chronicle* is published. He calls you his thorn."

Ronnell laughed. "In his side, no doubt."

"Or elsewhere," she said, and they both smiled.

"But it will be hard for me to separate what I have learned in this capacity from what I gather in my duties as a scribe."

"Yes, I realize that. I have already contacted your publisher, Mr. Rinkins. He is offering you a paid sabbatical. The *Chronicle* will say only that your injuries sustained during the attack have lead you to seek an extended absence."

"So this has already been arranged?"

"Short of your acceptance, yes."

"It's as simple as that?"

"It is, dear Ollo, perhaps the only thing that remains simple at this dire hour."

"And if I choose not to abide by your terms, Vivian?"

"Then we will never speak again, you and I."

The throbbing in his bad knee now extended to the whole of that leg. "Given how little we've spoken in the past 30 years, I'm not sure how that gives you leverage."

"It is not meant as a threat. It is a simple statement of fact. I ask for your help. Whether I deserve it, now, after three decades — that is for you to decide."

She rested her head on his shoulder, and her hands reached out for his. He felt the weight of her body. The warmth.

"For you to decide," she repeated.

He stood with a jolt, pushing her hands aside. Searing pain enveloped his entire lower leg. "When do you need my answer?"

"I give no deadline. But there is little time."

He rose gingerly, putting most of his weight on the hardwood cane, then donned his hat and made his way to the door.

"Ollo," she called.

"Yes." He turned back.

"We saved the continent, the three of us. We were young and idealistic, and we saved the entire continent. We did it together. History will judge you well for that."

"No, Vivian." He shook his head. "History rarely remembers those who are trampled in its march."

Outside, he ordered his carriage driver to take him to Schawmount Stadium. Press identification in hand, he made his way into the visiting team's locker room, and found a sturdy bat that had been left near the batting cage.

He grabbed a bucket of balls and a short locker room stool, then hobbled out to the batting cage, using the bat as a cane. He placed the stool down, the bucket next to it, and for 30 minutes he sat, tossing balls into the air with one hand, then swinging the comforting bat with both.

Bat to ball. Bat to ball. And again.

The throbbing of his leg was unrelenting, but the motion was soothing, restorative, as Ronnell sprayed the vacant field with imagined two-baggers, each hit easing the pain ever so slightly.

MICHAEL BARBATO-DUNN

SCHAWMOUNT CITY

ANDREW NAUGHTON RETURNED TO SCHAWMOUNT City by a combination of public carriage buses and cable cars, rather than a rented cab. Not having bathed or shaved in days, he probably looked wretched. So public transit was not only less expensive, it provided some sense of anonymity, as other passengers were apt to avert their eyes.

Anonymity. The words of the Helderan detective echoed: "You are a wanted man in your own homeland." If true, anonymity was a good thing.

Yet he remained unsure about the best course of action upon his arrival. The options were few: arrive at the League Headquarters and proceed to his office, as if it were simply a routine day back at the job, or ask a guard to announce his arrival. Or perhaps he should first return home to Amelia and the boys.

Over the course of the return he settled on the latter option. He craved seeing his family. The poor boys: what were they thinking? What was Amelia telling them? Certainly to little Isaac she'd be discreet, probably telling him that Papa was very busy at his job and would be home when he could. But Jack, about to turn 13, was old enough to understand far more. How much of this peril could the boy handle? Naughton felt himself well up.

Their two-story house was in a hamlet just beyond the Schawmount City limits, tucked away on a quiet road that rarely saw much carriage traffic. By the time he disembarked the last bus, night had fallen. The neighborhood was quiet, save for crickets chirping in the distance and the rustling of high branches. After just a few blocks, he was sweating profusely.

Ten minutes later, he turned down two short streets and arrived at his own, Brendfall Lane.

Their street. Their home.

He stifled a short cry. Four armed guards stood at attention, posted on and in front of the perimeter of his property. Three Schawmount City police carriages were stationed outside as well.

Naughton fell into a crouch and skirted behind a tree to avoid detection. His hands shook and clawed against the bark of the tree. He wanted to scream. He wanted to run to the house and burst open the door to reclaim Amelia and the boys. He wanted this nightmare to end.

Inside the house, gas lamps were lit only upstairs. *She's putting the boys to bed. She's reading them a story.*

One of the guards abruptly turned and took a few steps in his direction as if alerted by a sound. Naughton remained still. The tree that he hid behind was a well-aged maple, broad enough in trunk to mask his entire body from their view. Other trees and shrubbery in the outcropping would shield him from sight of the neighbors.

The guard, who Naughton judged by size and girth to be of Monystian descent, stood still, peering and listening for some further sounds. He wore a patch on his right upper arm: the League security logo. Naughton held his breath, clasping the back of the tree with both hands to steady himself. After a few moments the man turned back, and resumed his slow patrol in front of the house.

The guard's retreat allowed Naughton to relax slightly, and to repress the intense wave of emotion. *Now is not the time for that. Now I must be strong.*

He resolved to remain in place for hours if necessary, lest any further sounds from his movement prompt the curious guard to move closer.

He would wait, as long as it took.

And he would formulate a plan.

August 14

SCHAWMOUNT CITY

THE DRIVER TAKING OLLO RONNELL to the League Office managed to ride over what was likely to be every crevice and gutter in the roadway. The carriage trundled to and fro, and the shaking of the cab wracked him with pain. He vowed to find a different doctor once he returned home, one that would prescribe a narcotic to finally deaden the pain.

He had earlier sent a message to Vivian by courier that he would arrive early, 30 minutes before the news conference, so they could speak directly. So he could convey his decision.

On his lap now lay the day's *Chronicle,* featuring his latest column, and he took a moment to re-read it:

> "...*But three things are left unanswered, and if they are not immediately divulged at the League's scheduled news conference, we*

plan to press for clarity. Firstly, who is in charge? Secondly, what is the status of the investigation into the All-Star Game incident? Thirdly, what was the role of the servohound's owner, Special Assistant Andrew Gilpin Naughton, and where is the man?

"Nothing less than clear answers on these crucial points will satisfy your faithful scribe, for we know that you, dear readers, need those answers as well. The future of our great continent depends on it."

Ronnell closed the paper as the carriage neared the League Office. There was a time when he would have thought such writing too hyperbolic. But the severity of the national crisis made this melodramatic prose appropriate.

The Twin Nations were exhausted by it all, so it seemed. The previous evening, at the bar at the hotel, positioned in a corner to greet well-wishers and have a full sweep of the room, Ronnell had sensed the fatigue. "Damned Scientificka," blamed Nan Fallon, who worked in the Rhinos' front office. "The Setherians brought this on," countered Clarence Clare, the Warthogs' Chief Statistician. But that had been the extent of it. Others had stopped by to inquire about his health, but no one else brought up the larger matter of the attack on Cunningham or the future of the Ceasefire.

Another crevice, another jolt to his woeful knee.

———————

Vivian stood at the front entrance as the carriage arrived, expression solemn. He stepped from the carriage with his crutches, and she greeted him with a slight hug and brush of cheeks. Days of worry were evident in her reddened eyes.

"I cannot do this," he whispered. "I cannot help you."

"I know," she replied. "I expected as much. In fact, I expected you would simply reject my request out of hand. Thank you for taking time to consider it."

"I wish there were some—"

She held up her hand and silenced him. "No. Say no more." Her thin lips quivered. "I will get through this alone."

"Do you understand—"

"Stop." She put fingers to his lips. "Stop. You don't need to explain."

"I do—" he began.

"No, Ollo. I am the one who owes you an explanation." She looked away, her eyes moistened and blinking. "You believe I left you because I loved Bartholomew Cunningham."

"Yes, but—"

"Let me finish, Ollo. You assumed I loved him. But I didn't. I don't believe I ever did."

"Then… then why leave me? Because of your mother?"

"Yes, because of my mother, though not because she disliked you. Indeed, that would have been reason enough to stay with you!"

"I don't understand."

"I left you for Bartholomew because I wanted to show her that I could become more successful, more powerful, than she ever was. I wanted to prove to her that I was better, and that I didn't need her. Once I told Lord Bart of your idea, I knew he could end the war with it. He was magnetic. He could change the continent."

"And by being at his side, you would be part of it."

"Yes." She wiped her eyes with her kerchief.

"And your mother would see you as being integral to it."

"Yes."

"And she would be proud."

Vivian looked up at Ronnell and shook her head. "Oh, no, Ollo. Not proud. She would be jealous. That's what I wanted — for my mother to envy me. To covet my success."

"Did she?"

"I suppose. We never spoke again."

"Never?"

"She disavowed me. Such was the depths of her jealousy. She ended the monthly stipend on which I depended and removed me from their wills." Vivian pursed her lips. "So that, in the end, is what I left you for. You: the dearest, sweetest man I'd ever met."

Vivian kissed his cheek again, turned and rushed back inside. A League guard, standing nearby, likely eavesdropping all the while, glanced in his direction.

Ronnell struggled to keep his voice composed. "I'm here for the news conference."

"Indeed, sir. So you are." The guard grinned as he opened the door. "Down the hall to the right."

———————————

MICHAEL BARBATO-DUNN

LIMITED BY THE CRUTCHES, RONNELL needed every minute to make his way to the League press room. He settled into one of the back-row chairs, easier to make a hasty exit if necessary, and better to watch not just the speakers but his often-unpredictable colleagues as well. His heart was pounding after the walk. After his talk with Vivian.

He took the open seat next to Maddy Looper. "Ollo, you're looking no worse off. How are you feeling?"

"Other than constant pain through my entire right leg, I'm faring fine."

"Well, you certainly put yourself in a difficult spot at the All-Star Game. What the hell were you doing?"

"Oh, I thought I'd be a hero for the day, Maddy. Too bad my body didn't cooperate. And you? What did you see?"

"I was up in the press box. Bizarre sight from there, I have to say. None of us could understand what was going on. Asgar starts off toward the commissioner, there's a commotion in the stands, you start running on the field, and then that dog-device knocks Cunningham to the ground and starts chewing on him. All within ten seconds, I'd guess. It was as if the world suddenly went haywire." She rolled her eyes.

"I think it has, Maddy. I think it has." Looper had been covering the Mad Dogs for 20 years now. The constant travel and deadlines had taken its toll; her skin was pale and wrinkled, her cheeks dotted with sunspots, her hair gray and wiry.

After a few moments the reporters hushed as a single League official came in to the room, and Ronnell recognized him immediately: Andrew Naughton's own assistant.

"Ladies and gentlemen, I am Roderick Coyle. I have just been appointed as the Special Assistant to the Commissioner of the Leagues of SIP and ALE. We have several updates for you on a number of fronts. Please let us review them before your questions. First and foremost, the health of the commissioner. Bartholomew Cunningham remains under constant medical care and his physician describes his condition as serious. Lord Bart has voluntarily relieved himself of responsibilities of running the Leagues—"

This immediately prompted at least four reporters to shout out questions, but the young man waved them off. "As I said, I will take questions when I am done. The commissioner has relieved himself of responsibilities for the operation of the Leagues. He remains alert and talkative, but he needs, more than anything, to be resting and free of stress. He will convalesce at a private location. We will say nothing further about the extent or nature of his injuries, and we will only provide further updates on his health if and when there are changes. In the meantime, you can assume that his condition is unchanged unless we state otherwise.

"Secondly, and as you know, the Leagues of the SIP and ALE have resumed their regular season despite the terrible events at the All-Star Game. The Office of the Commissioner is now overseeing the continuation of the season in full consultation with both Setherian and Helderan owners—"

"Are you now the commissioner?" shouted one scribe.

Coyle scowled. "Bartholomew Cunningham remains the commissioner. He is simply stepping back, for now, from decision making. Again, please no interruptions. The season will continue as scheduled. Helderan and Setherians owners have agreed to put all political discussions aside until the off-season. Attendance is down throughout the continent. People are, understandably, in a bit of shock. We did have a few incidents of name calling at some of the ALE League games yesterday in which the Helderan clubs were hosting Setherian city opponents. No fights, though, no fisticuffs. All team general managers have been keeping us updated and remain on the watch for any incidents.

"And finally, the incident itself. Our security chief, Inspector Enoch Gill, is overseeing the full investigation. I am about to tell you two facts, but we will not answer any further questions about the incident. First, we are certain that the servohound was sabotaged, essentially programmed to attack the commissioner. Second, we do believe it to be linked to the crash of the Airship *Lady Crym*. How the two are linked, we cannot yet say. A full report on the investigation will be made public once it is complete. We do not expect completion until after the conclusion of the Continental Series of both the SIP and ALE leagues."

Coyle looked up. "Now I will take your questions."

Ronnell leaned forward. This would be the most difficult part for the young aide. He'd handled other public matters for the league before, but none of this magnitude. The questions flew at the new special assistant with a fury, from every corner of the crowded room.

"Did Andrew Naughton, your predecessor, sabotage the hound? Is he part of some broad conspiracy?"

"We are not sure. We know he commanded the device to attack the Squirrels' hurler, Asgar. Ostensibly, he thought the hurler, Asgar, was going to harm the commissioner."

"Was the Count, in fact, going to do that? Why is he still being allowed to play?"

"We have questioned the hurler closely. He denies any ill intent."

"So Naughton was wrong?"

"No comment."

"What does that mean?"

"It means no comment. There is an extremely fine line between what I can tell you as hard, irrefutable facts and what is, at this point, conjecture. I can say without any doubt that Asgar denies any ill intent. Beyond that is speculation."

Ronnell was impressed. He actually enjoyed the deft manner with which Coyle was handling the crowd, fielding the questions almost as cleanly as a sterling short-bagger scoops up line drives.

"Is the commissioner dead?"

"The commissioner is very much alive. I spoke to him this morning."

"How do we know you're not lying?"

"That's an absurd proposition. He survived, and he is convalescing."

"When will we see him?"

"When his doctors approve his return to public appearances. That could be many months."

"Mr. Special Assistant, your office has previously attributed the crash of the Airship *Lady Crym* to this mysterious Jellum character. Where is he? Has he been questioned?"

"As I stated, I will not answer any further questions about the investigation. That will come in due time."

Then a non-stop barrage: "Did Jellum sabotage the servohound?" "What about Halloway, the Squirrels' manager? Didn't he know about Asgar?" "Has Halloway been suspended?"

To all of these, Coyle simply scowled. "Does anyone have further questions about League operations? Otherwise, we are complete."

Ronnell raised his hand.

"Yes, Mr. Ronnell," signaled Coyle. "Good to see you here."

"Mr. Coyle, you seem to have received a promotion. Yet you've been noticeably quiet on the status of your predecessor, Mr. Naughton. Where is he?"

Coyle stared directly at Ronnell. Seconds went by, as if for dramatic pause.

"In fact, sir, I'm glad you asked that. I can confirm the following facts regarding the status of Mr. Andrew Naughton. First, as you may be aware, he was

placed into custody by Helderan officials immediately following the attack on the commissioner. What none of you know is that five days later, Helderan officials had no choice but to release him. Our understanding is that investigators felt that they lacked sufficient evidence to file formal charges, and as you know, no person may be held beyond five days without a formal criminal complaint.

"However—," and again Coyle paused, "Mr. Naughton has been relieved of all official duties with the Leagues of the SIP and ALE. He is considered a person of interest in the Leagues' formal investigation into the heinous attack on the commissioner. And most importantly, his whereabouts remain unknown to us. Guards have been posted at his home.

"So I close with this declaration: Andrew Naughton is now considered a fugitive. If he hears these words, we beseech him to turn himself in to the closest law enforcement agency. If he chooses to remain free, he should consider himself warned that our investigators will utilize every resource to find him. Trust me when I say that he will surely find the results of cooperation far more preferable."

The room erupted in a cacophony of shouts and declarations, and questions to which there would be no further response, for Coyle — the new spokesman for the Leagues — had left the room.

Ollo Ronnell waited a bit, 10 or 15 minutes, for the others to disperse, then slowly picked up his crutches and made his way back to his waiting carriage.

There was no need to hurry. For though he had another column to write, the words of Vivian Lynam slowed his pace.

August 15

Outside Schawmount City

NAUGHTON LET A ROOM IN a dilapidated boarding house in Quintell, a hamlet about 1700 fieldlengths southeast of Schawmount City. He'd found a hand-written 'room for let' posting on the notice board in the town square.

The owner, a sour, squinting woman who identified herself only as Mrs. Drebb, needed one week's rent in advance, but fortunately the rate was low enough that he could pay it with the cash he had on hand. There seemed to be no evidence of a Mr. Drebb, not any autonomic help, no half-butlers nor sweepsters, and the house bore evidence of poor upkeep: broken faucets, loose floorboards, dustballs in the corners and a sloping, creaking bed.

The woman served the guests the same fare each morning: poached hen eggs, wheat biscuits topped with a smattering of butter, and extremely bitter coffee. The morning meal was served at a long table in a chilly, dank room off her cellar, and Naughton was fairly certain that rats feasted on the crumbs once the guests left the room.

But it was the type of place where no one asked questions of you. And that was what he very much needed.

Three other men sat at opposite corners of the table, each mumbling a gruff greeting to the others, then disappearing into their thoughts. A copy of the Finchenland *Steampress* had been left on the table. Finchenland, home to the Mastadons of the ALE League, was a pleasant town on the River Valencroft, about two hours southwest of Quintell by carriage. Likely that the locals here preferred the *Steampress,* a feisty tabloid, to the staid Schawmount City broadsheets.

His head throbbed and he forced himself to finish a second cup of the coffee in hopes it would ease the ache. He glanced at the front page: the edition was August 14, the previous day, and front page bore an artist's rendering of Coyle, standing at a podium, depicting his news conference that morning. The headline blared above him: "Very Much Alive": Coyle's description of the status of Lord Bart. Naughton put down his fork and began to read, and when he finished, the acidic coffee was more welcome.

"Fugitive," Coyle had pronounced him. *Our investigators will utilize every resource to find him.* None of it came as a surprise; he had steeled himself for this very word from the moment he had found the guards posted outside his house.

But were they really trying to find him? Naughton had his doubts. He had spent the better part of a week in Setherian territory, relatively close to Schawmount City, yet never once had he been stopped, never once had a citizen studied him with suspicion. No wanted posters could be found. And the guards at his house? With police carriages parked in front? What was the point of that? If they wanted to capture him by luring him home, a far more effective tactic would be to post agents in hiding.

No, the search for him was likely a sham. It was possible that Coyle and Lady Lynam had no real desire to see him placed in custody, that they had declared him a fugitive simply to appease the public.

Or, it was possible was that the two had placed Gill in charge of rounding him up, and the security chief was doing his best to make sure he was *not* captured.

He pushed the cold eggs away. He was tired. The world had collapsed around him. He couldn't see his family. The commissioner to whom he had devoted the last 20 years was fighting for his life. The Ceasefire which he had worked endlessly to preserve was now a hair's breadth away from collapsing.

Does my freedom even matter?

Mrs. Drebb ambled into the breakfast room with coffee. "Last pot. No more after this."

"Yes, m'am," replied the others. Coffee would fuel their silent reveries. Perhaps they simply spent their days mulling lost ambitions. Lost loves. Mistakes and bad choices.

What were my mistakes?

AFTER BREAKFAST HE RETURNED TO his room, washed, then donned his coat and left the inn without so much as a nod to the woman. He'd bought a full-brimmed cap and he was growing a beard; that was the extent of any attempt he made to mask his identity. Down the lane toward the center of the hamlet, a light blanket of fog hovered over the neighboring fields. Carriages passed by, the drivers scowling in his direction. Friendliness had given way to a bleak mood here. Perhaps over the entirety of the continent.

At the publick square he bought some fruit from a street vendor and a copy of this morning's *Chronicle* for more recent updates, then found a bench. The headline was more jarring than the previous day's story about Coyle's news conference.

FITTON MOBILIZES FORCES, DEMANDS PROOF OF CUNNINGHAM'S HEALTH

(Crenshaw City, August 15) — The Helderan Executive, his Excellency Alexander Fitton II, today announced a partial mobilization of national forces in the wake of heightened tensions between his sovereign nation and the nation of Setheridge.

Exec. Fitton said currently conscripted men would be called up to

active combat duty by week's end. The total number of reservists being activated is estimated by officials at approximately 20,000.

"I take this action with the utmost caution, and with a heavy heart. I pray fervently that none of the conscripts will ever face actual combat. But after a lengthy examination of recent events, I can only conclude that Helderan defenses need to be mobilized. I ask the families of those who have been summoned to pray with me for a speedy and peaceful resolution to this crisis, and I thank you for sharing your sons with our nation."

At the same time, Fitton derided the announcement by the Office of the Commissioner earlier this week as 'purposely vague,' and demanded what the executive called "proof positive" that the assessment of Bartholomew Cunningham's health was accurate.

"What the peoples of both nations need at this point is certainty that the commissioner is convalescing as described. Statements given by lower League officials without such proof are only cause for further concern."

The executive stated that the Office of the Commissioner had one week to offer such proof. "Short of seeing the commissioner himself, the only definitive proof would be to hear directly from his physicians," Mr. Fitton said.

Finally, the executive clarified that all SIP and ALE League teams in Heldera would continue to participate in the season, even as the military forces are mobilized. "We'll keep the games going. It is vital to the entire economy and spirit of the continent," said Mr. Fitton. "Even if the Eternal Ceasefire hangs precariously at this historic juncture, we will continue to honor it."

Naughton put down the paper. A group of schoolchildren passed him, then a mother pushing an infant in a pram. He shut his eyes briefly. Fitton, keeping pressure on the Office of the Commissioner. Keeping the Setherians on guard. It was an astute gambit.

Fitton's demand was legitimate, he supposed. Both nations needed to know more about the commissioner's health than the few sentences Coyle had offered. Would his physicians speak to the press? Naughton couldn't imagine why they would not. Unless—

It was too horrible to imagine: unless Cunningham was already dead, or so completely incapacitated as to be incapable of leading. Both were very real possibilities, but both would mean that Coyle's comments were either outright lies or, at best, bald exaggerations.

The enormity struck him. *Lord Bart could be dead, or dying, and I am not able even to see him.*

A robin fluttered down in front of him. It looked for scraps, then sang a few notes that sounded almost a question. Then it was gone.

Amelia. Jack. Isaac. And the old man. I cannot see a single one of them.

It was a fine summer day in a quiet park in the hamlet of Quintell, a glorious day in fact, and those who passed by a solitary man on a bench could not help but wonder why he was crying.

KERN

HALLOWAY RETURNED TO HIS FLYING Squirrels just as the team boarded a carriage coach for a two-hour trip to Kern. It had been three days since his meeting with Ruthie. Three days to summon the will to do this.

The players stared at him without words, without greetings, as he boarded. He had expected nothing more.

He settled in to one of the front most seats on the long coach, in the rows reserved for the coaching staff. Next to him, the veteran infielder Lucius Cameron murmured, "Welcome back, Coach," but quickly leaned back and closed his eyes to cut off any possibility of conversation.

So be it.

He returned with the squad in first place in the Helderan South Division. The Screech Owls and Monkeys already had losing records and had long ago fallen out of contention. Only West Somerchester could challenge the Squirrels at this point; the Rhinos were just two and a half games back. First place: it was, he presumed, the only thing preserving his job right now.

Halloway peered at the coach seats around him. Though late morning, most of the boys seemed to be napping.

That was a relief: he'd expected some amount of whispering once he'd stepped on the bus. But the ache of his back pounded without let-up, a relentless reminder of the fall down the steps at the All-Star Game. He leaned back in his seat and tried to rest.

THEY FACED AN AFTERNOON GAME against the Screech Owls. Halloway stood on the small strip in front of the visiting team's dugout where strikers would take cuts during a game prior to their own at-bats. He called out for Keating. "How's he look?"

"Sharp as ever."

Asgar was warming up for his first start since the All-Star Game. The hurler wore his socks high today, to just below the knees, and from a distance it gave a sense of greater height to an already towering frame. *He has always looked imposing.*

"What has he been saying?" Halloway asked.

"Saying? About today's game?" Keating cocked his head.

"Gabe, please. You know of what I'm speaking."

Keating nodded. "He was questioned at length the day after the incident. He started throwing again two days later. His usual boisterous attitude is absent."

"Please bring him over."

"What? Now?"

"Yes. Bring him in. We have to talk. And I'd rather do it before the game than on the mound."

"But—"

"Bring him in."

Keating summoned the veteran with a whistle and Asgar lumbered over to dugout. Halloway led him to the visiting manager's office.

"How's the shoulder feeling?" Like many hard hurlers, Asgar had battled shoulder soreness much of his career, though he had had few instances of having to be placed on the injured roster.

"It's fine coach." Asgar's stare did not waver. "Anything else?"

"Yes." Halloway looked to the right and left, ensuring no one else was nearby to overhear. "I owe you an apology," he admitted.

Asgar picked at his cleats and said nothing.

"I owe you an apology, Ketter Asgar. Whether you accept it is up to you. Whether you choose to accept me as your manager going forward is up to you. But I owe you at least that much."

Asgar picked at the brim of his cap and looked everywhere but at the manager. "I suppose you do."

Halloway swallowed hard and leaned forward. "The truth, Ketter, is that I don't trust you. I've never trusted you. That's why I did what I did."

The hurler was equally fast with a response. "What you did was cowardly."

"How so?"

"You should have just come to me. Or go to the authorities and have me questioned. You did neither. Instead, you ended up looking foolish, and ended up precipitating the very thing you were apparently trying to prevent — an attack on the commissioner."

Halloway fumbled with the papers on his desk. Nothing Asgar had just said could be refuted.

Asgar looked back at the field, where other team members fielding taking ground balls. "Can I go now, Coach? I need to warm up more."

"Yes, Ketter. Go ahead."

The hurler adjusted his cap and turned to leave, but then stopped. "Oh, and coach, one more thing: if you're so sorely in need of a person to distrust, take a close look at your little boy Marsh."

THAT AFTERNOON KETTER ASGAR THREW with ferocity. High heat, down the middle, with an array of sliders and change-ups mixed throughout. Then to further flummox the strikers, a nasty curve that dipped down and in. Halloway stood in his favored spot in the dugout — against the brass railing nearest the steps — and studied the hurler. The Count held nothing back.

But the Screech Owls' starter, 33-year-old Jody Harmon, was equally sharp, and by the end of the fifth inning, the Kern club had a 1-0 lead. Halloway's boys went out in the top of the sixth frustrated, but first bagger Gillighan Alley got things going with a base on balls. Marsh was next up, and worked the count full before flying out to center. Next, the third bagger Wrye lashed a double on Harmon's 1-0 fastball, sending Alley to third.

With a chance to tie the game, up came the 24-year-old second bagger, Frederick Dunbar, full of potential but struggling so far this season to hit above

.250. Here, though, the youngster proved equal to the task, lining Harmon's first throw to right for a single, scoring Alley and advancing Wrye to third. Game tied. The boys in the dugout, pensive until then, burst out on a row of applause as the Kern fans groaned.

Silas Berbery, the stout right fielder, struck out swinging for the second out. Two on, two outs. Halloway was relieved to have the game tied, but felt his gut tighten at the thought of letting Harmon escape with just one run allowed.

Next up: the eight-hole batsman, the switch-hitting short bagger Ike Gamp. He laid off the Kern hurler's first offering, just outside for a ball. Then, with Harmon focused entirely on Gamp, Dunbar on first took off running, easily swiping second bag without even a hint of a throw from the Screech Owls' backstop.

Halloway shook his head. Dunbar was ambitious, but he should not have run, for first base was now open. And sure enough, Screech Owls' manager Hendry Smallwood did precisely what Halloway expected. He intentionally walked Gamp to load the bases, taking the bat out of Gamp's hands, and leaving Harmon to face the hurler, the Count himself, Ketter Asgar, for the final out.

It was a by-the-book move, a percentage play. Asgar had notched just seven hits all season to that point, and his batting average was a microscopic .082. It was not a fair match up: Harmon could induce Asgar into the third out with his eyes closed.

The Count, like many hurlers who had no prowess as a batsman, was prone to swinging at the first offering in hopes of a fastball. In this instance, though, he didn't swing but it cost him anyway. Harmon hurled a splitter, low and away, for a called strike.

The second throw was identical in form and location, so Asgar swung and feebly popped up, the ball curving foul into the stands near the home team dugout, just out of reach of Kern first-bagger Marion Desmond.

Two strikes. Two outs. Bags loaded. Harmon undoubtedly wanted to be done with this long inning; he had already thrown 24 times. So his third throw to Asgar was a fastball, straight down the middle, the type of throw that would leave no room for guessing from the arbiters. A throw designed to coax a mediocre batsman into swinging hopelessly late.

But the Count wasn't late. He timed his swing perfectly, connecting on the heart of the bat with a sound that was pure and golden, and the ball sailed out of the stadium with such speed that the outfielders didn't bother to give chase. A high rocket that cleared the center field fence. A slam of the grandest sort. Later they would measure the shot at 359 footlengths, a distance that would make even the most grizzled slugger proud. For a hurler to connect in this way was astounding.

The Kern crowd was silenced. Some began to leave.

With those runs providing a solid lead, Asgar went out in the bottom of the sixth inning, plowed through the Owls' line-up, and continued through the seventh, eighth, and ninth. One-hundred-seventeen pitches, 76 of them for strikes. A complete game. Three runs yielded, all earned. Four runs batted in. Final score: 7-3.

A masterpiece.

When it was done, Asgar stalked off the mound, accepted quick offers of congratulations and made his way directly to the clubhouse. Halloway, on the dugout steps, offered a hand, but the hurler pretended not to see it and trotted down the tunnel steps.

The manager saw others in the dugout, even the coaches Ferns and Keating, looking at him, studying his reaction. Halloway ignored the stares and slowly made his own way down to the silence of the visiting manager's private office.

It should have been the most satisfying of wins, for it meant the Flying Squirrels remained safely in first place. But he felt bile in the back of his throat and suppressed a gag.

That was Ketter's cleansing, he thought. *His catharsis.*

And Sander Halloway wondered if he'd ever experience his own.

QUINTELL

BETWEEN SLATS OF A WINDOW blind slim shafts of sunlight crept into the otherwise dim room, and it warmed him so much that he felt drowsy. He had slept with difficulty yet again, so additional sleep was a welcome thought. But time was crucial to Naughton; he could ill afford to be rising late.

He needed a plan. The options were few: turn himself in voluntarily or attempt to somehow find the true conspirators on his own. Neither choice was likely to yield a resolution to the continental crisis. Neither would necessarily result in his exoneration. The stark realization prompted him to finally bound out of bed.

On the first floor, Naughton peered around into the kitchen for Mrs. Drebb to inquire about a fresh pot of coffee, but she was not to be found. A servochef sat rusting in the corner, long since out of service. Its eyes, though, seemed to be studying him. He turned back toward the common room and stopped cold.

MICHAEL BARBATO-DUNN

A hooded man sat at the table watching him. Staring directly at him, wordlessly. Not one of the boarders.

In that instant he pondered whether to flee or give himself up. But the figure pulled back his cover. "Naughton."

"Gill."

"I am glad I found you."

"Are you here to arrest me? If so, let us be done with it. I'm in no condition to try to outrun you."

"No, sir. I'm not here for that."

Naughton cocked his head. Then he sat down across from the Monystian.

"Is it safe to speak here?" asked the inspector, glancing at all portions of the windowless room.

"It'll be fine."

"You were easy to find, actually."

"No doubt. I fully expected your men would have rounded me up a day or so ago."

"I've kept Coyle at bay, so he thinks you are well underground." Naughton cringed. The reality of Coyle's unbridled ambition was jarring.

"How is the commissioner?"

At this Gill scowled and shook his head. His dreadlocks, which had been bundled under the hood, shook free to his shoulders. "I do not know."

"You've been removed?"

"Not formally. I still sit in on certain meetings with Coyle. But I'm excluded from his discussions with Lady Lynam, and Coyle is giving me little if any information on matters related to the commissioner or the political situation. I'm getting only commands. Working blindly."

Naughton leaned back, perplexed. "But does he truly want me brought in?"

"Yes. He would relish that."

Naughton's demeanor faltered. He covered his eyes with his hands and lowered his head. Both Crandy and Cunningham — lost in the same instant. And Coyle, a traitor.

The two sat silently for a few moments as he composed himself. Naughton wiped his eyes and looked up. Gill narrowed his gaze in a look that was both suspicious and sympathetic. Then he surveyed the room as if to reassure himself of their privacy.

"Sir, we have identified at least three witnesses — all of them Helderan —

who were in the VIP box for the All-Star Game, all of whom distinctly heard you command the servohound to attack Asgar. And they are willing to testify publicly to that effect."

"What? Who are they? Helderans, you say?"

"Yes, including one team owner."

"Would that end the suspicions?"

"As they are Helderans," said Gill, "I would certainly hope so. But one cannot tell."

"Does Coyle know this?"

"Yes."

"And?"

"And I don't know if he shared that with Lady Lynam. I do know that their official stance toward you is unchanged."

At that moment, Mrs. Drebb walked in and scowled. "Mr. Timber," she addressed Naughton with the pseudonym he had given her upon letting the room. "I told you my house is not a place for entertaining!"

Naughton scowled. "My apologies, Mrs. Drebb. My guest is here for just a few more minutes."

"Very well, but more than five minutes and I will be charging him! Do you understand me? I don't run a social parlor."

"Yes, m'am. Absolutely." The woman scuffled off, muttering to herself. There might have been a time when Naughton would have found the exchange humorous. Now was not that time.

"This leaves us, it would seem, with few avenues," Naughton said. "The attack on the commissioner came before we could question Coyle or Lady Lynam, and now, obviously, I am in no position to do so. Jellum remains at large. The information I gleaned from Hood concerning possible involvement of Dr. Henry has also led nowhere, and it would be ill-advised for you to directly question the Scientificka, as it would arouse Coyle's suspicions."

Gill waited until the woman's footsteps could no longer be heard, then replied in a hushed tone. "There is one thing, sir, concerning Henry." The Monystian looked solemn.

"Go ahead."

"Hood's minions told you that a shipping company had employed Jellum's three accomplices."

"Correct. Drewel Coast Lanes."

"With our esteemed Dr. Henry named as a partial owner."

"Yes."

"Well it seems that Drewel Coast Lanes was not the first shipping company in which Henry had a financial interest. He also owned a stake in another such firm. But Helderan officials shut it down two years ago."

"Shut it down?"

"Yes, a local matter. It drew little attention, and the matter was only reported once, in a brief item in the Kern newspaper."

The inspector reached in to his overcoat and withdrew a newspaper clipping from an inner pocket for Naughton to read:

Shipping Venture Shuttered Amid Controversy

(Kern, July 14, 1921) — Constable Chisel Bassington IV today announced that a Kern dockworks company has been padlocked and closed for business pending an investigation into what Bassington said are shipments of illegal materials.

Bassington refused to say what was being shipped that prompted the closure of Valencroft Shipping and Express. One police source, though, indicated that some of the shipments included cadavers. Bassington, as is his custom, refused to comment on that aspect. Company officials could not be reached.

No arrests have been made, pending a full investigation, said the Constable.

Naughton looked up, then in both directions, hoping that neither the housekeeper nor any of the guests were in the vicinity, then leaned in. "Cadavers?"

"Cadavers," repeated Gill. "They were being shipped to Kern. Apparently, they were not found out until several slipped off a skiff in front of a group of tourists. My sources said most likely prior to that point, local Helderan officials were being paid off to look the other way. But once the mishap occurred, with out-of-towners witnessing it, they had no choice but to take action against the shipping firm."

Naughton reeled back and fought against a wave of nausea. Gill sensed his reaction. "I'm sorry, sir."

"And did the newspaper report anything further?"

"Not as far as we could tell. Most likely everyone was paid off to simply let the matter disappear."

"Disappear, like the bodies."

"Yes."

"So then Henry simply created a new shipping company?"

"Yes. Six months later, Drewel filed for a local business license."

"Can't we just have Henry arrested—" he stopped mid-question. There was no 'we.' He had no power to order an arrest. He had no position.

Footsteps signaled the return of the boarding house owner. The inspector rose and shook his head in disgust, clearly not at the impending interruption, but at the new facts at hand. "But there is an answer. And by virtue of being a fugitive you are, ironically, in the best position to find it."

Naughton nodded. "Because I am, for better or worse, outside the law. That is what is needed."

"Yes."

"In the meantime, do your best to keep Coyle at bay."

"Sir, I absolutely will endeavor to continue to search for the fugitive." At this they were both able to raise a brief smile.

September 13

WIDMERTOWN

HALLOWAY STRODE THROUGH THE POORLY lit tunnel that led from the clubhouse to the Squirrels' dugout. The game was to begin in one hour; the visiting Monkeys of Gregorson were on the field taking striking practice and he wanted to watch.

He chewed on pulpar seeds and fidgeted with his timepiece. He tried to convince himself to relax: the Flying Squirrels had a three-game lead over the Rhinos of West Somerchester, with three games left to play. His team needed to simply win one out of three contests against the Monkeys to clinch the Helderan South Division and ensure a spot in the play-offs. One victory among the final three games of the season.

But Halloway found no solace in the simple mathematics. The possibility that his team could lose all three — and then see the Rhinos sweep their opponent — would constitute a collapse of historic proportions. It would guarantee not only the end of the season, but a degree of ignominy that would last for decades.

And then, of course, there was the bigger picture: it had been nearly one month since Fitton had re-instituted a military draft and ordered the activation of thousands of reservists. And the latest reports showed that Setherian forces had quickly responded in kind.

He paused at the tunnel's terminus, where it opened out to the field. He closed his eyes and took in the relentless churning of the pneumatic piping that snaked through the bowels of the stadium, powering the lights, scoreboard, and public address system. It pulsed as if an organism.

It is only a matter of time before the games are suspended.

He took three quick steps up and out of the tunnel and into the dugout, beyond which he found blazing sunlight, lush grass, and the comforting sound of bats striking balls.

"SANDER, WE NEED A FEW minutes." Halloway turned. It was Langford, trailed closely by the team owner, Sir Willison Caffrey. He followed the two men back to the clubhouse.

Perhaps this is it after all, he thought. *Perhaps they are not going to wait. I am being fired.*

The trio proceeded in a line through the locker room and the outer clubhouse, then up a narrow corridor to a gas-lit conference room.

Halloway started before either man had a chance. "I can spare you any need to be apologetic, gentlemen. I understand the need to make a change now. I will not make a scene. The difficulties of this season have been borne by many people, so I have no desire to make this move even more difficult for you, for the team, or for the fans. Thank you for the opportunity to have served you."

The owner and general manager looked at each other in confusion, then smiled. "Sander," said Caffrey, "We have no intention of firing you. The All-Star Game is not at all why we are here. I actually wouldn't mind if it was that simple."

Halloway relaxed, but only slightly. "I see. Then what is it?"

"The draft. We are not sure what it means for the remainder of the season. We

are not certain, in fact, even if there is a post-season, whether we will able to field the team as we know it."

"Why not?"

"Because some of our players will be eligible. Anyone under 23 and of able body. And we highly doubt that ball-players, no matter how vital they are to our national pride, will be exempt. Fitton's announcement made clear that the political needs would take precedence over anything else, including — and perhaps especially — over the needs of the Leagues."

Halloway counted to himself the youngsters on the Squirrels' active roster. Three were under 23: the little-used utility infielder Samuel Cook, who owing to a fortunate dearth of injuries had played in only a handful of games; the outfielder Ambrose Goldwell, who hit for average and offered solid defense in center; and of course, Pyce Marsh. The budding star. The strongest offensive threat on his club. With just three games left in the season, Marsh, at 22, had tallied 16 home runs, 68 runs batted in, and 44 stolen bases. He was a threat both in terms of power and speed. Halloway's ambivalence about the young man was strong, yet the thought that the club could suddenly be stripped of its primary offensive powerhouse was unsettling.

"There is, unfortunately, more," said Langford.

Halloway braced himself. "Go ahead."

"Hard-line rebel groups have again mobilized along the border. We don't know if, at this point, they have been prodded or even funded by Fitton. But we do know that there have been new reports of clashes, and one of them took place just 4,000 footlengths from the city of West Somerchester."

Caffrey leaned forward. "The League Office has decided it is not safe enough to allow fans to travel to today's games. They are being urged to stay home. The situation is becoming too volatile."

"So the game is canceled? Will it be made up?

"No, it's not canceled," replied the owner, Caffrey, apparently in disgust. "The League insists the games go on."

"What does that mean?"

"It means, I would imagine, that some fans will ignore the warning and come anyway, but we can expect that today's games, and perhaps more to come, will be played in nearly empty ballparks."

AFTER SEVEN INNINGS THE MONKEYS boasted a four-to-two lead. But the bottom of the eighth brought him relief.

With the Monkeys' right-hander Seth Calle on the mound, Squirrels catcher Jeremy Minnocks reached on an error, then Gillighan Alley smoked a double up the middle to drive in the backstop. Marsh, batting clean-up, fell behind in the count, no balls and two strikes, but then proceeded to lash his own double down the right-field line. Alley scored without a throw, Marsh was at second, and the game was tied. Cook, who Halloway had earlier inserted at third base, flew out to right, deep enough for Marsh to advance to third.

The few fans in the stands — maybe two hundred had shown up — seemed to simultaneously exhale. Dunbar was intentionally walked, Berbery singled, driving in Marsh and sending Dunbar to third. After the third bagger Cameron struck out swinging, Halloway dispatched Ike Gamp to pinch hit for the hurler, Harald. Gamp laced a shot to center for a single, advancing Berbery.

Now the bases were loaded and the Squirrels were up by a run, five-to-four. The Monkeys' manager, Peter Horn, went to the bullpen and summoned his excellent middle man, Monty Merganser. Merganser, with a sub-3.00 earned run average, was known throughout the league as a great rally killer, and he relished these opportunities to shut down squads that were threatening.

"Blengin' Goldie," Ferns, hovering next to him, muttered. Halloway understood why the striking coach was fretting: for even though bases were full, their next batsman was Ambrose Goldwell, small and spry, a rookie with great promise, but lately mired in a terrible slump. Halloway had insisted on sticking with him, playing him every night, but the 22-year old struggled with breaking balls and the opposing teams seized on that. In fact, on this day he had gone hitless in his first three trips to the home bag.

"Watch for low and away," Halloway advised Goldwell as the youngster made his way to the home bag. Low and away: it was precisely where Merganser would locate his pitches to the kid. The middle man had great control, able to target pitches with a degree of precision that left other hurlers in awe. He doubted Goldwell could hit anything if Merganser made his mark.

The first throw, to everyone's surprise, was low but inside, and the young batsman had no trouble holding off. Next Merganser ventured into the middle of the strike zone and Goldwell fouled it off. The third toss: again down the middle, but with a curious dip at the end. Also fouled off.

Virtually everyone in the Squirrels dugout began yelling: "He's cutting!"

"Check the ball." "Where's the blade?" Mergenser long had a reputation for cutting the ball: using a tiny blade hidden in his glove to nick the leather globe and prompt it to make surprising twists and turns, just as they'd seen in his previous throw. But the arbiter paid them no mind and play resumed.

Now Goldwell was down in the count, one ball and two strikes. At this point, Merganser shook off his catcher's signaled suggestions and went to where Halloway had expected he'd go from the start, on the outside corner of the strike zone. A nasty fastball, low and away.

And Goldwell, to Halloway's surprise, showed the sort of patience that he'd been lacking as a batsman all season. He held off on that throw and the next, each determined by the arbiter to be outside the strike zone. Now the count was full.

Merganser, frustrated, danced around the back of the hurler's mound and fumbled with the rosin bag. He'd expected to make quick work of the light-hitting youngster. But now the count was full, the bags were loaded, and he had no choice but to target his next offering down the middle. He knew it, his backstop knew it, and everyone in both dugouts knew it. He would go in with all the speed he could muster and hope that the ball would blow straight past the kid.

Halloway and Ferns slipped closer to the railing at the front of the dugout. Merganser settled himself, dropped the rosin, wiped his brow, then positioned himself for the throw.

His wind-up was smooth, his delivery fluid, and the ball emerged from his mitt like a musket shot.

Sander Halloway was able to follow the path of the ball as if time had slowed, and he could see in that split second that the ball inched upward as it hurtled toward the home bag, directly into the heart of the strike zone. Young Goldwell was ready with an equally smooth swing and smacked a line drive.

The ball skimmed just over the arm of the Monkeys' leaping short bagger, arcing out toward left field just along the foul line, then rattled around in the dark corner as their left fielder gave chase. By the time he retrieved it, there was little he could do but toss it back to the infield.

The bases had been cleared. Goldwell ended up on third, tipping his cap as the adulation from the sparse crowd stretched on for several minutes. Three more runs were in, six total in that inning, and the Flying Squirrels had an eight-to-two lead. In the top of the ninth inning, the Monkeys' final chance, Halloway's closing hurler, Ryan Foreman, yielded a solo home run to Gregorson's lead-off man but then recovered to shut down the next three strikers.

The game was won.

The division was clinched.

The smattering of fans bellowed cheers, and the players tumbled out onto the field in jubilation. They surrounded Goldwell, who, with his surprisingly smooth swing, had won the biggest game of his life.

Halloway watched from the dugout, flicking seeds into his mouth, nodding as the other coaches walked by and patted him on the shoulder. After a while the teammates made their way down into the clubhouse, where the traditional bottles of Helderan sparkling wine awaited. The celebration would go deep into the evening.

LATER HALLOWAY WAS SURROUNDED BY the scribes and answered the perfunctory questions, and then retreated to the quiet of his cramped office, where he began his immediate preparation for the first round of the play-offs. The opening series, for the Helderan title, would be a best-of-seven against the Hammerheads of Bereton Park, who had clinched the North Division earlier in the day. The winner would then advance to the best-of-nine SIP League Continental Series.

The play-off was to begin in four days, on the 17th, with two games at home. He charted out a pitching rotation for the entire series. He would use a three-man rotation, just Harald, Asgar, and Skelly. For now his fourth starter, Broughan, would not be needed.

He put down his pen and rubbed his eyes. Wild screams and giddy catcalls resounded from the locker room. He was glad the boys were able to celebrate. He was relieved to have clinched, to have made the play-offs. But his relentless foreboding intensified.

War is coming. And I may have helped precipitate it.

Sander Halloway laid his head in the cross of his arms on his desk and tried to rest. Then he rose and moved over to his office cot. He'd continue his planning in the morning.

September 15

GREGORSON

FOR THE SECOND TIME IN two months Andrew Naughton made an incognito trip to Gregorson to see the Magera leader, Phangorious Hood. But unlike the July journey, he now opted to travel by airship.

He boarded not at Schawmount City — the risk of recognition would have been too great — but west of the city, at a coach carrier in the township of Selenbend that offered cut-rate travel. Like the cable car, he would have little chance of being spotted, but it was infinitely faster. The craft would arrive in Gregorson in just two hours.

"You want a window side?" the ticket master asked. "I have one still open. Not much of a crowd today. Seems folks are afraid to fly, what with all the talk of warring."

Naughton, his cap pulled down low over his eyes, nodded wordlessly, then slid over some bills in payment. Gill had given him extra cash to get through the next few weeks.

He had not been on a dirigible since before the crash of the *Lady Crym*. The ship held 50, seated on a single level. Accommodations were sparse compared to the ships to which he was accustomed: no restaurant, no pub, no private rooms. Instead it simply held five rows of seats, a lavatory, and spacious windows from which to view the flight. Most of the dozen or so passengers were families, couples with children in tow. After the entry door was secured by the wingman, the youngsters squealed with delight as the pneumaticist activated the primary generator and the commander announced that the passengers should prepare for ascent.

Within minutes they were above the cloud line, and the children looked at their parents in surprise as the steam engines kicked on. Their expressions were jolts to his gut: he had done his best to sublimate his yearning to see Amelia, Jack, and Isaac, but several of the children on this flight were nearly the same ages as his boys, and their presence now was a stark reminder. The children pointed in delight as they could see Schawmount Stadium in the distance, gleaming in the sunlight.

He remembered Ernest Winder, for so many years the head grounds keeper at the stadium. After Naughton had been hired by Cunningham he moved to Schawmount City, and had taken to attending Jackaloupes home games when the time permitted. On weekends he arrived early and took notice of Winder's attentiveness to the field, watering, weeding, perusing every incline and crevice until forced off by batting practice. The man cared immensely about every blade of grass, as if the field was his child. Eventually they struck up regular conversations, and Winder told him he was a widower, that he in fact did have a child, who was by then a young woman. Amelia.

His gut tightened at the memory. *Amelia.*

Their courtship was brief and fueled primary by Amelia; he supposed he had been more focused on League matters. She learned to forgive his frequent lack of attentiveness; she understood his duties. More so, she understood the game: not just its rules and its way, but its allure. That had been instilled in her by her father.

They married two years later, in 1910; Jack arrived a year after that.

Now the airship took a sharp turn eastward and pulled away from the teaming city. It glided over the River Valencroft, dancing in and out of clouds. Once it was above Helderan territory the craft pulled south, and the morning sun now engulfed his view. It warmed him. The ship would soon be over West Somerchester, and then would push further down to Gregorson and the southern edge of the great Continent.

Amelia's father had retired a few years ago and still lived in Schawmount City, not far from the ballpark, and often helped with the boys while Naughton was away. He imagined Earnest was helping his daughter now. He imagined Earnest was as worried as she.

His thoughts turned to Jack, now 12: old enough to understand what was happening. To understand that his father was embroiled in the crisis. But did he know his father was a fugitive? Did he know his father could face trial? Did he know that he himself could be subject to the military draft in just five years?

The dirigible turned westward. The sun dropped away and the river came back into view. Naughton could spy the tiny figures of rowers, five to a boat, training on the waterway. A few sailboats meandered through. And off to the east, further into Helderan territory, he made out a series of four large encampments, arranged as a square. He spied tents and horses, cannons and carbines.

Naughton shuddered. Military forces on a scale not seen in 30 years were being organized, yet rowers practiced on the river. Children flew in airships. Ballgames were being played. Life — leisurely life — was somehow still continuing on the divided continent. He was not sure if that should be a source of solace or discomfort.

DESPITE ITS LACK OF OPULENCE, the craft was regal in its silent descent. The children aboard bounced in glee as the airship emerged below the cloud cover and glided to the ground. After the crew confirmed its land ties were secure, Naughton stepped down a path of wooden steps from the bay and found carriages for hire waiting. But he chose to walk the rest of way.

He had memorized the street plan of the waterfront district for his first visit in early May, and that effort served him well now. He was able to navigate the narrow, winding pathways with enough ease that passersby would think him a resident. Gregorson was abuzz with activity, particularly the open air markets, and he wondered how many families were stocking up in fear of a return to warring and the blockades of trade goods that would create. It was late afternoon when he arrived at the store-front. He rested on a stone ledge across the way.

He waited. He calculated he would not have to wait long.

Fifteen minutes later, a hulking man in a black leather overcoat emerged and walked directly to him. "What is your business here?" the figure barked.

"Please tell Mr. Hood that Andrew Naughton seeks a few moments of his time."

"I know no Hood."

"Spare me your deflections. I have been here before. If Hood is not in, I will wait."

The guard furrowed his brow and leaned closer, studying Naughton's eyes. He turned, retreated inside, and then reappeared after a few minutes. "Come."

⎯⎯⎯⎯⎯ ⎯⎯⎯⎯⎯

"YOU'RE A WANTED MAN, ANDREW Naughton. I would do well to turn you in to the authorities. Perhaps I would earn a reward." Phangorious Hood sat on a long leather couch, a bull-faced hound nestled at his feet. He filed his fingernails with an emery board. The four rings that adorned the fingers sparkled even in the dim light.

"I suppose you could," he replied.

The guard who'd brought him in sat nearby, his gaze of suspicion unrelenting. The Magera leader smirked. "A fugitive! Who'd have thought a quiet, devoted, and loyal bureaucrat could become subject of a continental manhunt? Surely, it's surprising that you were able to travel here undetected."

Naughton nodded. "I have little time for your verbal prancing, Hood. I need answers."

"You presume I have them."

"Absolutely."

"Fine, Mr. Naughton. I believe you to be an honorable man. We have worked together well over the years. And I have always appreciated your office's continued, shall we say, willingness to allow me to pursue my business interests unimpeded."

"Absolutely."

"Then go ahead."

"I never had the opportunity to pursue the information your men provided in August. I never was able to question Henry or Lynam about the shipping company."

"And now, I suppose, it would be quite difficult for a fugitive to do so."

"There is no doubt of that."

"So you then come to me again, in further desperation."

"Get me Jellum."

"Jellum?"

"Yes, Jellum. The bookmaker."

"Well, Naughton, we told you we could not locate him. He's disappeared."

Naughton gritted his teeth. "I have known you for years, Phangorious Hood. I have no doubt that if you were to seriously search for this miscreant, you would be able to find him. The tentacles of the Magera are long and broad."

"Ah, flattery. Always a welcome tactic. However — and I'm not saying that I can do this — but if I were to find this Jellum character for you, it would take far more than flattery to repay me."

Naughton leaned back in frustration. Unlike his past visits with Hood since the airship crash, he now had no leverage. He had no position, no power, no clout, no ability to offer further riches. "You always have your price, Phangorious Hood."

"More flattery. Thank you."

"And this time? What is your price now?"

"Well, given that you are a fugitive among your own people, and are probably not welcome here in the sovereign nation of Heldera, I'd imagine that you have little to offer."

Naughton nodded without comment.

"Actually," Hood leaned toward him and narrowed the gaze of the green eyes. "There is one thing…"

Naughton knew immediately what the man wanted. It was the only thing he had left to give. His pulse quickened.

He remembered Amelia, comforting him not long after the airship disaster, just after he had first visited Hood. *"Don't let our boys down. They depend on you too much. Don't get yourself into something that has no good outcome."*

He sighed. "You are taking advantage of my desperation."

"I know what it is like to be desperate. It only builds you stronger. Relish the chance."

"I need this information to save the commissioner," he pleaded. "To save the Leagues. Don't ask this of me."

"We have our price. You know that."

"But what good am I to you?"

The Magera leader flashed a broad smile. "Oh, Naughton. With your background, your intellect, I've no doubt you will prove valuable indeed."

"Please, Hood. No. Not this."

"Yes." He filed his nails and grinned broadly. "I don't do favors. I make deals. I am a businessman."

Naughton swallowed. A bead of sweat trickled down his right temple. *I'm sorry, Amelia, I have no choice. I need to solve this. I need to save the Leagues.*

He nodded, and swallowed again.

"Do you agree?"

"Yes."

"You will be afforded no chance to change your decision later."

"I understand."

Hood smiled and rubbed several of his rings. He nodded to the guard, who then slipped behind a curtain and returned with a tray. It had clearly been prepared in advance. On the tray lay a bowl, a candle and a gleaming knife.

The lights dimmed and the candle was lit. Four other Magera appeared and circled around him.

"We have our little customs, Andrew Naughton. I'm sure you are familiar with them."

He could not reply. His lips quivered.

I have no choice.

A guard took his left hand and placed it firmly on the tray. "To the Magera, we pledge," chanted Hood.

No choice.

His bowels loosened as the knife perforated. He bit down on his lower lip, then uttered an anguished wail.

No…

His knees buckled and two of the guards steadied him. Two others applied a salve to the wound and wrapped his hand. His wedding ring clattered to the ground.

"You bore that well, my friend," said Hood. "You will prove most valuable. Now we need your vow."

The guards released him and, still quivering from the pain, the former Special Assistant to the commissioner of Leagues of the SIP and ALE placed his right hand over his heart and uttered the words that Hood wished to hear, words that Naughton could never have previously imagined speaking.

"I give you my allegiance, Phangorious Hood." He swallowed and gasped for a breath. "I give my allegiance to the Magera."

"Is that until death, Andrew Naughton?"

"Yes." He saw blood seeping through the layers of the bandage.

"Say it."

"Yes, you son of a bitch. I pledge to the Magera until death."

September 16

WIDMERTOWN

"GENTLEMEN," HALLOWAY BEGAN. "I HATE blengin' speeches." A few of the boys laughed. *A rare sound in this club house,* he thought. "You don't need to hear from any coaches. You especially don't need to hear from me." More laughter.

He had called them in after a light workout, one day before the start of the play-offs. It was the first time he'd addressed the team since his return after the All-Star Game incident.

"You boys won the division despite me, despite the enormous distractions of which I was part." He shifted and propped one foot up on an empty chair, then looked down at his hands. "I had an issue with some players. They know who they are. But I didn't handle it very well. And that culminated in a major misunderstanding at the All-Star Game."

Several players avoided his gaze. He peered into the eyes of those who still looked toward him. "Some of you, I know, have a lot of questions about that, and you have kept from coming to me. I appreciate that. You have kept the game your focus, and you won the division handily, and that honor is truly — and only — yours.

Halloway stood fully. "That's all I'm going to tell you. You don't need me to do anything but fill out the line-up card and swap out the hurlers. And stay out of your way, so you can keep winning ball games. We're going to open up the first round against the Hammerheads tomorrow. This afternoon we'll go over our scouts' reports on their hurlers and strikers. But I'm giving you fair warning: your ability to stay focused will be sorely tested. You've been able to block out the political matters of late, but the press won't. They'll keep coming at you with questions about it. What each of you says is your choice, of course. But we are here to support you, and to the extent that you want us — the coaching staff, the front office — to shield you from that, we will be here for you. Just let us know.

"That is all. If you can do that, the baseball part will be damn easy. Because I know you guys are good enough to win it all."

He was done. He turned away, started back toward his solitary office, when one of the players called out. "Coach!"

Halloway swung back toward the players. It was Asgar. His right hand was outstretched, just as he done toward the commissioner at the All-Star Game. "Good luck to you, Coach. Thanks for getting us here."

After a moment's hesitation, Halloway returned the handshake. "Thank you, Ketter." The others applauded, and there was more laughter, and the Widmertown Flying Squirrels made their way back out to the field.

LATER, AFTER WATCHING BATTING PRACTICE, he returned to the alcove that was his office in the basement of the stadium, and found Langford waiting for him.

The two had barely spoken since the All-Star Game, and certainly not about that game itself. Now the general manager waited, a single sheet of paper in his hand. His expression morose.

"That was quite a nice little speech you made, Sander."

Halloway peered down the length of his reading glasses. "You were there?"

"No. But it was relayed to me in sufficient detail. It was needed, perhaps overdue. But I understand why you waited, and you handled it well."

Halloway settled in behind the desk. He had no stomach for pleasantries. "How can I help you, Eldon?"

Langford passed the paper to him. "We received this communique via messenger this morning. Fighting has flared anew. Four companies of Helderan forces clashed overnight along the border area due west of LaValleyford Prairie. At least seven men were killed, perhaps a dozen injured. The Helderan military command says Setherian forces incited the clash with long-range cannon fire. The Setherians are claiming the opposite."

Halloway felt dizzy as he looked at the paper. The information had been sent by the Office of the Commissioner, but was unsigned.

"And the play-offs?"

"Still scheduled, at this point. Whether or not fans are allowed in, we don't know. Whether or not the play-offs can be completed, we also don't know. The League has said only that they are monitoring the situation." Langford rose to leave. "I will keep you informed. You need to tell your players this as well."

"Agreed," Halloway replied, and then the general manager was gone.

There were few throughout the continent who didn't sense that this day was coming, that Fitton's decision to begin a military draft and mobilize new guard units would create a political tinderbox. Yet the reality was startling.

The ceasefire was over. Gone, in a matter of weeks.

In a matter of minutes.

Halloway eyed the baseball memorabilia scattered on the shelves of his office: old gloves and balls from his playing days, programs and plaques, line-up cards from his years as a manager. A painting of him delivering his famed speech three decades ago. *We could win the Continental Series, even as our world collapses around us.*

BOUNDYMOUNT CORNER

THEY LAID NAUGHTON ON A cot and he thrashed for hours. The pain in his maimed hand seared through his shoulder and chest. He dripped sweat, and still more blood, and tears. Eventually, he slept, but it was in a delirium, a feverish rest.

He woke to the noon sun, stared at the hand, and cried more.

Then he rose and told a Magera aide he was ready.

PHANGORIOUS HOOD WAS NOWHERE IN sight, and Naughton did not ask for him as he left. They would see each other again.

The private carriage, arranged by Hood's minions, waited for him on the street, three storefronts down from the nondescript Magera headquarters. The driver would take him from Gregorson to the western Setherian port city of Boundymount Corner.

He stepped in, carrying a small duffel in his good hand, his right hand. He'd been given a change of clothes and enough cash to secure his needs for several weeks, as well as narcotics and bandages for the wound. Traveling by charter offered several advantages, not the least of which was to greatly reduce the risk of being detected. Also, he was determined to use the respite of a private journey to recuperate as best he could.

Thirty minutes into the trip Naughton asked the driver, a heavyset Amandean by the name of Pumelton, to stop so he could purchase the latest broadsheets. Both the *Gregorson Bugle* and the *Chronicle* contained detailed and unsettling accounts of the border clashes near LaValleyford Prairie earlier in the week. The bodies of the seven killed — three Setherians and four Helderans — had been transported back to their respective home towns for burials. The Commissioner's Office had issued a statement describing the clash as an anomaly and urging calm. The tone was of desperation.

Yet in the past two days no further skirmishes were reported; no new crises had presented themselves. It was as if everyone was simply exhausted. The play-offs, he read, would begin the next day despite the violence. The press also seemed relatively well behaved, as if the scribes realized the dangerous precipice on which the continent now rested.

After reading a while the throbbing of his injured hand was ferocious, so he put the newspapers down and closed his eyes.

They arrived in Boundymount Corner seven hours later. It was the westernmost of the major cities of Setheridge and, other than Tredgemond Butte, it was the most remote, situated on a triangular peninsula that jutted into the ocean. Residents called it simply 'the Corner.' For centuries the city had been large and vibrant, for the peninsula's shape, the wind, and the currents provided a perfect launching spot each day for hundreds of trawlers and schooners. The fishermen had a passion for the sea and for baseball. The population may have been small compared to

MICHAEL BARBATO-DUNN

other SIP League cities, but the Boundymount locals adored their Racoons, and Nonmeth Field was always sold out.

He handed the precise address, scrawled on a scrap of paper by Hood, to Pumelton. The apartment was in the eastern portion of the city, a newer development that was one of several made possible by a noticeable population boom in the vicinity of Boundymount Corner. The buildings were tall, six stories or so, and block-like, featureless and uninspiring.

Four narrow streets led them to the apartment complex. The carriage master had some trouble navigating the turns. Naughton smelled the fried dough rounds of the local street vendors. He heard the cable cars, part of a fairly extensive transit system in the Corner, operating on tracks parallel with the streets.

Finally, after the fourth sharp turn in as many blocks, the carriage stopped in front of his destination: 674 Garrond Way. Naughton ordered to Pumelton to park further down, to feed the horses, but otherwise to wait discreetly for his return.

A bus stop bench was positioned at the curb in front of the building. He stood near it and studied the structure: clay and brick, painted white, with rusting metal ornaments providing the only taste of color on the apartment's facade.

He waited. He had arrived perhaps 10 or 15 minutes early. That was fine. It gave him time to compose his thoughts.

At eight o'clock, three figures appeared at the top of the street and walked toward him. All were dressed in dark overcoats and high-brimmed caps. Their hands were gloved, their faces hidden in the shadows of the brims.

"Naughton?" the tallest asked. "I'm Kellender. That's Trentworthy and Englehard."

He nodded. They were local Magera, dispatched by Hood to assist him in the questioning. They knew only that they were to obey Naughton, to provide protection if needed, and to hear nothing. Hood had assured him they were his very best men in Boundymount. Loyal beyond reproach.

The apartment itself was on the fourth floor, toward the rear. The four men kept a brisk pace, Naughton leading the way, but without sound. Within just a few minutes they were at the door, and Naughton looked to Kellender to determine if his men were ready. The Magera nodded, and all three men drew their side clubs.

Naughton then turned to the door and knocked.

"What?"

The voice was harsh yet resonant. Not that of an elderly man, as Naughton had imagined.

"It is the Office of the Commissioner of the Leagues of SIP and ALE."

"Go away."

"Open the door."

"Who is it?"

"I repeat, sir: open the door."

Silence.

"I have three members of the police force with me, and they can easily break this down. There's no need to make this more difficult than it is."

A few more seconds of silence, and the shuffling of feet. Then the door was unlocked and opened.

"I work for the commissioner of baseball," Naughton said.

"Well," said the bookmaker Hardwin Jellum, leering at the four visitors from behind thick glasses. "It certainly took you long enough to find me."

NEAR MT. WAYLANDTOWN

OLLO RONNELL SAT AT HIS desk, fidgeting and fussing, again on deadline. Always, the deadlines.

He had returned to the *Chronicle* newsroom at the beginning of September, some two weeks after the All-Star Game catastrophe. Since then, he had been to three different doctors about his knee and none had provided much help. Two of them simply wanted to increase the level of narcotics to ease the pain. A third had recommended some odd procedure in which the leg was inserted into a tubular, pressurized chamber for hours of what the man called "pneumatic intensification" of the knee joint. He'd claimed dozens of successful cases ridding patients of chronic pain. Ronnell had glanced around the office, observed no medical certifications, and bid the man farewell.

Oddly enough, he discovered that the pain of the leg eased considerably when he sat at a mechascribe to compose his column. Perhaps it was the operation panel, festooned with an array of buttons representing individual letters, which forced him to sit upright as he composed. When he wrote longhand, he tended to hunch over the desk. "You look like you're actually working for once," Candless, one of the crime reporters, had joked. He snarled in return, irritated at the irony that the very device he long loathed now provided some comfort.

He tried pecking out a lead. "*The play-offs have proved a welcome respite, dear readers, a distraction—*" He leaned back, frustrated. He had no idea where he was going with this column, what his ultimate point would be, and it was due in less

MICHAEL BARBATO-DUNN

than two hours. Sometimes he envied the general reporters, for they simply wrote about what happened. The obligation to craft opinions into entertaining columns three times each week felt increasingly like a burden.

He tried again. "*The esteemed Office of the Commissioner, and whoever may be in charge of matters there these days, certainly must be—*" He glanced up from the device and was startled by the sight of a copy boy, standing silently, and waiting for Ronnell to afford him attention. "What?"

The boy handed over an envelope addressed to him, then scampered away. Ronnell ripped its seal and found inside a signed, handwritten note.

"*4 pm. Look for me on a bench at Hedgeworthy Park.*"

"Damn." He spit out the butt end of his cigar as others in the newsroom took notice.

"Need help with your spelling again, Ollo?" one of them called.

"No, your sister helped me enough, with that and other matters," he shot back, grabbing his jacket, cap, and cane. "Crom!" he shouted, "I need two more hours."

He was gone before his editor could object.

"How does it feel, Ollo, to be making decisions rather than questioning them?" asked Fitton.

They sat on a bench that was one of about a dozen lining a gravel pedestrian path. The park was east of Mount Waylandtown, home of the *Chronicle,* and extended further east to the McKinmond Lakes that lay amid the Setherian-Helderan border. At the lake's shoreline, down a sloping hill from where they sat, Ronnell could make out the figures of armed guards pacing. Waiting for signs of an incursion.

"I'm not sure of what you're speaking, Mr. Executive."

"My information is that Lady Lynam has convinced you to act as counsel to her during this, uh, difficult time."

"Your information is incorrect."

"That I doubt."

"It is, sir. Do you think your intelligence network infallible?"

"Did she not ask—"

"She did ask. But I said no."

"Oh. I see."

"Are you disappointed?"

"Perhaps. I thought your new status could prove mutually beneficial."

"I'm sure you did. In fact, it occurs to me that you expected her to ask, and that is why you sought me out at the hotel in West Somerchester shortly after the All-Star Game. You sensed an opportunity."

Fitton, dressed in a workman's overcoat and a baseball cap so as not to attract attention, eyed him with a smirk. "Ollo, one does not become chief executive of a nation without sensing, and seizing on, opportunities."

"And that is why you sought today's meeting? You thought I was now advising the Lady?"

"I am certainly curious about your perspective on the situation. What is with this fellow Coyle, now making public pronouncements? I certainly don't appreciate him speaking for all Helderans in saying we're content to wait until the season ends to press our concerns."

"He never said 'content,' Mr. Executive, if I recall correctly. But he did say you will wait."

"And how, pray tell, does he know that?"

"I'd imagine he — they — realize you have no choice but to wait. Lady Lynam won't allow another peace conference, or whatever you choose to call your little exhibitions, until the commissioner is recovered."

"Won't allow? She doesn't control me, Ronnell. She certainly doesn't control the Helderan people. That's the type of typical arrogance that you Setherians have heaped on us—"

Ronnell raised his voice for emphasis. "I will tell you precisely how she will control your people as you mobilize your troops: like it or not, the peoples of the Twin Nations still love Bartholomew Cunningham. And they fear for his health. And they will mourn him if he dies. Do you understand? Not just Setherians. Helderans too. They will mourn him if he dies. And any sign of aggressiveness from you will have a tremendous backlash, including from your own people."

"So she intends to use the continent's love and admiration for the old man to her devices?"

"If you choose to characterize it that way, so be it." Ronnell reached into his coat pocket for a cigar, but found none; he'd left them in his desk.

Fitton scowled. "So the commissioner is her leverage."

"Just as the army you are now forming throughout the Helderan countryside is yours."

"We are a sovereign nation, or so we've been told for 30 years. Have not we the right to bear arms?"

"I am simply saying that Lady Lynam's effort to use the continent's great esteem for Lord Bart for her own aims is no more repugnant than the speed with which you have chosen to pick up arms. Though it is, I daresay, a good deal less costly. And less potentially bloody."

Fitton's aides and bodyguards, until now hovering further down the path in two small groups, inched forward, alarmed at the rising voices. The executive waved to ease their concern, then rubbed his mustache.

He is a bit scared by all this, Ronnell thought. Without the facial hair, without his baritone voice, Fitton's anxiety would be painfully apparent. "I need to be going now, Alexander Fitton. I have a column to write."

Fitton took a deep breath. "Ollo, I need to find out if Lord Bart will live. Everything hinges on that."

"I can't help you. I have no good information about that, any more than you do. Even if I did, I have no desire to be assisting either side. Why would I possibly do that?"

"Because it could help stave off war."

"You have the ability to prevent that without my help."

"Damn it, Ollo. Do you think the other Helderan owners want war? Of course not. They're too wealthy. Can't she see that?"

In the distance, at a curve of the lake, a flock of migratory birds swooped down toward the water, searching for their meals. Ollo allowed them to distract him from the unpleasant discussion. In a few months they would travel further south, beyond the continent, to lands no one has seen.

Fitton broke the silence. "Fine. So be it. Stay out of the fray, Ollo Ronnell. It's what you've done your whole life. But your friend Lady Lynam may very well learn that the wave of sympathy for the commissioner will not last. Go into the publick houses that dot the landscape and listen to what is being said. That little news conference the other day did little to silence the skeptics."

"I am, rest assured, well aware of what is being said in the publick houses. Liquor is indeed the best fuel of revolution."

"Perhaps. And three decades of lies to my people provide ready fuel indeed." The Helderan tipped his hat, bowed, and left.

Off in the distance, Ronnell heard the gulls cawing in delight. They'd found their next meal.

And then further off — what sounded like a mortar shell.

"Sit him down."

The Magera sprang forward and grabbed Jellum by the arms, forcing him into a small chair near the apartment's kitchen table.

"How can I help you, Mr. Naughton?"

Naughton stood over him and glowered. "How is it you know my name?"

"You are a man of prominence of late. Aren't you wanted by the law? In fact, I should assume now that these men do not, in fact, work for the local police, or they'd be arresting you."

"That is not of your concern. I am here on behalf of Commissioner Bartholomew Cunningham."

"Well, then. My condolences."

"He's not dead."

"As I said: my condolences."

Kellender raised his hand as if to slap the man, but Naughton blocked his arm. "No," he told the man. "I don't want that." Then, he turned back to Jellum. "Sir, if your snide remarks continue, I can't promise I can keep these men off you, do you understand?"

"Well, I guess I'll just have to be polite now, won't I?"

"I don't need manners, Jellum. I need the truth."

Kellender turned and rooted through the one-bedroom apartment, looking for others in hiding. One of his henchman, Trentworthy, extinguished all gas lamps save one on the wall nearest the kitchen table where Jellum had been placed.

Naughton took the empty chair next to him. The light now fully illuminated Jellum's face: gray-blue eyes set back in shadows, further masked by high, pale cheekbones. Stubble of a gray beard peppered his cheeks and chin, and closed-cropped hair accentuated his gaunt pallor.

"Is this an interrogation? Am I not entitled to the representation of a barrister?"

"All in good time. This is a conversation."

"A conversation in which I am forced to participate?"

"It would be in your best interests to do so."

"I can only imagine."

"Mr. Jellum, you have been implicated in the crash of the Airship *Lady Crym*."

"I am aware of that."

"You have intentionally evaded authorities for several months."

"If only your investigators were competent, they would have found me."

"We had a few other matters that needed attention."

"Apparently so. You and your boss — or should I say, former boss — seem quite intent on plunging the continent into another civil war through your ineptitude. Sixty years this time, perhaps?"

"We have worked diligently to avoid exactly that. But this isn't a political discussion."

"Everything, Mr. Naughton, is a political discussion."

"Very well. Let's start." He slipped a piece of paper across the table. "Here are three companies through which League money was channeled. And we have determined that those funds were ultimately sent to you."

"'We have determined'?"

"I don't care to hear my words repeated. I want answers, and my associates—" he motioned to the three Magera, "—are here to ensure that I get them."

"I know nothing of the payments. Perhaps your good friend Hood is being less than forthcoming."

Naughton caught his breath. With his good hand, he ran his fingers through his hair and wiped a line of sweat from his forehead. He had expected a guttural man, crass and vulgar. Instead, Jellum was articulate, quick thinking and poised. "The three Amandeans who died in the crash — Dodd, Newton, and Fishbourne: were they working for you?"

"Yes."

"In what capacity?"

"In this instance, I was an intermediary, and hired them to deliver a shipment on behalf of another."

"Tell me who hired you to attack the Airship *Lady Crym*."

Jellum squinted at Naughton, as if trying to gauge the seriousness of the question. After a few moments, he responded. "I don't accept the premise of your question."

"In what way?"

"I did not attack the dirigible."

Naughton clenched his fists, and a bolt of pain shot through his gloved, maimed left hand. "Mr. Jellum, let me explain this to you. This process can be difficult, or it can be easy. It is up to you. My goal is to determine who planned this. Who sought the disruption. We know you are not political, we know you are only a hired hand. If you think those who you are protecting care about you, you are sadly mistaken. They would easily see you locked away for many years rather than find themselves exposed. So I wonder why you would bother to care about them."

"You presume, however, that I was involved."

Naughton paused, uncertain how to respond. The bookmaker, unfortunately, was correct. This entire inquiry was predicated on that presumption. "Go on."

"Did it occur to you, Mr. Naughton, that in accepting the findings of your internal investigation, you implicitly trusted the least trustworthy person on the entire Continent?"

"Who?"

"Gill. Your inspector. How was he vetted? He suddenly is brought in to handle League security immediately after the airship disaster, and now you look at his findings as infallible?"

"How do you know of Gill?"

"Oh, his father Hargate was a well-known figure among the Amandeans. Never well liked, truth be told, but my people are usually distrustful of Monystians. Anyway, my information is that it was Gill who concocted that report, cobbling together scraps of circumstantial evidence."

"And you're basing that on pub chatter?"

"Of course not. I have my sources, sir. A vast network, in fact. How do you think I was able to remain out of your reach for long?"

"But we found you."

"Thanks to Phangorious Hood, I can see." Jellum stared at Naughton's gloved left hand. "Besides, it was time."

"What do you mean?"

"It was time for me to make myself known to you. I know you were jailed in Heldera and are now a fugitive from the foolish Setherians. I know you're in with Hood now. Don't bother hiding that mangled hand below your glove. Do you think me so ill-informed that none of this would be known to me? Honestly."

Naughton steadied himself against the table. The man had actually expected him here. He had chosen to be found out. "Why— why after hiding for months did you now want to be found?"

Hardwin Jellum grinned, his thin lips stretching hauntingly across his countenance. "Because the events of the past month have made it clear that you need help. You need *my* help. And so, we can help each other."

"How so?"

"I have information that will allow you to unravel the mess that began with the crash of the Airship *Lady Crym*. It will be, frankly, invaluable."

"You're trying to negotiate a deal."

"You are observant, aren't you? Yes. That's what I do. And trust me when I say that it will be a very good deal for both of us."

"Why would I trust you? You're a man of ill repute, you have been for years and you are implicated in at least one if not two of the most horrible crimes that have befallen our land in the past 30 years. You expect me to agree to a deal?"

"I understand your skepticism. Indeed, I have predicted it. So I will tell you this: I will give you a morsel of my knowledge now. It will be of some interest to you. Free, no charge."

"And the larger deal?"

"I will tell you everything. Everything I know. I will answer your questions."

"For….?"

"For full and absolute immunity from any accusations, charges, or imprisonment."

"You know I cannot promise that. That is out of my control. As you yourself stated, I am now a fugitive."

"Fine. But your promise that you will do everything under your control to provide such immunity will be sufficient. That's not so much to ask, is it, Mr. Naughton? Regardless, you need not decide now. All I ask for the moment is that you simply keep me here, rather than turn me over to League authorities. Post one of your henchmen here as a guard if you so desire. I have no intention of going elsewhere."

Naughton looked down and shook his head in disgust. None of this had gone well: Jellum had sought the meeting, had controlled the conversation and was now trying to dictate the terms of their relationship. Kellender, sensing Naughton's discomfiture, stepped forward, grabbed Jellum by the shirt collar, raised him out of his seat and shoved him again the wall. "I think Mr. Naughton has heard quite enough of your nonsense."

"Naughton," responded the bookmaker, "I'm trying to be cooperative. Get your thug off me."

Naughton sat and stared at the two. Jellum struggled, kicking his arms and legs, but Kellender's grip remained firm.

"Please, I *am* trying to cooperate."

Naughton bit down on his lower lip. The Magera looked at him for direction. "You're not trying nearly enough, Jellum. Not nearly enough." He raised his good hand and signaled to Kellender. The other two Magera lifted the bookmaker by his arms and pinned him against the wall.

And the beating began.

WIDMERTOWN

THEY PRACTICED ALL MORNING, AND then went over strategy and lineups in small groups in the afternoon. The boys seemed loose, that much Halloway could tell. The speech had clearly helped. He sat at his desk, the door to the cramped office open, and waited for Asgar to walk by.

"Count."

"Yes, Coach." The hurler stepped inside.

"You didn't have to do that, but I appreciate it."

"Coach, you apologized to me last month. But, truth be told, there was no need to. You owe me nothing. I am complicit."

Halloway's eyes widened. *An admission? A confession?* "Complicit in what?"

"In sowing your distrust."

"Go on."

"I don't like Setherians. You know that. I do believe in the Kender Hypothesis. I believe all of the difficulties of this season have been carefully orchestrated by the Commissioner's Office to prompt a backlash against the Helderans. I believe we Helderans are being duped—"

"And...?"

"And so you were right to be suspicious. I had no intent to harm Cunningham when I approached him. None at all. But I was going to shake his hand and tell him how I feel."

"What would you have said?"

Asgar now fiddled with the bill of his cap and thought. "With our hands clasped, I was going to look him in the eyes and tell him, 'We will tolerate your subjugation no longer.'"

"That was it?"

"Yes. That was it."

Halloway swallowed hard. There was the truth. That was the extent of Asgar's plotting. A simple, though bold, political statement. "That would have been inappropriate, Ketter."

"A lot of what the commissioner has done for the past three decades has been inappropriate."

"Perhaps, but that is not your place to say. Nor mine. We're just ballplayers."

"That's where you're wrong, Coach. I am a Helderan first, a ballplayer second."

Sander Halloway stood and walked closer to the hurler. "No. *You* are wrong. When you are on the field, in a uniform, you are just a ballplayer. If you want to be more, leave the team and take up arms. That is your choice. Do you understand?"

"But when you made your famed speech 30 years ago, promising to play for a Setherian owner: were you just a ballplayer then?"

Halloway swallowed. "Ketter, I never intended to be anything more. The founding fathers of these leagues wanted us — the players and coaches — to simply be the miniatures, harmless little soldiers, playing out the little wars each and every night with bats in place of guns, so they could end the big war. That is our role, and nothing else."

Asgar sat silent, scowling.

"Do you understand?"

"Yes, sir. I understand."

———————————————

LATER, AFTER THE CLUBHOUSE EMPTIED, after Halloway had returned to the dingy apartment, he thought over the hurler's words, "I am a Helderan first." He walked slowly to the mirror hung over the rented wooden dresser and looked at himself, rubbing the stubble on his chin with his right hand.

I am neither Helderan nor ballplayer, he thought.

He changed into his nightclothes, drank a small glass of whiskey from a bottle in the top dresser drawer, and lay on the bed. After a long while he extinguished the solitary gas lamp on the otherwise empty nightstand.

There was a ballgame tomorrow. A play-off game. An important game. Yet he lay in the dark pondering how insignificant it seemed.

BOUNDYMOUNT CORNER

NAUGHTON WAITED IN AN OUTER room and tried his best to block out the sounds: punching, shoving, shouting, pleading.

He caught his reflection in a window. What am I doing? What have I become?

Eventually, the noises subsided, the door opened, and Kellender looked out and nodded.

He found Jellum on the floor, propped in one corner of the room, moaning and writhing, his shirt bloodied. The bookmaker cradled his left arm with his right. The sight of another arm injury caused his own maimed hand to pulsate in pain.

"I ... need water." Jellum spat out some blood.

Naughton nodded and one of the guards left to retrieve a pitcher and glass. Another handed Jellum a towel, which he held against his bloodied lip and right ear.

"That was unnecessary, Naughton."

"I've no time for your nonsense. Tell me what happened." He motioned to Kellender and another Magera to carry the bookmaker back to his chair. "I'll make no deal. Tell me everything. You have ten minutes. Or my friends here will start over."

The bookmaker nodded but waved in the direction of the thugs. "They need to leave." Naughton signaled to the Magera to wait outside the room.

Jellum drank from the glass, emptied it, spit some more blood, then began.

"You see, Naughton, I have always made my living by being careful. It has kept me out of prison except for perhaps one or two incarcerations that were, shall we say, quickly remedied. And I manage to avoid problems with the law by carefully choosing not only what locations I work in, but with whom I engage. In short, if I can't be sure you can be trusted, I don't do business with you."

"Trust is an elusive matter," Naughton interjected.

"Indeed. And my standards in that regard have caused me to, over the years, pass up quite a few opportunities. I don't like risk."

"Yet you work in a risky business."

"Which, by intelligently minimizing the risks, becomes quite lucrative. So, shall I continue?"

"Please."

"I have, over the years, had the occasion to be engaged for oversight of various shipping activities throughout the Valencroft River's southern basin, the area that is least regulated by provincial Helderan and Setherian authorities."

"Thus a lower risk."

"Correct. And over the years I have found a rewarding subsidiary trade in arranging discreet shipping operations for members of the Scientificka, many of whom need materials that are, shall we say, not readily available at open-air venues."

"Such as cadavers?"

"Yes, that would certainly be one such item."

"And so you became acquainted with the illustrious Dr. Iphonious Henry?"

"Ah, Mr. Naughton. There you err. I have never met nor even exchanged any messages with Dr. Henry, though I have certainly heard of him."

"Then who wanted cadavers?"

"If you would allow me to finish my tale. Two years ago an unfortunate mishap occurred at one dock, wherein some shipments of that material unfortunately fell on a loading dock and opened at precisely the moment that a group of tourists from Red Mine were passing by."

"I can only imagine their surprise when the boxes opened."

"Yes. Even some of the male tourists were said to have fainted. Suffice it to say, local law enforcement officials with whom we had a previously amicable relationship had little choice but to close down the firm. Fortunately, they were cooperative enough, and the local press forgetful enough, that the matter quickly receded in the public's mind. After an appropriate period of time, the operations resumed."

"Under a different company's name."

"Yes, but that is routine. We regularly change the names of our firms lest any single operation become too prominent. Anyway, last fall, many months after operations resumed, I received a visit from an agent representing your good friend, Dr. Henry. Mind you, he was not named in this conversation, but being careful as I am, my intelligence sources later were able to ascertain with a high degree of certainty that it was Dr. Henry who my guest represented."

"Your guest's name?"

"You don't need to know that."

"What did your guest want?"

"He wanted me to arrange the transport of a particular shipment to Schawmount City, to be delivered surreptitiously to the stadium one day before the 30th Anniversary Celebration."

Naughton sat forward. He was finally getting to the truth. "What was the shipment?"

"I wasn't told, and I didn't ask."

"So you hired the three Amandeans for the delivery?"

"Yes."

"Were you there yourself?"

"No. I hired them, and took a percentage of the fee, and was done with it. It was — I thought — a routine transaction. I was told the three would pose as workmen during the installation, which would take place just prior to the start of the festivities, while your League workers were actually preparing the park for the celebration."

"You knew of this, yet you did not ask whoever had hired you for its purpose? Did you not care?"

"Mr. Naughton, surely you understand that a businessman such as me makes it a practice *not* to ask questions, that the people who are hiring me don't want questions."

"Fine. Go on."

"After I hired the men, I arranged for delivery of the item to them on March 6th, a day prior. They were to transport it to Schawmount Stadium that afternoon. They would be met by another operative unknown to me, who would allow for their admittance to the ballpark and receive it. That operative would then oversee the installation. But in the days leading up to the anniversary celebration, I became concerned that Dr. Henry had nefarious goals, and that a disruption of the event could lead to a return to warring across the continent. I have no desire to facilitate that."

"So you suddenly developed a conscience?"

"Your moralizing is a bit hypocritical, wouldn't you say, Naughton, now that you're pledged to the Magera?"

Jellum's barb dug as sharp as Hood's knife had against his finger. "When you took this job, you knew it involved the Anniversary festivities. Yet you agreed to it."

"That was a mistake. I should have steered clear. I ignored my own instincts, and that was a lapse I regret. As with your good friend Hood, my operations would only suffer in wartime. Moreover, I knew that any unfortunate event would lead to a broad investigation that could easily implicate me. As I said, I make it a practice to avoid incarceration at all costs."

"So then…"

"On the evening of March 6th, after my three hirelings had completed the task, I contacted them. They explained that the shipment contained only a small object — all tubes and brass and clockworks — and that they'd been directed to install it on a rafter of a distant section of bleachers."

"What was it?"

Jellum wiped more blood from his ear and mouth, then shook his head. "Oh, Naughton, I think you know full well what the shipment was. Another one of Dr. Henry's strange inventions."

"The beam weapon that he demonstrated publicly? He sent one to Schawmount Stadium? Surely my security forces would have spotted that monstrosity…"

"No, not the one he displayed in Kern. That, I believe, was simply a ruse. That was large, and not particularly effective. This one… this one was a miniature, yet somehow far more powerful. I don't believe Dr. Henry showed publicly what he had truly accomplished. It's amazing what members of the Scientificka do with gears and pneumatics nowadays."

Naughton collapsed back into his seat and pressed his hands to his temples. He spoke in a whisper. "So…so that's it. Henry used a beam device to shoot down the airship. And it was installed right under our very eyes."

"Oh, no. You don't understand."

Naughton cocked his head. "What do you mean?"

"The plan was never to use the beam device to shoot down the airship."

"What then?"

"The plan, I realized, was to use the beam device to fire upon the commissioner. I had aided and unwittingly abetted in an assassination attempt."

Naughton shouted an obscenity and lunged at Jellum, pushing the man backward in chair. The Amandean broke his fall by lurching sideway, off the chair and onto the ground. Naughton landed on top and being pummeling punches into the man's ribcage. "How could you do that! How could you allow that!" But the melee was brief: Kellender and the other Magera burst back in and separated the two. Naughton dropped back onto the floor against a wall. "How could you?"

Jellum returned to his chair and looked down at his interrogator. "I stopped them, Naughton. I didn't want Lord Bart's blood on my hands. I dispatched my most loyal aides — not the miscreants, but others — to the stadium to prevent the use of the device on the commissioner. They arrived during Cunningham's speech."

Naughton reeled back. He remembered an altercation during the old man's speech, Section 351. He'd dispatched Crandy to investigate the fisticuffs. "A fight erupted."

"Yes," Jellum said.

"And your men stopped the assassination attempt."

"Yes, they were successful."

Naughton's thoughts were racing. "And in the fracas, the device shifted—" He couldn't bring himself to say the words.

"Yes. Amid the fight, Dr. Henry's device must have been jolted and the beam re-directed."

"And it struck the Airship *Lady Crym*." The words felt like bile in his mouth.

"Yes. The Commissioner lived, Andrew Naughton. I saved his life. But by my noble intercession, many others died."

———————————

Naughton had the carriage driver stop to the side of a farm road, under a bridge. He got out and vomited. He retreated back to the cab, wiped his face, and closed his eyes. His maimed hand throbbed.

The carriage jostled him to and fro. The driver was taking him back to his boarding house outside Schawmount City, by back roads, a journey of at least nine hours. The tumult of the uneven roads paled to the horror of what he had just learned.

An assassination attempt on the commissioner, gone awry. Thirty dead, instead of one.

He encased his face in his hands, the nine fingers stretching from his eyebrows down to his jaw. His stomach churned again, but now it was empty.

The names swirled. Jellum. Hood. Henry. Fitton. Lynam. Coyle. All of them at various points through this tortuous period had asked for his trust. And— Gill! Jellum had said Gill's own report — finding that the airship itself had been sabotaged — was false. But was it knowingly false?

He remembered the words, spoken to him now six months ago: "Whoever perpetuated this heinous act knows plenty. And knows enough to play off our own inherent failure to trust." Gill himself had said that, as a warning to him not to be overly trusting.

Naughton considered the words. *Our own inherent failure to trust.* They had been on Lake Leoran, six months ago. Gill had brought up the question of whether he'd been lax in readily accepting Crandy's initial repairs, after the hound was demolished in the airship crash. "You are wholly laying your trust about this with a group of people you don't even know," he had chastised.

It struck him: Gill had assured him he had checked out the repairs on the servohound and found them proper. "Don't worry, sir," he had said. "I've already had the hound checked over. He's fine. There's been no compromise."

But there was a compromise. Crandy had been sabotaged.

So: either Gill missed the sabotage, or the inspector was trying to divert him away from sabotage he knew to have occurred.

Naughton thought of the supposed illicit payments made by Coyle that Gill said he discovered: Naughton had no independent corroboration. And he had not ever questioned Coyle; he hadn't had the chance before the All-Star Game attack. What if Gill had concocted that whole matter as a further diversion?

He leaned back and closed his eyes. He thought of the knife that had claimed his finger. He thought of the beating he'd ordered on the quick-witted bookmaker. He thought of Jellum's answers, which had only led to more questions. And he knew the time he had left to find those answers was quickly diminishing.

Through the window of the carriage Naughton saw dusk had arrived; the roads were wider and full of bustling traffic. Soon, though, they'd be riding in darkness.

September 25

WIDMERTOWN

T HE MANAGER OF THE WIDMERTOWN Flying Squirrels sat at his desk two hours before the first throw of the most important game of the season and wrote out his line-up card. The veteran Jerome Callison was throwing for the Hammerheads, a right hander, so Halloway kept his three best left-handed batsmen, Alley, Marsh, and Dunbar, bunched together in the third, fourth, and fifth holes. *No, check that, he thought. Better to put Wrye, the right-handed short bagger, after Marsh. It'll break things up a bit.* He wrote in the change.

There had been a time when such minutia excited Halloway. This sort of fine tuning could account for two or three extra victories over the course of a long season. Or so he believed; there'd be no way to actually know for certain. Now, though, the comfort of this fairly routine aspect of managing was absent. It seemed a chore.

He had never had that problem before.

Attendance had diminished amid word of the fighting. Widmertown was far from the border, where the clashes had been centered, on its own island. But the escalation of tensions was sufficient to keep many families home. Even a promotional event two nights ago — each fan under the age of 16 received a ticket for a cream soda or a souvenir cap — failed to boost activity at the turnstiles.

Moreover, his speech to the team nine days earlier, and Asgar's handshake, had dispelled the dour mood of the clubhouse for only a brief time. Now there was no levity among the players, nor any practical jokes or catcalling during batting practice. No one spoke to him much anymore, neither his coaches nor the players, even the veterans like Wrye or Minnocks, who'd been with him for years. Perhaps it was the looming tension of the play-offs.

More likely, he thought, *they still don't trust me.*

The Squirrels had battled the Hammerheads for six games in the best-of-seven series and came out even: three wins, three losses.

The right to advance to the Continental Series would be decided with a single game. Tonight's game.

Halloway felt only hollow.

———————————————

THE FIRST SEVEN FRAMES OF the game proved uneventful, with each team scoring two runs by the end of the fourth. Benny Harald, starting for the Squirrels, was a bit wild at first, walking four in those early innings. But then he settled into a rhythm, as did his counterpart Callison of the Hammerheads, and the fifth, sixth, and seventh innings left both sides without a hit.

Halloway paced in the dugout and watched the veteran start off the eighth inning. Harald got two quick outs, inducing easy grounders from the Hammerheads' right-fielder, Ora Aubrey, and their backstop, Will Biddle, on just three throws. Benny had never been a strike-out master, but he consistently avoided hitting the upper part of the zone. The balls stayed on the ground, and his teammates did the rest.

For the potential third out came the first bagger, Rob Shackleton. One of the greatest players in the history of the league: a career .286 striker who averaged about 30 home runs and 100 runs batted in each season. Thirty-eight years old, and in his 19th season, all with Bereton Park. And he was showing no signs of slowing down.

Harald versus Shackleton.

The hurler waited for Minnocks to give him the sign. The backstop glanced toward the dugout, toward Halloway, who touched his right ear, the tip of his cap, his left shoulder, then his right ear again and, finally, his nose. For this particular game, only the second motion mattered, the rest were distractions. Tip of his cap: fastball, inside.

Minnocks relayed the instructions to Harald with two flicks of his index and middle fingers hidden in the gap between his crouching legs. The hurler nodded, went into his wind-up, and delivered. Shackleton was waiting for it and swung, but the spinning ball came inside, just where Halloway wanted it, a few thumblengths from the batsman's chest.

Shackleton jammed his fists inward and the ball somehow connected with the bat, then caromed out into a high bounce out to the third bagger, Lucius Cameron. But the shot bounced a bit higher than Cameron expected, and though he was able to grab it by jumping, he threw slightly off balance to Alley at first.

Easy out, Halloway thought in that instant as Cameron's throw sailed over the infield to Alley's waiting glove. *Shakelton can't run.* He grinned.

But then: "Safe!" shouted the arbiter at the first bag, Colin McElhatton. The Widmertown fans erupted in boos. Halloway shook his head and trotted out of the dugout to argue the call.

He stood close to McElhatton and spoke in a near whisper. "Are you watching the same game as me, Colin?"

"He was safe by a footstep, Sander. You best be getting back into the dugout."

"He was out by a footstep, Colin, and you best be paying attention to the game from here on in. I don't need you to be handing gifts to the Hammerheads."

McElhatton reddened, and Halloway knew he'd overstepped a boundary with the reference to gifts. "Excuse me?"

There was no going back. "You heard me."

"Sander, you're the last person who should be throwing around accusations."

"What does that mean, Colin?"

"Listen here. We know all about you. There's not a single person in this stadium who thinks you were not somehow involved in the attack on Lord Bart."

"Excuse me?"

"Don't feign ignorance. You know what you did. You start shouting from the stands, and then the commissioner was attacked—"

Halloway moved a step closer to the arbiter, careful not to touch the man's protruding belly. "You don't have any idea—"

Fredrick Abernathy, chief of the arbiter crew, stationed for this game behind the home bag, had made his way over and broke up the conversation. "Halloway, get the hell back to the dugout, you don't want to be here on the field, out in the open. You never know what some fan may try to do."

Halloway tried to keep his voice from rising. Fans in the lowest seats, the ones nearest the field, could easily hear. He leaned in close to the two. "Neither of you have any idea what you are talking about. You don't know."

"I know," said Abernathy, "that you'd better get your ass back to the dugout or I will toss you."

Halloway turned and tugged down on his cap, biting his lower lip. Some in the crowd cheered, others hooted, a few clapped.

Harald was not well served by the delay, though. The hurler served up a no-nonsense fastball to the next striker, second bagger Walter Brackens, who slapped a high line drive that just made it over the left field fence, aided by the wind. As Shackleton and Brackens crossed home, the arbiter Abernathy took off his protective mask, looked over at Halloway, and smirked.

ODDLY, THOUGH, THE ON-FIELD ALTERCATION with the two arbiters lifted the mood among his players. They greeted him warmly after the argument, with handshakes and backslaps. Asgar moved down from the perch held by the starters. "Nice try, coach." The words came without a hint of animosity or sarcasm. Cameron walked by and patted his shoulder in support.

It was as if a storm cloud had passed. As if by his arguing, their spirit had been restored.

Down four runs to two, Squirrels strikers began the bottom of the eighth with backstop Minnocks reaching on an error by the Hammerheads' second bagger. The misplay clearly irritated the hurler Callison, who began shaking off the signs of his backstop. His unraveling had begun. Alley smashed a first-throw double, driving in Minnocks, then Marsh doubled to drive in Alley. Next: a fly-out, an intentional walk of Dunbar, and then a single by Berbery to score Marsh.

With that, the Squirrels owned the lead, five runs to four.

This brought the Squirrels to the seventh spot in the line-up, held by the short bagger, Ike Gamp. Halloway, for a moment, considered a pinch striker, someone with a bit of power like Comber or Flaherty. But Gamp had been connecting well of late, and in fact the previous day had notched three base hits.

Callison, on the mound, was by this point clearly winded and fretting. Sweat poured down his forehead from beneath his cap. Into his wind-up, the hurler danced a fastball inside for a called strike. Gamp stepped out of the box, wiped his bat on the inside of his right arm and looked to the dugout for the sign. Halloway tapped his cap, his left shoulder, then his chin. Swing away. Which Gamp promptly did, slapping a sneaky line drive through the gap between third and short. The runners advanced but held and, with the bases loaded, Beech emerged from the dugout. Callison was done.

The Bereton Park manager signaled to his bullpen for his All-Star reliever Brewster Mangan, a lanky youngster with phenomenal stuff and excellent control. The Squirrels were now up by one run, but threatening to break the game wide open, so Mangan had one task only: stem the bleeding. Prevent further damage.

Facing him was Lucius Cameron, the 34-year-old third bagger hitting in the eight hole. Mangan stared in for his sign and then threw high for a ball. Cameron took a hack at the second throw and managed to foul it off. That was followed by two throws low for balls, another hacking foul, and suddenly the count was full.

The hurler took several deep breaths and waited for his sign from the catcher. Cameron began to take his place in the box, then stepped back. Halloway smiled. The veteran striker was trying to force Mangan out of his rhythm. Finally Cameron held his bat aloft, as if pointing at the hurler, as if making a statement, then crouched into his stance and swung at the reliever's cutter. The ball slammed into the wood and reversed direction, sailing out toward the Hammerheads' right fielder and then past him, dropping several footlengths in front of the wall.

Dunbar scored from third.

Berbery scored from second.

Gamp, on first yet fleet of foot, made his way to home base without even drawing a throw. The Hammerheads' right fielder instead threw to the third bag. But Cameron arrived a good half-second sooner. A base-clearing triple.

The boys in the dugout erupted. The players hung on the rally and cheered as the three jubilant batsmen bounced down into the dugout. Several slapped Halloway on the back, acknowledging what was obvious: he'd managed the inning perfectly. Ferns, the striking coach, walked over and shook his hand as the base-runners bounded into the dugout amid more cheers. "Nice work, Coach. Great job."

A half inning later, after reliever Ryan Foreman shut down the Hammerheads with relative ease, the victory was locked in. The Flying Squirrels of Widmertown were Helderan Champions, and the best-of-nine Continental Series against the Jackaloupes of Schawmount City would begin in two days.

The celebration in the clubhouse was already underway when he returned from offering quotes to the reporters. The boys shouted, laughed, poured ale on one another. Halloway watched from the doorway. "Come on in, Coach," Cameron called out. "We're waiting for you."

Halloway thought at first he should avoid the revelry. He needed to plan for the Continental Series; there was little time. He needed to read scouting reports about the 'loupes strikers and hurlers. He needed to plan strategy.

"Coach!" repeated Cameron.

He smiled and waved at the third bagger, then entered the locker room and joined his boys for a drink or three.

September 26

SCHAWMOUNT CITY

O N THE MORNING OF THE 26th, Naughton took a public carriage car to the heart of the business district in Schawmount City. He disembarked near an open-air market, then made his way through the crowds, head down, shoulders hunched. With his good hand he tipped his cap to ladies and the elderly, as custom dictated, but he otherwise avoided eye contact.

Nine days had passed since Hood's men had returned him to the boarding house in Quintell. The Magera, at his request, had deposited him a dozen blocks away so as not to arouse the suspicions of Mrs. Drebb and the other boarders. They gave him money and narcotics. They would not return until he needed them again.

Phangorious Hood, he was told, would be patient.

He had used the time to convalesce. The boarders, all men, unkempt and bleary-eyed, mercifully kept to themselves. His body was still healing and he slept at least twelve hours each day. Each morning he had risen early, made his way to the common room for Drebb's unchanging breakfast, then returned to his room for more sleep, his dreams infused with the cries of Jellum being beat. And of a knife bearing down on his hand.

Each afternoon he had ventured out to find a supper and a newspaper. Over the course of those days, the pain began to subside and he worried less about the threat of infection.

Now, after more than a week, he felt sufficiently recovered to press on.

Along the roads into the city he saw evidence of the growing Setherian mobilization ordered by Executive Clay: caravans of what appeared to be military supplies carted on horse-drawn trucks with armed guards hanging off the sides.

They carried uniforms, perhaps. Food and tents. Ammunition. And behind the trucks: lines of raggedly dressed conscripts. The street hawkers and fruit vendors stopped to stare at the disturbing convoy, and the pace both of pedestrians and carriages was quickened. Daily life had been altered.

Eventually, he arrived at the park across from the headquarters of the Leagues of SIP and ALE. The public square was unusually empty — another indicator of the anxiety of the citizenry — and Naughton had no trouble finding a vacant bench.

He watched the headquarters building. For 20 years he'd entered its front gate with a nod and greeting from the guards; now he risked arrest merely by sitting across the boulevard from it. Yet he was not overly concerned about detection: his beard was full, his cap kept his eyes in shadows, and he held a newspaper aloft. And, of course, he wore gloves.

It was a massive structure, built over the course of three years after the declaration of the Eternal Ceasefire. Its architecture was dictated by Lord Bart to reflect the optimism of those heady days: a gleaming granite façade that stretched four stories high. Above the top story rose an ornate gable and two columned towers on each side. On the street level, three pointed arches covered imposing entryways with steel doors and rose-glass windows. On the spires, on the third-floor arcade, and on the banding under each archway were detailed figures of ballplayers, of families, of children, cut in stone. The headquarters seemed like a cathedral, and he supposed that was as Cunningham had intended.

But now, amid the military assemblage and residents hiding in their homes, the building's boastfulness, grandeur and pretension felt sadly ironic.

"You realize you should have directly messaged me to meet. It was indiscreet."

The Monystian security chief, Enoch Gill, sat on the bench space next to him.

"Yes. So be it," Naughton replied.

Gill opened a book and placed it on his lap as if engrossed in the story. Naughton kept the broadsheet open in front of him. "Nor should we be seen in such a public space."

"I can't take the time to row out on a lake. We need to talk."

"Sir, you located the bookmaker, correct?"

"Yes."

"And does he claim innocence? What is his story?"

"Before I tell you, Enoch Gill, I need answers from you."

The Monystian paused and contemplated Naughton's reply. "I see. Fine. Proceed."

"Did you program Crandy to attack the commissioner?"

"No."

"How do I know you're not lying? You oversaw the repairs of the hound after it was destroyed in the airship crash. Then you assured me that you had found those repairs without issue. And they proved not to be! He was sabotaged at some point, and your words at the time caused me to believe the hound was rebuilt properly. To trust that Crandy was fine."

"Well, then, you and I are in similar positions, wouldn't you say?" Gill swung his long, braided hair back over his shoulders.

"How is that?"

"The peoples of the continent believe you sabotaged Crandy. And you believe I did. And neither of us has sufficient means to prove otherwise."

"True enough. But if I take you at your word, Enoch Gill, that the hound was not compromised during his reconstruction, what then is your theory? When was Crandy sabotaged? And by whom?"

"I have no proof of this, sir. But I suspect it came when you visited Lord Bart late in the evening of June 12th, when you went to inform him of the first border clashes."

Naughton remembered that he had left Crandy outside the commissioner's estate for that difficult meeting, rather than bringing him inside. "That was when I noticed Dr. Henry arriving at the estate as I departed."

"Yes. It is entirely possible that the commissioner's apparent delusional episode was concocted as a distraction."

Naughton shook his head. A young mother, pushing a pram, passed them with her toddler following. The little boy stopped and stared at them, as if somehow cognizant of the gravity of their discussion, then ran ahead to catch up with his family. "So where does that leave us?" he asked.

"It leaves you, sir, with a decision. You can resume placing your trust in me, and we will continue working in tandem to reveal the conspiracies. Or, you choose to accuse me. In that case, I point out that I have three of my guards positioned discreetly around the park. At my signal, they will move in and have you arrested. Quietly, of course."

"You wouldn't, Enoch Gill."

"I do still have my official duties, sir, and you remain a most-wanted fugitive."

"So you leave me with no choice but to trust you."

Gill sighed and turned a page of the book. "Andrew Naughton, did you ever wonder why so few Monystians pursue the sport of baseball? Why only a dozen have succeeded in the Leagues of SIP and ALE over the past 30 years?"

"I have always thought the sport is simply not to the liking of your people."

"But do you know why it is not to our liking?"

Naughton shook his head. "No. I admit I do not."

"Because players cheat. It is that simple, sir. You know full well the sort of low-level cheating that is rampant in the Leagues, that is accepted: a runner at second relaying the backstop's signals to the striker, or a hurler cutting the ball with a hidden blade. A batsman putting tar on the top third of his bat. A grounds keeper tilting the field to leave a visiting squad off-kilter. The arbiters look the other way, and no manager complains because every team is doing it."

"Yes. It is, in those ways, a very dirty game."

"But Monystians find it hard to countenance that cheating, Andrew Naughton. It is against our very nature. Those who do play still cannot bring themselves to cheat, and thus rarely do they rise to the level of your professional leagues."

Naughton exhaled and wiped at his eyes. He understood: the security chief, by virtue of his lineage, should be beyond reproach.

Down the boulevard that separated the park from the League offices rumbled three large flatbed trucks, each pulled by a galloping, whipped team of mares. The material they carried was covered by cloth tarpaulins, but Naughton could discern the forms of cannons.

"I need to stop this war from coming, Enoch Gill. I need to get to the truth of things. To do so I need my freedom, and so I choose to trust you."

"An astute choice, sir."

"But I need information, Gill. I need to know the location of the commissioner, of Coyle, and of Lady Lynam. I need to know what their plans are."

"Unfortunately I cannot help, as Coyle has successfully ostracized me from discussions of import. But my own operatives have confirmed that shortly after the commissioner was transported back to Schawmount City, he was moved again. I do not know where, but two weeks ago, Lady Lynam traveled to Kern — she has long owned an apartment there — and she has not returned here since."

"Kern."

"Yes."

"In which our dear friend Iphonious Henry operates."

"Indeed."

Naughton folded the newspaper and placed it on his lap. Gill looked down at his left, gloved hand, then glanced directly at him.

"Yes," Naughton replied to the unspoken question. "I have pledged to the Magera. I did so in order to get to Jellum."

The security chief turned away. "I am sorry."

"As am I."

"No. You don't understand. I am not expressing sympathy for you. I am saying I am sorry because I can no longer help you, Andrew Naughton. I can no longer be of assistance. For the Magera is antithetical to the very existence of the Monystians. They epitomize what we despise. Their illicit ways are anathema to us."

"I know that, Gill. And I'm sure you know that historians believe the Monystians share a common ancestry with the Rebular, who dominate the ranks of the Magera. Very likely, before the Wide Cataclysm, those peoples were one."

Gill looked out, not at Naughton but straight ahead, at the crowded boulevard and beyond, at the cathedral-like edifice that was the home to the Leagues of SIP and ALE. "That is no matter to me now, Andrew Naughton. You are Magera now. And a fugitive as well. You have two minutes to leave this park or I will have you seized."

"But—"

"I can't be involved with whatever you're doing. You're going to do what you need to do, but I can't be part of that. So go. Go to Kern and resolve this damnable mess. And until you do so, do not seek contact with me again."

WIDMERTOWN

SIP League Continental Series Opens Amid Mobilization
By Blakeford Gash, Noble Daily baseball correspondent

(September 26, 1923 — Widmertown) The 30th Anniversary Season of the SIP League — marked by tragedy and uncertainty — culminates tomorrow with the start of the best-of-nine Continental Series pitting the Setherian champions, the Schawmount City Jackaloupes, against the Helderan titlists, the Widmertown Flying Squirrels.

This pinnacle of baseball comes after both divisional rounds went the full seven games. In the Setheridge, the 'loupes advanced by winning

their deciding contest over the McKilligan Terriers in resounding fashion, 11-2, thanks in no small part to a wild seven-run sixth inning. In the Helderan, the Squirrels also won the seventh game, although their victory over the Bereton Park Hammerheads was by a slightly slimmer margin, 8-to-4. That contest featured an outstanding performance by hurler Benny Harald and some timely hitting by the hero of the day, Lucius Cameron.

As this edition went to press, it remained unclear whether Commissioner Bartholomew Cunningham, still convalescing since the attack of the All-Star Game last month, will appear at the Continental Series. As most of our faithful readers know, Lord Bart has not been seen publicly since the incident. But he issued a statement two days ago proclaiming that the games will go on, despite the continued border clashes and the mobilization of forces by both of the Twin Nations.

"The Eternal Ceasefire is challenged as never before," said Cunningham in those prepared remarks, "but I vow that it will not crumble. We call upon our Helderan brethren, including their esteemed national Executive, his Excellency Alexander Fitton II, to lay down their arms and join in the celebration of our continental past time, the most wondrous sport of baseball!"

Sources close to the commissioner's Office indicate that Cunningham has not even appeared in person for internal meetings, and many on staff speculate that the statement was drafted by the new Special Assistant, Roderick Coyle. Coyle replaced the disgraced Andrew Gilpin Naughton, who is a fugitive from the law and remains at large amid a national manhunt.

Halloway put the paper down and sighed.

"What?" Ferns sat on the small couch in the manager's stadium office.

"I can't bear to read it."

"You expected otherwise?"

"No, but still. Enough." The rest he left unsaid. He had spent years working for

this very moment, to bring his team a championship. And to find the continent's attention diverted from the game itself: *Why this year? Why now?*

Ferns leaned forward. "It's out of your control, Sander. There's nothing you can do. Just try to enjoy the ride."

Halloway appreciated the words. "Archie. You never asked questions about what happened."

"What do you mean?"

"You know damn well what I mean. The All-Star Game, the affair with Asgar. You never questioned me."

"'Tis not my affair, Sander. And it is past, it is beyond us. We've still got some baseball to play."

"But—"

Ferns scowled. "But what?"

"I would have expected you to want to know more. To ask questions."

"Are you looking for absolution from me?"

"No—"

"Good, because if you are, you'll have none. I don't understand why you handled this the way you did. But that's past, and what is present is that we are now about to battle for the Continental Series crown, and our players have to be ready, have to focus, have to block out the turmoil."

"I know, but—"

"And you have to do the same. Block it out. Move on, Coach." He turned and left, shutting the door behind him with a touch of force.

Halloway sat for several moments, then realized he'd been holding his breath and clasping papers on his desk. He exhaled and let go of the sheets.

He knew he had lost Ferns. The man either would move on to another club next season, perhaps with his own managerial job, or would take over here in Widmertown if Halloway was dismissed. Either way, it was clearly in the striking coach's interest to distance himself from his own manager.

———————————

THAT NIGHT, THE NIGHT BEFORE the start of the SIP League Continental Series, the night before one of the biggest games of his managerial career, Sander Halloway dreamed he was walking out from the dugout to relieve Asgar during a game, and the hurler started laughing at him, and then the other players did, and the arbiters, and the ushers and vendors, and then the fans, hundreds of them, thousands, nay — tens of thousands. They showered him with ridicule and catcalls. They hooted and called names. *You can't take him out, they called. He's the Count! And he's throwing a no-hitter!*

He woke panting. A circle of sweat marked the pillow case. He checked his timepiece: five o'clock. Sunlight would be coming soon enough.

After dressing he made his way out onto the deserted, dew-covered cobblestone streets. The game would begin at two in the afternoon: nine hours away. The walk to the Stadium took twenty minutes. He passed fruit and vegetable purveyors setting up their curbside stands. A few stray mutts, some real, some autonomic, dashed into alleys, perhaps chasing rats. The sun poked through a thick layer of clouds.

The team entrance to Catalinaside Stadium faced the docks, and at this early hour only one guard was posted at the team entrance. He didn't look familiar, but the man clearly recognized him. "Coach Halloway. Its early. Trouble sleeping?"

"Yes, actually. But that's fine. More time to get ready." He tipped his cap as the guard held the door open.

In the dim corridors that led to the clubhouse, four janitrons rolled by, each applying some sort of wax solution to the cement floors. He cursed quietly; he'd have to wait now a half hour before going to his office. Then, above the rumble of the cleaners' wheelchains, he heard a noise from the field above.

Thwank!

It echoed through the corridor, and before the echo faded, it came again.

Thwank!

Halloway turned to the left, dodged two more whirring devices, and then took a set of steps to the first level of bleacher seats behind the home bag. The sun now firmly sliced through a large section of the cloud cover.

Thwank! The ball flew out to right field, landing in the midst of what seemed like two hundred balls that had yet to be retrieved.

The striker heard Halloway's footsteps, looked up and waved. "Good morning, Coach! A great day for the play-offs."

"Yes, Pyce. A great day."

A gas-powered steel box with a catapult-like arm was positioned on the hurler's mound, and every 30 seconds the device flung a baseball toward Marsh. At each automated hurl he swung and made contact, and the power of his attack was sufficient to send each ball careening high into the early morning air, beyond the outfield, over the fences. The direction of the shots varied little: virtually every ball made its way to the seats in right field, or center right.

"Choke up, boy," he called out. "Choke up a bit and you can spray the ball to all fields. I've been telling you that for months now."

Marsh listened, moving his hands up the bat about the distance of half a fist. Immediately, the direction of the hit balls began to vary, and many now landed in left field.

"Good. That'll keep 'em guessing."

"I don't like it, Coach. It feels uncomfortable."

"Yes, and it'll feel uncomfortable to the hurler when he watches the ball sail past the second bagger."

"But I like hitting home runs, Coach."

Halloway laughed. "Why are you out so early, Pyce?"

"What do you mean?"

"Why are you practicing this early? Its not even six o'clock."

"I'm here every morning this hour, Coach. Except when we're traveling, and the other team's stadium crew won't let me in." Marsh stepped back in to the striker's box and resumed his ritual.

Halloway removed his cap and fiddled with its brim. Most young players arrived with abundant talent, yet took for granted that the skills that allowed them to dominate in school ball, in university ball, would carry them as easily in the major leagues. They'd never had a need to work at improving. Years later, they'd wonder why they descended into mediocrity.

Not Marsh, apparently.

This, he thought, *this is the stuff of greatness. This is how legends are made: in thousands of hours of early morning practice, with no one else watching. With even the coaches unaware.*

He watched the boy another few minutes, then went into his office, treading carefully over the wet floors, and began charting out defensive alignments for the Jackaloupes starters. He'd refer to them throughout the game, shifting the infielders repeatedly to adjust for the hitting tendencies of the opposition. Anything for a slight edge.

Thwonk! Bat on ball.

Thwack! He lay his head on his desk and focused on the steady rhythm of the ball being released by the catapult, then struck by Marsh. The boy didn't miss.

Thwonk! The repetition was soothing, and within minutes Halloway found the sleep that earlier, amid tormented dreams, had eluded him.

Thwank!

  MICHAEL BARBATO-DUNN

September 27

DOWNTOWN KERN

THE APARTMENT BUILDING WAS RELATIVELY large — seven stories — with a brick and brass-plated facade. A high fence, a grand semi-circular driveway, guards at the front gates, carriages and their horses hovering with ornate carriages at the curbside in front: it all spoke of grandeur, of exclusivity.

The rain, which had fallen in torrents during the overnight ride, had dissipated. Naughton pulled the collar of his overcoat tightly against his neck and walked at a deliberate pace across the manicured lawn.

He reasoned that if it appeared deliberate, sure of himself, he would not be challenged.

A single concierge waited at a podium in the lobby, and a doorman hovered behind him.

Naughton tipped his cap. "Good morning, sir," came the immediate reply, and the concierge's tone of familiarity was sufficient to prompt the doorman to open the second set of doors. "Thank you," he pronounced, without looking in the man's direction. Inside, to the left, another attendant sprung open the door to the conveyance carriage. "What floor, sir?"

"The penthouse, please." The man switched two levers. Naughton entered and offered another word of gratitude. He avoided the operator's eyes. His hand throbbed. The carriage stopped with a lurch, the operator slid open the door, and within seconds Naughton was alone, in the narrow hallway of the topmost floor.

He found the door, caught his breath, then knocked.

"Yes?" came the female voice behind the door. "Who is it?"

"Message from Mr. Coyle, m'am."

Vivian Packer Lynam opened the door a sliver. In one swift motion he placed his shoulder against it, pushed his way inside and covered her mouth to stifle a scream. He hoped he would not need to bind her or gag her mouth. "I ask ten minutes of your time, Lady Lynam. That is all. Then you can have me arrested."

She stopped kicking and he removed his right hand — his good hand — from its hold over her mouth.

"To hell with arrest — I will have you strung up!" she shouted. The hand went back over.

"I will not hurt you, m'am. I simply need to talk to you, unobstructed, for ten minutes. Please cooperate."

After a few more minutes of struggle, she settled down.

"You—" she sneered. "You will pay for this in ways you cannot imagine."

"Trust me, I am already paying."

"I will give you five minutes to say your piece and then I will summon security to have you immediately arrested, jailed, and tried."

"I understand."

She was sitting now on a green velvet couch, and took to straightening her dress after the altercation.

"Lady Lynam, I must inform you: I have information that the Helderan scientist Iphonious Henry planned to assassinate the commissioner, that the plan went awry, and the airship was accidentally felled from the skies. And I have proof that you helped channel League monies to fund Dr. Henry's research. You have been acting in concert against the best wishes of Commissioner Cunningham, and may in fact have sought to have him slain."

"Oh, that's beautiful. A traitor calling me a traitor."

"I am not a traitor, and you, of all people, know that."

"Your servohound attacked my dear Bartholomew."

"And I am sure the suspicions against me will follow me forever. But you know it was not me that reprogrammed the hound."

She started to blurt out a response, but then stopped, and Naughton could see her combative demeanor crumble. Her lower lip quivered. "I know. Bartholomew, dear Bartholomew, never would have doubted you, Andrew, and I suppose I should not."

He paused. His heart was racing. He took a deep breath and summoned his courage to continue. "I have struggled since April to get to the root of this and have come up with only one bit of clarity: that you, Vivian Packer Lynam, are at the center."

She sniffled, dabbed her eyes, straightened her back, and pursed her lips. "No. I have been as allegiant as you, Andrew Naughton." She erupted in sobbing. "I don't understand how it all came to this. How he planned all this. How I agreed to all this."

"Who did the planning? Of whom do you speak? Coyle? Henry?"

She cocked her head to the right. "Oh, dear Andrew, you don't understand, do you?"

Tillbrookson Bluff

The gray mist cast a mournful pall over the cityscape of Tillbrookson Bluff, the highest city in the entire continent. Clouds and rain visited daily, and the best conditions the residents could hope for came in the early morning, when the eastward sun sometimes managed to burn through the mist. Sometimes.

Ollo Ronnell couldn't imagine living in the Bluff. It was hard enough visiting even a few times a year. But he knew plenty of former players who would not think of living anywhere else, because the mountain air and enveloping damp mist were, they believed, curative.

So it was to the Bluff that Ronnell fled in hopes of finding some relief from his aching right knee. A narcotic prescribed by his physician had done little. Nor had the salt baths of Sandbanna Woods. The Bluff was his latest hope.

The cable car, powered by a flexible steel tubing system, snaked its way both across and up the primary mountain, Keybursford Peak. This was the only route to the Bluff, unless a visitor managed to hire an ambitious carriage driver with an athletic mare.

Ronnell rode in one of the back cars, in one of the rearmost seats, to stave off any nausea that might arise as the travelers ascended in elevation. Across from him were two teenage girls, schoolmates perhaps. They spent the ride amusing each other with strange antics, each frequently dissolving into hysterics. Ronnell had hoped to sleep during the ride, and initially he shot them critical stares in hopes they'd quiet. But the two were oblivious to his remonstrations and eventually he relinquished any hope of rest. By the second half of the journey, as his body acclimated to the rapid ascent, he became accustomed to their outbursts of levity.

In a way, he was jealous. Their world was undoubtedly a small one, limited to family, school, and close friends, and thus their worries were limited as well. He yearned for such simplicity. Everything now seemed so horribly complicated. He couldn't recall the last time he had laughed so.

The cable car was swinging forcefully as it approached the final peak: the pod was pointed nearly straight upward, and Ronnell felt himself pressed against the back of his seat with such force that he closed his eyes. Then the car lurched forward and was finally, mercifully, horizontal, and the passengers were upright. The last leg of cable guided the tram to the waiting station platform. Ronnell waited until the others disembarked before stepping out.

A vivid vista and biting breeze greeted him. The Bluff: it was, in both a practical and an emotional way, a world away from the harsh realities of the sea-level cities. *Perhaps this is where the peace conference should have been held.*

"Ollo! Over here! Ollo!" That would be Rowland Warde, the longtime baseball columnist for the *Tillbrookson Bluff Register Times,* who had convinced him to visit the spa at the Peak.

"My friend, you look well," Ronnell greeted.

"I wish I could say the same for you, Ollo. You look like a wretched old man. I hear you took quite a spill at the All-Star Game. Chasing after demons, huh?"

"Chasing after something, I suppose. Not quite sure what got into me."

"No matter. This mountain air will cure that ache in no time. Why do you think I never left this godforsaken town? Anywhere else I travel, my back acts up. I've told my paper to get some youngster for the road games. I'm staying put."

"Thank you, sir. I will give it a try."

The two boarded Warde's waiting carriage for a short ride to the Keybursford Hotel, a grand mansion that housed the spa guests. Ronnell had requested a first floor room, to save his knee from any flights of steps, and he was fortunate that the hotel had had a vacancy for the weekend.

"How long will your stay be?" Warde asked.

"I suppose just a few days, though that could change if the air and the spa regimen prove helpful."

"The *Chronicle* doesn't mind?"

"They don't have much choice, Rowland. I need time off after the … the incident."

Warde, who was some 20 years younger, leaned forward and whispered to him as the carriage lurched forward. "What is going on, Ollo? Rumors abound that the commissioner is dead. That Fitton is demanding full control. That the Setherian owners are preparing to announce a retraction of Helderan autonomy. That the games will be canceled. Confusion is rampant up here on our little mountaintop. Surely you have some insight."

The old scribe scowled and looked away. "You know as much as I do, Rowland. I wish I could tell you more."

Downtown Kern

HE BROUGHT HER A GLASS of water after her crying subsided. Her hands shook as she drank.

"It was two years ago that I left Bartholomew, Andrew. You know that."

"Yes."

"But do you know why I left? Or why I returned?"

He shook his head.

"The reasons are one and the same."

"Go on."

She clenched a white handkerchief in both hands as she spoke. Her voice was in a whisper, as if to speak the words louder would only increase the pain they caused. "It was two years ago that my dear Bartholomew informed me that he planned to stage a disruption of the 30th Anniversary Celebration."

Her words hovered in the air. The confirmation of his greatest fear.

The old man is the culprit. The old man is mad.

Naughton's hand throbbed; he felt dizzy. He resolved to press on. "Why a disruption? To what end?"

"He sensed that the owners were tiring of his stewardship. It worried him. It consumed him."

"It warped his perspective."

"Yes. He believed that only by bringing the continent to the precipice of warfare could he ensure his continued hold on power. The owners, the peoples of the Twin Nations — everyone would rally around him."

"What did you tell him?"

"I tried to talk sense into him. I tried everyday. Everyday for weeks after he concocted this horrible scheme. But he would have none of it. I told him if he insisted on going forward, I would leave him."

"Which you did."

"Yes."

"And you were not complicit?"

"Not any more than you."

"Yet you said not a word to me. Nor to anyone."

"No one. He swore me to confidence, and I held to that oath. I kept it to myself. I know now that was wrong. But I did not believe there was anyone else to whom I could trust the matter. And I couldn't bear the thought that he would think I'd betrayed him. Like you, I have been loyal to a fault."

Naughton stood and paced across her living room. "Lady Lynam, it was you who brought in Gill. It was you who demanded the preparation of a false report, to confuse the supposed conspirators — and you knew they did not exist!"

"Yes. I wanted Gill here, to be a voice of reason; Lord Bart trusted the

Monystian's father. I expected him to be able to uncover Lord Bart's plotting without my having to reveal it. He failed. He never made that connection, and I was too afraid to simply reveal it."

"Afraid?"

She looked down at her lap and twisted the kerchief. "Afraid I'd lose him."

Naughton rubbed his maimed hand, then retracted it from view before she saw it. "But Dr. Henry's device — if it was not to assassinate him, then what?"

"The plan was that Henry's beam device would only injure Lord Bart. He would be hurt, but would survive. Neither Lord Bart nor Henry believe the beam was capable of more than a minor injury."

"So it would appear as a failed assassination attempt."

"Yes."

"And he would elicit the sympathy of the two nations."

"Yes. As I said, he feared there was a growing sentiment among the others in both nations for a successor. A failed assassination attempt—"

"—would halt that in its tracks."

"That is what he believed."

Naughton rushed to a window and cracked it open. He gasped in the fresh air, and his spiraling dizziness eased. "That is — insanity."

She stifled more sobs, and then took a deep breath. "That is not the half of it, Andrew."

"Of what do you speak, Lady Lynam? Is the commissioner in danger?"

"We are all in danger, if this continues. We are all in very grave danger."

TILLBROOKSON BLUFF

AFTER LUNCHING WITH WARDE, RONNELL took a charter bus to a mountain overlook. There he could spend the day in solitude, rest his knee, and put the tumult of the last few weeks out of his mind.

A small tour group was on the bus as well, mostly young couples, and at least half of the seats were empty. Ronnell imagined that the threat of war was wreaking havoc on the tourist industry, not just in Tillbrookson Bluff, but throughout the continent.

The bus arrived at the overlook within an hour. The driver parked in a gravel-strewn lot about 200 footlengths below the peak, and two separate sets of stone steps allowed the visitors to make their way to the summit. Ronnell walked the steps at a deliberate pace, grabbing a railing with his right hand as he clutched his carry bag with his left. An attendant asked if he needed assistance, but he waved him off. The dozen or so others arrived at the top well before him.

The peak was barren of vegetation. Steel benches inlaid with brass were bolted to the rock face in small arrays, each facing outward. A railing encompassed the perimeter of the rock. Ronnell caught his breath after the final ascent, then found an unoccupied bench and settled in.

It was said that the peaks of Tillbrookson Bluff allowed visitors to grasp a sense of the entire continent. That was an exaggeration, of course. But on this particular day, with spectacular clear skies, Ollo Ronnell saw the landscape as he had not in years. To the north, MacKaness and Goodwyn Fork. To the west, the trio of port cities of Bottom Brook, Mount Jarviswell and Boundymount Corner. Steam liners and sail boats could be spied without great effort in the waters beyond them. And then to the east, the teaming metropolis of Schawmount City, home to the Office of the Commissioner.

A waiter came by offering assorted fruits and prime cigars for sale. "Sir? Anything for you today?" He shook his head. Nothing for now, not even a cigar. Nothing would provide the solace he sought.

Except baseball. Oh, how he missed its sounds and smells. The simple slap of the bat, the murmurs of an expectant crowd, the artistry of a curveball. Even the arbiter bungling a call at first was somehow part of the game's beauty.

It was the best game, the one that had saved two nations.

After a few minutes, he rose and walked to an unoccupied spot of the railing. The bus would be leaving shortly. Down below, across the great swath of the beautiful, tormented continent, baseball was still being played. In the SIP League Continental Series, the Flying Squirrels — winners of the Helderan Division — would face the Jackaloupes of Schawmount City. In the ALE, the Jackrabbits of Bottom Brook and the Goats of McKinmond Lake had advanced to that league's Continental Series.

Through the political tumult, the games had somehow, mercifully, continued.

Ronnell turned again eastward, toward Schawmount City. He saw whiffs of smoke rising from the dense concentration of buildings in the city's core. Then he heard in the distance the muffled sound of gunfire. He wondered if the fighting, heretofore limited to the sparsely populated border region, had spread inland, if it had reached the capital of the Setherian nation.

He wondered if Vivian was safe.

I left when she needed me most, Ronnell thought. *Am I that bitter? That vengeful? Doesn't everyone, at some point, deserve absolution?*

An urgency, an alarm, rushed through him. Vivian had reached out to him six weeks earlier, and he'd pushed her away. But since then the political tumult has only worsened.

And her need for my help is even greater.

Ronnell looked again into the distance; the smoke was spreading. Schawmount City was likely under siege. He grabbed his cane, steadied himself for an instant against the railing and began making his way down the stone steps back to the waiting bus.

A couple to his left, a middle-aged man and woman, also peered toward the escalating smoke. As he passed them, they broke in to cheers.

Ollo Ronnell scowled. "You're celebrating a war?" he spat at them. "You should be ashamed."

The two laughed. "No, sir," they explained as they too made their way toward the steps, down from the peak of Tillbrookson Bluff. "That's not gunfire. It is only fireworks. The Jackaloupes have beaten the Flying Squirrels in the first game of the Continental Series!"

September 28

KERN

S LIGHT BEAMS OF SUNLIGHT PEAKED up from the distant horizon. Naughton squinted and turned away as he walked.

The city was quiet as dawn arrived, save the fishmongers down at the docks on Lake Leoran, shouting jokes amongst themselves. A sudden breeze brushed past him, but he was sweating and left his overcoat open. Further down, on a narrow roadway several blocks away, two Magera — his Magera — were about to carry out a necessary task. He pulled out his timepiece: 6:18. It was likely taking place at this very moment.

Down and across several alleys and walkways he went, then to the intersection of Barton and Tomlin Avenues: the appointed meeting spot. He stood at the

MICHAEL BARBATO-DUNN

southwest corner, leaned against the front of a closed shoe repair shop, pulled out a broadsheet and hid his face in the pages.

He stood unnoticed by the early-rising food purveyors, truck drivers, and delivery boys on bicycles. Slowly the pace of activity escalated, conversations and carriage rides consumed the quiet, and the smells of baked goods wafted past him. At one point a servohound, creaking and rusty, perhaps an abandoned stray, rushed past him. He tightened his grip on the sides of the newspaper.

And he waited.

The carriage came a half hour later, driven by Trentworthy, one of the Magera henchmen. Though based in Boundymount Corner, the trio of thugs had — with Hood's assent — stayed with Naughton to assist as needed. "All is well, sir. Climb in."

Inside the carriage was Kellender, the Magera who had carried out the beating of Jellum.

On my command, he reminded himself.

"Good morning, sir." The thug spoke with a cheerful lilt. "It was perfectly executed. We commandeered the driver as he left the stables. He is being held by Englehard at a discreet location. He was not harmed, but he understands the need for cooperation."

"I'm sure."

"Trentworthy is fairly close to the man in body type and is now wearing the driver's uniform," Kellender said, pointing to his colleague. "We should have no problem."

Naughton offered a slight smile. *They are efficient, these Magera.*

The downtown traffic was voluminous and meandering, and the short trip to their destination seemed interminable. His mouth was parched, his back ached, his left hand still throbbed, and his resolve to continue on was fueled only by his belief that the ordeal was nearing an end.

He was nearing the truth.

They arrived outside a modest townhouse in a quiet, residential portion of downtown Kern. The homes dated, he imagined, from the late 1700s, well before the start of the Great Insurrection. Kern had been a key battleground during the war, with both sides valuing it as a strategic necessity, a potential chokepoint to incursions both east and west. Yet somehow these homes had survived and still maintained their unassuming beauty.

Trentworthy slowed the team as they reached the address, a nondescript townhouse in the middle of the block. The henchman dismounted from his perch and walked to the front door while Kellender left the cab and waited behind it, hidden. Once he was in position, Trentworthy knocked on the front door, called out to a voice behind the door, and then returned to the carriage box. Naughton remained in place, but shifted lower in his seat so as not to be viewed from any of the cab's windows.

Two minutes later the door opened and Iphonious Henry emerged. He strode down the short walkway to the waiting cab and tipped his cap to the driver without as much as a glance at the man. Then he opened the carriage door.

"Dr. Henry," Naughton said, "We meet again."

The Scientificka cocked his head in confusion, then turned to flee, but Kellender and Trentworthy were already upon him, holding his arms back and shoving him into the carriage before Henry could even cry out.

"Damn you, Naughton. Have you lost your senses?"

"I was going to ask that of you."

Kellender jumped in next to them and locked the door closest to the inventor.

"You're a fugitive, Naughton," Henry spat. "Have your thugs release me now if you know what's best."

"What's best, Doctor, is that you start explaining."

Henry gaped at his captor. "Naughton, you're a wanted man in your own nation. But I do believe that Executive Fitton has granted you clemency for your crimes here in Heldera. Do you really care to risk that by holding me hostage?"

"My legal status matters not. You will cooperate."

"Or what?"

Naughton took a deep breath. Threatening was not his way. But neither was ordering a beating, or a kidnapping, and he'd managed to do both in the last few days. He held up his left hand, his maimed hand. The wound where his ring finger had once been was still red, though less swollen. "Or you will never be seen again."

Henry flinched and became pale. "You have—"

"Yes, I have pledged to Hood. An unfortunate necessity."

Henry removed his top hat and brushed back a shock of reddish brown hair. His forehead glistened in sweat.

"Do you now understand your predicament?" Naughton pressed. "If you value your future, you will cooperate."

Dr. Henry slumped back in the leather seat and nodded. "I do. I will."

Naughton tapped on the front window and called up to the Magera driver.

"To the University of Kern. The good doctor is going to take me to see the commissioner."

KEYBURSFORD PEAK

OLLO RONNELL LEFT TILLBROOKSON BLUFF with haste. He demanded that the hotel concierge summon a carriage, then dashed a note of apology to Warde and rushed to his room to pack before the hired cab sped him to the cable car terminal. The final run down the mountain departed at 10 o'clock that evening, and he arrived at the terminal with just minutes to spare.

The car, nearly empty of passengers, lifted off from its mooring and swung wildly at first. Ronnell clenched his teeth, nearly biting off the cigar's end. He fought back a wave of nausea.

The ride down Keybursford Peak proved interminable. He rubbed his throbbing knee and gnawed on the cigar. Smoking was not allowed on the cable car system, so he had no choice but to leave it unlit.

He cursed the fates. At the very moment he realized he wanted to be back by Vivian's side, he was in one of the most remote locations on the continent.

He needed to find her. To help her. To support her.

Even at ten times its speed, the cable car traipsing down the mountainside could not move quickly enough.

KERN

THE UNIVERSITY OF KERN WAS situated in the hills on the periphery of the city, and dozens of horse-drawn buses carrying students to and fro clogged the roadways. Naughton's carriage ascended the narrow thoroughfare that led up a steep incline to the college's immense front lawn. Ahead, an open-air bus pulled by a team of six horses carried two dozen students toward their classrooms, limiting their pace.

Henry's countenance remained ashen, his hands clenched. Naughton leaned toward him and spoke in a whisper. "Dr. Henry, Lady Vivian Lynam tells me that the commissioner has been under your care virtually since the attack at the All-Star Game, that his personal physician acquiesced to that change. Is this correct?"

"It is, yes."

"Why, after Lord Bart was transported from West Somerchester back to Schawmount City, did you not care for him there? Why risk further degradation of his health to have him here in Kern? And why is he even in your care?"

"That is difficult to answer here, in this carriage. It is best to wait until we are at my research facility."

"So you will allow me access, then?"

"Yes."

"And you will permit me to see him?"

"Yes, Andrew Naughton. The Commissioner will be quite pleased to see you."

"Is he conscious?"

"He is under sedation, but will shortly be brought to."

"Today?"

"Yes, in fact. This very day."

"So he will live?"

Color returned to Henry's face, and he offered the hint of a grin, the edges of his mustache arching upward in matching exclamation points.

"Oh, yes. Quite so."

The carriage swayed side to side as it made its way up a steep, gravel-strewn drive amid enormous oaks and pine. At the gated entrance to the facility, two guards stood at attention. One opened the double-wide doors to the carriage, then gasped as he recognized Naughton. The other, sensing the alarm, drew his musket and assumed an attack pose. "Halt!" he shouted.

Dr. Henry waved the two off. "It is fine, it is fine! At ease! I bring him here of my own volition."

"Dr. Henry, he is the fugitive. The League wants the traitor seized! He is to be arrested!"

"Yes, I am aware of that. However, I am allowing him to come with me."

The second guard lowered his weapon. The first continued to hold the door for the two of them, scowling at Naughton as he passed. "Wait here," he told the two Magera.

Inside, they walked by the entryway where two of Henry's assistants stood in equal amazement, then followed as Henry led Naughton to a series of private rooms on the second floor. At the third such door, the inventor halted his pace, and waved off his assistants. "Wait downstairs."

Henry reached down and swung a lever that revealed a bronze lock box with an array of buttons. Naughton found his heart pumping furiously. It was not from the exertion of the flight of stairs.

The doctor activated several of the buttons in a precise pattern. The door clicked and automatically swung open.

"He is recovering, Naughton. He will be fine. And shortly you will see why all of this was necessary."

SCHAWMOUNT CITY

IT WAS DAWN AS RONNELL arrived in Schawmount City. He went first to her apartment on the west side of town. He'd not been there in years. The doorman, a dour overweight man, looked him over once or twice before answering.

"She's not in."

"Do you expect her back?"

"And you are?"

"A friend."

The doorman squinted at him. "I don't recognize you one bit. Why don't you move along?"

Ronnell sighed, reached into his pocket and produced two crisp doubleweights. He extended them toward the man, who glanced in both directions, then grabbed the bills.

"She hasn't been here in weeks. Several weeks, in fact."

"Is that all you have?"

The doorman looked around once more, saw no one within distance of hearing him, and whispered, "As I understand, she left Schawmount City for her place in Kern, and did so shortly after the attack on Lord Bart, after he was transported back to his estate."

Ronnell stared and said nothing. The doorman knew more, he suspected. The man looked at his feet, then around the bright lobby. Two residents passed through, waved to the worker, then left the apartment building to hail a carriage.

They locked eyes, and the doorman bit down on his lower lip.

There is more. Ronnell produced two more doubleweights and the man snatched them away. He lowered his voice further and leaned in. "I hear she is with him. Lord Bart was taken by ambulatory carriage to Kern weeks ago. She accompanied him, they say. She has not been back here since."

Ronnell retreated to the quiet street, unsure of his next step. The aching desire to return to Vivian had only intensified since it first struck him atop the peak at Tillbrookson Bluff. If only he had agreed to her offer to serve as counsel during Cunningham's convalescence... Ronnell signaled for his driver.

Inside the cab, he pondered his options. A trip to Kern would take three hours, but once there he would be uncertain where to go. He did not know the location of

Vivian's apartment there, nor did he have any idea where the commissioner would be convalescing.

He needed help.

The scribe leaned forward and tapped on the pane, then commanded his driver to take him with haste to the League Headquarters.

"Do you have an appointment?" asked the receptionist in the lobby.

"No, but the matter is urgent. Please tell him Ollo Ronnell is here."

The woman scowled, then pecked out a message on a mechascribe, inserted the printout into a 'tube, and within one minute came a reply. "He will see you. You are to wait."

Ronnell lowered himself onto a guest chair in the ornate lobby. He had little contact with Coyle when the youngster was simply the assistant to Naughton. Now, though, with Lord Bart under medical care, perhaps in Kern, with Vivian there as well, and with Naughton a fugitive, it seemed as if Coyle was the last person in charge. And the feeling that Vivian was in danger, that she needed him, was as relentless as the throbbing of his mangled knee.

How has it come to this?

"Mr. Ronnell." The reverie broken, he looked up.

"Coyle."

"Why are you here? There's no news conference planned—"

Ronnell stood and whispered, so as not to alarm the receptionist. "Where is Vivian Lynam?"

"I'm not offering comment, Ronnell. I will likely be available to the press later this week. Wasn't my providing that report to you back in June sufficient?"

"You don't understand." His voice began to rise. "I'm not here for a story. I need to find Vivian. I have reason to believe she is in Kern, with the commissioner."

Coyle looked around the lobby, checking for anyone who might be eavesdropping, then leaned in. "And you base that on what evidence?"

"I have none."

"You are alarmed then, because of simple intuition?"

"I suppose you could put it that way."

Coyle grinned, exposing a slight and unbecoming gap between his upper teeth. "Then you are in luck today, Mr. Ronnell. For I will confirm to you privately — not for use in a column — that the commissioner and Lady Lynam are indeed in Kern, and I was about to depart at this very hour to see them. With your promise not to report any of this, I will let you accompany me."

Naughton stepped inside. The room was white and sterile, lit by dozens of gas lamps. Stacked along the walls, rows of metallic boxes rose to the ceiling like hulking beasts, heaving and vibrating, their purpose unknown to him. Four attendants, faces covered in surgical masks, scurried about. An enormous glass chandelier, intricate and ornate as one would find in a formal dining room, dominated the center of the ceiling. The reflections of its glass drops danced across the floor and the walls like shooting stars.

Below the chandelier lay a long table, surrounded by more pieces of odd equipment, tubes and cables protruding from their front and sides.

On the table was a bedsheet, under which was the form of a body, prostrate and unmoving.

Lord Bart.

Naughton felt his knees weaken, his hand throb, his pulse quicken.

I have found you, old man. I will save you.

Henry stepped in after him, snapped his fingers, and the attendants looked up from their duties. "Leave us be," the scientist commanded. The others filed out.

"He is sleeping now," Henry said. "He needs to rest, and is under a mild sedation. You can stay for ten minutes." And then he, too, left.

Once the door closed, Naughton stepped toward the table with a measured pace, glancing at the equipment that surrounded him: masses of steel and dials, pipes and beams. Lord Bart lay with eyes shut, breathing at steady pace. The face was pale; the wrinkles of the years seemed more pronounced. Occasionally, a cheek or nostril would twitch slightly, but otherwise the body was unmoving. Only the rhythmic breathing, the rise and fall of his chest, conveyed life.

"I don't know if you can hear me, sir. It is Andrew. I am back."

He waited for a sign of response, but there was none. "I am told you have been sedated. There may be a degree of understanding. I will assume so."

With the lightest of touches, he placed his hand on the commissioner's arm beneath the sheets. "My servohound attacked you from behind. I believe that he was sabotaged. Others wonder if I was the culprit. I assure you that that was not the case. My allegiance to you is unwavering.

"Yes, I know I earlier suggested that you step down. I had believed the time had come, for the good of the continent, for new leadership. Now, though, I do not know what to believe. I am told you planned to stage a failed assassination attempt to secure your hold on power. If that is true, sir, it was beyond foolhardy. It was madness. It is indeed proof that the time for succession has, in fact, arrived.

"But I also know that you are still greatly loved throughout the length and breadth of the continent and among all of its races. You brought peace to a land that had endured five decades of warring. You brought hope to generations of families. You brought baseball to the land that needed teams to cheer."

Andrew Naughton buried his face in his hands as the tumult of the past months washed over him.

"So tell me you have not betrayed your accomplishments, your life's work, through such bizarre treachery. Tell me you have not done what I was told."

The old man's eyes opened.

"It is true, Andrew. I have done this. And much more."

Downtown Kern

She opened her door and allowed Ronnell to enter. Her eyes were red and moist; her hair, normally immaculate, was tousled. She clasped a thin robe to her chest. "Ollo. Are you—"

"I should have come when you asked, Vivian. It was selfish of me. I was harboring a 30-year old grudge."

She grimaced and shook her head. "Stop. I deserved your refusal. But now, things have gone too far, beyond my ability to exert even a modicum of control."

"And that is why you've been crying.

"I cry for him. Bartholomew. He is… changed."

"Changed?"

"Yes. In more ways than you can imagine."

"Where is he now?"

"The University. He cast his lot with a deranged member of the Scientificka, and their scheming is beyond the pale of reason."

"Vivian, you are being cryptic. What are you saying—"

"You need not worry. I have taken care of this ungodly mess. Andrew Naughton found his way to me, and I explained to him what has been done."

"Naughton? The fugitive? He came here?"

"He came here for answers. I gave them to him. And if this goes as I hope, Naughton is at this very moment with Bartholomew, and will expose his treachery to the continent."

Ollo rubbed his jaw, confused. He felt as if both knees would give way, and

 Michael Barbato-Dunn

took a seat on her couch without asking. "Treachery? Scheming? Dear woman, what has become of the old man?"

"At some point, he lost his way. And I could not save him."

He sighed. "And that is why you asked for my help? To save Lord Bart from peril?"

Lady Vivian walked over to him and cupped her hand under his jaw, then leaned forward and kissed his forehead. "No, Ollo. To save him from himself."

The University of Kern

The Commissioner of the Leagues of SIP and ALE activated two levers at the side of the bed. The upper portion of the mattress and frame shifted upward, the lower section downward, and steam plumed from its sides as the entire contraption swiveled toward Naughton. It had become, instantly, a chair, and the old man now sat upright, the bed sheet still covering his lap.

Lord Bart's voice was firm, his gaze direct. "I realized years ago that the Eternal Ceasefire would only remain eternal if I did. So I sought out the young Dr. Henry, funded his research, and waited for the appropriate time."

"Henry."

"Yes, indeed. A brilliant man. I was wise to choose him. His research: his biomechanical hound, his beam device, all manner of advancements. He tried to prepare you for this. He tried to lay the groundwork for your acceptance. His lecture at the Opera House — Coyle prodded you to personally attend — that demonstration was very much intended for your eyes."

"Coyle." Naughton felt himself overcome with dread. *It was a broad conspiracy, right in front of me.* Bile rose up in his throat and he started coughing.

"Coyle oversaw all details of the preparations," Lord Bart explained in a buoyant tone. "Henry lead the scientific route. Hood provided logistical support, of course, but he was unaware of the full scope of the planning."

"But— you... you hired them to fire upon your very self? What warped mind—"

"Andrew, no, no. It was a brilliant idea. It was to look like an assassination attempt, but the beam would not be powerful enough to claim my life. The attack would cause both political unrest and sympathy throughout the land for my very being, making it more difficult for those who would clamor for succession."

"And you kept this from me?"

"That was deliberate. Coyle was certain you'd oppose it, that you'd stand in the way. It was difficult enough to have Vivian resisting us. Besides, we needed you to be unaware, for you'd not be able to keep this from the press. We needed you to be the innocent."

"And Gill?"

"The Monystian? He knew nothing. But his presence enhanced the credibility of our denials."

Naughton clenched his throbbing left hand, looked up at the old man, and spoke in a whisper. "What of the airship crash? Is that your doing also?"

"That was not part of the plan. We don't know what happened. The doctor's beam device was to have been aimed at me, and me alone."

"Thirty people died, Commissioner. Scores more were injured. What of them? What do you say to them?"

"The toll was unfortunate, I do admit."

"And it was Coyle who leaked the Monystian's report to Ollo Ronnell?"

"We needed to foment unrest. Our original plan had been derailed, so we improvised. It succeeded brilliantly."

Then Naughton swallowed and asked the question he dreaded most. "The servohound attack? Was that more improvisation?"

The old man nodded with a grin, evidently pleased with himself. "Yes, in fact. When the staged assassination attempt at the Anniversary Celebration went awry, we needed a different incident that would lead to my hospitalization. Your hound provided the appropriate means. I directed Henry to have Crandy reprogrammed—"

"— to attack you."

"It was an unfortunate necessity, Andrew. Only by bringing the continent to a crisis — back to the cusp of another continental war — could we make our citizens realize the true value of my continued leadership."

"Your... continued... leadership..."

"Yes, Andrew. For the Ceasefire to remain eternal, it is vital that I am as well.

Naughton gasped for breath. "That you are—"

"Behold, Andrew. I am eternal."

The sheet fell away as Lord Bart stood from the bed-chair with a gleeful grin. He wore a hospital gown, and below its hem Naughton saw metallic legs, gleaming and shimmering, rotating and flexing.

Naughton's vision blurred. His temples ached. "What— what is all this?"

"I am renewed."

  Michael Barbato-Dunn

The old man walked with a brisk gait across the room. The sounds struck Naughton like a hammer to his groin.

The clicking of levers.

The contraction of ligaments.

The whirring of gears.

The arcing of condensers.

The very sounds of Crandy — but now they emanated from the commissioner himself.

"What have they done to you?"

The Commissioner grabbed a wooden chair with one hand, then lifted and carried it to him. "Sit down, Andrew. You do not look well."

Naughton complied and Lord Bart stood directly in front of him, without even a cane or hand on the table to steady himself.

And then he raised the gown.

The metallic legs, hinged at the joints with multiple tubes and gears, rose fully up to his hips, and the sheeting continued to where his navel would have been. The transition to skin was seamless. On his sides, glowing tubes ran the full length of his torso, disappearing into the shadows under his arms.

Naughton gasped. "What is left of you?"

"Portions of his torso, shoulders, and arms remain, Naughton." The answer came from behind him, from Iphonious Henry, stepping in to the laboratory, carrying a large roll of parchment. "And of course, most importantly, his mind. The rest, including key organs, has been integrated."

Naughton stood again and glowered at the scientist. "Integrated?"

The doctor stared back, undeterred. "Yes. I showed you my altered hound several months ago. Sally. She was just the start — I've tested this more since then, much more. On hounds, felines, and simians."

"And on cadavers?"

"Well, yes. Suffice it to say that testing on dead bodies is always a precursor to live ones."

"That is sick—"

"I told you many months ago, Andrew Naughton, that the clockworks always move forward. Come see how they do." Dr. Henry opened the parchment roll, unveiling a detailed, hand-drawn design across the breadth of a nearby table. It showed a man's body, or at least a portion of the body. In place of the rest — the limbs, the lower torso — were specifications for miniature pneumatics, logic circuitry, steam compressors and condensers. "My crowning achievement," said Dr. Henry. "My pneumorg."

Naughton looked at Lord Bart, then Dr. Henry, then back again to the commissioner. He thought of the day they'd first met, in 1903. Cunningham's magnetism was palpable; the light in the interview room seemed to shimmer in his aura. A brilliant man, a man of accomplishment. A noble man. It was intoxicating, and Naughton had known in those first few minutes that, if given the chance, he would devote his life to Lord Bart's goals and needs.

"That is me, Andrew." The commissioner walked to the table, the steel of his legs and feet clanging against the floor. He moved without hesitation, with awkwardness, as though these appendages were, in fact, his own. "I am now truly eternal. And this will guarantee the continuation of the Ceasefire, the continuation of baseball, the continuation of peace throughout the Twin Nations and whole of the continent!"

Naughton looked down at his maimed hand. It still throbbed from his sacrifice. The finger — gone. His family — gone. His very purpose — gone.

"Oh, you are indeed a monster," he whispered. Then Naughton swept his arm, pushed the blueprint off the table and lunged forward, slamming his maimed hand against Lord Bart's still-human chest. "Monster!"

As his hands reached for the old man's neck, the outer door swung open. Ollo Ronnell rushed in, and Coyle, trailing behind, raised a musket and fired a single shot.

October 9

WIDMERTOWN

THE FIRST EIGHT GAMES OF the Continental Series encapsulated the emotional tumult of Sander Halloway's entire season.

At the start, the Squirrels' bats had gone silent, resulting in losses in the first three games, shut-outs in two of them. The Jackaloupes looked overpowering, particularly in throwing. But then the tide shifted: the Widmertown strikers returned to form and the throwing was resilient. Squirrels victories of 2-1, 4-3, and a 12-10 ruckus were enough to tie the series. That was followed by dramatic extra inning affairs in the seventh and eighth games with the Squirrels and Jackaloupes each coming away with a victory.

There it was: the series was tied at four games apiece. The entire season would be decided by a single game, a ninth game.

This very evening.

Tuesday, October 9th, 1923: seven months since the anniversary celebration that began the continental nightmare.

Seven very long months.

Halloway, in his windowless office four hours before the first throw, stared at his line-up card.

A. Goldwell CF
J. Minnocks C
G. Alley 1B
P. Marsh LF
F. Dunbar 2B
L. Cameron 3B
S. Berbery RF
I. Gamp SS
K. Asgar P

Yes, Asgar. *How appropriate.* His play-off performance had matched the team's: poor early (he'd given up five runs early in game two, which ended as a 5-0 loss) and better in the middle games (in game five he'd yielded just one unearned run and lasted nine innings in a 2-1 victory). Halloway had no reason to be disappointed at the way the Count had thrown.

Nor could he fault the way Asgar had conducted himself in the wake of the All-Star Game affair. He'd been reasonable, cordial, positive. He had apologized. He'd extended his hand.

Halloway could not have asked for more. Yet he still found the hurler's presence unsettling.

Catalinaside Stadium was at capacity for the evening game. Thirty-nine thousand had purchased tickets and, surveying the park from the dugout, it seemed to Halloway as if many more had been let in. He had no idea how many were Setherian, traveling into what was now enemy territory in support of their

Jackaloupes. It was possible to see a smattering throughout of 'loupe banners, shirts and caps.

And scattered on every level of the enormous park, military guards with muskets prowled. It was impossible not to notice, and he had no doubt that it would dampen what would otherwise be a festive atmosphere.

He traipsed back down into the tunnel that led from the dugout to the clubhouse and his office. The coaches, who shared a separate office, were gathered around an audiocaster, listening to some sort of announcement. Halloway peered in.

"What? What is it?"

"They're saying the opening ceremony is being delayed," said Ferns. "One hour. We don't know why."

"Is it... fighting?" On the cusp of the ninth game, the final game of a long and tortuous season, an outbreak of fighting would derail the game, and thus, the championship.

"No, it doesn't appear to be. We're not sure."

Halloway dispatched an attendant to seek out Langford. In the meantime he went to the clubhouse and found Asgar. The original start time was two hours away, and normally the hurler would be about to begin his dedicated warm-up regimen. "Hold off, Ketter."

"What?" The Count looked suspicious.

"There's a delay, one hour to the start time. We're not sure what's going on."

"Actually, we now know." Halloway turned. It was Langford, holding a communique from the Office of the commissioner. The general manager held it out to Halloway, who read it aloud.

"The Leagues of SIP and ALE are pleased to announce that the esteemed Commissioner, Lord Bartholomew J. H. Cunningham V, will attend today's final and deciding game of the SIP League Continental Series. This marks the commissioner's first public appearance since the unfortunate incident at the All-Star Game. As the contest is being played in Widmertown, this marks the commissioner's first journey to the sovereign nation of Heldera since that day. Lord Bart will address the audience before the start of the game."

———————

THE CENTERFIELD WALLS OF CATALINASIDE Stadium parted, and in strode the

elephant. Tens of thousands of fans from all corners of the cavernous park bellowed in delight.

Nellie. She's been repaired. Restored. Rebuilt.

Much like the old man himself.

Naughton watched, not from the familiar VIP seating behind the home bag, but from a section high above right field. Further back, at the last row of this section, stood Gill, watching him. Ostensibly, Naughton was under arrest. But Lord Bart had approved the outing so long as it was under the security chief's personal supervision. He was untethered by chains or handcuffs. Gill knew he would not flee.

Then Nellie moved, and the crowd gasped. One front leg and one back leg rose upward then forward and down. Then they held firm as the other pair replicated the laborious action. Bright plumes of steam emanated from the mechaderm's many hinged joints. With each step loud cracks resounded as metal struck metal within the aging steel frame. Its trunk swayed right to left, up and down, then rose like a mark of exclamation when the construct reached the center point of the ball field.

The announcer's tinny voice echoed, "Behold! A monument to progress! To peace! The return of Nellie, the mechanical pachyderm!" Applause erupted as fans focused on the small cabin atop the elephant, embossed with red velvet and gold leaf. It opened and a small platform emerged from the device's side below a small door.

A figure emerged. "Ladies and gentlemen, we present the founder and Commissioner of the Leagues of SIP and ALE, our national hero, his most excellent Master and Gentleman, Lord Bartholomew Cunningham!"

Once the thousands realized it was him, their beloved Lord Bart, they stood and cheered. Rumors that he was to appear had been rampant for days. So Naughton knew the cheering, hollering, and whistling were not of surprise but of adulation. Sheer, unmitigated adulation.

A ladder projected out from the side of Nellie and cascaded down to the field's green grass, and Cunningham — to the astonishment of all paying attendees — hopped down to the ground without hesitation, as if a young man. Then he trotted to the small stage that had been erected just behind the second bag.

The crowd saw the old man no longer needed assistance to reach the podium. Or to climb stairs.

Or to command a continent.

Naughton's left arm was bandaged and supported by a cloth sling. The narcotics that the doctors had prescribed after Coyle's musket shot struck his shoulder had dulled but not eliminated the incessant pain of his hand. They also made him feel sluggish, lifeless, without emotion. *At least it dulls the horror,* he mused.

The applause continued unabated, and Lord Bart stood to the side of the podium, waving both arms to acknowledge the cheers. After a minute another figure walked out from the home team's dugout, in black tie, tails, and top hat: the Helderan leader, Alexander Fitton. He leaned down to the old man and the two embraced, then clasped hands and raised them above their heads. The steady roars of the thousands watching escalated in intensity.

Gill and Naughton exchanged glances of apprehension as Fitton and Lord Bart approached the podium.

Fitton spoke first. "I thank the great people of the nation of Heldera for their support and cooperation throughout these difficult few months. I proclaim now that I have ordered all Helderan forces to withdraw from the border region. I have ordered an end to the military draft. The sovereignty of the great nation of Heldera will continue!"

Wild cheers rang out. Naughton pressed his monocle to his right eye, and could distinguish members of the Flying Squirrels applauding. In the bullpen the hurler Ketter Asgar had put down his glove to offer an ovation. In the VIP section, Setherian and Helderan team owners whispered among themselves. They wore an array of expressions, from anger to relief to confusion. It seemed as if none of this had been made known to them beforehand.

"The Kender Hypothesis is proved wrong!" Fitton declared. "The doubters, the nay-sayers, the cynics: all should be silenced. The continent will remain that of two nations! Helderan independence is, more than ever before, a right, a guarantee, a certainty!"

Now the crowd was rhapsodic, and Fitton basked in the cheers.

Next came Cunningham, who had donned a top hat and evening jacket provided by an aide after his descent from the mechaderm. He took the podium, grinning and waving as the applause continued. Naughton was certain that no observer could discern the whirring and clicking of Cunningham's mechanicals above the din of their worship, and he imagined that everyone was marveling at his recovery, his sureness, his pace and steadiness.

Perhaps some are wondering if the man is ageless.

"Kind people, when I addressed you seven long months ago at the 30th Anniversary Celebration, none of us had any idea what terrible events would transpire. But we did know that the Eternal Ceasefire was threatened. I had used these very words: 'We all know there are forces throughout the continent that would have us return to our warring ways.'

"Within minutes, of course, that warning proved all too horribly prescient. Those forces — criminals who to this very moment still elude us — were successful in the short term. They brought out the fears and suspicions of both nations. And that, in turn, caused us to militarize, to threaten, and even to attack. In all, dozens of lives were lost, scores more injured, and the Ceasefire hung in a precarious balance as it never had for its first 30 years.

"But — as my dear Helderan friend Alexander Fitton has told you — the Ceasefire survives!"

The old man paused, providing an opportunity for the tens of thousands to again erupt in shouts of euphoria. After a few minutes he continued.

"We did learn a thing or two in these past seven months. One is that the majority of peoples of both nations truly hate war. I knew that, of course, 30 years ago. But over time it became too easy to forget. Now — we remember!

"Those that would see a return to warring are the minority! They are not representative of either nation! And we will not allow ourselves again to fall victim to their insidious ways."

Now Cunningham, sweating slightly, removed his hat and wiped his brow as the cheers rose to a crescendo. He sipped from a water glass and continued.

"The other thing we've learned is that the unfair treatment of the Helderan people — which lasted for centuries — cannot simply be swept under the rug. That horrible history cannot be ignored. The nation of Heldera needs more than a simple assurance that its freedom is a true and permanent thing. I today acknowledge that the skepticism of the Helderans is warranted, that the Eternal Ceasefire is not enough to resolve those doubts.

"So I announce the first amendment to the Proclamation of an Eternal Ceasefire — a declaration that upon my death, the Helderan Executive — be it Alexander Fitton or whoever should be leading them — will become the Commissioner of the Leagues of the SIP and ALE! We pledge to share power! We pledge to share governance! We pledge to ensure that the Ceasefire is indeed, forever, eternal!"

On that cue Nellie, still in centerfield behind him, raised her trunk and trumpeted. This sent thousands to their feet, some dancing, others waving their arms in unison, some shouting Fitton's name, others Cunningham's. Those seated around him were hugging one another, strangers embracing across seats. A woman next to him reached out, and Naughton raised his injured right arm to demur.

On the platform, the two leaders had clasped hands and acknowledged the cheers with broad smiles. Cunningham was buoyant in a nearly literal sense: he was, at moments, jumping amid the shouts. Next to him, Fitton appeared overcome with the emotion of the moment.

He seemed to be crying.

Gill walked down to Naughton's row and motioned. It was time to leave; attending the opening ceremony was all Cunningham had approved. He could not stay for the ninth game, the final game of the anniversary season.

———————————————

HALLOWAY WHILED AWAY THE HOUR by staring at the clock and the line-up card. The boys were out on the field, and the crowd was drifting in. He heard an announcement, and then a groan, and then a cheer, and he knew the audience had been informed of the delay in the start.

They'd groaned at the delay, he surmised.

They'd cheered the word that Bartholomew Cunningham was returning.

He felt the muscles of his stomach and buttocks unwind, his fists unclench. It was an odd sensation: relief. He couldn't recall the last time he experienced it. Certainly not since before the All-Star Game. Relief. He let it wash over him.

And then Sander Halloway did what had long needed to be done. What he'd put off doing since that terrible day, since his return to the team.

He called out to the clubhouse boy. "Cheesely, get me Marsh. Now."

Eventually, the young striker entered, cap in one hand, glove in the other, lanky and awkward as ever. "Sit down, Pyce. Close the door."

"How are you today, Coach?"

Halloway leaned back and ignored the attempt at pleasantries. Pyce Marsh had had a phenomenal year: a .303 striking average, a slugging percentage over .500, 16 home runs and an astounding 44 stolen bases. Among the league top five in hits and runs scored. The team would not now be a single victory from the championship were it not for Marsh. And he was not yet 23.

"I want to talk to you, Pyce, about our conversations earlier this season."

Marsh drooped down into a chair. "Yeah, Coach. I don't know why I did that."

"Did that?"

"Made up that story about the Count. About him planning to hurt fans. It was just— he was terribly mean to me. He was very nasty. I wanted to get back at him."

"You made it up?"

"Yes. I'm sorry. I hadn't planned to. It was a spur of the moment thing."

"Why are you waiting until now to tell me?"

"I—I thought you knew. I thought you'd realized."

Halloway's hands shook. "And what made you think that, Pyce?"

The boy seemed to shrink in the chair as he recoiled from the question. "I—I just assumed. It was a crazy story, after all."

"Well, Pyce, these are crazy times. And your words precipitated a... an incident."

Marsh raised his head and looked directly at his manager. Halloway saw his eyes were moistened, his lip quivering. "Can I still play today, Coach?"

He's just a little boy. He plays baseball, and he plays pranks.

"Yes, Pyce. You can still play. But after the season ends, after tonight's game — whatever the outcome — you and I are going to sit down with the team's general manager and owner. They need to be fully aware of your actions. They will determine if any discipline is necessary."

"Thank you, sir." The boy stood to leave, his glove still firmly on his left hand.

So much talent. He could become a Hall of Famer.

But in that instant Sander Halloway was certain that despite his work ethic, Pyce Marsh would end up as so many others he'd seen, arriving with abundant natural talent, yet not bright enough to adapt to the inevitable declines in ability. As the seasons wore on, he would become confused by increasingly frequent slumps, flummoxed at the home bag by young and crafty hurlers, frustrated by failing to compete at this level — at any level — for the first time in his life.

He would become his own worst enemy. He would be finished by age 30. And he would grow old and angry, always wondering what had gone wrong.

"Marsh."

The outfielder turned back. "Yes, Coach?"

"You're sitting tonight."

"Excuse me?"

"I've just had a second thought. You're not playing tonight. You're riding the bench."

"But coach. It's— it's the ninth game. It's the final game. I'm your best striker. I helped get you to this point!"

"I'm well aware of all of that, Pyce. I'm letting you know now, rather than have you find out by reading my line-up card."

"But— I deserve this."

Halloway shook his head. "You will sit on the bench, Pyce Marsh, and you will watch the game, along with thousands of others, and you will think about the consequences of your actions."

Marsh snatched his cap off and held it to his chest. He opened his mouth to reply but no words came, and as the boy fled the room all Halloway heard was a muffled sob.

<hr />

It took Naughton and Gill a full half-hour to exit the stadium. The festivities had enveloped every portion of the ballpark; stairwells and corridors were jammed with celebrants. As they reached the lowest level, off the right field line, they paused at a railing for one last look at the jubilant scene.

Out on the grass, just below them, the hurler Ketter Asgar has resumed his warm-ups. The bullpen catcher crouched 60 footlengths away, snagging each of Asgar's throws with ease and tossing them back to the Count. Fastball, low and away. Fastball, down the middle. Curveball, up an in. Another fastball, this one chest high. The two, the hurler and his catcher, continued on without let up, oblivious to the roaring jubilation and the lengthy delay in the start of the game.

They could have been children quietly having a toss on a rock-strewn sandlot. Tossing a ball and dreaming of playing in a Continental Series.

"Hello, Andrew."

He turned back. Standing next to the security chief was Lady Lynam. "Chief Gill was kind enough to arrange for a brief meeting before you depart." She nodded to the Monystian, who replied with a small bow and took several steps back, affording them privacy.

Naughton thrust his left hand into his pocket. "Does the Commissioner know?" he asked Lady Lynam.

"That we're meeting? No, of course not." Her face was gaunt and pale to a degree that even makeup could not mask. "I have convinced Lord Bart not to charge you. You will soon be released."

"I'm sure that decision was not difficult for him, given that a trial could bring his scheming into the public record."

"Of course," she said. "But you still have that opportunity. You could reveal the truth. You could go to your friends in the press."

"As could you."

"No, Andrew, I can't. I cast my lot with this man three decades ago."

"But, Lady Lynam, he is not the same man. Nor is he the man who hired me 20 years ago. At some point he convinced himself that he was more important than the Leagues, that he was irreplaceable. Megalomania infected his soul."

"I know. But to reveal his duplicity now would cost me everything. You are well aware I receive a regular League stipend. It is all I have. I rely on it for my lifestyle. And..." She looked away.

"And?"

"Andrew, my mother passed away years ago, but I still cannot bear to have her think that she was right."

"Yes, I'm sure." Naughton nodded. "And what of the press? Are they pestering with questions? Are they suspicious of the old man's newfound gait? Of his now-boundless vitality?"

"They seem to be oblivious. They are quite focused on the supposed peace agreement, and the amendment to the Eternal Ceasefire."

"Even Ronnell?"

She shook her head. "I have asked for, and received, his cooperation. His understanding."

"So the Twin Nations may never know."

"Unless you tell them."

"Is this why you're here? To dissuade me from speaking out?"

"I'm sure you realize that to reveal all would, ironically, bring the continent back to the precipice of warfare that you worked so hard to avoid. Is that what you want?"

Naughton looked back out to the ball field. The tiny figures of the commissioner and Fitton could be seen, still on the stage, still leading the celebration. "Poor, foolish man," he said.

"Lord Bart?"

"No, Fitton."

"Foolish, because he doesn't realize that Lord Bart's pledge of succession is a false promise?" asked Lady Lynam.

"Indeed. The pledge is based on the premise that Cunningham one day will die."

"Do you doubt that day will come, Andrew?"

"Lady Lynam, now that the commissioner has elevated Dr. Henry to head the Association of Scientificka, they will devote even greater resources to ensure that the mechanization will continue. As each part of old man's mortal body fails, it will become machine."

Gill moved a step closer, apparently anxious over the duration of their conversation. Lady Lynam reassured the Monystian with a nod, then turned back to him.

"Where will he stop, Andrew? Will he let Dr. Henry go further with his... his..."

"...pneumorgs? I suppose. Perhaps we'll see them in uniforms on the ballfields one day. The clockworks always move forward."

Lady Lynam dabbed her kerchief against her moist eyes and leaned against him. "He was a good man, once."

Naughton placed his arm across her shoulder in comfort. "I know. He solved an endless war. But now he wants to solve that very inconvenient matter of death."

Lady Lynam nodded and stifled a sob, then retreated back into the crowd. Gill stepped forward and placed his hand on Naughton's elbow.

On the field, Fitton and Cunningham strode forward, with chests upraised, to take their seats behind home base for the start of the deciding game. A band had struck a rousing fanfare, and dozens of spectators in the bleacher seats, carrying horns of their own, joined in.

Fitton's grin was immense.

Foolish man, Naughton repeated to himself. *He thinks he's won this thing, but he's just struck a deal with the devil.*

HALLOWAY TIGHTENED THE BELT ON his uniform trousers. The pants were baggy, as custom dictated, but lately he'd noticed that his waistline was no longer snug. He had lost weight since the mishap at the All-Star Game; between the constant ache of his back and the anxiety of the bizarre situation, he rarely had much appetite. Now, without a belt, the trousers would have simply fallen to the ground.

He stood from his desk. From above, from the stadium, he had heard the roars of the crowd for the past half-hour. Both Executive Fitton and Commissioner Cunningham had spoken. The resounding cheers were enough to tell him that the two leaders were amicable. That peace had returned.

That the ninth game would be played.

Halloway had been tempted to go up to the dugout sooner in order to hear the speeches. But he needed first to rewrite his line-up:

  MICHAEL BARBATO-DUNN

A. Goldwell ~~CF~~ LF

J. Minnocks C

~~G. Alley 1B~~ F. Dunbar 2B

~~P. Marsh LF~~ G. Alley 1B

~~F. Dunbar 2B~~ L. Cameron 3B

~~L. Cameron 3B~~ S. Berbery RF

~~S. Berbery RF~~ I. Gamp SS

~~I. Gamp SS~~ M. Flaherty CF

K. Asgar P

Dunbar, who had struggled to hit most of the year and been relegated to the five-hole in the line-up, would now strike third. Gillighan Alley would move down to clean-up in place of Marsh. Morris Flaherty, usually a late-inning defensive replacement and occasional pinch runner, would start in place of Marsh, batting down in the eight-hole and covering the outfield from center. Goldwell would shift from centerfield to left. Others in the bottom half of the line-up would move up a spot.

He stood, put on his Squirrels cap, and grabbed the unsightly card. He would not write a fresh copy. He would leave the card as is, with the names scratched out and rewritten for all to see.

The din of cheers grew as he ascended the steps to the dugout. Out on the field he could see the small riser erected at the second bag, and spied Executive Fitton and Lord Bart, arms upraised, the Helderan leader towering above the old man. But the commissioner, even from this distance, looked spry and hail.

The manager took a deep breath. He had not expected as much, but the sight of Lord Bart was a comfort. His was a healing presence. *If only he could be with us forever.*

Then Sander Halloway turned back to the cement dugout, and took in the long line of players, most leaning against the railing watching the grand ceremony. Marsh was nowhere in sight. But the others, his boys: not a single one of them would ever understand why he was benching the team's best striker in the final game. Nor would the scribes, nor the fans, nor the general manager.

Nor the owner.

He tacked the line-up card to a corkboard at the near end of the dugout.

Hell, he thought, *it's only a blengin' game.*

October 11

TWO DAYS AFTER THE NINTH and deciding game of the SIP League Continental Series, Sander Halloway walked into Catalinaside Stadium. He slung a large canvas bag over his shoulder and trotted down the short flight of steps to the empty locker room, then into his office, soon to be empty as well.

On his desk lay his score sheet from the final game.

He stared at the numbers on the marked sheet, the array of boxes denoting the runs tallied in each inning: four in the bottom of the second for the hometown squad, four more in the bottom of the eighth for good measure. The rest of the boxes were zeroes.

Flying Squirrels 8, Jackaloupes 0.

The absence of Marsh in the line-up had caused a momentary furor in the dugout and, no doubt, in the press box. His coaches had shot furtive glances while the players whispered amongst themselves. An attendant delivered an urgent note from Langford: "What are you doing?"

Halloway crumpled the slip of paper and tossed it aside.

The only team member to approach him directly was Asgar himself, and he did so with a broad grin. "Are you certain, Coach?"

"I am, Ketter," he affirmed. "Now get out to the mound and throw me some strikes."

Throw, Asgar did. His every hurl had nipped the edges of the strike zone, arriving at speeds that varied wildly. The Schawmount City batsmen walked away flummoxed, several pounding their bats in frustration. More pronounced was the Count's demeanor on the mound: he glowered and stalked, pounding his glove with intensity between strikers, and throwing with a pride that rose as the innings went on.

Perhaps, Halloway thought, that was the greatest irony of the Squirrels' 1923 season: his suspicions of Asgar, fully baseless and without merit, prompted by a boy too immature to know better, led the Count to seize the championship moment, to throw as if he had something to prove to the entire continent. The ferocity of his fastball, the duplicity of his change-up, the deception of his slider: all were at a level of effectiveness that exceeded any prior start of his seven-year career.

Halloway's strikers responded as well: they bloodied the Jackaloupes' starter Wilber Giles with those four in the bottom of the second, and that proved to be all that was needed. Even Flaherty, given a start only because of Marsh's benching, contributed to the offensive output with a double that drove in two of the runs.

By that point, not a single person was thinking about the missing slugger, Pyce Marsh.

So it became, after all, a lopsided game, and near the end Halloway did not want to pile on. In the top of the eighth, after Asgar yielded a lead-off walk, the manager emerged from the dugout and walked to the mound, then took the ball from the Count.

"Thank you, Ketter. You were magnificent."

"Let me finish this, Coach. It's my game."

"It's already your game, Ketter. You have nothing more to prove. Go walk to the dugout and take in the cheers."

"But—"

"Take in those cheers, son. Remember them. Soak them in. Because some day you may find yourself alone in an empty apartment, with little else but the memory of that sound to keep you going."

The hurler raised an eyebrow and studied his manager, then walked off the mound as thousands in the stadium showered him with a standing ovation.

Asgar's final line: eight innings, three hits, three walks, eleven strikeouts, no runs. A shutout in the most important game of his life. A capstone to what was already an impressive career.

Now, in his office, Halloway placed the score sheet into a binder that held those from the entire season, then lowered the notebook into his canvas bag and hoisted the duffel over his shoulder.

The Flying Squirrels were the champions of the Setheridge Island Professional League of Baseball. A championship for the players. For the city of Widmertown.

For the nation of Heldera.

I managed them to victory in the Continental Series. Sander Halloway had formed those words to himself several times over the past two days, and he did so again as he made his way down a stadium corridor, then up several flights of stairs to the suite of offices shared by the general manager and the owner. He hoped the repetition of the phrase would make the accomplishment seem satisfying.

It did not.

STABBING PAINS STRUCK OLLO RONNELL's damaged knee as he made his way down the short flight of steps. He had looked in the Tap and Cork's two drinking rooms on the main floor without success, so there was no choice but to try the third room, in the basement.

It was a brilliantly sunny day, but because the room was below ground, only thin horizontal windows near the ceiling let in any light. Plumes of dust and smoke danced in the shafts of sunshine. The room was nearly empty; it would fill soon enough, when the Continental Series victory parade was over and fans sought to continue their revelry.

Ronnell squinted at each of the patrons. And there, sitting alone at the far end of the bar, he found him. He hobbled over and extended his hand. "Well, if it isn't the manager of the continental champions!"

Sander Halloway sneered and looked away. "I have no comment, Ronnell. Leave me be."

"I am not here on business today, Sander. May I sit down? My knee can take no more."

Halloway pushed the stool next to him out toward him. Ronnell propped his cane against the underside of the wooden bar, hoisted himself onto the stool, and waved to the bartender. "Whiskey, please."

"Last time I saw you, Ronnell, you were poking around about the fisticuffs in my locker room."

"Which you denied."

"I didn't need that written about in your rag of a paper."

"Maybe if I'd written about it, you might have been spared the mess at the All-Star Game."

Halloway scowled but said nothing.

The owners of the publick house had placed audiocasters in each of the drinking rooms so the patrons could follow the descriptions of the parade. Ronnell cared not to hear it, and he assumed Halloway did not as well, but the few other men in the room seemed fixated on the large brass-and-steel box.

"I thought you'd be out on the streets," Halloway sneered, "composing witty barbs about the parade."

"No, thank you. Parades are for the young scribes. Besides, my reporting days are done."

"Oh?"

"Yes, I am no longer in the employ of the *Chronicle*."

"Why is that? Have you tired of placing thousands of lives at risk in order to publish an exclusive?"

"You don't much care for reporters, do you, Halloway?"

"I'm a baseball man, Ronnell. Or at least, was."

"Excuse me?"

"I too have tendered my resignation. Caffrey and Langford called me in this morning to fire me, but I never gave them the chance. I left them a letter and packed my things."

"Are you certain they intended to let you go?"

"Quite. Langford wanted nothing more to do with me after the All-Star Game. I don't blame him. So now they can announce that I left of my own volition. I made it simpler for them."

From the speaker came bubbly chatter of the two announcers, describing the members of the Flying Squirrels escorted on regal carriages down the main thoroughfare of Widmertown. Fans leaned out the windows of office buildings, showering them with confetti. The players were now heroes.

They would become, at least to Widmertown, and perhaps to all of Heldera, immortal.

"How did you know I was here?" Halloway asked him.

"Word got around fairly quickly that you were not taking part in the parade. I suspected something was afoot. Finding the publick house in which you'd chosen to hide was simple enough."

"But you won't be reporting on my resignation?"

"No. I told you: I'm done."

"Then why did you seek me out?"

"Curiosity. What happened with Marsh? Why did you bench him in the final game?"

Ronnell watched the manager swirl the ice cubes in his glass and stare straight ahead, as if recounting a memory, perhaps a conversation. "He didn't deserve to play. And that's all I'll say on the matter."

"What did he do? And why are you walking away? They love you now. The whole blengin' town loves you."

Halloway finished his drink, waved to the barkeep, then rubbed his hand through his thinning hair. "Did you ever have children, Ronnell? A family?"

"No. I suppose I never made time."

"Have you been in love?"

Ronnell twisted his cigar in his hand and shifted on the stool. "Yes. Once. It was a long time ago."

"I've been in love," the manager said. "But it was with this damned game. Baseball. With bats and balls and mitts and caps. Hurlers and strikers. Wins and losses. I've loved everything about it. I had two wives, and I paid them little mind. It is small wonder they stayed with me as long as they did. I was always just chasing victory, chasing a championship. I thought that would be enough."

The chattering of the box continued as the announcers described every moment of the wondrous parade. One quoted the commissioner's words from the ill-fated Anniversary celebration: "As baseball endures, so will the continent!" The few others in the taproom cheered.

"And you?" Halloway asked. "What will you do?"

Ronnell shook the whiskey glass so the ice chips spun. "I have an idea or two."

"Such as?"

"For one, I want to do something about the plight of the steamsmen."

"The steamsmen? What of them?"

"They work in horrible conditions. Both nations ignore the situation. Even I never gave it much thought until meeting one such worker months ago. They need better safety precautions. They need better pay. I believe they can achieve this through unity."

"Unity?"

"Yes, a union of the workers. Through solidarity, they can demand improvements."

"That's quite an idea, Ollo Ronnell."

"I know." He laughed and plucked his cigar from the corner of his lips. "I suppose my ideas only get me into trouble."

"What do you mean?"

The scribe turned away. "Never mind. No matter."

Ronnell ordered a third round for the two of them, and they clinked their glasses in a silent salute. Now the announcers were musing about the glaring absence from the parade of both Halloway and Pyce Marsh. The young slugger had disappeared during the ninth game two days earlier and had not been heard from since.

"Will you miss it?" Ronnell asked the former manager.

"Of course," Halloway replied without hesitation. "Every waking minute. And you will as well."

October 15

Gregorson

...and that, Amelia, is how I came to this point: I pledged to the Magera in order to uncover the truth, a truth that proved as horrible as the pledge itself: Bartholomew Cunningham convinced himself that the only way to preserve his hold on power was to stage a threat against himself. So with the help of others, he created one threat, then another. And he chases immortality.

Now I am lost to you. And to Jack, and Isaac. If I were to try to return, the Magera would seek me out, and that would endanger you and the boys as well.

You may hate me now for the decision I made. I hate myself for it, for I placed my devotion to the Leagues, to the preservation of the Ceasefire, above my allegiance to you.

I said this at the onset: I am not so bold as to ask for your absolution, nor your compassion. I am owed neither. I move now to a new existence, a terrible one, and the only solace I have is the knowledge, the certainty, that you will be strong.

With all my love,
Andrew

NAUGHTON WIPED HIS SLEEVE AGAINST his eyes, careful not to let the tear drops spoil the handwritten sheets. He folded the papers, twenty four in all, into quarters, then slipped them into a square white envelope.

Onto which he wrote her name.

Crandy lay outstretched in front of him, his tail swishing side to side as steady as a metronome.

After he and the security chief had left the championship game, Gill revealed what he'd done: every part of the hound that was still usable after the All-Star Game incident had been saved and repaired. Components that were beyond repair were replaced with new ones. Programming was carried out by a new firm with impeccable credentials, then checked and re-checked by Gill's own staff. He had done all this covertly, without the knowledge of Coyle or the commissioner.

At first, Naughton had refused to take the hound. "It is my gift to you, sir," Gill had insisted. "For all you've done for me, and for the Leagues. For the continent. Besides," Gill added, "he's your boy." And at that moment Crandy had bounded toward him to lick his face.

Crandy was back.

Now, four days later, formally released from League custody, Naughton powered down the servohound and unscrewed the metallic plates that formed his lower back. The topmost plate was hinged and he swung it upward, revealing a slim compartment.

He slipped the envelope inside, bending it in order to make it fit. Then he pushed the plate back into position. When the hinge snapped in, he folded the fur back over, then returned the hound to a full power state.

Crandy opened his eyes, blinked, and wagged his tail.

Naughton knelt down and stroked the underside of the hound's snout. "I know you remember me. I know. You've been rebuilt twice, yet you remember. But you must leave me now, Crandy. You must make your way back to Schawmount City, to our house, to Amelia and the boys."

Crandy lowered his head, trying to avoid Naughton's eyes.

"No." Naughton lifted the hound's head upward. "Look at me. You are to go to her. Give her my letter. Stay with her and the boys. They need you now, far more than I."

Naughton stood. His lower jaw quivered. The hound peered upward. "Now, Crandy. You belong to them now. You must go."

The servohound stayed in place, sitting, head bowed, tail swishing across the ground, but otherwise unmoving.

"Go!" he commanded.

Crandy rose, ears and tail at alert, then turned and galloped down the darkened street, thin plumes of steam rising from his hide. The hound stopped at the entrance to an alleyway, looked back at his master for an instant, uttered a low cry, and wagged once more.

Then he was gone.

Naughton raised his right arm, his healthy arm, and buried a sob into the crook of his elbow. Then he turned back, walked a short ways up the road, and stepped into the waiting carriage of Phangorious Hood.

Acknowledgments

GRATEFUL APPRECIATION TO READERS TERRY Lohr and Mark Bangela, for their insight and advice, and to editor Judith Redding, who made me realize how little I understand about commas.

Thanks also to Markus Heinsohn and Andreas Raht, creators of Out of the Park Baseball, the simulation software that served as the genesis for the Leagues of SIP and ALE, and to Brad Cook of OOTP Developments for his promotional efforts.

And of course, my heartfelt thanks to Clarice and Olivia, for their support and encouragement over the past four years.

Appendices

THE SETHERIDGE ISLAND PROFESSIONAL
LEAGUE OF BASEBALL (SIP)

Setheridge North		
Binney	Foxes	Bragbinney Stadium
Kendall	Griffins	Prolent Park
McKilligan	Terriers	Bannon Field
Mount Waylandtown	Fighting Camels	Wayland's Cove Park
Setheridge South		
Boundymount Corner	Raccoons	Nonmenth Field
New Ungerapolis	Fisher Cats	Fischer Cat Park
Schawmount City	Jackaloupes ('Loupes)	Schawmount Stadium
Tillbrookson Bluff	Lizards	Summit Branch Stadium
Helderan North		
Bereton Park	Hammerheads ('Heads)	Ernestmont Field
Crenshaw City	Warthogs ('Hogs)	Wilddon Field
Red Tummlyn	Grizzlies	Flintover Park
Skate River	Mad Dogs	Jared Lake Stadium
Helderan South		
Gregorson	Monkeys	Teresa Center
Kern	Screech Owls	Gardengreen Park
West Somerchester	Rhinos	Rebaley Field
Widmertown	Flying Squirrels	Catalinaside Stadium

Fans are expected to wear semi-formal attire: sport jackets for men, skirts and blouses or dresses for women and girls, knickers and caps for boys.

Most SIP League ballparks are regularly renovated and offer first-class accommodations for those purchasing the most expensive tickets. Many of the parks have installed pneumatically-controlled scoreboards.

Most fans arrive by carriage or cable-car.

Food is to be purchased at kiosks throughout the ballparks. No food may be brought in. Many families picnic at tables outside the parks before the games begin.

Alcohol is strictly prohibited, though men commonly carry small flasks in their jacket pockets, to be sipped then passed down the row and shared, even among security guards. The tradition is appropriate given the league's acronym, the SIP.

Gambling on games is common, despite the best efforts of law enforcement agencies.

THE AMANDEAN LEAGUE OF EVERYMAN (ALE)

Setheridge North		
Blue Square	Gophers	Birchley Grove
Goodwyn Fork	Hedgehogs	Waterunion Park
Red Beach	Mules	Joleneing Park
Sandbanna Woods	Orcas	Donalddale Stadium
Tredgemond Butte	Hounds	Zephyrglen Field
Setheridge South		
Bottom Brook	Jackrabbits	Jayway Park
Finchenland	Mastadons	Willowdale Field
MacKaness	Octopi	Glenland Field
Mount Jarviswell	St. Bernards	Irismore Park
Red Mine	Pirhanas	The Park at Claybury
Helderan North		
Fanningana Falls	Toads	Orangeham Stadium
Folgerley Bluff	Pandas	Altadon Stadium
McKinmond Lakes	Goats	Lilaton Park
Pear Falls	Stone Crabs	Aviswick Park
Powlet Creek Summit	Great Danes	Freeford Field
Helderan South		
Buck Falls Heights	Woodpeckers	Greenwick Field
LaValleyford Prairie	Loons	Wolf Bridge Park
Hot Bear Bend	Turtles	Jackmond Stadium
Leadland	Mudhens	Karynlin Park
Murrichswell Cove	Gators	Coraton Field

Fans wear all types of attire, from formal to casual. A few are known to wear costumes and paint their faces.

Given the lesser financial status of the league, parks are usually in poor condition, with hard wooden seats and limited amenities.

Some fans arrive by cable car, but those who can't afford that arrive by bus or on foot.

Food can be either purchased at the ballpark for nominal prices or brought from home. Vendors dot the perimeters of the park, often hawking lower-priced fan favorites, such as billy-bread rounds and fried calbur strips.

Ale is sold throughout the park and by vendors who walk up and down the aisles. No other alcohol is permitted.

Fist fights among fans are common, particularly in later innings after many ales have been consumed. Vendors rarely refuse beer sales to even the most inebriated fans.

Timeline of History of the Known World

Editors Note: *Historians on Setheridge are famous for their academic sparring, particularly over the roots of our civilization. The following timeline is limited to areas on which there is general agreement among leading historians. Areas of dispute are italicized.*

Setherian culture is thought to have begun approximately 5,000 years ago, or 3,200 years before the adoption of the current calendar system, created by the mathematician Aaron Preote. It was at that point, 50 centuries ago, that the world suffered what we now refer to as the Wide Cataclysm.

PRIOR TO RECORDED HISTORY: DISAGREEMENTS over the precise nature of the Wide Cataclysm are as numerous as there are historians. Some ascribe a climatological change over hundreds of years that decimated whatever civilizations existed at the time. Others hypothesize a seismological disaster lasting mere months. Less frequent are the arguments for otherworldly intervention — with theories of other races traveling to the world from the stars. And, of course, the religious arguments abound — and the Rebular are known to hypothesize that a god-like power reformed the world in a single day, as penalty to a race of people that had lost its moral compass.

Alas, we will never know. What is certain, however, is that the world that existed in that day was gone, in the cosmic equivalent of an instant. It is from this event that we date our current calendar.

Modern Era, Year 47: Antecedents of the Setherian writings, found on coastal caves of Tredgemond Butte, are dated to ME (modern era) 47. Linguists theorize the writings are accounts of hunting exploits by the indigenous peoples.

Year 192: Accounts of earliest Amandean civilization. It is believed that Amandeans were the dominant race on the continent during a period lasting roughly Years 150-300. This was the first great civilization of the post-Cataclysmic Era, and at its height the Amandeans ruled over three-quarters of the continent.

Year 450: Remnants of Amandean civilization are scattered throughout the Northern Tier. Setherian Croxus (leader by inheritance) is established in what is now New Ungeropolis.

Year 500: First surviving accounts of a stick-and-ball game are dated to the sixth century. Drawings show children running across what appear to be squares, or bases, after striking a small ball with a stick. The drawings include adults watching nearby.

Year 572: Helderan democratic tribunal established at Leadland. Historians believe the First Tribunal, lead by *Conrath Brendland*, lasted approximately eight years before dissolving in acrimony. Helderan factions engage in four decades of 'low-level' civil strife.

Year 600: Rebular mathematician Aaron Preote proposes a calendar system dating from what had, by this point, become the accepted time of the Wide Cataclysm. Years prior to this time are given the nomenclature B.C., for Before the Cataclysm.

Year 612: Exhausted by the warring, Helderan tribes agree to establish The Second Tribunal. This was a two-tiered democratic body, with the upper body encompassing just 11 elected representatives, known as *Solonus*. These 11 had veto power over the lower chamber, *Perimus*, which had an ungainly 26 members.

Year 674: First Helderan military incursion, later dubbed "The Battle of Hot Bear Bend," is launched on the main continent. It is quickly repulsed by Setherian volunteers supplemented by Monsytian mercenaries hired by *Croxus Harrion the Third*. (*Two key points here are under dispute by modern historians: whether this invasion was in fact the first by the Helderans; and whether the incursion was provoked by covert Setherian acts, including espionage. These two disputes, in fact, form a core historical controversy of the continent*).

Year 715: *Croxus Harrion the Fourth* decrees Setherian sovereignty over the whole of the continent. Heldera Island, in the southeast, remains the only stronghold of the Helderan people.

Years 715-1759: Duration of the thousand-year reign of Setherian House of Harrion, a succession-based monarchy. It is over the course of these ten centuries that relative peace is brought to the continent of Setheridge, though at a tremendous cost. First, through what was at times sheer brutal aggression, the Setherians successfully claimed control of the entirety of the continent and of the Island of Heldera, not just the traditional Setherian strongholds to the east.

Second, it was over the course of the reign of the House of Harrion that the Helderan people were ruthlessly assimilated into the Setherian empire, losing their land and their businesses. Starting in about the 1200s, the Helderan tribes became the de facto working class for both the Harrion ruling houses as well as other nobility, including the remnants of the Amandean people.

1600s: First recorded mention of the term 'baseball' is dated to the early 17th century. Rules include a limit on the number of missed swings, described as 'strikes,' and an independent arbiter to determine rules disputes. Historians agree that by the latter 17th century, baseball was commonly played by children at schools and adults after work, particularly by Amandeans, Setherians, and Helderans.

Year 1757: *Croxus Harrion the 104th, nicknamed "Deranged Harry,"* is assassinated outside LaValleyford Prairie, after a ferry ride across the Valencroft River. As he has no male heir, this leads to disarray among the Setherians, with growing disputes over whether the monarchy should continue. The assailant is not caught, as insurgent groups that separately had tired of the monarchy conspired to ensure that the investigation would be fruitless.

Year 1759: The House of Harrion is formally dissolved as a ruling entity. A bicameral parliamentary government is installed, with representatives from all regions of the continent and of the Island of Heldera. Thousands hail the peaceful transition to a more modern government, but multiple political parties spring up and the parliament is largely dysfunctional.

Year 1801: The first of what would prove to be four major Helderan insurgent groups is formed in the eastern port city of Leadland on Heldera Island. Lead by a indentured machinist named *Earvin Wren,* the group calls itself Free Heldera, and espouses nonviolent means to achieve sovereignty. The group is quickly declared to be illegal and Wren is imprisoned for several years.

Year 1805: The dissolution of Free Heldera backfires on the ruling Setherians in that it leads to the creation of three new insurgent groups, each dedicated to achieving freedom, each willing to use violence as a means to that end, and each operating in total secrecy. Setherian intelligence agents are unable to learn the leaders, locations, and funding sources of the groups, and in fact their exact number is unclear. Only later were historians able to surmise that the insurgent groups did number three: the Helderan Liberationists, the Army of Islanders and Helderan Unity.

1800s: The 19th century brings the first formal baseball leagues, most of them amateur. The teams dot the countryside, and the rivalries among various cities and towns bring a welcome respite from the political turmoil. A few leagues claimed to be professional and paid players based on that day's ticket sales; fights over whether the owner was paying out the proper share were frequent.

Year 1807: The various leaders of the three primary Helderan insurgent groups meet on a heavily guarded boat off the coast of McMurichswell Cove. The session though is disrupted by an attack of the Setherian military, and casualties on both sides number in the dozens. The Helderan rebel leaders successfully escape, leading to open debates in the Setherian Parliament about the competency of the Setherian military and the eventually sacking of the Navy commander. This incident becomes known as The Battle of Murrichswell Cove and is memorialized in song and prose.

Years 1808-1835: Relative calm throughout the continent lulls the Setherian people into the belief that the insurgency has run its course. Historians now think that to have been anything but the case. In fact, all three insurgent groups see their ranks swell during this period as the Helderan people — furious over the Battle of Murrichswell Cove and the treatment sympathetic Setherians — became increasingly supportive of a revolt. This pronounced change in sentiment prompts each of the insurgent groups to quietly stockpile armaments, money, and supplies.

1820s: Semi-professional baseball teams grow in number, resulting in loose, regional confederations. At least three such groups, two Setherian and one Amandean, become profitable. Young men began who excel at the sport are able to earn relatively stable incomes by associating themselves with the more successful teams, and some become known nationally — the continent's first baseball stars. A few female baseball teams spring up as well.

Year 1837, August 4: The continent erupts in full-scale warfare as the Helderan insurgents launch coordinated, pre-dawn attacks on Setherian military outposts. The Setherian military is caught by surprise, and is understaffed, under-supplied, and woefully trained. This allows the Helderans to immediately claim control of vast portions of the southeastern tier of the mainland. This date marks the start of what came to be known as the Great Insurrection.

Over the next five decades, the Setherians try unsuccessfully to reclaim those areas, while the Helderans are able to gradually increase the lands they control over the whole southeastern portion of the mainland. The cost is incalculable, with hundreds of thousands of casualties, the decimation of historic sites and natural wonders, and entire generations of people living out their lives knowing nothing but war.

Year 1847, September 29: Bartholomew Cunningham is born on the outskirts of Sandbanna Woods, the only child of Braley and Ellie Cunningham, two struggling farmers.

Year 1887: The war reaches its 50th anniversary, and that dubious milestone gives new impetus to long-stalled discussions on a ceasefire. Still, both sides are unable to even agree on a framework for such discussions. The Setherians insist as a precondition for talks that Helderan forces surrender all territory on the mainland; the Helderans refuse that point and insist on a Setherian admission of human rights violations for centuries of abusive treatment. Formal talks are never held.

Year 1890: Cunningham, by now a successful promoter of sporting and other entertainments events, conceives a solution to the political strife: a continental, professional baseball league made up of teams based in cities controlled by both

Setherian and Helderan forces. He proposes this in April, prompting six months of debate across the continent. The two sides, exhausted by war, eventually agree.

Year 1891: The Proclamation of an Eternal Ceasefire is declared, and ratified by both the Setherian and Helderan military leadership. Helderan peoples are granted their own sovereignty, the Nation of Heldera, compromised of their native Island and much of the eastern half of the continent.

Year 1892, July 23: Lord Bart announces the Setheridge Island Professional League of Baseball, or SIP, is formally announced, with the inaugural season to begin the following spring.

Year 1892, November 14: Spurred by popular demand, the Amandean League of Everyman, or ALE, is ratified as a second continental league, with 20 teams in smaller cities. Cunningham, declared commissioner of both leagues, establishes offices in Schawmount City. He quickly asserts broad political powers, with the support of the suddenly-prosperous team owners.

Year 1893, May Second: Opening Day of the Inaugural Season of the SIP and ALE Leagues.

Year 1923, March 30th: the 30th Anniversary Celebration of the SIP and ALE Leagues is held in Schawmount City.

About the Author

MICHAEL BARBATO-DUNN WORKED FOR MANY years as a City Hall reporter for an all-news radio station. He enjoys reading science fiction and playing fantasy sports, and has managed to combine both passions in this sprawling novel. Mike lives with his wife, daughter and their two dogs in Philadelphia. For a free story, and to discover more of his writing, visit michaelbarbatodunn.com.

www.ingramcontent.com/pod-product-compliance
Lightning Source LLC
Chambersburg PA
CBHW051313250626
47155CB00007B/2300